WITHDRAWN

my brain
escapes me

Robert Steven Rhine

my brain escapes me

sun dog press
northville, michigan

MY BRAIN ESCAPES ME

Copyright ©1999 by Robert Steven Rhine

Cover design by Grey Christian

Back cover photo by Lon Bixby

Book design by Judy Berlinski

All rights reserved. No part of this book may be reproduced or utilized in any form or by any means, electronic or mechanical, except for brief quotations and reviews, without permission from the publisher. Inquiries should be addressed to Sun Dog Press, 22058 Cumberland Dr., Northville, MI 48167.

The publisher wishes to thank Dan Waldron and Judy Berlinski for their professional help and guidance in the preparation of this book.

Library of Congress Cataloging-in-Publication Data

Rhine, Robert Steven
    My brain escapes me / Robert Steven Rhine. — 1st ed.
       p.   cm.
    ISBN 0-941543-18-8. — ISBN 0-941543-19-6 (pbk.)
     1. Fantasy fiction, American. 2. Horror tales, American.
I. Title.
PS3568.H497M9   1999
813'.54—dc21   99-19398
                                                  CIP

Printed in the United States of America   First Edition *to* J.D.

■ TABLE OF CONTENTS ■

ACKNOWLEDGEMENTS 9
FOREWORD 11

CHAPTER ONE
FAST ACTING XILOTRIPIMENE 15
CONJUGAL VISIT 37
RAOUL, LOW-LIFE EX-COP "HEARTLESS" 49
HOWLING WIND 61
TAKING OUT THE GARBAGE 69

CHAPTER TWO
SASQUATCH IN CENTRAL PARK 81
RAOUL, LOW-LIFE EX-COP "THREE SHADES OF BLUE" 103
MURDER SCHOOL 113
EXCURSION TO INSANITY 123
THE BRAIN EXCHANGE 133

CHAPTER THREE
RAOUL, LOW-LIFE EX-COP "BAD BOYS & ALLEY CATS" 139
SOMETHING IN THE AIR 153
MY BRAIN ESCAPES ME 175
SPARE PARTS 179
HE WHO DIES WITH THE MOST TOYS 191

CHAPTER FOUR
ANXIETY 199
STRESS 209
DEPRESSION 220
RAOUL, LOW-LIFE EX-COP "FLAMINGO MEAT" 228
THE EVIL YEKNOM SNIARB 239

Chapter Five
Andros   249
What if Clouds Were UFOs?   263
Killing Spree   279
Raoul, Low-Life Ex-Cop "Wrong Hole"   283
Twister Sisters   293

Chapter Six
Grenetta, Queen of Loyns   309
Raoul, Low-Life Ex-Cop "Duh, We're Hookers"   326
Reflectionites   339
Regular Can   347
Extreme of Consciousness   350

BUT WHAT HAVE YOU DONE FOR ME LATELY?

I would like to thank my best friend and often wife, Julie, who lives with the moods of a madman and endures sleep deprivation by flashlight and frantic scribbling at three a.m. Thank you J.D. for your faith in my writing and for bringing a slice of sanity to an insane world. Also, thanks to: my friend Brad Zutuat who greatly encouraged me; Norman Merrill who brought introspection to new depths; my sister Vicki who lived with me through the wars; Rafael Robledo, my fearless guide into the seedy underbelly of L.A.; my fourth therapist, Roberta, who hung in there with the best of them; Phil Davis for the pro bono; Bob Henson at the National Center for Atmospheric Research; Lon Bixby for the back cover photo; John Boegehold for the computer assist; Rob Cohen, who bravely published three of my stories in his radical coffee house magazine, *Caffeine*; and, most importantly, Sun Dog Press publisher Al Berlinski, who saw my stories in *Caffeine*, asked if I had some more, and subsequently funneled the stories I mailed him into this book, thanks to the superb editing and tireless dedication of his wife, Judy Berlinski.

Finally, to all the publishers who gave my writing a second glance and stuck a story in their magazines and books . . . What the hell were you thinking?!

They are as follows:
Bad Guys Finish First, Bandicoot, Blackmoon Magazine, The Blue Lady, Caffeine, The Cimmerian Journal, Dark Kiss, Deathrealm, Dragon's Dreaming Magazine, Eulogy, Fell Swoop, Forbidden Lines, The Fringe, Graffiti Off the Asylum Walls, Heliocentric Net, His Garden, The Iguana Informer, Insidious Tales, Medusa's Hairdo Magazine, Midnight Zoo, Mind in Motion, Moonletters, Naked Kiss, The Oak, Obscene Cuisine, Outer Darkness, Over My Dead Body, Parlour Papers, Potpourri, Prohibited Matter, Rictus, Scream When You Burn, Sinister, Spellbound, Strange Days, Stuff, Symphonie's Gift, Thin Ice, White Knuckles, Wicked Mystic.

Herman M. Swafford Fiction Award for "Andros."

FOREWORD

To read these stories is to take a dare—a dare to erase them from your mind once you have read them.

This is vivid stuff. It is imagination at its most extreme. Robert Steven Rhine is a writer who looks at life with an unflinching eye, seeing where our present-day obsessions are taking us. In case you fear this casts his stories as tracts, be reassured: they are not. He is first and foremost a story-teller. You will be vastly entertained.

Yet invisibly underneath is a view of life that exposes our communal nerve-endings. Our fixation on the implacable march of science ("Fast Acting Xilotripimene"), the denouement of our collective hungers ("The Evil Yeknom Sniarb"), nature's wrath ("Twister Sisters"), the race for ideas ("Something in the Air"), and our belief that "education" is a remedy for everything ("Murder School")—these are a few of the contemporary shibboleths he takes on. Then, there is that remarkable series of darkly humorous adventures of "Raoul, Low-Life Ex-Cop." They're Rhine's answer to the TV-spawned self-righteous upholders of the law, and neatly and uproariously skewer the fantasies we attach to those whose mission is the euphemistic "to protect and serve."

You don't have to be weighted down by these psychological considerations, of course. You can read these stories for the pure pleasure of it. Individually and as a whole they give no vibrations of ulterior motive. Call them "escapism" if you wish. But if you are looking for the strain that holds them together, that makes them so solid in conception and so right-on in style, it's there if you care to discern it.

Like Edgar Allen Poe, Rhine has conceived a time, place, and mood for each individual story and stuck with it. He has mined a rich ore of images and feelings ranging over a wide field of subjects. Nearly all of them tend towards the bizarre, but neither Poe's nor Rhine's is a one-note operation. Rhine's stories may take place in past, present, or future, but he speaks exclusively in words tuned to today. This is true of everything he writes, whether a quirky fable like "Grenetta, Queen of Loyns," which takes place in some mythical land, or "Andros," a realistic tale of fisherboys, a barracuda, and human compassion.

There are thirty stories here, each with its own character and personality. Their order of appearance has no particular significance, other than providing variety for those who wish to start at the beginning of the book or those wanting to dip in at random. Whatever your preference—you are in for a treat. Robert Steven Rhine is a name you will not soon forget, nor will his stories leave your mind, ever.

—Daniel Waldron

my brain
escapes me

1

Fast Acting Xilotripimene

Xilotripimene had left test market a resounding success. A synthetic drug, Xilotripimene, when poured into the middle ear, much like Hamlet's hemlock, would prolong experience. There were other drugs which enabled the consumer to feel things for a few extended minutes or hours but the TOLM corporation had researched and designed Xilotripimene for semi-paralyzed patients, to allow them to retain minor sensations for weeks or possibly even months. Whatever pervading emotions and sensations experienced precisely at the time of taking Xilotripimene, would stretch out like taffy.

Private John Milford awoke feeling very cold. He was lying completely naked on a steel surgical table. He opened his eyes and squinted in the harsh white light. His head throbbed like the remnants of a nasty hangover and he thought of grabbing an aspirin but discovered that his hands and feet were strapped down by leather restraints.

His shaved head felt heavy as he slowly rolled it to the left scanning the walls, painted a blinding white. He saw a single white door cut into the left or west wall but there were no windows or even visible lights in the small airless room. As Milford gingerly rolled his head to the other side he spotted a digital camera pointing towards him from the corner. By his right arm, hovered an empty surgical tray table.

Private John Milford had no idea what he was doing strapped naked to a steel-guttered surgical table in a totally white room devoid of anything but a single door, a security camera and a surgical tray . . . but he was becoming extremely curious.

When Xilotripimene was invented, back in the early two thousands, the formula leaked out. Word was, it was someone in the military, a disgruntled scientist, interested in finding fortune as a synthetic drug dealer. No one ever found the source of the leak, which was quickly plugged. But Xilotripimene soon created a whole new society of street addicts and rich players. For a sexual experience there was nothing better. Imagine an orgasm which lasted for a solid week. A virtual coma locking the body in a tense wave of orgasmic pleasure. There would be orgasm dens much like the opium dens of old where the consumers could lie for weeks on a stained mattress quivering in eternal ecstasy.

The white door opened. Private Milford heard footsteps and turned his head to the left, barely catching a glimpse of a figure quickly exiting, his shoes fit with white surgical coverings.

Milford's thin body shivered on the steel table as he now observed, taped to the outside of the opened door, a small, white sign with the word "Scenario," followed by the number "One."

After a few minutes, Milford heard whistling followed by an overweight Latino man who entered the room wearing a white germ-containment outfit, wheeling in a mop bucket.

Milford was relieved to see another person in this antiseptic white box in which he was imprisoned. Maybe now he would get some answers.

"Hey," uttered Milford, sounding hollow to his ears.

But the Latino man was busy mopping and didn't hear him, or didn't care to.

Milford, being mildly anxious at best, wasn't about to give up. "I said, 'hey'."

No reply, only more mopping and whistling. *This could drive a fellow nuts*, thought Milford, trying to keep a level head, though growing more annoyed by the moment. *Maybe this guy's deaf?* he pondered.

"Hey, you fat fuckin' freak . . . I'm talking to you!" shouted Milford.

This got a response. The man stopped mopping.

"The name's Carlos," hissed the Latino, wielding his mop like a weapon, his heavy eyes rimmed with red.

Milford felt somewhat embarrassed, though more vulnerable than anything, lying there so completely defenseless and naked.

"Sorry, dude, I thought you were deaf or something," apologized Milford.

"Well, I'm not," informed Carlos who resumed mopping, though he had ceased whistling.

"Hey, Carlos, what's the trick? I mean, what am I doing here, amigo?"

"I can't talk to you," said Carlos.

"Please," pleaded Milford, "I'm getting a little nervous. You see, I don't know how I got here."

Thick lips curled over capped teeth in a knowing smile, "You'll find out real soon *amigo*, adios," grinned Carlos as he shut the door behind.

It was the last face Milford would see for the next seventeen hours.

When taken in conjunction with another drug, Xilotripimene would prolong that drug's effect as well. Same when combined with alcohol, or the savoring of fine cuisine. If taken in an elevated mood, that mood could continue indefinitely, hence of great relief to those with manic depression. Eventually comedy clubs would get into the act, selling Xilotripimene ear shooters to audience members, figuring that if a comedian got a big laugh up front, the audience would never stop laughing. The only drawback was that if a comic's first joke bombed, the audience would just stare like a convention of zombies.

Milford lay in a puddle of his own piss. He was thankful, however, that was the only bodily function which had thus far escaped him. He now thought fondly of Carlos and their brief repartee. He had memorized his pudgy pockmarked face and Brillo pad goatee. But the memory of Carlos wasn't enough to subdue the demons wreaking havoc in Milford's overactive mind.

The last thing Milford remembered was a trial—his trial back in his home town of Purvis, Mississippi. Milford had murdered his girlfriend, something which would be eventually proven in court, though you didn't need Perry Mason to solve this one. Milford's girlfriend, Nancy, had succumbed to strangling fingers, leaving purple choke marks on her lithe neck. Milford hadn't meant to kill her, at first; but it felt so darned good feeling her pulse beat slower in her carotid artery, as she finally puffed her soul from her lips.

Nancy wasn't what you would call a "good girl" though it took a summer of dating and Milford's broken heart to determine that fact. It seemed that while Milford was dating her, so was most of the varsity football team and a sizable portion of the marching band. But she was Milford's first crush, and he had lost his virginity to her, so he was blind to such matters, reasoning that she just had a lot of "close friends." Actually, Milford was the laughing stock of Robert E. Lee High School. A tall gangly kid with connect-the-dot-pimples, Milford was a social misfit, preferring to spend his time playing re-enactment battle games and marching with the Army Reserves.

Milford was working at the Stop and Go convenience store and gas station on Highway I-13 when Nancy Bernadette stopped in one evening for a pack of Virginia Slims. They got to talking and made a plan to meet the next night after work. Nancy didn't care much for Milford, but she had a somewhat self-destructive personality following a decade of sexual abuse by her father, a local pastor.

Milford and Nancy only did it twice. Once in the Stop and Go storeroom, with Nancy seated on a carton of Huggie diapers, and once after midnight on the grassy knoll behind the Frosty Freeze, where Nancy would sometimes go with her friends to smoke cigarettes. Both times happened the same night.

Anyhow, the following week, when Milford got wind of Nancy's sexual proclivities, he snapped. He waited until she was walking home from school, then jumped from the bushes and strangled her in front of about fifty witnesses. Milford, having not properly premeditated the murder, choked her directly across from an entire bus load of ninth graders, and a seventy-year-old crossing guard, with one glass eye, who all witnessed the heinous act.

Unfortunately, it was too late to stop the crime. The crossing guard tried to pull Milford off of her, but his fingers were clamped around her neck like a moray eel. The bus driver, an ex-Marine, intervened, hammering Milford unconscious with an industrial Eveready flashlight.

The case was a prosecutor's dream except that Milford had technically managed to kill Nancy in the "heat of passion," something which would afford the public defender certain latitudes in Milford's defense. The only snag was that Milford had written precisely three hundred and seventy-two times in his spiral notebook, that he intended to strangle her (the District Attorney grandiloquently pointed out) the night before the murder. When this notebook was discovered in the school's bushes during the trial, it all but pounded the nails in

Fast Acting Xilotripimene

Milford's coffin. He was convicted of Nancy Bernadette's murder and sentenced to death.

But then something happened which saved Milford's skin. The government program was called "L.H. studies" or, as known by those with higher security clearance, "Laboratory Humans." Evidently, due to heavily armed animal activist groups, it had become suicidal to test new drugs on lab animals and it was increasingly difficult to find voluntary human guinea pigs. There were, however, several death rows full of "testers" should they *be interested*. Of course, the decision was up to the convict: "Pop a pill, get a chill," or "a date with the Hangman." Milford, offered the choice, naturally picked "L.H. Studies." I mean, what could be worse than death?

At a secret military base, Milford's blindfold was removed and he was lined up in his skivvies along with other testers. He was given a once over by an Army nurse, stamped on the rump with a bar code, and quickly given a blood test.

Or was it? Milford could have sworn the doctor injected something into his vein before withdrawing his blood.

That was the last thing Milford recalled before waking up naked on the cold steel table. At least now he remembered why he was there ... to test drugs too horrible for laboratory rats.

Xilotripimene became the choice drug of longtime lovers wishing to hang onto whatever love they had. On the other end of the spectrum, someone in a murderous rage, who took the drug, would become a homicidal maniac until stopped with a hail of bullets.

Milford's stomach was a whining knot. He was wondering if perhaps the test was to starve him to death on the surgical table when he heard something in the hall. It sounded like gurney wheels. The door opened and a man dressed in a white chef's uniform, complete with a cylindrical chef's hat, entered the room pushing a long cart covered with a rounded steel lid.

The chef wheeled the cart beside Milford and opened the lid revealing a portable kitchen: stove, sink, cutting board, refrigerator. The chef immediately went to work lighting the pilot on the stove and chopping ingredients on a white Lucite cutting board.

"Whatcha making?" asked Milford, his mouth instinctively watering.

"Do you like seafood, Milford?" asked the chef with a thick French accent.

Milford was stunned. It was like his mind had been read, "I love seafood! My favorite is . . ."

". . . Lobster Newburg," interjected the chef, completing Milford's thought.

"How'd you know that?" inquired Milford, amazed.

"Oh, we know lots about you Milford, lots. You had lobster Newburg for your fourteenth birthday at the Fisherman's Grotto restaurant in Hattiesburg, Mississippi. It was the best meal of your life."

Milford numbly nodded as the chef continued, "I'm making all your favorites—lobster Newburg, macaroni and cheese, a Ball Park Frank with sauerkraut and, for dessert, a Pop Tart covered with peanut butter."

Milford was stunned. They were absolutely, hands-down, his favorite foods of all time and he rightly had to keep back the slobber as he fought against his restraints. The chef went about preparing the food with quiet expertise. Milford watched doe-eyed as he began to smell the glorious chow permeating his nostrils.

The chef, who seemed to wish he had more creative dishes to work with, turned off the stove. He ladled the lobster Newburg onto one plate, placed the hot dog on a second plate, the steaming macaroni and cheese on a third and the Pop Tart on the last plate.

The chef lined up the four plates on the stove top and asked, "Are you hungry?"

"Uh-huh," Milford replied.

"Real hungry?" prodded the chef.

Milford nodded like an obedient puppy.

"Then you must select one, and only one, of these foods to eat," instructed the chef.

"Only one?" asked Milford, his eyes dancing over the plates.

This game was rather ridiculous but Milford was a captive to his appetite and he knew if he could just eat something, he would think more clearly. Most of the foods he could have eaten anytime at home, except for one dish, the most expensive on the menu, which seemed to be crying out to Milford.

"Lobster Newburg!" announced Milford, like a game show contestant.

"Splendid choice!," applauded the chef as he placed the white porcelain plate with the lobster Newburg on Milford's hairless chest. The warmth of the plate felt good at first but began to grow hotter and hotter the longer it rested on his chest.

"The plate's kind of warm," voiced Milford.

"Yes, well, I wouldn't think about that right now," advised the chef.

The heat wasn't completely intolerable, and Milford's hunger was overriding all other emotions, as the chef dipped a sterling silver spoon into the rich creamy lobster Newburg and fed Milford a wondrous spoonful.

The flavor caressed Milford's taste buds. The richness of the mellow cream with the sweetness of the fresh hot lobster was pure nirvana. It was even better than he remembered on his fourteenth birthday. Then, just as Milford's eyeballs fluttered backwards in ecstasy he felt something cold pour into his ear. The chef abruptly removed the plate from Milford's chest before he could ask for another bite, whisked the portable kitchen out of the room, and slammed the door behind.

Milford, floating in lobster heaven, realized that although the chef had fled, and he wouldn't get another spoonful of lobster, he still felt locked with the pleasurable experience of the first bite. It was an exceedingly intense feeling.

Milford was high on lobster Newburg . . . and he wasn't coming down.

It didn't take long for government agencies to learn of Xilotripimene. The U.S. Government has tabs on every new patent and invention and their potential uses, particularly for the military. The Pentagon was *extremely* interested in Xilotripimene. The executives at TOLM were equally anxious for a lucrative government contract, although several scientists there feared the ominous consequences of government

Fast Acting Xilotripimene

involvement, warning, "Remember atom splitting?" But TOLM had laid off nearly two thousand employees in the past year and needed a winner. TOLM sold a contract for Xilotripimene to the Pentagon.

Three hours later, Milford was still riding high on lobster Newburg. He had savored the flavor for so long, he could almost think like a lobster. Finally, the door once again opened and a middle-aged nurse wearing white orthopedic shoes and a starched white nurse's cap, entered carrying a small white satchel.

The nurse unrolled the satchel on the surgical tray table as Milford observed.

"What's for dessert?" inquired Milford with a friendly tone.

The nurse wasn't talking, all business, avoiding his eyes as if he was the condemned. But so far as Milford knew he was just a "food tester." Besides, he was feeling pretty darn great with those crustaceans crawling around his senses.

A doctor, mid-fifties, balding with thick eyebrows entered and quickly approached the surgical table, no time for bedside manners. He seemed particularly interested in Milford's bare feet, examining them through a micro-surgery lens he wore around his head. He appeared to be making a decision, like where to start carving a holiday turkey, when he finally selected a serrated scalpel off the surgical tray.

Milford would have been feeling mildly jumpy if he wasn't so overwhelmed with lobster Newburg, seemingly pumped into his nostrils with blow-dryers, rising up in his throat like high tide at Fisherman's Wharf on a muggy day.

The doctor, while humming, used the scalpel to quickly slice the skin off the bottom of Milford's left foot, as quick as a sheep shearer removes a pelt, leaving raw flesh underneath. You might think Milford screamed in agony, but the lobster had its claws on his psyche.

"Does that hurt?" inquired the doctor, between hums.

"I'm not sure," pondered Milford. "Maybe a little," adding with trepidation, "Wha . . . what are you doing?"

But the doctor was too busy humming to answer, methodically using his surgical peeler to scrape the flesh off Milford's little piggies . . . one by one.

The Pentagon formed study groups, or Xilotripimene "think tanks." Their study concluded that if a soldier was given Xilotripimene when he was hell-bent for battle, before the bullets started flying, he would never surrender before death. Battle fatigue would be replaced by kamikaze soldiers. This made the generals at the Pentagon giddy as schoolgirls.

Milford puked the tablespoon of lobster Newburg onto his chest. It had taken over three hours but the doctor had successfully peeled Milford's skin off both feet and legs all the way up to his waist, mercifully leaving the skin on his fear shrunken genitals. Milford felt naked in a way he never thought possible.

The nurse dabbed the sweat from the doctor's brow, then handed him a syringe which he injected into Milford's arm. The nurse collected the tools in her satchel, and followed the doctor out of the room without comment.

Slowly the lobster sensation began to wear off, and, equally, Milford began to feel a mild pain in the skinned portions of his body, like a mild sunburn, but nothing as bad as you might expect, had you just shaved your legs with a giant vegetable peeler. But the pain was slowly creeping up on him and he knew he would be begging for lobster Newburg if he stayed this course for long.

Just then, Milford heard circus music coming from outside the room. It was a comforting sound, reminding him of the time he went to the circus as a boy, the happiest day of his life. Suddenly, the door burst open and six clowns entered followed by a miniature pony. This took Milford so off guard that a smile elevated his lips. But he doubted they could ever cheer him up, what with his skinned legs and lobster breath.

Each clown was dressed in his own comedic way—bright orange dreadlocks, bulging eyes, buck teeth, giant shoes and red bulbous noses. They took turns doing ridiculous pratfalls and zany, hysterical stunts with the pony and Milford felt his spirits lift. Sure, Milford was in hell, but why not have a moment of pleasure? At least the doctor was finished with his bizarre experiment in human skinning and Milford would be sent home, without having to spend one minute on death row.

While the short goofy looking clown with a huge belly made silly balloon animals, a tall clown with a tiny head played a Bach concerto by expelling air out of his orifices. It was this kind of humor that really got Milford going and he momentarily forgot about the increasing pain in his lower extremities. He started a belly laugh which shook him all the way up his neck to his mouth until he actually *guffawed*. It was somewhere in mid-guffaw that the funny farting clown bent down and squirted something from his trick daisy into Milford's ear.

Milford immediately noticed that the lobster Newburg taste and all pain was eliminated, and what a relief it was . . . only that now his face was pinned ear to ear in a huge, face-splitting grin. The clowns and pony, suddenly sullen, quickly exited the room and slammed the door behind.

Milford tried to lower his lips which were now peeled over his teeth like a deranged jack-o'-lantern. He also, distressingly, continued the manic guffaw that the clowns had induced . . .

"Guh-hu . . . hu-hu . . . hu-hu . . ."

After twenty minutes, Milford's face became a cramp with a hole. Even worse, the door opened, and guess who was back. Yep, Dr. Skinner and Nurse Emotionless. Milford noticed, before they closed the door, that the sign on the front had been changed to read: Scenario Two.

The doctor snapped on his latex surgical gloves and calmly took up where he left off, at Milford's waist, skinning him back in large sectional slices much like you would peel a navel orange. The work on his stomach and chest went much more quickly than his toes and legs. Worst of all, Milford was apparently finding this extremely funny. Side-splitting, gut-busting, eye-tearing, face-cracking, hee-haw funny.

The doctor and nurse weren't sharing his amusement.

The Pentagon commissioned another study group to further examine ways to use Xilotripimene against the enemy. One problem would be getting the enemy to consume the drug. You couldn't just ask them to pour it into their ears. You might put

Fast Acting Xilotripimene

it into their water supply, so they would become infected during a shower. But then you ran the risk of them being in a positive fighting mood when they showered. One imaginative tactician suggested filling the vaginas of prostitutes with Xilotripimene and sending them to the enemy who would become infected and locked in an orgasmic state, unable to perform in battle. However, it was hard to imagine a situation where a prostitute's vagina and a soldier's ear might come into contact. Nevertheless, these strategies were on the list of top secret plans from the Pentagon.

Milford was still a one man laugh factory as the doctor expertly finished his work, and dropped a translucent sheet of epidermis into a bucket. Only Milford's head and, thankfully, his private parts remained unpeeled. Milford's jaw was still aching from non-stop laughing; God knows his torso and arms should have been killing him. But he apparently found the whole experience uproariously funny. *Maybe they should gut me like a trout, for a real belly laugh,* painfully grinned Milford.

"Guh-hu . . . Hu-hu . . ."

The nurse solemnly filled another syringe and the doctor again injected Milford in his peeled triceps. The smile began to mercifully loosen on Milford's face, replaced by a distant pain faintly echoing across his body. But somewhere, in the far recesses of Milford's nerve endings, were planted the seeds of unspeakable agony.

The Pentagon finally came to the conclusion that the best use for Xilotripimene would be for interrogations. Any inflicted pain could be amplified and continued for weeks. The pain from a mere pinch could become unnerving after a few days. But there were studies to be done and they needed subjects to test their theories. They made a deal with the Department of Justice to appropriate condemned prisoners, those without families or friends, for experimental purposes.

There were few who fit the bill so nicely as Milford.

Carlos was back mopping the floor around Milford's surgical table. There was blood, sweat, piss, excrement and lobster Newburg which had accumulated since he was last in the room. Carlos seemed accustomed to such sights. Even Milford, peeled on the surgical table, smiling like a deranged maniac, didn't give Carlos pause.

"Help me! Guh-hu . . . hu-hu . . ." implored Milford, the tortured Joker.

"Hey, don't give me your grief," Carlos replied, "I got a wife and five kids to feed."

Carlos noticed the stupid-ass grin on Milford's face for the first time. "You think that's funny?"

"No . . . guh-hu . . . I don't," replied Milford, unconvincingly.

Carlos shook his head as he left with his mop, "Everybody's a comedian."

After a few moments, the door opened and the most stunning woman Milford had ever laid eyes on, even in his jerk-off magazines, entered the room. Before she shut the door, Milford noticed the sign on the front had again been changed to now read: Scenario Three.

The woman, who looked no more than nineteen, paraded around the surgical table studying Milford's peeled body. As she strolled past, Milford ogled the outline of her astonishing body beneath her tight red, silk dress. His limp loin began to gather itself together, engorging with blood beneath its pink finger-puppet glove.

The young temptress had her eyes fixed on his crotch much the same way Milford had looked at the lobster Newburg, like something hot you hunger to taste.

"You want to fuck me, don't you, Milford?"

"Guh-huh," Milford eagerly nodded, his eyes never leaving her body as she stalked him in ever tightening circles. She finally stopped, her loins a millimeter from his face. Milford could smell her heady sex perfume emanating like a drug through her silky dress.

She stroked a finger across his sweaty creased forehead. "Poor, poor baby. Can Candy make it better?"

Milford weakly nodded as Candy lifted her dress between her coral pink fingernails, exposing white lace G-string panties hugging perfect tanned legs. A few golden hairs waved to Milford from above the elastic as she began to lightly stroke herself with her fingernail while gawking at Milford's attentive flesh flute.

"I want you *sooo* bad, Milford. Do you want me?" she naughtily pouted.

Milford dully mumbled, "Guh-Huh . . . guh-huh . . ."

"Have you ever had a blow-job, Milford?" she asked licking her full ripe lips.

Milford didn't have to think too long, the answer was a resounding "no." It was the one and only thing that Nancy had refused to do. Something about smearing her make-up.

"Nancy never gave you a blow-job, did she?" said Candy, the ever-understanding slut.

"Guh-huh," gobbled back Milford.

"I know all about you Milford," toyed Candy, "What you like sexually, what you don't. You've rented *Deep Throat* twenty-seven times, am I right, Milford?" She was sucking her thumb now, and Milford was on the verge of erupting like Krakatoa.

Candy slowly and seductively stripped down to her birthday suit while Milford, strapped to the table, moaned in expectation as she took a cotton-candy pink lipstick out of her dress pocket, twirled it up and thickly spread it onto her slightly parted mouth. She then reached over and lightly circled the lipstick around the tip of Milford's purple, swollen mushroom cap.

"Just in case it rubs off my lips," explained Candy.

And with that . . . she was down on him. It was the most intense pleasure Milford had ever felt as she worked him like a blow pop. He built and built to orgasm, his body beginning to uncontrollably shudder.

"Are you coming?" she breathlessly gurgled.

"Guhhhh-huuuh . . ." whimpered Milford through clenched teeth.

Milford's semen was shooting up his epididymis like the guns of Navarone as Candy poured an icy liquid into his ear. The remaining smile instantaneously vanished from Milford's face and was replaced with the most excruciatingly pleasurable orgasm imaginable . . . only the damn thing wouldn't finish.

"Ugghgggghggggg . . ." groaned Milford in the throes of the longest uncompleted orgasm in recorded history. It was enough to drive a man insane. Candy, meanwhile, wiped her mouth on the back of her hand, pulled on her silk dress and silently exited.

Milford was all too familiar with what would come next ... and it wouldn't be him.

The door opened and bad news again entered. The mirthless nurse officiously opened her satchel and laid out the carving knives like a caddy for the doctor who made his selection and quickly skinned Milford's penis like a rattlesnake, fortunately unfelt, so overpowering was his orgasmic state. Then, the doctor went about the more delicate work of peeling off Milford's face and detaching his scalp.

Two hours later the task was completed. There was not a speck of skin left on Milford's body.

He was, in fact, skinned alive.

The Pentagon decided to test Xilotripimene to see how the enemy would endure torture. They knew that a soldier, under the influence of Xilotripimene and inflicted with extreme pain, would reveal any information they required. But the strategists at the Pentagon also had another scenario. What if Xilotripimene fell into enemy hands? How would we train our soldiers to keep from talking?

That's where Milford got to give service to his country. He may have taken the life of Nancy Bernadette but he would save the lives of many countrymen if he could simply prove that pleasurable thoughts coupled with Xilotripimene could withstand the most hideous torture performed in the time of war.

That's if ... Milford survived the final scenario.

"*. . .* Uuuunnnugggghhhnnnuuuuggggg . . ."

Milford lay on the table in the throes of orgasm. The doctor undid the restraints on Milford's arms and legs, but he still couldn't move, so incapacitated with carnal incompletion.

A burly attendant entered the room wheeling in a steel tub filled with liquid, "Ready for scenario four, Doc?"

The doctor solemnly nodded, turned and calmly spoke to his peeled patient for the first time, "Have you ever had lemon or salt poured on a wound, Milford?"

Milford was rendered speechless by the orgasmic plateau.

"Well," continued the doctor, "this tub is filled with forty gallons of lemon juice and ten pounds of sea salt."

Milford's eyes widened as the attendant easily lifted his peeled body off the surgical table and lowered him into the solution.

But Milford felt nothing, the orgasm overriding all other sensations. He was mighty thankful too. *Can you imagine the pain?*

The doctor seemed fascinated, waiting for a reaction from Milford. Finally, he gazed up towards the digital camera in the corner and shrugged.

A deep voice permeated the room, "Move to scenario five."

The doctor seemed hesitant, contemplating, then spoke towards the camera, "I think we've established scenario four, sir. Why is five necessary?"

"We need to determine subject sensitivity," the voice answered.

"There's a high mortality risk," warned the doctor.

"Our prerogative, Colonel. Proceed with scenario five . . . that's an order," the voice commanded.

"Yes, sir," the doctor crisply responded.

The nurse filled another syringe and handed it to the doctor.

"Uuunnhhgggg . . ." Milford erotically groaned.

The doctor gave Milford a comforting smile, the kind you might give before putting an animal to sleep, and explained, "This is the antidote for the drug we are testing, it will immediately stop the exaggerated symptoms you've been experiencing."

"But we already gave him that," noted the nurse.

"No, clarified the doctor, the injections he received were merely a transitional pain reliever mixed with a small amount of the antidote to make him susceptible to each scenario. This full dose of the antidote will completely remove the effects of Xilotripimene, returning him back to his normal sensory state."

Milford's eyes widened as the doctor continued, "Don't worry, I'm only giving you a dose to last a few seconds. This way we can test your normal pain threshold."

"Uggnnuuughh!!! . . . ," pleaded Milford.

"Sorry, you have no choice, Milford. A deal's a deal."

The attendant held him down in the the lemon-salt solution as the doctor squirted the Xilotripimene antidote into Milford's ear. Almost instantaneously, Milford ejaculated onto the front of the nurse's starched uniform; then, within another millisecond, Milford experienced agony beyond any conceivable cosmic pain. It was an indescribable, searing pain in every fiber and nerve ending of his entire raw being. His scream almost tore out his esophagus as blood teared from his eye sockets. A needle was jabbed into Milford's arm and, just as quickly as it started, the pain ended.

Milford's peeled, ravaged citrus-soaked body was lifted from the tub, placed on a gurney and rushed out the door of the white room.

In the sterile hallway, a line of doctors, nurses and high ranking military officers applauded as Milford was wheeled past. Milford spotted Candy, now in a military uniform with silver Captain's bars, gazing down and applauding.

The gurney was pushed into another surgery room where a team of eight surgeons stood ready. Milford wondered what fate awaited him now—*a slow beheading?* But instead, he noticed a nurse unloading sheets of synthetic skin from a nitrogen cooled container. Another shot in the arm and Milford went, happily, unconscious.

Milford, with his synthetic skin, and new identity as Randall Troutmeyer, returned to society and moved to a trailer park in Modesto, California where he would never speak to anyone of the horrible scenarios he experienced in the white room. His brain never functioned entirely the same way again, experiencing occasional flashbacks of pain and pleasure much like a heavy LSD abuser.

He was terrified of clowns, became violently ill at the smell of seafood and was never able to have an orgasm to completion.

Though Milford had freely chosen to be a "tester" over execution, sometimes, as he tossed and turned in his trailer late at night, unable to get Nancy's tortured face out of his mind, he wondered . . . had he made the right choice?

Conjugal Visit

The walls would sweat on humid nights inside Louisiana State Penitentiary. Condensation would form into tiny beads which escaped down the walls in rusty stains. The inmates at Angola said it was the tears of those who died in their cells.

Jackson DesValle lay naked on his cot in the dark, on a sweltering ninety degree August night, feeling the occasional drip on his forehead from the tears of the dead.

Drip ... drip ... drip ...

You might think that the droplets on Jackson's forehead drove him crazy, but actually he found comfort in the touch of something outside himself, a reminder that God was still there, tapping a gentle reminder on his skull.

The minutes melted with agonizing slowness that August night as Jackson counted down his prison sentence with each monotonous drip ... drip ... drip ...

Ten months, two weeks, six days, five hours, one minute and thirteen seconds at last drip and that was just until his next parole hearing. He had thirty-one years left on his original sentence and it was likely that, at the age of forty-four, his tears would someday drip on the forehead of the next prisoner to occupy this very cell.

Jackson was all alone in the world and for that he was thankful. He was even alone in his eight by nine cell and felt lucky not to have some psycho bunk mate who could slit his throat one arduous night with a sharpened spoon.

The air grew particularly heavy as the night wore on, like cream curdling to cheese. You could almost chew on the molecules, thought Jackson, wishing he had a window like the inmates on B-block. They could see sky and clouds and an occasional sparrow swoop by, which might break the stupefying routine. If you were lucky enough to have a crack in the glass, you could smell the sweet scent of freedom. But Jackson didn't need a window. He had another way of escaping the confines of his cement cell.

He flicked on his flexible reading light illuminating the pale green, sweating walls. He slowly sat up his bulky frame on the cot, which creaked under his weight, and lowered his bare, brown toes onto the cool cement. He wished he could have laid on the floor but there was hardly room to walk, let alone stretch out.

Around his bed were piled stacks of dusty books, some old, some new, all with cracked bindings from overuse. These weren't legal books intended for Jackson's defense. Though he was up for parole in less than a year, Jackson knew his case was hopeless. He'd been to the *inquisition* several times before, always with the same result.

"Maybe next time, Mr. DesValle . . . Maybe next time." But next time he would predictably hear, "Parole denied."

It amazed Jackson the questions the committee routinely posed as if this time, finally, he would answer correctly and they could all go home.

"Are you sorry for what you did?" reiterated the double-chinned matron with the malignant mole on the side of her nostril.

"Yes ma'am," solemnly replied Jackson, "Sorry as sorry can be."

The woman sniffled, unconvinced, as an emaciated man with a pencil-thin mustache and a Marine tattoo on his forearm jumped in, "She means . . . " (as if Jackson was too stupid to understand the question) " . . . are you remorseful, Mr. DesValle?"

It took every ounce of strength not to leap across the table and smash their heads together like coconuts, watching the warm milk pour out the cracks. "Why yes, yes sir, remorseful as remorseful can be," lied Jackson, doe-eyed.

His favorite question usually came towards the end of the proceedings and involved his future job prospects. The parole chairman, a dour man in his late sixties, who had tufts of hair growing out of his ears and a nasty case of psoriasis on his neck, drawled, "Have you managed to locate gainful employment on the outside, Mr. DesValle?"

Talk about your Catch-22's. Jackson actually did try calling once for a job from the prison pay phone. He called an automotive garage in Gretna and a buddy he used to work with who ran a small repair shop. Jackson considered Bubba one of his few friends left on the planet. They had both "done time" at the same Catholic orphanage. But Bubba paused a good while when he heard Jackson's voice on the other end of the phone. The last time Bubba had seen his ex-friend was on the six o'clock news: "The man nicknamed 'the Tarot card rapist,' Jackson DesValle, has been captured after a brutal two year spree. One of his victims died following DeValle's vicious attack."

Jackson had been tagged the "Tarot card rapist" because he would always leave a different Tarot card behind on the nightstand. His M.O. was to select women from aerobics classes at various work-out clubs where he temporarily became a member. A muscular specimen himself, DesValle would follow his prey home from the gym, carrying his Nike gym bag.

All of his victims were young single females living by themselves. But not one of them ever suspected they were being trailed by a serial rapist on a black Honda Rebel motorcycle driving behind their cars through the streets of New Orleans. But they found out, soon enough, what was in the gym bag . . . a ski mask, eight feet of nylon rope, a chromeplated Raven .25 ACP, and a deck of Tarot cards with several missing.

Jackson wiped the sweat from his brow onto the back of his pudgy arm. He had lost a lot of muscle tone in prison preferring not to exercise in the yard with the others. He wouldn't take part in that musclebound freak show or go cruising for new arrivals, "chicken wings" as they were affectionately called. He'd much rather stay in his cell and read. It's how he escaped.

Conjugal Visit

The temperature felt like it was rising as the night wore on and Jackson's labored breath echoed off the slick walls.

He glanced down at the titles of the books stacked closest to the bed: *A Soul's Journey, The Fourth Dimension, Disembodiment, Adventures in the Spirit World, Projecting the Astral Body, Documented Out-of-Body Experiences* and *The Search for the Astral Plane.*

Jackson selected a book off the top of the stack, from 1927, entitled *Handbook of Astral Travel.* His fingers caressed the cracked binding and he took out the book mark, a greasy black comb with several teeth missing. Jackson hadn't been one much for literature before he launched his prison career, but the chaplain had taught him to read children's books, and over the years, Jackson had advanced to high school proficiency.

Though he failed to mention it to Father Reyes, the only reason he wanted to learn to read was so he could enjoy his voluminous mail. It had started even before the trial. Hundreds of letters, many from out of state, all from women. There were pen pals, lonely hearts, offers of financial assistance, proposals of marriage and even a few nude photos.

These letters were the greatest of mysteries to Jackson who could never seem to get a handle on the opposite sex and was responsible for no less than twenty-nine rapes. *Who were these women?* Jackson wondered. *And where were they before his arrest?*

Jackson had raped the first girl he ever dated when he was sixteen. It went unreported. Jackson actually dated her twice, but after the first ten minutes, watching him wolf three hot dogs at a Lucky Dog vendor, she wanted nothing more to do with him. That's what the second date was for, to let him down gently. At six-three, two hundred and eighteen pounds, Jackson wasn't the kind of boy you wanted to upset. There was something brewing beneath those inset eyes, an inner energy which his female pen pals, who were drawn to him on the news, mistook for sexual magnetism.

What it was, was anger.

Jackson was angry at the system, angry at his father for deserting him when he was five, angry at his alcoholic mother for blaming and abusing him, and angry at her for dying of an overdose, leaving him orphaned at twelve.

The twenty-nine rapes he committed were the release of that anger. Most of his victims were hospitalized afterwards with concussions and broken bones. One later died from a collapsed lung.

At his highly publicized trial, Jackson felt betrayed by his victims for giving the police the details that led to his downfall. He hated the cops who arrested him, he hated the state-appointed lawyer who incompetently defended him, he hated the publicity seeking Assistant D.A. who prosecuted him and he hated the woman judge who sentenced him.

And Jackson had a long, long memory.

He took a deep breath and laid back on the cot with his book, trying to block out the incessant ranting diatribes of his cellblock neighbors.

He opened the *Handbook of Astral Travel* to chapter nine. He had spent more time on this chapter than any other. He read to himself, his lips moving, caressing every word. He closed his eyes and repeated the page verbatim. He had been painstakingly committing the entire chapter to memory. After repeating the page several times he reached overhead and switched off the reading light, then laid back on his cot with the book opened across his bare chest.

It was time to go out for a spin.

Jackson regulated his breathing, slowing his heart beat. He focussed on the drip on his forehead, concentrating with all his being on the desire for "projection."

Drip . . . drip . . . drip . . .

He fell into a trance and his mind wandered back to his fourteenth rape. Her name was Kathleen LeMont, a petite blonde who lived in a subdivision of Lafayette. He knew where she lived because he had trailed her home on several occasions after her aerobics class at a gym called Sweats.

He knew her body in minute detail, the way her small nipples would harden under her spandex as she exercised, the way her thong leotard sandwiched between her firm butt cheeks, and the perspiration ring which would spread between the legs of her tights.

His mind suddenly dissolved to the trial, watching her testify and the undeniable terror as she tried not to lock eyes with him. She was the only victim who could I.D. him in a lineup, because the night of the rape she had inadvertently pulled off his ski mask.

She would never forget his eyes. Burning rage in the dark.

The scars had not yet faded from her face as she took the stand, and when it came time for the moment the prosecutor was waiting for, Kathleen drew a breath, pointed a shivering finger in Jackson's direction, and declared, "That's him . . . that's the man who raped me."

Jackson's conscious mind reentered his body. The astral projection wasn't working. He had followed the book's instructions precisely, even fasting for a day to increase the inflow of cosmic energy.

He focused again on the monotonous drip, his mind clawing up the water droplets like a ladder towards the ceiling . . . rising . . . rising. It was an exhausting experience and Jackson tightly squinted in the dark as he subconsciously willed himself to leave his body, imagining steam emanating from all of his pores.

A cold numbness began spreading over his limbs and he heard a faint ringing in his ears.

The process had begun.

He began detaching from his physical body. First, he separated out of the soles of his feet, disconnecting from each tendon along his body, hearing the faint snapping of innumerable small cords as his astral body contracted like an elastic band. He at last emerged from his head like a translucent soap bubble rising towards the ceiling. It floated higher and higher until it finally tapped the ceiling and popped into a cloud of bluish mist.

The mist molecules began moving together, forming into the phantom shape of a man.

Jackson was at last free of his body.

He fought to open his eyes, desperately wanting to awaken in the astral but knowing that this was an extremely difficult stage. Finally, with intense concentration his astral eyes popped open.

At first he was frightened he would fall, as his spiritual body hovered six feet above his physical body, near the ceiling. But as he gazed down at his pathetic shell on his prison cot, weak and balding, looking all but dead, he was glad to be rid of it for awhile.

He tried to move through the air but found himself floating uncontrollably about his cell. He eventually relaxed into the preliminary stage of exteriorization, and was able to glide back and forth horizontally, discovering that motion was reversed in the astral plane. It you thought "upwards" you'd go "downwards" and if you thought of turning "left" you'd turn "right" and visa versa.

Once he mastered propelling his phantom, all he needed to do was escape the confines of his cell. *This shouldn't be too tough*, speculated Jackson. But for some reason the bars formed a formidable mental barrier even to his fleeing astral being. Something was holding him back. He soon discovered what it was. A cord was connected to the back of his astral skull, tying him to his physical body. He reached behind his head and touched the whitish cable, feeling the heartbeat of his physical body through the ghostly cerebral life line.

But Jackson wasn't going to be trapped by some string cheese connected to his cranium. He considered ripping the cord, then remembered from his book that severing the psychic cable could bring immediate death to the physical body. So, instead, he concentrated with all his will, projecting himself beyond the cell bars.

Suddenly, the bars passed right through his luminous body and he was now observing his physical body from outside his cell. The cord was still connected to the back of his head but it had grown thinner as it was stretched further, like a lucid strand of cobweb.

He was free!, laughed Jackson loudly, then covered his mouth as if someone would hear him. But the correctional officer, patrolling on duty, only rubbed his neck as a cold draft blew past. Odd, thought the c. o., on such a muggy night.

Jackson's astral body was now soaring over the penitentiary towards the stars. The air was delicious. He felt exhilarated as he traveled at lightning speed along the Mississippi, over Baton Rouge towards New Orleans, over the crumbling cemeteries, the drunken revelers on Bourbon Street and the seedy slice of Magazine Street.

Little did Kathleen LeMont know that the "Tarot card Rapist" had kept track of her, as he did all his *girls* and knew where each were living. It was heck-of-a-lot easier than finding a job, chortled Jackson, as he set his evil soul on a course for her quaint guest house in the Garden District.

St. Charles Street was empty and quiet. Never had the city looked so mystically beautiful. The stately mansions, draped in tangled vines, were shrouded in a dense mist like a terrarium.

It was a little after three in the morning as a bluish vapor infiltrated Kathleen's kitchen window. All the dishes were washed and put away. Everything neatly in place.

Jackson floated through the small living room and eagerly moved towards the bedroom, still aware of the nagging pull at the base of his phantom skull.

Kathleen was lying on her stomach, on her four-poster bed, under a lace canopy. The sheets had been pushed back in the sultry night, her damp nightgown bunched up over her ivory hips.

Back in his cell, Jackson's soulless body began to get a hard-on.

Meanwhile, in Kathleen's airless bedroom, Jackson hovered inches over her sleeping body. He blew into her ear and she swatted at the tickle, then rolled over onto her back.

She was a few years older and had gained a couple pounds since her gym days but was still in great shape from her workouts in the safety of her secluded guest house.

She breathed through her open mouth in her sleep, her legs slightly parted. Jackson ran his ghostly fingers over her flesh. She didn't flinch, though she mumbled something in her sleep. He lowered his luminous astral body on top of her and, with a radiant tendril of sexual energy, willed himself inside of her.

Kathleen's forehead crinkled up as a horrible nightmare began to form in her subconscious.

Jackson DesValle had returned.

She desperately fought to pull herself from the depths of slumber as Jackson began to beat her face with his fists as he had done during the rape, her head tossing from side to side with each punch. Finally, she dragged her subconscious from molasses and opened her terrified eyes.

For the briefest of moments she thought she saw the angry eyes of Jackson, burning in the dark.

Kathleen LeMont sat up and screamed the air out of her lungs.

Lights popped on in the main house.

Moments later, her landlord, Grace, was knocking on the door. Kathleen was at first too shaken to unlock the deadbolt but Grace finally convinced her it was safe.

When she opened the door, Kathleen collapsed into Grace's arms, sobbing, confiding to her that she had just had a vivid nightmare of her rape.

"It seemed so real," sobbed Kathleen.

Grace nodded and patted her tenant's icy hand, comforting her. But Kathleen decided not to mention that her face was hurting, as if she was feeling the bruises all over again, from eight years ago.

Jackson was jolted back to his cell and snapped backwards into his empty shell as if by an invisible elastic cord. His physical limbs jerked spasmodically. Then his body lay still, breathless for almost a minute. Suddenly, his fingers twitched alive like spiders on their backs. He took a deep gasp of breath and his eyes fluttered open. He felt thoroughly exhausted, had a splitting headache and a deep pain slicing down the center of his body like he'd been hacked in two.

When the ache began to dissipate, he leaned forward on his cot, cradling the back of his head, and noticed that his body had experienced a nocturnal emission. He didn't even bother wiping himself off, he just lay back down, feeling the comforting drip . . . drip . . . drip . . . on his forehead.

It had been a good night. But there were more ahead. Tomorrow he would visit another of his girls.

Who needed conjugal visits?

He could drop by anytime he wanted.

Heartless

Another "Raoul, Low-life Ex-Cop" Adventure

The warm acid rain fell unmercifully, dropping needles on Raoul's deeply furrowed forehead, rolling down the creases like a maze. He jammed his thick hands deep into his pockets as if they were warmer down at the bottom. He smelled of mildew and cheap bourbon.

His heart beat a war drum in his chest as he stood in the shadows of a graffiti-scrawled alley smoking a Lucky, watching an apartment across the street, the one with the blue light shining through the dingy curtains. He tucked his Saint Christopher medal into his shirt so it wouldn't reflect, then checked his watch knowing it was three minutes slow and too early for the show to begin. A crack of thunder startled Raoul, his heart skipping like a needle across a record. He chuckled at himself as he smoothed down the coarse hairs on the back of his neck which had bristled up like a pig at the slaughterhouse.

He was sick of being a private dick and missed the beat. Watching seedy sex from the sidewalk had its moments, but he would have rather collected his pension and moved to warmer climates.

Unfortunately, Raoul had a penchant for screwing up, and rather largely. Six charges of excessive force, drinking on the job, accepting bribes, and the kicker . . . shagging a teenage prostitute in the back of his squad car. Raoul suspected that was the final straw.

He raised his face to the storm, feeling much like the turkey who watches the rain until it drowns.

This, regrettably, was Raoul's last conscious thought.

Suddenly, a familiar sound sent a shiver through his spine, slapping his vertebrae together like a row of shuffleboard discs. It was the unmistakable click and tumble of a .38 special followed by the metallic slap of a hammer against a firing pin. Then, a blinding flash like lightning.

He didn't even hear the "bang." The bullet beat the sound.

Like a manic cartoon, Raoul's legs flung out from under him and his body tensed into a rigid ironing board, facing the pavement. He noticed a yellow dandelion poking out of a sidewalk crack, approaching rapidly. The last thing he heard was his Saint Christopher medal clinking to the pavement . . . followed by a dull thud.

The anesthesia was not as effective as he had hoped. He felt himself descending to a depth where he couldn't form words, but nevertheless, could numbly feel the compression in his chest as his ribs were pried apart, like cracked crab. He heard sirens faintly in the background as other unlucky stiffs were delivered on confused gurney wheels, like wobbly shopping carts racing for the frozen meat section.

Raoul could smell his own blood, a savory gravy smell, while a sucking sound like a dentist's spit-bowl gurgled behind his head, and he objectively wondered whether it was pumping something in or siphoning something out. The nurse, with harried footsteps, left to retrieve a sharper scalpel, Raoul hoped, as his blood squirted in thin jets on the latex- gloved white-masked surgeons who struggled to restitch Raoul from scraps of flesh.

Raoul kept reliving the flash of the gun, the slurping sound of the bullet peeling apart his pectorals and the heated lead hurtling between his ribs, fired by a man he had never met —or was it a woman? No matter, bullets were sexless. Besides, there were any number of trigger men, or women, who would have liked to use Raoul for target practice. An ex-con, a vengeful husband, Raoul's own girlfriend or ex-wife, or both, holding the gun and laughing simultaneously as they pulled the trigger. Hell, let's not rule out suicide.

Raoul felt a draft across his gaping incision as more equipment was wheeled in and he was surrounded by the numbing voices of dread. He felt suspended between two worlds, floating on this sterile steel table holding his soul aloft, halfway to heaven and halfway to hell.

And then, he was heartless.

For a brief moment he had the realization that his still beating heart was out of his chest while his brain continued to function normally, like a radio that continues to play for a second after it's unplugged. It was an accurate notion, and not a pleasant one at that.

Raoul was about to become a donor. That damned card in his wallet. He had filled it in at a bar as a joke. Bunch of drunk cops shooting Cuervo at Ernie's while holding their donor cards and flipping coins, "Heads, they can take my head, tails, they can bite my ass." A bit juvenile, but cops in bars were like that. Anyway, Raoul's toss came up heads and he drunkenly scrawled the epitaph, "Take me, I'm yours" on his donor card. The guys got a belly laugh out of that one as Raoul drunkenly stashed the card in his wallet. And there it remained for three years with a Ramses's reservoir-tip condom pressed firmly against it.

Beep . . . Beep . . . Beeeeeeeeeeee . . .

Raoul was still alive, barely, on the operating table but he suspected his heart was already in a stainless steel bowl used at hospital Christmas parties for guacamole dip and was about to be plopped into an Igloo ice chest for a flight on the "Friendly Skies."

The doctors were still at work in his gaping chest and Raoul wondered why, then bleakly remembered the *other* organs. Raoul suddenly felt like he was in the middle of a medical shopping spree: "Spleen, check . . . Liver, check . . . Eyes double check . . . Oh, and cock and balls, did anyone order the cock and balls?"

Heartless

A nurse's maniacal laugh faded as Raoul fell backwards into the dark place screaming, "Don't take my cock and ballllllllsssss!"

The end. Or was it?

Raoul swam towards the surface through thick congealed liquid, tangled kelp grabbing his limbs like waxy alien fingers, holding him back from a much needed breath.

He bolted up in bed and gasped. Disoriented, a pain burning his chest like napalm, Raoul squinted in the harsh fluorescent lights, his eyes adjusting to a canary yellow hospital room.

He was naked, both arms connected to IVs, and had an angry purple wound stitched down his chest that would make Frankenstein wince. Raoul had just noticed that his Saint Christopher medal was missing when he felt a stream of hot liquid squirt between his legs, the warm pool spreading around his thighs. Raoul sighed like he'd untapped a keg of beer.

A Philippine nurse, her name tag reading Angel, entered, pushing a draped metal cart. He hoped she was hiding some highly hallucinogenic substances in that cart, the more illegal the better. Angel leaned over him. She was badly in need of a lip wax.

"And how are we feeling?" she smilingly asked.

We? Raoul calmly thought. If *she* were feeling what *he* was she wouldn't have to ask because she would be writhing around on the linoleum pissing in her panties and screaming for someone to grab a fucking fire extinguisher and put out the forest fire in her chest.

Raoul uttered a "muh" as Angel smelled the urine and continued unabated, like a mother who can understand her "goo-gooing" infant.

"You've been out for three days," she answered as she ripped back the sheets, revealing Raoul's pale nakedness. They both studied his wrinkled member, a mere replica of its former self. Nevertheless, Raoul was pleased to see his old pal, Gomez.

Angel whistled as she yanked a Handiwipe and heartily wiped the urine off his genitals.

"You're a lucky man," Angel chirped, "the bullet missed your heart by this much, the doctor say." She held her thumb and forefinger together, with no space in between, and Raoul wondered if she was exaggerating or just phenomenally stupid.

"Did you know you were dead when you came in here?" Angel cheerfully informed as she balled up the urine stained sheets, lifted both his legs with one hand and wiped off his bare bottom like a baby being diapered.

Raoul, helpless, formed his first word, "Dead?" She threw the damp sheet on the bottom shelf of her cart and took out a clean one, "The doctor tell you all about it. But you're a lucky man. Very, very lucky." She was out of the room with her cart before Raoul could utter one more pained word . . . "Drugs."

For five days Raoul lay in bed staring at the acoustic ceiling, playing connect the dots until his butt began to itch and he decided it was time to go after his killer. The doctor advised him to stay a few more days, but Raoul didn't have insurance and knew the doctor would change his prognosis when he found out. Raoul figured that gave him about a week to capture his would-be assassin and skedaddle out of town before the checks started bouncing.

Raoul took the Pico Union bus from County General back to his hotel on Seventh and Alvarado. He sat on his swayback bed, scratching his stitches and making a list of everyone who had out for him. He had to continue on a second page.

Letting his fingers do the walking, Raoul made calls to his cop-drinking buddies who were stunned he had pulled through. The word was apparently out that Raoul was cooling like fudge on a marble stab. The department hadn't even assigned a detective, yet, to the case. But Raoul knew they were on overload and he was a "low-pri" anyhow, an ex-cop with a nose for trouble, a rap sheet and few friends in the department. But he was appreciative of the head start afforded by his past.

He swallowed two Percodans dry, appropriated from Angel's pill cart, as he narrowed down his list of suspects to a half a page. Many were dead. Drug overdoses, murderous lovers, drive-bys, and suicides. Twelve had left town, the country or perhaps the planet. Another seventeen were still in jail and one was muerto, shanked in the eyeball during a Chowchilla riot. Raoul knew his ex-wife wouldn't kill him before getting an alimony payment . . . and she was still waiting. That left the man who had hired Raoul to watch his wife while he worked graveyard, the wife with the insatiable itch, or her young scratch. Also, regrettably still making the list: Raoul's current squeeze, the police chief, and Raoul's mother.

Raoul rode the midnight bus not knowing exactly where to start but suspecting the beginning was an appropriate place. He got off the bus and walked down Eighteenth to Bonnie

Brae Street past the rows of dingy barred apartments, Pentecostal churches and heavily tattooed gang members dealing five dollar bags of black Mexican tar heroin.

Raoul located his dried blood on the sidewalk. He had lost a lot of red that night and wasn't particularly surprised that in this neighborhood no one had cleaned it up.

Raoul studied the graffiti-coated alley where he had been hired to stand by the jealous husband who suspected the crusty stains on the bed sheets weren't his own. The husband and wife hadn't had sexual relations for five months before the husband dialed Raoul's "AAA Detectives," the first detective agency listed in the Yellow Pages. Raoul's agency used to be "Abracadabra Detectives" but he changed his name to "AAA" when "Aardvark Detectives" tried to muscle ahead of him in the phone book. Raoul knew that desperate clients often called the first agency listed in the phone book and in his business, they were all desperate.

Raoul yawned and checked his watch; still three minutes slow, it now read twenty past one in the A.M. He reached into the holster concealed behind his back underneath his trench coat, and removed his Tangfolio-Spa BT 99. He checked the magazine. Thirteen rounds. He snapped one into the chamber, comforted by the sound, and pushed the safety off with his thumb before placing the weapon back in its holster.

His chest was itching like crazy and he fought like hell not to scratch, though at that moment he would have given anything for a salad fork. Instead, he bit back a Percodan and watched a man in his mid-twenties park his VW bug down the block, walk to the subject's apartment and leap up the steps two at a time.

Heartless

The wiry young man, wearing a Grateful Dead tank top which showed off his sinewy biceps and a Tweety Bird tattoo, smoothed back his long greasy hair and rang the bell for number five. He was promptly buzzed inside.

Shortly after the barred security door clanked shut, a black Pontiac Fiero slowly glided down the street, pulled in front of the apartment building and turned off its lights. The windows were smoked black and Raoul wondered if it was the suspicious husband checking on the "missus." But Raoul remembered that the husband drove an '83 Buick and set his sights back on the apartment window as two figures entered the illuminated bedroom, one wearing a Grateful Dead tank top.

Raoul had learned from watching the duo that this wasn't a romance built on conversation and the action would be hard and fast. Raoul pulled the pair of Army Surplus binoculars out of his trench coat pocket and blew hot breath onto the lenses rubbing them clean against his shirt. He climbed the stairs of an apartment stoop opposite the suspect's apartment and waited until the lights flicked off before raising his binoculars.

Moonlight shone through the parted bedroom curtains as Raoul observed the young man seated at the foot of the bed, his 501's around his knees, an expression of near pain on his face, as the woman kneeled in front of him fellating him like a well-oiled steam piston. These are the details that Raoul would rather not provide to jealous husbands, preferring to say they were seen "together."

Raoul was distracted from the porno loop in apartment five by a distinctive spraying sound. He lowered his binoculars and peeked around the doorway as a gang member in a plaid shirt, White Sox baseball cap and a blue handkerchief covering his face from the nose down, tagged the brick wall. The tagger artistically sprayed his street mark while Raoul slowly backed into the entranceway, inadvertently tapping his binoculars against the wall. The tagger, startled by the sound, immediately whirled around, pointed a gun in Raoul's direction and shouted, "Venga aqui!"

"Shit," Raoul hissed through his nicotine stained teeth. He stepped out of the doorway palms at his shoulders, staring down at the snub nose barrel of a chrome plated .38 special. When the tagger saw Raoul's face he reacted as if he was seeing a ghost.

"Usted estas muerto," the tagger uttered.

Raoul didn't know how this gang-banger knew him, or why he thought he was dead, or even care. But he was happy to introduce him to the nine millimeter in his holster.

They stood like this for several unsettling moments, Raoul anticipating another quick trip to the hospital, though he expected this time he wouldn't be so fortunate. The tension was broken by a woman's muffled moan emanating from the apartment across the quiet street and Raoul could only imagine what he was missing. The tagger made a slight turn of his head, indicating he heard this too. Raoul smiled his best knowing smile, raised his eyebrows and nudged his head in the direction of the moans, like a drinking buddy pointing out a babe in Spandex pants.

Raoul couldn't tell if this was working, and whether the tagger was lecherously grinning back under the handkerchief, or preparing to blow his head off, but he took the chance anyhow and offered his binoculars for a closer look. The tagger seemed curious and put out his free hand. Raoul, his neighborly grin starting to waver, tossed the binoculars.

In that fraction of an instant, as the tagger used both his hands to catch the binoculars, Raoul reached behind his back and pulled his 9mm from its holster. But before Raoul could say "freeze," a sudden burst of automatic gunfire burst out, violently pinning the tagger against his graffitied wall. Raoul whirled around to the black Pontiac parked across the street as a gang member leaned out the back window firing a Mac 10. The teenage shooter finger-flashed his street numbers and then screeched off in the Pontiac packed with bangers.

The bullet ridden tagger collapsed face first on the sidewalk onto Raoul's dried blood, the back of his shirt displaying the wet paint imprint of his placaso, his gang moniker.

Raoul stepped over the body. The front of the tagger's face was Smuckers. He placed two fingers against the kid's carotid artery. Nada. He tentatively lifted the blood-clotted handkerchief off the tagger's face and saw that one cheek was blown clean off, leaving him with a grotesque grimace. The other side of the kid's face displayed the plump collagen cheeks of a boy no more than twelve. Raoul noticed something glittering around the tagger's neck. He wiped off the sticky blood and could see it was a gold Saint Christopher medal. Curious, he turned over the medal and read the inscription, "I am a Catholic. In case of an accident, notify a priest." The flowery inscription was dedicated "to Raoul, from Rosa." It was a gift from Raoul's mother.

Case closed. Apparently Raoul had been standing in front of the deceased tagger's moniker, was mistaken for a rival tagger in the dark and shot. Possibly a "bomb run"—a graffiti duel between gangs. The streets weren't safe anymore, even for thugs like Raoul.

Across the street, the married subject and her bump breathlessly poked their heads out the window of apartment five. But Raoul had already started down the sidewalk as sirens wailed like coyotes in the distance.

The couple craned their heads further out the soiled curtains, watching Raoul as he strolled down the graffiti-scrawled street, scratching his chest.

Raoul had left the medal on the boy's neck.

Its luck had run out.

Howling Wind

They lived up in the Chesapeake mountains where the snow was deep, winters brutal. After a particularly severe blizzard, which dumped a record sixteen feet of snow, the only sign of Ben's cabin was the river-rock smokestack and a telltale wisp of white smoke.

Ben had been snowed in for twelve days and his food rations were down to three Ritz crackers, a can of Crisco and a jar of jalapenos—the killer kind that made your eyes burn and sweat beads burst out on your forehead.

Ben, a burly logger with tree-trunk biceps and heavy red beard, had fallen on hard times long before the blizzard. But he wasn't alone. It seemed that a white spotted owl had put two hundred loggers out of work. Ben would have liked to fricassee that dumb bird, with a cream sauce of "environmentalist," but they were "protected." Ben feared the logger would be next on the endangered species list. Then *he* would be "protected."

Ben felt his stomach chewing on itself and sliced a sliver of jalapeno with his hunting knife. He noticed Buck staring and offered him a piece. But Buck wouldn't touch the stuff. Made him sneeze.

Buck was half timber wolf, half German shepherd, with jet black fur, a thick white mane, and eyes like a forest fire. Buck had been the biggest puppy Ben had ever laid eyes on. Paws like horse hoofs and a mouth full of calcium stalactites that could crush bone. The old Zuni woman who bred wolves with domestics assured Ben he was tame as a kitten. But Ben knew better. Kittens could grow to be mountain lions and breeding was tricky stuff. You had to water down the killer without making him weak.

Buck grew into his feet by the following spring and his muscular back rose nearly to Ben's waist. The gangly pup would teethe on pine cones, snapping them in two in a bite; and Ben sensed that Buck's instincts for survival were as strong as ever. Now, trapped with dwindling food and lousy prospects, Buck had begun to stare with hungry eyes . . . and Ben thought about those teeth.

Ben closed his eyes from the hound's unnerving stare and listened to the fire crackle, feeling the warmth on his face. He thought back to the winter chariot races where wolf dogs pulled homemade chariots of timber. Ben and Buck's team was christened "Ben-Hur" and after three straight wins they had become legend up in the mountains. The next year was a different story.

Howling Wind

Frank LeGrand had brought his gray wolf, Shadow. Though smaller than Buck, Shadow was just as strong, fast as lightning, and one hundred percent timber wolf. Ben knew it would be a race.

The contestants, nine men and two women, waited unsmilingly on the starting line. Some deep in thought, trance-like, others offering last minute words of encouragement to their wolf dogs.

The starter pistol sounded and the dogs bolted off, towing their one-man sleds behind. LeGrand got a slow start, cut off by a Siberian husky, but Buck quickly got in front of the pack just as Ben planned. By the second mile, Shadow hit his stride weaving through the pack like a slalom. LeGrand spotted Ben and worked Shadow up behind their sled. LeGrand held back a length and stayed there for seven miles.

With the finish line a quarter mile ahead, Shadow pulled alongside of Buck and LeGrand flashed a toothy smile, Ben noticing that he could use some dental work. They were still neck and neck when they spotted the finish line ahead. Ben whipped fire into Buck's eyes, who needed little encouragement, as he dug his powerful paws into the snow.

A yard away from the finish line LeGrand pulled out his secret weapon, a three foot long cattle prod. He gave Shadow a single jolt on the haunches and Shadow surged ahead, beating Buck by a nose.

LeGrand proudly held the trophy cup overhead, with pats on the back all around as Buck's angry breath burst from his nostrils like a steam engine.

Ben was tilting beers afterwards at Willie's Watering Hole when he heard the ruckus outside. Snarling wolves, snapping teeth, and the howl of death. Ben ran outside without his jacket—shivering with an icy premonition.

LeGrand was on his knees beside Shadow. Blood was sprayed on the snow like spin art and Shadow's soft neck was ripped clean out. "Looks like a badger attack," Willie the bartender said. But it soon became clear from the steaming blood on Buck's muzzle who had done the dirty work.

LeGrand screamed that Buck should be destroyed, "There's something about that dog that ain't right." But Ben said it was LeGrand's fault for leaving the dogs chained so close. A circle of men gathered, shouting drunken encouragements, egging them on. LeGrand threw the first punch and Ben was glad because it gave him sportsmanlike reasons to flatten Frank with a right hook as Buck watched . . . wagging his tail.

A piece of birch bark cracked like a blackjack firecracker, jarring Ben and sending a spray of sparks over Buck. Ben noticed that Buck had moved closer to the fire, his unrelenting stare giving Ben the shivers.

"Need another log," Ben whispered. But Buck was guarding the fireplace and Ben didn't want to disturb him. "Not now. Better save the wood for later," he added out loud, wondering if there would actually be a later.

It was deathly quiet in the cabin. Ben could almost feel the weight of the snow, smothering him, pushing on his lungs, a vise tightening on his chest. The clock over the mantel tick-tocked . . . tick-tocked . . . tick-tocked . . . with agonizing slowness as minutes melted. The fireplace was now just a pile of angry embers as the clock suddenly hurled against the wall shattering into pieces.

Ben rubbed his fatigued eyes, drugged by the fire's hypnotic dance. When he looked up, the clock was still on the mantel . . . tick-tocking . . . tick-tocking . . . tick-tocking . . . Buck still staring.

Ben shook off the stare competition with Buck and decided to start reading his book over from the beginning again. *Call of the Wild.*

Buck's savage eyes soon grew weary and he dropped off to doggy dreamland. Though beckoned by exhaustion himself, Ben feared that Buck was just pretending to be asleep and was waiting for him to shut his eyes. A trick to lull him to sleep and then go for the jugular. Meanwhile, Buck's snoring, whether real or fake, grew more annoying, and Ben could actually feel his exhale being sucked into the wolf dog's snorting black nostrils, with precious air left to share.

An arctic whisper blew down the chimney and Ben inhaled a deep breath of sweet pine air before Buck stole it all.

Then, the wind died.

The cabin creaked with arthritis and Ben heard a rattle by the back door. Someone was breaking in! But that was impossible; they were ten feet under the snow. Unless . . . unless . . . they were being rescued! *Well, it was about time.* He had been fearing that all the neighbors were dead by now, their chimneys stuffed with snow clots cutting off their last gasps of breath.

The doorknob rattled again. *Maybe there were looters outside waiting to pick him clean like vultures on a rotting carcass.* Well, these looters would have a surprise in store. If Buck didn't tear them to shreds, he had the "ole Pacifier" over the fireplace.

Ben glanced at his twin barrel shotgun above the mantel. To get to it he would have to step over Buck. He gently placed his book on the arm rest and, walking heel to toe, silently approached his wolf dog. The floorboards creaked. Buck stopped snoring. Ben froze.

It seemed like an eternity until Buck started snoring again. When he was certain Buck was asleep, Ben gingerly stepped one foot over the furry beast. His fingertips could just barely touch the butt of the shotgun. He raised his other leg over Buck realizing he was in a rather precarious position, one leg stretched over Buck, leaving his manhood hovering like a meaty dog treat for his starving wolf pet.

The clock tick-tocked . . . tick-tocked in rhythm with Ben's pounding heart . . . totally terrified of Buck who slowly opened one piercing red eye.

A low growl began somewhere in Buck's kidneys and rose up his esophagus to a throaty earthquake. Buck's black nose pleated back like an accordion, his dark lips lifted a curtain call over his gargantuan canines and a thick thread of drool flooded over his gums, puddling on the rag rug.

Ben's fingers desperately fumbled for the shotgun. If he could get control of the weapon he planned to aim straight down and give Buck both barrels in the head, putting the beast out of its misery. He imagined at this range the impact would be terrific, scattering bone and brain tissue everywhere.

Suddenly, as if Buck could read his mind, and with blinding speed, the beast leapt up, clamped Ben's crotch in his canines like a vicious moray eel, and bit through the crotch of his Levis with the sound of a snapping pine cone.

Howling Wind

Ben lurched up in bed, perspiring, soaked in fear beneath his cozy down comforter. Moonlight crept through the torn curtains. Perhaps it had all been a dream, like in a bad B-movie.

Ben dabbed the spittle that had leaked from his lips during sleep and studied the wetness. It was purple in the moonlight. Ben realized that the snow had melted below the top of the window. He reached up, placing his palm against the cold glass, feeling the moonlight through the pane. For a moment the weight of the snow lifted. But, as he pulled his hand from the glass, he noticed an ominously dark handprint. He involuntarily gulped as he wiped his hand on the comforter leaving shadowy smudges. Ben suddenly recalled the movie, *The Godfather*, which he had watched five times on mountain cable, as he slowly pulled back the covers. Fortunately, nothing unusual awaited him, though his pajamas were drenched as if he had sweat out a fever. He checked his crotch, which had shriveled in fear, but otherwise appeared in proper order.

Relieved, he got out of bed and stepped into something sticky, like molasses. Concerned, he desperately tried to whistle for Buck, his mouth stale and dry, but the pitiful sound was drowned by the wind—howling like a wounded animal surrounded by a pack of hyenas.

Ben followed the bloody tributaries along the hardwood, into the living room. The clock had been bashed into pieces, the book's ashes glowing in the fireplace. He noticed that the shotgun was missing from the mantle and dried blood was splattered against the river rock hearth. He immediately crouched into a fighting stance, preparing for the worst.

"Who's there?," he shouted. But his voice caught in his throat, making him sound as weak as he felt.

He tiptoed towards the kitchen, cringing at each squeaky plank, anticipating the horror that might greet him.

He wasn't let down.

Ben's wail of agony clawed up the river rock chimney and was released into the night. But there was no one to hear him. Only the ice crystals floating and dying.

Buck lay on the kitchen floor, gutted . . . his insides devoured. The shotgun leaned against the locked back door.

Dazed and nauseous Ben brushed bloodstained fingertips over his trembling lips as he felt a horrible ache rise from his belly.

With a twisted, knotted bubble of sorrow and regret . . .

He belched.

Taking Out The Garbage

Marty's mother was suffocating . . . in the Hefty garbage bag by the kitchen door.

The craftsman house was eerily quiet, except for the occasional moan from the Hefty bag. The quiet was nice. Marty was glad not to be arguing with his mother, as he had done for the last thirty-nine years. He had finally acted like the man she had always wanted him to be.

That's when she wound up in the Hefty bag.

He planned to take the bag outside and place her by the curb for the morning pickup but for now was satisfied to have her close at hand. He went to the back door and compulsively checked the lock for the eleventh time, furtively glancing at the hunter green, plastic trash bag. It could be filled with chicken bones or garden leaves or old newspapers but instead it was filled with mom. It gave Marty a comforting feeling.

He decided to watch some television and dragged the Hefty bag into the den where Leona's nineteen-inch Magnavox awaited.

"What do you want to watch, Ma?" asked Marty as he rapidly surfed through the channels with the remote. There was a groan from the bag and Marty felt a twinge of guilt. Maybe he should loosen the top, give her a sip of air? But he was terrified that she might spring out and slit his throat with her sharpened fingernails. It was a disturbing thought and Marty tried to divert his attention with double Jeopardy. He played along with the game show, occasionally uttering to the bag, "Hey, Ma, I got another one right! Did you hear?"

Silence from the bag.

But Marty wasn't fooled. She was listening, no doubt, formulating a dark plan for revenge.

It was past midnight. Marty had six hours until trash pickup and he nervously chuckled as he pictured the trash bag lifted over the back of the garbage truck and Leona, in her fetid bag of glory, spilling into the stench. A poetic end.

Yet, Marty wondered, was it right? Killing your mother was nasty business. He liked his job at the post office and didn't want anyone to take it away from him. Just let them try! But he was jumping ahead of himself. He hadn't even been caught, yet. Hell, he hadn't even really committed a crime, yet. Unless, you consider drugging your mother's Listerine and dumping her convulsing body in a Hefty bag a crime. But what would that be with no prior record and plea bargained in today's lenient courts? Assault and battery? A couple years on parole, at worst, with some community hours served. The real

Taking Out The Garbage

crime wouldn't occur for another few hours when his mother would be added to the local landfill.

You might be wondering at this point what Marty's childhood was like. It appeared quite normal. School, toys, ice cream cones. But Marty also had a mother who would pop his pimples before school, perform minor dental surgery to save money and once even made him drink a vitamin milkshake made from his One-a-Days and his pureed pet hamster, Mr. Peepers.

Yes, Leona was truly a card, as others used to say.

When Marty was really bad, at least in Leona's twisted mind, she would stuff him in a garbage bag to sweat it out until he apologized for some perceived transgression.

Apparently, Marty's mom hadn't wanted him. It was quite clear from the moment she became pregnant that Marty was an *accident*, though Leona was hardly the promiscuous type, cautioned by her mother that, "Men and the devil are bedfellows." Leona would have likely died a virgin, if . . . on her way to high school one cold morning during the Depression, she hadn't been raped by an indigent farm hand, two days before her eighteenth birthday.

Up until that point, Leona had never had so much as a date. She was a matronly looking woman even at the age of nine and as she grew into adulthood she was one of those people you couldn't picture young. Maybe she never was. So her pregnancy was regarded by the local townsfolk as incontrovertible evidence of an immaculate conception.

Marty sometimes felt sorry for Leona and her tales of woe for which he was clearly "responsible." He was constantly reminded how Leona's alcoholic mother beat her with a switch when she discovered her daughter's pregnancy and would lock her out of the house during booze binges . . . all because of Marty.

The Hefty bag stirred. Or was it his imagination?

"CAN'T YOU SEE I'M WATCHING TV?!" Marty bellowed at the bag.

He settled back in his La-Z-Boy recliner, feeling drowsy. But he caught himself. She was probably just waiting for him to doze. Oh yes, and then she'd open his throat like baby veal.

He switched the channel to a religious program. A woman dressed like Little Bo Peep with blue hair and surgically enlarged tear ducts was expounding how Jesus had spoken to her and said that he needed some hard cash . . . in the next half hour. A phone number, meanwhile, incessantly flashed on the screen.

Marty wondered how Jesus, a man with no earthly possessions, who wore sandals and a tattered robe, could get so behind in his bills. Nevertheless, feeling an impulsive need for redemption, Marty reached for the phone and dialed. It rang.

"I'm doing this for *you*, Ma," informed Marty as he waited on the phone. The bag remained silent.

Marty, startled by a voice on the other end of the phone, took a moment to speak. ". . . Uh, yeah, my name is Mar . . . never mind. I would like to pledge . . . um fifteen . . . no, twenty dollars. Can I donate it in my mother's name? She *recently* passed away. L-E-O-N-A E-M-E-R-B-A-L-M. My name? . . . um . . . anonymous. Yes, the check's in the bag . . . I mean mail."

Marty abruptly hung up. They were asking too many questions. He collapsed back in the recliner, his eyes glued to the set. On the religious program they now introduced a silver

Taking Out The Garbage

haired, emaciated man in his mid-fifties with an overbite who sounded orgasmic, "We would like to thank yuuu all for your pledges. Jeeeesus blesssses yuuuuu. I see yuuuuu . . . I see a woman, Mrs. Isaiah Furth, with liver cancer . . . Hallelujah . . . touch the screen and I will heal you . . . yessssssss . . . Mr. Frank Gordon, though you can hardly rise to your six hundred and eighty-seven pound feet, drag yourself to the TV screen . . . Jeeeeesus luvs yuuu for your donation . . . and to the man in pain over the dearly departed passing of his sweet mother Leona Emerbaum . . . Jeeeesus luvs yuuuuu!!"

Marty was ecstatic, "You hear that, Ma? You're on TV!"

There was a sigh from the bag.

Marty paused for a moment marveling at the television screen.

"Hey, Ma, can I borrow some money?" he sheepishly asked.

The bag wasn't speaking.

"WELL, YOU KNOW I'M BROKE!" Marty suddenly boomed.

Without knowing what he was doing, Marty began clawing at the twisty garbage tie. He opened up the bag and lurched back at the sight. His mother's face was upturned, her eyes rolled back in their sockets, her blue lips parted in a frozen scream. The bag was already beginning to smell and he was glad tomorrow was trash day.

Perched on Leona's lap, clutched between her rigor mortis claws, was her vinyl imitation Gucci handbag. Marty leaned over and apprehensively reached inside the garbage bag trying to get at the purse, until his ear was practically over her mouth. His mother's beefy cellulite thighs were parted, displaying thick support hose. Marty's fingers finally reached the purse strap but she had a death grip on it with her icy fingers and wasn't about to let go.

"Come on, Ma, give it to me. GIVE IT TO ME!"

Marty tried peeling back her rigid fingers but it was no use.

"You don't want me to get the poultry shears, do you?" cautioned Marty.

At that moment, Leona's pudgy fingers released the strap.

Marty was relieved, but as he started to stand up, he thought he heard a faint exhale in his right ear. He moved his head an inch closer to Leona's gaping mouth.

"Ma . . . you're alive—."

Suddenly, Leona clamped her teeth onto Marty's ear and bit down with a vicious crunching sound.

"MA, LET GO OF MY EAR!" screamed Marty, as she held on like a pit bull.

He propelled his body backwards, dragging the garbage bag across the hardwood floor as Leona tenaciously chewed his ear between her jaws. It reminded him of when he was a little boy and Leona would grab hold of his ear and drag him to the bathroom where she would give him an enema. She would pump him so full of water he thought he would explode. Then, she would make him hold the liquid until he tearfully begged for relief. If he disobeyed and released so much as a drop, she would force-feed him a bottle of castor oil. Marty wondered what his mother's psychotic preoccupation was with his bladder and bowels. Was it the ultimate control?

Marty forcefully yanked back his head from Leona's mouth. There was a sucking sound like a shucked oyster and

Taking Out The Garbage

Marty fell to the floor, dizzy and nauseous. He turned towards the plastic sack where his mother's bloated face peeked out. All her teeth were missing and he noticed blood on her pink grimacing gums.

Marty staggered to his feet and gazed into the gilded mirror on the den wall. Leona had nearly bitten his ear clean off but he had managed to pull away just in time, with her foul dentures firmly affixed to his earlobe. He reached up and pried open the hideously salivating earring.

Marty walked back to the rubbish bag, "Lose something, Ma?"

Leona stared at him with a smirk of satisfaction on her puckered mouth. Marty began whimpering. Was she going to take away this moment too? He took a deep breath and, gathering his courage, approached her, "Time to take out the garbage, *Mother*."

Marty tossed Leona's dentures in the bag and then firmly planted the sole of his slipper on top of her head, smashing her down like a pile of mulch. He tightly tied the twisty over her head, sealing the bag . . . and her fate, he hoped, forever.

He dragged the trash bag through the living room and out the front door of Leona's house.

"I told you not to be bad, didn't I?" scolded Marty. "Look what you made me do!"

He dumped the sack against the front curb, paused, kicked the bag once and then strode back into Leona's house.

"Night, Ma."

The house was devoid of sound, except for the ticking of Leona's antique clock collection. Marty strangely missed having someone to talk to as he sat back in front of the TV, his torn and bloody ear on fire. But the emotional evening had sapped him and his eyelids soon began to grow heavy.

After awhile, Marty got up, rubbed his eyes, and peeked out the living room curtains. He was horrified to see that the trash bag was gone. Frantically, he scanned up and down the street. All the neighbors' trash cans were by their curbs. Just then, there was an ominous knock at the front door, frightening him. Terrified, he opened the door and saw . . . Leona . . . her decayed face swarming with maggots. She was holding an enema bag.

Marty awoke from his nightmare with a jolt. A pair of tomcats were fighting outside. He checked his watch. Five-twelve A.M. The garbage truck would be there in less than half an hour. He had been sleeping for over three. Still jumpy from the dream, Marty stood up and peeked out the window. It was dark out, the garbage bag by the curb. Just then, a shadowy movement caught Marty's eye near the trash.

"Now what?!" Marty tiredly exclaimed.

Marty sighed, threw on his muffler, so he wouldn't catch cold, and went out the front door. It was freezing outside, his breath making thick clouds in the early morning mist.

As he approached the trash bag he saw what appeared to be a wagging tail. "Ma?" Marty tentatively inquired.

Halfway across the front lawn he saw that it was a stray dog, digging in the trash.

"Shoo! Shoo!" shouted Marty. But the ravenous, shivering pooch wouldn't budge, munching on something at the top of the garbage bag. Marty, horrified, fired the toe of his slipper into its protruding ribs. The mutt yelped and

Taking Out The Garbage

galloped down the street. Marty felt badly as he watched the emaciated mongrel limp off, carrying something hairy in its mouth.

He hesitantly approached the bag, whispering, "Ma, you okay?"

But Leona wasn't talking and Marty, frankly, didn't blame her. The pooch had chewed off the top of the bag and . . . the top of her head.

"Damn it, Ma!" reprimanded Marty. "Why'd you let him do that?!" Marty softened a bit, "Oh well, you always had a thing for strays, didn't you?"

Leona was comatose, her brain a victim of a canine lobotomy.

"Come on, let's get you inside," proposed Marty as he dragged the Hefty bag back inside Leona's house, checking over his shoulders to make sure nobody was watching. Nobody was.

He locked the front door, checking it eleven times, then dragged the bag into the living room, past the plastic covered furniture, over to the linoleum kitchen floor.

"Cold night, huh, Ma?" said Marty as he rubbed his palms together. "How about some hot tea to warm you up?"

Marty poured water into the tea pot and then cautiously opened the top of the trash bag with a pair of ice bucket tongs. Much of the top of Leona's scalp was missing and it looked like the dog had lapped up some of her cerebrum, as well. But, leave it to Ma, the old gal was still breathing.

"You look pretty silly, Ma," said Marty, stifling a giggle, then adding solemnly, "I guess this is our last breakfast together before your ride comes."

They stared expressionless at each other for a moment.

"Hey, Ma, remember when you used to send me off to wait for the bus in the snow? You wouldn't give me a jacket because you said it would toughen me up, make me a man. It toughened me up alright . . . but I still felt cold."

The tea pot whistled. "Tea time!" exclaimed Marty, pouring two steaming cups. "Cream?" "Sugar?"

No reply.

"Just like old times," reminisced Marty.

He walked over and bent down, pouring the piping hot tea past his mother's chapped lips. Most of the boiling chamomile just poured down her bloodied chin.

"That's a good girl."

They sat quietly drinking tea together. Time passed.

Marty checked his watch.

"Well, Ma, looks like this is it. Better get you out by the curb." Marty took a step towards the bag.

"Don't!" gurgled a raspy voice.

Marty froze. Leona had spoken.

"Don't wh . . . what, Ma?" stuttered Marty, sounding like a hurt little boy.

"Don't throw me out like garbage," hissed Leona.

"Why do you want to do this now, Ma?" cried Marty. "I've got it all planned out, I'M DOING SOMETHING ALL BY MYSELF!"

"No, Martin, you'll never go through with it. I command you to stop," Leona chanted like a carnival hypnotist.

Marty was whining, "Pleeeease don't start, I've made up my mind."

Taking Out The Garbage

"You're being a *bad boy*, Martin. Do you know what happens to *bad boys?*" Leona wickedly asked, like the Hansel and Gretel witch.

"They get enemas, Ma?" Marty quietly answered.

"NO!" They go to *hell* Martin. JUST LIKE YOU!" spat Leona.

"It's not going to work, Ma," Marty retorted, "I'm already in hell."

Marty forcefully pulled the plastic sides up over her oozing skull and sealed the top with the twisty tie.

Leona's desperate voice wailed through the bag, "What have I done to deserve this, Martin? What?"

Marty paused.

"It's called childhood, Ma. But it's time to put childish things behind and move on with my life," triumphantly replied Marty.

He waited for a response, a final objection as the distant sounds of a garbage truck and banging trash cans approached.

But Leona had rested her case.

Marty resolutely dragged the bag back outside and placed it by the curb. He watched the garbage truck turn down their tree-lined street in the warm glow of dawn. He sighed. It was almost over.

Marty sniffled, then turned to walk away.

"Are your wearing your muffler?"

Marty stopped in his tracks and grimaced.

He didn't even turn around. "'Bye, Mom."

Marty continued up the cobblestone walkway.

There was a final desperate plea through the bag, "Please Marty! . . . please! . . . I beg you! . . . I . . . I . . . love you."

Marty winced. How long had he waited to hear those words? Across the street he could see the shivering dog, hungry for more. He closed his eyes and shook his head, not believing what he was about to do.

He dragged the bag back inside the house.

Marty and his mother had another cup of tea as the garbage truck roared outside.

Then, he dragged her back outside . . . .

Just in time.

2

SASQUATCH IN CENTRAL PARK

Sheila liked to wear fur. She especially liked to wear it on blustery days on her walks through Central Park. And so it was on a twenty-six degree Tuesday in January that Sheila bundled herself up in her full length white mink coat, chinchilla cap, winter ermine stole, harp seal boots, and white fox gloves and left her apartment on Park and 63rd for a brisk walk to the zoo.

Alvin, the doorman, saluted Sheila as she exited the shiny brass doors of The Tower with her toy poodle. Though Alvin hadn't served in the Armed Forces, he felt it his civic duty to salute the inhabitants of The Tower whom he assumed had struggled as he had to make successes of themselves.

Sheila, admittedly, hadn't done much struggling. Her father was Jacob Stein of Stein/Weller, one of the largest plumbing suppliers on the East Coast. An only child, Sheila had been pampered her entire life. She had attended Smith

College in Northampton for two semesters before deciding that higher learning was a waste of precious shopping time. Besides, there wasn't even a "Bloomies" near Smith. So, she returned to Manhattan where her father purchased for her a three bedroom penthouse on Park Avenue and that's where Sheila Stein had resided for the last sixteen of her thirty-seven years, along with her deaf and blind toy poodle, "Mr. Piddles."

Sheila yanked the rhinestone dog leash as Mr. Piddles sniffed a homeless person on the sidewalk. She stepped around the indigent, holding her breath, so as not to inhale the stink molecules. *They're worse than doggie poo*, thought Sheila, who would practically faint from the malodorous odors which wafted into her tweezed nostrils from these desperate souls. Over the years, Sheila had become increasingly annoyed by the homeless who would sprawl on her sidewalk, where she went for her strolls. It had become so bad that Sheila would have to hold her breath almost all the way to Central Park lest she take in the fetid stench of failure. Just for such sensory intrusions, Sheila carried a vial of Chanel Number Five which she sprinkled on vagabonds. It was her own small way of contributing.

"Good Boy," encouraged Sheila, as Mr. Piddles squatted, with furrowed brow, eyes rolling back in his coiffed poodle head, as he noodled out a strand of steaming foie gras with truffles paté, six inches from the vagabond's nostrils.

Sheila smiled with accomplishment, her chubby cheeks blossoming out like Dizzy Gillespie as she clipped down the street in her snow-white, six hundred dollar baby harp seal boots, sprinkling Chanel Number Five like Lourdes water.

Sasquatch in Central Park

For the most part everyone stayed the hell out of Sheila's way. She was a formidable figure, burly you might say, and with heels, she rose to an intimidating five foot eleven. The homeless dodged Sheila as she defiantly swept past, cocooned in her minks, slumped against the wind like Sasquatch in Central Park.

Mr. Piddles stopped to sniff every leaf in the park. The only sense the emaciated poodle had left was smell and even that was failing. Sheila should have mercifully put the sixteen year old poodle to sleep, but she couldn't live without him and had paid plenty to keep him alive, including a third cataract surgery which her veterinarian told her wouldn't improve his vision. But Sheila wanted his eyes crystal clear and sparkling, just like her Beanie Babies.

Mr. Piddles stopped at another leaf, lifted his shivering leg from beneath his mink sweater, and squirted a teaspoon of urine onto his paw. Wagging his mangy tail, Sheila directed him through the ornate iron gates of the Central Park Zoo.

When Sheila entered the zoo she was in another world, as if she had wandered into heaven. Well, maybe not heaven, heaven was Bergdorfs. Nevertheless, the zoo was wonderful, like one of those beautiful Hallmark cards her father sent her on Valentine's Day. Sheila had never married, and her father doted on his only child as if she were still a teenager. Sheila adored him. Her father had arranged things so she hadn't a care in the world and would never have to work a day in her life. Rent, food, taxes, insurance and her heart-skipping credit card bills were all paid automatically out of her trust fund. She had a wallet stuffed with platinum and knew where to use them. Manhattan was her oyster and she, its pearl.

The cold gray, stone buildings of the zoo lined the path and Sheila could hear the playful bark of sea lions up ahead. Sheila felt safe inside the zoo. Odd, she thought, that she was more afraid of the animals on the street than the ones at the zoo. The animals in the zoo were just as dangerous and smelly as the homeless, *but at least these beasts are on the other side of bars,* she chuckled to herself, thinking that the homeless should be kept in a zoo all their own. Her impromptu snicker caused a thin jet of saliva to squirt from her mouth and quickly freeze on her Estee Lauder powdered chin. She chipped off the frozen icicle and then placed a quarter in the turtle feed dispenser. She turned the dial, but no pellets were forthcoming. The machine ate her quarter! Agitated, she shoved in another quarter. The stupid dial jammed and Sheila desperately tried to pry out her stuck quarter. *Why was life so unfair?!* Sheila thought, as she helplessly checked around for help. But the entire zoo seemed deserted. Litter and tree branches were strewn about from the previous nights storm making the zoo seem even more ominously unattended.

"YEEWWW WHHOOOOO!" bellowed Sheila into the wind.

No response. Maybe everyone was indoors? It *was* rather frigid today. Sheila shivered, momentarily feeling the cold through her fur. First, no turtle pellets, next, God only knows. The afternoon was definitely not going as Sheila had planned and Sheila didn't like it . . . she did not like it one bit.

Just around the bend, Zazgen Miagenovich was feeding the polar bears. Zazgen hated his job, feeling it was just one step above a circus shit-shoveler. As a child he had dreamed of the big top at the Moscow Circus and someday being the lion tamer. Perhaps that dream was still lingering at the cortex of his subconscious when he applied for a job at the Central Park Zoo. But life hadn't gone *exactly* as Zazgen had planned. There were no lions or tigers at the Central Park Zoo, he soon discovered, and the closest he would ever get to interacting with wild animals was cleaning their pens and at feeding time.

Zazgen was running late, as usual, and furiously belched as he removed a caribou thigh from his aluminum feed cart. He sheepishly checked around to see if anyone had heard his resounding gut-gas, while slushy drops of caribou blood dribbled onto the toe of his grimy Air Jordans. Fortunately, no one was around to hear him belch. As a matter of fact, Zazgen hadn't seen any zoo-goers all day, though that wasn't terribly abnormal considering it was a Tuesday with a wind-chill factor of twenty degrees.

Zazgen blew hot breath through his knitted gloves and involuntarily belched into his fist, this time conjuring up a bit of green chile which he chewed and reswallowed.

How many times will I have to eat that burrito? pondered Zazgen who had forgotten his bag lunch and made the regrettable error of eating a spicy green chile and pork burrito from the vending machines. The damn burrito had been riding high for the past hour, reminding him why he avoided the food machines. He pounded his fist against his breastbone as two fifteen hundred pound polar bears approached the front of their enclosure, licking their lips. The polar bears, Misha and Snowflake, fixtures at the zoo for sixteen years, reacted to Zazgen's chest pounding as if he was asserting that *he* was king of the arctic circle. This was not something polar bears liked to see on their own turf, especially when it was Zazgen, who would occasionally taunt them before tossing them their meals. Their black, agate eyes studied him, measuring his weight and watching the blue vein pulse in his neck.

Zazgen pounded up another belch and smiled, relieved, as the hot bubble burst past his bluish lips. Only this time the belch sounded different, off key. Even the bears seemed to notice as Zazgen felt a warm liquid course over his lips. He dabbed at the fluid and then examined the red fluid on his gloved fingertips. Feeling panicky, Zazgen started to say something, then suddenly felt a hammer blow to his chest and fell to his knees, dropping the caribou thigh in front of him. Meanwhile, Misha and Snowflake watched with hungry eyes.

As Zazgen's eyes fluttered back in their sockets, the last thing he observed was a broken tree branch precariously dangling over the fence. *It must have snapped in the storm*, thought Zazgen, making a mental note to notify Mr. Kim, the zoo gardener.

Then Zazgen hit the icy pavement with a stony thump.

Sheila was excited that day to see the temporary special exhibit featuring a rare albino great ape named Bonzo.

Sheila stood at the fence staring at the group of mountain gorillas but couldn't find Bonzo whom she had seen on the news. As the gorillas stared back at Sheila, she was amused by how human they seemed. She waved at them and they waved back. Bonzo, meanwhile, dispassionately studied Sheila with hooded eyes from the shadows of his heated cave.

Sheila, excited with her new found friends, spotted a another feed dispenser and impatiently dug into her Louis

Vitton purse for a quarter. She didn't carry much money, what with all the homeless hounding her. Besides, when you have credit cards for every major department store in Manhattan, who needs cash?

As she rooted around in her purse she heard a strange sound, glanced up and was startled to see a gorilla jerking his *thingy*. *How horrible*, thought Sheila who, for some reason, couldn't avert her eyes.

"Stop that, you sick monkey!" ordered Sheila.

The gorilla grunted and hurled something which stuck in a glob on the front of her fur coat. She looked down in horror, not even wanting to *think* of what the goo might be. She was terribly flustered, muttering to herself as she frantically wiped at the monkey gunk with her monogrammed silk hankie, spreading it deeper into the downy hairs of her natural white mink.

Zazgen was sprawled on top of the caribou thigh, his body heat thawing out the meat as the bears anxiously paced on their island, gazing across the icy water at the twenty foot wide by thirty foot deep ditch which ensured their permanent incarceration.

The polar bears were losing their patience as they waited for Zazgen to toss them something which would quell the ravenous yearning in their bellies. Zazgen usually made them perform a circus trick, like turning in a circle, or standing on their hind legs to beg for food which they were now doing to no avail. Misha and Snowflake put up with Zazgen because he was their meal ticket and also because they were separated by a deep gorge that prevented them the pleasure of dining on his beating heart.

Misha and Snowflake were mere pups when they were shot with tranquilizers in the wild and awoke in a sixty by ninety foot reproduction of the Antarctica. Whereas on the icy tundra they would eat whenever their mother could catch a walrus, seal or a fish, here at the zoo, they were on a more regular schedule. Hence, their mouths would water and their bellies growl like Pavlov's dogs when they spotted Zazgen. Even though the meals he tossed them quelled their hunger, something was missing—a gnawing emptiness caused by their instinct to hunt their own prey. But today, things would be different.

The bears could presently smell the hearty caribou blood just beyond the fence, which had separated them from freedom for over a decade. But this time Zazgen wasn't having them perform their tricks and . . . a broken tree branch was dangling over the moat.

Sheila was in tears, her mink *ruined* . . . RUINED! She would make them pay. All of them! Her father's attorney would sue the zoo, then the city, and finally those bad monkeys would have to be put to sleep. She took a stuttered breath, removed her chinchilla cap and patted her dyed blonde hairdo. *Don't let them get the better of you,* thought Sheila. *You're not going to let a couple of filthy monkeys spoil your whole day, are you?* Yet she couldn't let it go, thinking of how her father should have been here to shelter her from such ugliness. It reminded her of that disgusting boy in junior high school who showed her his *thingy*. As if it was something she wanted to see! Boys were all the same, just like those dirty monkeys ready to pull out their *thingies* at a moment's notice and spray their gunk all over your fur. She felt better for her decision to leave men out of her life for good. Except for Daddy. He was different. But she could easily live without the rest. She had done just fine, so far, without them, thank you very much.

Feeling decidedly better, Sheila snapped her fur covered fingertips and made herself forget all about the gorillas, then she headed, with Mr. Piddles at her heel, towards her favorite attraction at the zoo, the penguins.

Misha and Snowflake swam across the pond and now hungrily paced along the edge of the empty moat, staring at the overhanging tree branch. They hadn't felt this ravished since they were pups and their mother was after a walrus when a killer whale crashed through the ice and took her away. After several days without their mother returning with food, the gangly pups were forced to chase down an ailing caribou. It was their first kill, and the gamy taste of blood filled their senses, as it was beckoning to them now, entwined with a throbbing rhythm—the final pulses of Zazgen's failing heart.

Misha and Snowflake gazed at one another, just as they had the first time they chased down that caribou. Then they made a desperate sprint for the fence.

Sheila loved watching the penguins. Their wobbly walk and tuxedo jacket reminded her of the debutante ball. She felt a sort of affinity for penguins who, like herself, were funny looking. She, too, had been stared at and poked fun of through school. Those evil girls at Smith College had been the worst. They were all so slim and pretty with their white gloves and she looked like a big ape by comparison. They got all the good looking boys, too, while Sheila was left alone in her dorm room leafing through Neiman Marcus catalogs.

Just then, the penguins started squawking and racing in circles around their enclosure, startling Sheila. *What could be disturbing them so?* wondered Sheila, unaware that she had inadvertently let go of Mr. Piddles leash, and he was blindly wandering down the path.

Zazgen could probably have been spared a horrible fate . . . *if* he had gotten a checkup in the last decade . . . and *if* he had ever used the Exercycle his ex-wife gave him for Christmas . . . and *if* he had stopped smoking when his father got throat cancer and started speaking out of a voice box . . . and *if* there was anyone with medical knowledge nearby to witness him collapse face first onto the pavement, knocking out his front tooth while suffering a massive myocardial infarction. Unfortunately, the *ifs* were stacked against Zazgen. The last sound he heard was the growling of a large animal, and then he dreamed he was at the Moscow circus, center ring, snapping a huge whip as he felt the hot breath of a lion on his face.

"PIDDLE WIDDLES!, PIDDLY WIDDLY!!, COME TO MOMMA," Sheila futilely hollered, her breath fogging the air.

Frankly, the tumor riddled pooch wouldn't have heard her if she had been screaming directly into his eardrum. But Sheila felt helpless and had to do something. The sun was quickly setting and the zoo was no place to be walking around at night. You could be mugged, or worse.

Just thirty yards around the corner from the polar bear enclosure, Sheila spotted something on the path. It was a soiled high-top basketball shoe, and as she approached, she noticed a bright red liquid on the rubber toe.

"Ick!" exclaimed Sheila, holding her breath as she realized she was standing in blood. She abruptly made a wide detour, thinking it might be from an infected, homeless disease carrier.

She continued down the path, calling for Mr. Piddles, unaware of the serrated ankle bone tucked just below the rim of the high-top.

A pair of steely eyes followed Sheila from twenty feet above as she continued down the path. Snowflake, resting in a eucalyptus tree, licked her paw and swabbed her face, cleaning off the sticky blood. She felt quite content. Her belly was full and she was free for the first time since she was a pup. She only wished Misha could have been with her, but he was at the bottom of the gorge. He had made a noble jump but missed the branch by nearly a foot. Snowflake, however, managed to get her claws into the branch and swing herself up and over the fence just before the tree limb broke. She peered at Misha below. Her brother was nursing a sore paw, but he would survive.

The same couldn't be said for Zazgen as Snowflake belched a burrito and observed, from her vantage point in the trees, a furry beast walking hunchbacked on the path below crying out "Piddles" over and over again. At first, Snowflake thought the white animal was another polar bear invading her territory. But this two-legged animal had an intoxicating honey scent, and Snowflake would have chased the animal down right then if she hadn't been cleaning off Zazgen's red juice. There would be plenty of time. Then she would hunt down the white walrus and tear it limb from limb.

Sheila was exasperated. The park was getting dark and there was still no sign of Mr. Piddles. Time was running out. Soon teenage gangs would roam in packs to spray paint their epitaphs to lost youth.

Sheila noticed something else on the path up ahead. It was a metal cart, sort of like the ones the maids push around at The Tower. On the other side of the cart, a dark shape was lying on the ground.

"Is that you, Piddles?!" cried Sheila, whose night vision was only a little better than her poodle's.

But as she got closer she saw it wasn't Mr. Piddles at all, but rather a human body. The person appeared perfectly intact except for a nagging hole in his back that you could dunk a basketball through. Also, she couldn't help noticing a gnawed animal bone jutting through the ragged crevice like a gamy swizzle stick. Handfuls of human organs were dashed about on the frozen pavement. Sheila held her breath, closed her eyes, and once again wildly snapped her furry fingers hoping it would all go away. But when she opened her eyes the morbid scene was still laid out for her like an autopsy swap meet. Even worse, on second glance, Sheila noticed something she should have spotted right off, only her brain preferred to ignore what her eyes were telling her . . . that the man's head was entirely missing.

Zazgen was, regrettably, still conscious as Snowflake chewed through his vertebra to get at the caribou meat trapped beneath his body. If Zazgen had his druthers, he would have preferred death by heart attack over being eaten alive. But this wasn't Zazgen's day, as he involuntarily belched, tasting the burrito one final time before he felt his head bitten off his spine.

Snowflake hadn't forgotten about Misha. Polar bears, unlike many people, were loyal to the core, and Snowflake had a deep love for her brother. She tip-toed back along the broken tree branch and dropped Zazgen's severed head into the ditch. It rolled back and forth along the walls of the trench, like a skateboarder, before finally tumbling to a stop by Misha's massive paws.

The polar bear batted the head down the trench like a soccer ball and playfully ran after it until it again rolled to a halt. Zazgen's frozen scream silently stared up at Misha. The huge bear appreciatively gazed up at Snowflake before leaning down and crunching Zazgen's skull between his powerful jaws.

Even if Sheila had known that running would have been the worst thing she could have done, she probably would have still been running. Unfortunately, there is no more attractive prey to a hungry polar bear than *moving* prey. Snowflake, only partially interested before, now had her rapt attention targeted on the fuzzy creature scurrying below. Snowflake climbed down from the tree and followed the strange animal, who wasn't too hard to track.

Sheila was wailing like a banshee. She hadn't know such terror in all her life. Actually, the most horrific thing she could recall was the day she found out she would have to get braces and wear headgear to school. But that was nothing compared to being stalked by a deranged killer, a psychopathic madman who cut off people's heads, ripped through their guts, and left an animal leg planted in their back as a hideous calling card.

Just ahead, Sheila spotted a pay phone. "Sweet Jesus!" she cried as she bee-lined for the phone, grabbed the receiver and immediately shouted, "Help me! . . . Please!! . . . A lunatic is after . . ." She suddenly stopped, realizing that she was blubbering to a dial tone and had neglected to put a quarter into the phone.

Standing in the yellow light of the phone kiosk, Sheila desperately rooted around in her purse for change. "Come on . . . come on," Sheila chanted like a gambler at the slots. Sheila had always kept three quarters in her purse, two to feed the animals and one for an emergency phone call, the very one she had used to buy snacks for those *disgusting* apes. She was doomed. Then, she remembered. Her calling card! She could use it to dial 911! She madly dialed her calling card number (not thinking to simply dial 911) when she heard a sound. She whipped around, heart thumping in her throat. Thankfully, there was no one behind her, though she couldn't ignore the creepy feeling that she was being watched. The wind blew a single leaf through the deserted zoo. It was eerie quiet, as if all the animals were holding their breath. Then, a pebble fell to the ground by Sheila's feet. She slowly tilted her head upwards to see, hanging from above the bathrooms, Mr. Piddles rhinestone leash.

"SHNOOKIE POO!" she happily cried as she grabbed the leather handle of the leash and gently tugged.

But the leash wouldn't budge.

"Come to Mommy!" she again encouraged her reluctant poodle, wondering how he got onto the bathroom roof.

Sheila was really yanking on the leash now but, for some reason, she couldn't move a three pound toy poodle. She was practically swinging from the leash when Snowflake stepped from the shadows on the bathroom roof with the other end of the leash dangling from her clenched canines.

Mr. Piddles, it appeared, had been an appetizer for this enormous drooling bear and Sheila, no doubt, would be the blue plate special. She released a blood curdling scream and scrambled down the path waving her arms over her head, leaving the phone swaying on the cord.

"YOU'LL ALL PAY!" swore Sheila as she furiously sprinted for her life, gulping frigid air and sobbing, *"I'll have the whole freaking zoo exterminated before I'm through!"*

Snowflake had been just about to leap when Sheila made the guttural shriek from her ample lungs. To the bear, the woolly woman suddenly seemed a bit more intimidating and apparently had very large lungs. Ever more exciting for the kill.

Snowflake chewed on the rhinestone dog leash, regretting having swallowed the malnourished looking rat with the long, extremely tough tail. The helpless little lump had simply stumbled directly into Snowflake's open mouth and sat down on her giant tongue. It wasn't exactly a challenging kill. Not much meat either. But the other one, thundering down the road on clicking hoofs, would leave plenty of leftovers to bring home to Misha.

Sheila tripped on her seal boots and fell. She took off one of her gloves as she checked her tender ankle and noticed that she had chipped a fingernail. She burst into tears. She had just had her nails done in majestic pink that morning at Rudolph's. She was sitting on the pavement, sobbing, when she heard a low growl. Sheila turned and saw the massive bear just a few yards away, rhinestones sparkling between its blood-stained canines.

Sheila knew she would wind up like the headless body with the basketball hoop in its back if she didn't move, and fast. She put on her glove, stood up and stepped backwards, her bulging eyes locked on the approaching bear. *My they move fast!*

Sheila felt like a roast suckling pig as she desperately searched for a means of escape. She took a cursory glance at the gorilla enclosure. There was no way she was going to get in there with those degenerate simians. Then again, what choice did she have? The fence was over fifteen feet high, but there was a large pile of decorative boulders outside the fence. She kicked off her heels and quickly climbed up the rocks.

Sheila was now only ten feet from the top of the fence. If she could climb over, she would be safe from the polar bear. The only obstacle was a discouraging trench dug around the inside perimeter of the fence, to keep the gorillas from escaping. On the opposite side of the gully there was a strip of grass, and if she could jump far enough, she *might* land safely. She was still weighing her options, when Snowflake roared, sending Sheila up the fence. Luckily, she had a head start because Snowflake leaped up the boulders just as Sheila struggled to pull her hundred and seventy-nine unexercised pounds onto the wrought iron bar near the top. It was just like her tryout for gymnastics in high school when everyone laughed at her because she got stuck on the horizontal bar, only now it was the gorillas hooting at her as Snowflake swatted her razor claws, shredding the back of Sheila's fur coat. Fortunately, the mink had billowed away from her body as Sheila leaped off the top of the fence, over the gorge.

Unfortunately, she landed a wee bit short, her white fox gloves clinging to the edge of the turf. She was rapidly losing her grip and feeling like she was about to pass out and plunge to her death when she heard rhythmic chest pounding and a powerful roar. Snowflake backed away from the fence and retreated down the path.

Sheila, meanwhile, fainted.

A hairy arm swept into the trench, caught her by the arm and effortlessly lifted her from the crevice.

Sheila woke up surrounded by half a dozen gorillas staring at her. She was about to scream when one of them reached out and stroked her thirty-two thousand dollar pelt.

"Don't mess with the mink, monkey," warned Sheila, returning to form. She gingerly sat up, feeling lightheaded, and glanced at the fence. Snowflake was gone. She didn't know how she made it and at that moment she really didn't care.

The gorillas were fascinated with Sheila, smelling her, poking her and rolling around like they had found the best play toy in the world. One of them suddenly punched Sheila's leg, hard, and then did a somersault.

"Ow," whined Sheila, "that hurt!"

Another gorilla ran over and punched her in the other leg, even harder. Sheila knew she would have to take control, quickly, or wind up a gorilla punching bag.

"You better leave me alone, YOU HEAR ME!? You know who my father is?!" threatened Sheila.

The gorillas shuffled away and pouted. Sheila stood up, thinking she would appear more authoritative on her feet, when another gorilla playfully slapped her across the flank. Sheila whirled around, her face crimson. It was harmless, the gorilla merely mocking her, dancing with his hands over his head, but Sheila didn't like to be teased . . . ONE BIT.

Sheila's voice now came in a throaty threat, "You heard me, buster, hands off! OR ELSE." And, with that dire warning, they began to do exactly the opposite of what Sheila had requested. They slapped her, punched her, and licked the makeup off her face. One began throwing feces snowballs. She was being assaulted by a gang of gorillas, hooting and hollering like drunken frat boys at a keg party when, suddenly, Sheila heard a powerful roar.

The gorillas parted and in strode Bonzo, all five hundred and ninety-eight pounds. He picked Sheila up over his head with one hand and pounded on his chest with the other. He was King Kong and Sheila was his, admittedly overweight, Fay Ray.

"Thank you, Bonzo, oh, thank you, Bonzo, my good friend," applauded Sheila.

The other gorillas stayed a safe distance back, their heads lowered in reverence to the great Bonzo. They hadn't seen their leader like this in years. Bonzo typically sat hunched over in his synthetic cave, rarely moving. Six months earlier Bonzo was in the news when he was at the Cleveland zoo and specialists from around the country had tried everything to get Bonzo to mate: Pheromones, a variety of attractive female gorillas, and even porno movies were used, but Bonzo, it was henceforth concluded, was clinically impotent. Now, the great albino ape had discovered Sheila and all of a sudden . . . *Bonzo had risen.*

The huge African gorilla carried Sheila to his plaster cast cave. He sat her on his huge knee and Sheila felt protected.

Bonzo made her feel safe, like no male had before, besides her father. The enormous ape stroked her chinchilla cap and deeply inhaled her honeysuckle perfume. Sheila giggled as he tickled her neck. He patted her hand. Sheila coyly smiled. Then, after a long pause, during which Bonzo picked an ant out of his nose and ate it, he suddenly shoved Sheila onto her stomach. Sheila prayed that Bonzo was just playing until he started sniffing her behind.

"BONZO, NO!" firmly stated Sheila, as she had learned in her women's assertiveness group. But Bonzo seemed distracted, stroking his red thingy which swelled into a King-Kong sized blood sausage.

Sheila could smell the rancid odor of his primate privates and again felt faint.

"Bonzo, LET ME UP," she commanded, conjuring up her most authoritative voice. "NOW!" ordered Sheila.

But Bonzo had other things on his mind as he began to poke his engorged member at the rear of her mink coat.

Sheila's eyes swelled as wide as a deer in headlights as Bonzo parted the torn strips of her fur coat and ripped off her Donna Karan undergarments. He firmly held Sheila by the back of her neck as he tooled around with his thick, wrinkled ape finger. He eventually located the moist slot he was hunting for, then grabbed both meaty cheeks of Sheila's plump buttocks and, with little fanfare, rammed himself into her with an animalistic grunt.

Sheila yelped in pain as the brute entered her, breaking her vintage hymen and staining her white mink scarlet. Bonzo furiously thrust in and out underneath her fur coat mating with Sheila, who had somehow managed to escape the nastiness of sex her entire life.

Sheila threw off her gloves and dug her pink fingernails into the dirt as Bonzo pummeled her from behind with all his suppressed jungle passion.

Though Sheila would never admit it until the day she died, in a horrible, indescribable way, it actually felt pretty good. As a matter of fact, it felt darn good. Better than peppermint ice cream and bouncing on Daddy's knee.

"That's it Bonzo . . . Ooooohhhh! . . . Yeahhhhhh! . . . Do it . . . STICK ME, YOU BIG FAT MONKEY!" thundered Sheila, as she climaxed, startling the animals at the Central Park Zoo.

At dawn the following morning, a homeless man, known fondly around the park as Rummy, woke up beneath his newspaper blanket and strolled to the zoo for breakfast. He knew that Zazgen would sometimes leave his cart unattended and he usually had some vegetables which could get Rummy through the morning.

Rummy wandered through the deserted zoo searching for the food cart and walked directly past the gorilla enclosure not noticing that Bonzo had finally found a mate, wrapped arm in arm with him, asleep in his cave.

But the press would be swarming within the hour after the police received a report from a homeless man named Rummy who stumbled upon a half-eaten body at the zoo. Police and Animal Control Officers were dispatched to the scene and found Snowflake hiding up in the tree above his enclosure, close to his brother, Misha. Snowflake subsequently became part of a huge public debate regarding destroying or saving her. Phone polls were taken across the country but Snowflake eventually prevailed after the coroner, a zoo patron, determined that Zazgen was not killed by the bear but rather consumed after he died of a massive heart attack.

Sheila didn't get off so easy.

The cover of the *N.Y. Mirror* featured Sheila, draped in her tattered furs, seated next to Bonzo in his cave, a dazed look on her rosy face. The headline read:

SOCIALITE SEDUCES APE MAN

The National Inquirer wasn't quite as subtle:

WOMAN TO BIRTH MONKEY BOY

The *Journal* had their own sleazy slant:

MILLIONAIRESS GANG RAPED BY GORILLAS.

And, as befitting the society page of the *New York Tribune*, they ran a photo of Sheila from her coming out party with the startling announcement:

STEIN WEDS BONZO IN PRIVATE CEREMONY.

It would be the last time that Sheila would make the society page.

THREE SHADES OF BLUE
Another "Raoul, Low-life Ex-Cop" Adventure

It was last call at the Starlight Lounge and Raoul's face had melted into his lap. His eyeballs floated in a warm plasma pool gazing up at the cascading goo which had recently been his face. It wasn't a pretty sight. It usually took about five shots of Cutty to create this effect, and Raoul was proud to have accomplished it in four tonight, a savings of two dollars and seventy-five cents, sans tip. Enough for a scratcher and a Sizzling Slim Jim from Jolly Jug Liquor.

The street lights were buzzing like June bugs on their backs as Raoul staggered down the sidewalk, tossing his Lotto ticket in the gutter. This was Raoul's hour: transvestite hookers on their knees in dim alleys, wild-eyed soul-savers admonishing God, crack whores picking their connect-the-dot vein scabs. It made Raoul long for the good old days on patrol with Metro. But it was now all a blur as

Raoul drifted down the sidewalk, trailing his puddled face behind.

Raoul glanced down, suddenly noticing he had messed his polyester shirt. Feeling decidedly better, after ridding himself of the rancid Slim Jim, he buttoned his trench coat over the stain and stumbled into the next bar on amnesia row.

The Blue Room featured some of the scariest strippers ever to bump and grind. Raoul worshiped the place, now as much as his first night as a rookie getting his cherry broken.

He took a chair at the runway and basked in the tawdry indigo lighting and the sweetly acrid smell of vomit and Love-My-Carpet. On stage, shrouded in a cancerous haze, danced Brooklyn, a mascara-drenched ass-wagger in her thirties, with cottage cheese thigh-divots you could slip your fingers into like bowling balls. She winked at Raoul, inadvertently knocking off a crusty cobalt eyelash into his near beer. Raoul stirred his drink with it, sucked it dry and handed it back to her. She appreciatively nodded and stuck the damp eyelash back on as she began a fan dance, leaving behind a trail of skeletal ostrich feathers, like the remnants of a hyena attack.

Raoul took another gulp of his tepid brew and studied Brooklyn as she slid down the tarnished fire pole leaving snail trails. She then slithered over to a pockmarked patron at the other end of the runway, who was holding a dead president between his rotting teeth. As Brooklyn leaned forward with her size forty-four silicones, to jimmy the buck from his teeth, the man hissed something in her ear which made her face go pale under her rancid pancake. She tearfully darted from the stage in a blizzard of blue feathers.

Raoul, dangerously woozy, watched the interaction with passing interest. He could barely make out the guy's face in the dark, but there was something about it which was uncomfortably familiar. Raoul considered chumming over to get a free drink. But, he wasn't sure if the guy was friend or foe and after nineteen years on the force, the foes had it.

Raoul winced as he took another swallow of the tepid brew. He then opened his soiled trench coat, liberated a pint of Early Times and hammered back a couple shots, chasing it with the fraudulent beer, then solemnly prepared for his face to start melting again.

Brooklyn, after a brief intermission, returned to the stage sporting a pair of tattered stockings and dragging a mangy faux bear rug. She plopped down on the shag in front of Raoul and proceeded to display her fallopian tubes and a rising yeast infection.

Raoul was about to advert his eyes when he spied something wedged between the rubbery folds of her womanhood. She moved closer, placing her heels on the rail, gyrating under his nose. Raoul inhaled a toxic whiff of peppermint disinfectant which made his eyes sting as she continued to spread herself like a deli platter. Raoul grew curious from all the attention, considering he hadn't placed a tip (to insure pussy) on the rail.

"Take it," she impatiently whispered.

It finally became apparent that she wanted him to remove a tiny rolled up piece of paper from her sluice. But Raoul was apprehensive, fearing what horrible surprise he might pry from her labia and, in his current state, into what vulgar creature it might metamorphosize.

Raoul tentatively reached into her cash box and slipped out a tropical drink umbrella. She quickly snapped her legs shut like a Venetian fly trap and moved down the runway towards a somber Korean with a two on the tarmac. As she ground her ample backside into the Asian's bifocals, Raoul slyly opened the tiny turquoise umbrella. Written in a circle on the underside of the paper umbrella was the following message: *My boyfriend at the end of the bar has a gun. He says he's going to kill me when this song ends.* Fortunately for her, they were playing "Whipping Post" by the Allman Brothers, the concert version, giving her a reprieved death sentence of at least fifteen minutes.

Raoul glanced around. At this hour everyone in the bar was probably armed with at least one gun. The tiny hairs on the back of his neck rose as if from static electricity. Raoul had learned to trust those little hairs and he quickly sobered up.

The flashing discos briefly illuminated the face of the shadowy figure at the end of the bar; and Raoul could see that it was a Latino, mid-thirties, with a jet black ponytail, and a scar from his forehead down his cheek, to his chin. He was wearing a midnight blue fishnet tank top and his steroid biceps displayed a tattooed cross with the faded letters V.L. Raoul remembered the Vato Locos from his early days on the force, as did every gang in L.A. who used to respect and fear them. But no more. Firepower was now king of the city and the V.L.'s were outgunned.

Through the haze caused by his shedding brain cells, Raoul felt reasonably certain he had busted this character before, but he was having trouble making the I.D.

Even though Raoul was no longer employed to "protect and serve" he felt a certain duty to the strip bars he frequented. So, he kept a bloodshot eye on the V.L., watching him force-feed himself with beer and stale pretzels until he finally beelined for the bathroom. Raoul tailed, tripping over the bar stool before continuing his surveillance.

On the way to the men's room, Raoul passed a cubical with a sweaty lap dance in the second act. The obese man's fly was at half-mast and an anorexic waitress who danced under the name Sapphire had a sawbuck folded over her dingy G-string. She yawned as her hand pumped methodically under his slacks like a dairymaid. Raoul studied them for a moment, the way an art student admires a Picasso before staggering past.

The floor in the leakery was an inch deep in kidney-filtered beer. The bathroom appeared empty. Raoul peeked under the bottom of the first two stalls. Empty. He stuck his face under the third stall and spotted a pair of rattlesnake boots. He dipped his head under further and found himself face to face with a blued steel Baretta 92.

"Muerte!" spat Raoul, placing the gun and the face at the bar together. Luckily, he had been in this predicament before, not in a strip club crapper but in numerous street encounters while working narcotics. He confidently reached under his trench coat for his Tangfolio-Spa BT 99, his eyes widening in panic as he realized his holster was empty. Raoul abruptly remembered that he had forfeited his concealed gun permit several days earlier. The D.A. had pulled his permit following an impromptu marksmanship exhibition which Raoul performed on a row of street lights at four A.M.

It appeared that this was not going to be Raoul's night.

"Uh, sorry, wrong stall," meekly offered Raoul, taking a large step backwards.

The hammer on the Baretta clicked back and Raoul mournfully realized that he could soon be sprawled on the urine-soaked floor with a bullet lodged in his cerebrum.

"Drop your drawers," ordered the voice on the other side of the stall.

Raoul did as requested, unbuckling. He unbuckled his chinos, which dropped to the floor and began to absorb liquid like a Huggies diaper.

Raoul had barely enough time to gulp before the stall door flew open, smashing him in the head. He landed on his butt with a splash.

The Latino leaped out of the stall, pointing the gun at Raoul. It was indeed "Muerte," an aging bad-ass who Raoul had arrested on more than several occasions, twice for murder. Raoul recalled, as the Latino's eyes began to burn with recognition, that he had smacked him around a bit to get information about a drive-by. It seems a six-year-old boy had caught a stray bullet in the head from a gang-banger. The bullet came from a Baretta 92. Everyone knew Muerte was guilty as shit, but Raoul had, nevertheless, been reprimanded for his "overzealous" interrogation, part of a personal rap sheet that booted him to an early retirement, with a reduced pension.

Muerte, on the other hand, was set free on bond.

Raoul's heart was beating in his throat as Muerte, pointing his Baretta, squinted so he wouldn't get brain tissue in his eyes.

"Remember me, Chota?" stated Muerte, with the arrogance of a man with a loaded gun.

"Gee, I can't place the face; might we have met at the country club?" innocently inquired Raoul.

"Don't fuck with me, pinche puerco!" Muerte sternly shouted, "I'm the one doing the fucking now!"

"Eloquent," retorted Raoul, "have we a poet laureate in our midst?"

"You were kicked off the force, weren't you, cop? For beating me up," proudly added Muerte with bravado.

"Not without getting this cool watch," smirked Raoul, displaying his retirement gift, a waterproof Timex.

"You look old, cop . . . and drunk," offered Muerte, stating the obvious.

"So do you . . . like Muerte warmed over," noted Raoul.

A steel boot toe suddenly connected with Raoul's recently healed ribs, ending the witty repartee and sending him hydroplaning across the bathroom floor like a frozen turkey on a Slip and Slide.

Maybe he had pushed the last comment a wee bit, pondered Raoul as he lay face down on the saturated floor, his skin cured to leather by the salty bladder brine. The good news was that Muerte seemed to be tiring after executing several spin kicks to Raoul's head.

Then again, maybe not.

Muerte pushed his boot heel down on Raoul's spine, who managed to sputter, "What do you want?"

"Your scalp, amigo," calmly answered Muerte, "right after I give you a nose job, a jaw realignment and a tonsillectomy." As if to highlight this point, Muerte put away his gun, pulled a double-bladed knife from his boot and approached Raoul as if he were a cutlet.

Raoul realized that things were going from bad to worse to an Andrew Lloyd Weber medley. He felt faint and worried that he might wake up in several places.

He thought fast. "I have something you want," interjected Raoul.

"Your huevos?" laughed Muerte, still approaching with his knife.

"No," replied Raoul, stuttering, "it's . . . it's in my wallet."

"This better be good, or I kill you twice," threatened Muerte as he yanked Raoul to his feet and shoved him back against the graffitied tile wall.

Muerte reached into Raoul's pants pocket on the floor while placing the blade point in Raoul's belly button. He lifted the piss-logged wallet and out fell a neon blue "Ramses the Third" condom.

"A condom?" incredulously spat Muerte.

"Look on the other side," suggested Raoul.

"Of the condom?" said Muerte.

"No, the wallet," sighed Raoul, wondering about the state of education in this city.

Muerte opened the wallet and his eyes lit up. It was Raoul's gold and silver detective badge, la placa, a high commodity on the streets. The glow from the badge illuminated Muerte's face like he was seeing the Holy Grail. It was at this spiritual epiphany that Raoul decided to seize control—*zero to sixty in seven seconds*—and abruptly jabbed the drink umbrella into Muerte's eye socket. Muerte dropped his knife and fell to his knees, clawing at the tiny umbrella stand lodged in his eyeball. Raoul thrust his knee forward, slamming the toothpick umbrella stand to an unreachable depth.

He must have hit a major nerve because Muerte shivered on the floor for a moment, then turned three shades of blue before puffing out his questionable soul.

Raoul retrieved his wallet and shook off the urine. He wiped his badge dry with toilet paper, pulled up his pants and headed back into the bar.

He returned to his seat at the runway. His beer was still warm. Brooklyn was just finishing her set, picking up her pasties, and nodded at Raoul, who nodded back.

Raoul knew the cops would be there shortly, not because someone would call, but because cops were always at the Blue Room. Following procedure, Raoul would be taken down to the station and vigorously questioned and this would be added to his ever-mounting rap sheet. Only this time they couldn't suspend him.

He actually looked forward to seeing his old detective buddies: Raker, Williams, Tinker and the others. They would have a chuckle, tell war stories, and drink Johnny Walker out of business. Raoul knew someday he'd push it too far and he'd serve some time. But what Raoul feared, even more than going to jail, was someday facing a hundred Muertes on the street seeking revenge against him or the system or both if nothing was done to abate the rising gang tide.

In the love-pit of the Blue Room, the music throbbed continuously in a scratchy loop. The next bored stripper strode onto the stage on towering ice blue satin stilettos and faded denim hot-pants to a pathetic smattering of applause, mostly from a crew-cut lesbian holding a Lincoln between her cleavage.

Brooklyn, now serving, sidled up to Raoul. "Lap dance?"

Raoul turned, paused, and asked, "On the house?"

Brooklyn smiled, her makeup cracking like the Mohave.

She wearily turned and headed towards the private booths.

Raoul followed.

Murder School

The Holiday Inn banquet room was packed to capacity with murderers munching on glazed donuts and sipping coffee while waiting for class to begin.

At eight A.M. sharp, a stocky middle-aged man, his transplanted hair slicked back, stepped to the front of the group and switched on the computer podium.

Max Palmer, an unemployed executioner, put on his amplifier headset and surveyed the audience, waiting for all eighty-three felons to take their seats.

"Welcome to Murder School," announced Max, the podium speakers emitting a thousand watt blast of high frequency feedback, causing everyone's eyes to bug out.

Max fiddled with the computer controls, lowering the volume before continuing, "Today will be murder . . . as you know."

There were a few nervous chuckles. Max knew the morning crowd could be a bit chilly, but he'd have them thawed out in no time.

Max cleared his throat and continued, "You've all committed various degrees of murder, some intentional, some involuntary, and you've opted to give up your Saturday to erase this felony from your record."

A man in the back row wearing a neon tube suit, anxiously waved his arm in the air.

Max pointed his index finger at him, "Yes?"

"Where are the bathrooms?" the man inquired.

Max sighed, "Out the door to your left, then take your first right and it's at the end of the hall."

The man hastily exited.

Max poured himself a cup of glacier water from the podium bar as he continued, "You may think you got off easy but this is an intense eight hour seminar to teach you how to stop killing and, most importantly, get this murder off your record."

He took a sip of water and continued, "Some of you may think that this course will take your name off the prison waiting list . . ."

Everyone was staring at Max like they wanted to murder him.

"Well . . ." paused Max, for comedic effect, ". . . it will."

This was Max's first set joke and it died.

"You're killing me, folks," said Max, as he always did when his material fell flat.

"HA . . . HA . . . HA," tauntingly laughed a burly bald man in the second row displaying eighteen inch biceps and tattoos of Armageddon around his thick neck.

Max, accustomed to hecklers, effortlessly fired back, "And what are you in here for . . . suicide? I'll have to give you an incomplete."

There were a few chuckles of approval and the muscular madman was momentarily silenced.

Always have a strong comeback, reflected Max, feeling in the groove as he plowed ahead:

"As I gaze around the room, I see some familiar faces . . . Mr. O'Donahue." An obese man in the back of the room sheepishly glanced up from his jelly doughnut with raspberry filling splattering his five chins.

Max paced in front of the podium, "Apparently, some of you are missing the message! Three strikes and you are out of this course, for good. That's two, Mr. O'Donahue. What this means, for you newcomers, is that you've got three chances to complete this course but you are allowed only one murder to be erased off your record per year. If you screw up, you'll go right back on the prison waiting list or wind up on funeral detail. For you murderous novices that means picking up body parts alongside the highway, trimming cemetery trees, digging graves and cleaning out cremains. That's not the stuff you put in your coffee, folks," quipped Max for the comedic rim shot.

There was another ripple of laughter and Max took a relieved breath. He had broken the ice.

"But seriously folks, this is 'murder one-o-one' and we have a lot to cover this morning. I will be showing you some short films today and—."

There was thunderous applause. *So predictable*, thought Max, *they always love the movies.*

He waited for the applause to die down before moving on.

"Some of the films are violent crime scenes showing the aftermath of heinous crimes. Others, are cartoons. We will also be bringing in some family members, victims of your rage. Then, from twelve to one, we'll have a lunch break."

Max waived a printout in the air as he droned on, "I have put together a list of inexpensive eateries in the area. I'd advise staying out of the Holiday Inn coffee shop. I wouldn't want to have another murder on my hands."

This struck a few more funny bones.

"But," added Max in a forbidding tone, "I must remind you to be back on time or I will not sign your completion certificate at the end of the day."

Just then, a teenager, dressed in extinct leopard prints, stepped through the door and noticed that there were no seats left in the banquet room.

"Sorry, we're all full up," Max explained, "You'll have to come back next Saturday. And might I suggest, on time."

The punk vigorously tapped the tips of his thumbs together, angrily "thumbing off" Max, before slamming the door behind him.

Max shook his head, "What does he think I'm running here, a Federal Prison?

Max, on a roll now, forgot what he was talking about before the interruption. He felt a trickle of sweat under his vinyl jacket, "Um . . . Where was I?"

A convicted ax-murderess, once a Miss America runner-up, helped Max out. "You were telling us to be back on time after lunch."

"Right. Thank you . . ." Max strained to read her name tag, ". . . Ms. Sandy Hacked Sister."

More laughs. Score another one for Max.

"You can just call me Sandy," she growled, glaring at Max with daggers.

"Touchy, touchy," pouted Max. Then to the group: "By the way, I'm glad you all followed my instructions and wrote the nature of your crimes on your name tags. So, let's go around the room and hear a little bit more about each of you and who you murdered."

"Let's start with . . . you," encouraged Max, pointing to a dour man in the front row.

The man glanced around with a *who me?* expression and then said, "The name's Glenn Moss, and, as you can see by my name tag, I murdered my mother-in-law."

Several whoops and catcalls of approval.

"Let's tone it down people," implored Max to the group. "Go on, Glenn," he urged.

"That's it, I killed my mother-in-law."

"That's never it," moaned Max. "How did you kill her?"

"I clubbed her with a frozen turkey drumstick and buried her in the backyard."

"And how were you caught?" prodded Max.

"How the hell did I know she was going to be building a swimming pool?" shrugged Glenn.

This one really busted up the class. Unfortunately, it was Glenn getting the laughs, not Max, who decided to move on to a shriveled woman in the second row.

"You, ma'am," prompted Max.

"Trudy Harper. Can't you read the name tag, sonny?" reprimanded the spunky spinster.

"I'm sorry, Trudy," apologized Max. "What brings you here today?"

"My daughter, Margaret," she replied, "said she'll pick me up at four thirty."

"Everyone's a comedian," mumbled Max over the giggles. "I meant, who did you murder?"

"Well, I'm one hundred and seventy-three and I—" the audience warmly applauded. Trudy meekly smiled and continued, "Anyhow, I was piloting my jetchair to a bingo tournament at the Church of Sins when a boy crossed my airspace in his turbo scooter."

"So it was manslaughter," concluded Max.

"No, I hit the wrong button," corrected Trudy.

Max appeared puzzled.

"You know, the gas instead of the brakes," she explained.

Max cracked a smile and cross-examined, "So it was still an accident?"

"No, sonny," clarified Trudy, "that hooligan needed to be taught a lesson!"

"I see," said Max, mortified.

"Smacked the little bastard halfway to Mars," she tartly added, to roars of approval from her classmates.

"Thank you, we get the idea," nodded Max, who decided to dispense with the rest of the introductions.

"Ladies and gentlemen, today I'm going to teach you ways to curb your murderous cravings and how to avoid the places you're most likely to get caught, called *death traps*, but first . . . a cartoon."

Murder School

Again the predictable applause.

"This one's a Disney favorite, which I think *you'll* remember, Mr. O'Donahue, entitled, *Goofy's Murder Spree* . . . Cartoon one," mouthed Max into his headset.

Instantly the lights dimmed and a three-dimensional Goofy, clutching a bloody sickle, appeared at the front of the banquet room.

Max, having seen the 3D-toon a zillion times, ducked out beneath the illuminated exit sign. He could hear the insane screams of laughter as he strolled through the halls to the swimming pool and collapsed on a lounge chair in the sun.

Since the atmosphere had been infused with Polaroid particles in the mid 20's, the enormous ozone hole was no longer a concern. (This, only after a group of sunbathers were disintegrated on Myrtle beach, August 7, 2023.) But now, just a few years later, you could stay outside all day without sunblock 900 and tan without tumors.

Max rested his head on the lounge chair, seduced by the sun. He knew he had about fifteen minutes until the cartoon ended. Plenty of time for a catnap. He closed his eyes and the last thing he heard was Goofy's distant voice chortling, "G . . . G . . . Golly, I think I committed a murder."

An ambulance siren startled Max awake.

"Oh God," cried Max, realizing he had overslept. He raced around the pool, an ominous feeling in his gut.

The banquet room was eerily quiet as he pushed open the door. Pure carnage greeted him on the other side. Body parts were strewn about like a messy kid's room, blood was splattered against the walls resembled modern vampire art as steam rose from the eviscerated corpses like the ghosts of the dead.

Glenn Moss, the man who murdered his mother-in-law, had been bludgeoned to death with the espresso machine. Mr. O'Donohue's windpipe had been stuffed with jelly doughnuts like an inner tube and he would not be returning to class soon. Perky Miss America runner-up had been gang-raped and then partially consumed. The hundred and seventy-three year old dowager had been impaled with the Americanadian flag. And, the *piece de resistance* . . . the bald, severed head of the tattooed man was perched atop the podium like a shiny apple for the teacher.

There were thirty-one dead and fifty-two likely suspects.

The victims had paid the ultimate price for their crimes, a life for a life, which is how Max recalled it used to be, before capital punishment was ruled unconstitutional in 2013.

The *whoop-beep, whoop-beep* of a mobile trauma center wailed through the sky towards the Holiday Inn, followed by a half dozen aging supersonic cop-choppers, a mobile morgue D-80 and over a hundred TV crews, including the number one tabloid show, *Death Watch*.

Max, meanwhile, maneuvered around the corpses to the podium. He cleared his throat and solemnly addressed the survivors, "I will be signing you out early today," stated Max, adding, "class . . . is dismissed."

There was a spontaneous cheer from the survivors, who now had the rest of their Saturday free. They quickly gathered their blood speckled sweaters and jackets (and a couple doughnuts for the road) then lined up at the front of the room so Max could endorse their completion certificates.

Murder School

Max waved his hand over their documents as they walked past, leaving his ultraviolet heat print. He released the last pupil, then stepped outside where he was nearly stampeded by a mob of international press. After answering a flurry of questions, Max found himself in the middle of a spontaneous rights' auction. After some fierce bidding, and a few gun shots, Max sold an exclusive to *Death Watch* for forty million pesodollars.

Max signed the contract and did a short interview. He then tiredly headed to his restored GE-Jet Star parked on the Holiday Inn tarmac.

Overall, it had been a great day. *Death Watch* was a real career-maker and Max now had the down payment he needed for the new Light Speeder by Hondaford, the one he had seen on the hologram billboard.

Max landed at his condo just in time to turn on Truth-Vision and catch a promo for *Death Watch*. He knocked back an R.J. Reynolds Beer Capsule, kicked back on his hover-couch and licked the froth off his lips as the announcer eagerly promoted "Murder School Massacre," promising an exclusive interview with the heroic teacher and slice to slice autopsy coverage.

Max swallowed another RBC and blinked three times for the Good News Channel, which he discovered had been preempted by some bad news about a mass murder inside a murder school classroom.

Just then, Max received another annoying beep on his brain pager, one of sixty-three messages left today on his cerebral message implant. But he knew this would all soon pass. Next weekend there would be another group of violators wanting to erase a few murders off their data files.

One thing for sure, Max had job security. Murder was in fashion and Max would be telling the same jokes for a long, long time.

Excursion To Insanity

A Psychology Master's Thesis by
Jerome Brambling

As Edited by Robert Steven Rhine

As a fifth year psychology student at Northwestern University, I have pondered a variety of subjects for my master's thesis, but I have finally decided to focus on the condition and affliction of INSANITY. The question I pose for my thesis is this: Is insanity purely genetic or can it be induced? Also, if others can drive you insane, can you drive yourself insane?

In order to explore this subject as thoroughly as possible, I feel it would be best to work from personal experience. To accomplish this I will try to temporarily induce insanity in myself. Having had a mother committed for schizophrenia, I admit I have a unique insight into this subject.

There are many methods to promote insanity. Genetic factors, naturally, play a major role, though I have disproven that in my personal history. I have often wondered why I didn't inherit my mother's schizophrenia either through genetics or proximity. Also, I recall as a child hearing rumors of a great uncle who had allegedly committed suicide with an industrial nail gun. But these family skeletons weren't discussed at the Brambling dinner table, nor, for that matter, was much of *anything*. But I digress.

The following is a diary of my Excursion To Insanity. For the purpose of this thesis, only the more significant days have been included. The complete diary is available at the Galter Health Sciences Library.

DAILY JOURNAL

Day One

I commence at dawn on a cool November morning. A chilly breeze ruffles the curtains of my dorm room window as I write the following report, which I will mail to my psychology professor, Dr. Harold Troutmeyer: I, Jerome Brambling, twenty-six, being of sound mind and body, will undergo a voluntary psychological experiment to analyze the impetus and etiology of insanity. Signed, Jerome Brambling.

I quickly packed a few meager belongings (including a human skull I *borrowed* from anatomy class) and caught the bus across town to a dingy apartment I've rented overlooking a cemetery (to set the mood). From my bedroom window I have a great view of the moss-tinted headstones and crumbling

Excursion to Insanity

mausoleums. I can practically smell the musty rotting corpses ... or is it only in my mind? (I laugh to myself.)

Since I need total isolation for this experiment, I have dropped all associations with friends and family, leaving no forwarding address. This is rather easy considering I have no friends to contact and most of my family is deceased, except for my dear mother, committed to Pleasant Oaks Sanitarium for the past seventeen years.

Day Two

I am eager to begin my experiments but I don't know where to start. I decide to begin by depriving myself of the comforts of home. I shall leave my apartment unfurnished, sleep on newspapers (when I allow myself to sleep), and eat off the linoleum kitchen floor, using no utensils of any kind.

I feel I'm off to a good start.

Day Five:

I've spent the last few days staring out the cracked window of my apartment at the cemetery below, drinking cheap whiskey as I plot my own insanity. I miss not having a radio or television. I'm bored and restless. Nothing's happening. How long will it take, I wonder, to drive myself insane?

Anxious, I escaped my apartment at dusk and wandered down the sidewalk. Within minutes I was offered drugs by a neighborhood crack dealer, no more than thirteen. I waved him away, then called him back. This could be the break I need.

I returned to my apartment with a ten dollar cocaine rock. The tiny crystalline lump looked like a piece of yellowish rock candy, the kind I used to suck on as a kid, when my mom would let me. But as she grew worse she began to refer to candy as "Satan's snacks" and forbid it.

I located a box of matches in the kitchen drawer, then suddenly realized that I didn't have a pipe. I scanned the empty apartment and my eyes fell on the skull I borrowed from anatomy class. I stared into the bony face. *Does madness lie herein?* . . . I wondered aloud before stuffing the skull's gaping mouth with a ball of yellowed newspaper. I next lined the nose cavity with a piece of blackened tinfoil that I scrounged from the stove broiler pan. Then I put the cocaine rock in the nose bone pipe bowl, placed my mouth over the face of the skull, lit the rock, and sucked the fumes from the eye socket. I enhanced the suction by placing my hand over the other socket, to create a drag.

The drug hit its target and I shuddered with an orgasmic wave that soon turned nasty. The newspaper inside the makeshift pipe suddenly burst into flames, transforming the skull into the devil's severed head, screaming in infernal hell.

I was distracted from the vivid hallucination as the drug jolted my nervous system and I collapsed, comatose, on the linoleum. I feared the crack had been cut with numerous chemicals, as I smelled Ajax on my breath. Nevertheless, the experiment had been moderately successful, I reassured myself, as I regained consciousness and stared up at the cottage cheese ceiling.

It is well documented that drugs can ignite the bottle-rocket launching towards insanity. It's an excellent way to set the mind adrift in rough seas without a paddle. But it won't lead to pure, 100% natural, insanity. Nothing like "the real thing," as they say.

Maybe if I murdered someone? I could hack them up and put the pieces through a meat grinder. Instead of writing a thesis, I could throw an impromptu barbecue for my classmates.

I now realized that the crack was making me stupid, not insane. There was no way I wanted to risk spending the rest of my life in prison, being a love doll for some tattooed loser (though it would drive me insane, no doubt, in short order). Murder, I concluded, was definitely excluded.

Day Seven

I have completed the first loathsome week in my dingy apartment. Tonight, after reading *Autopsy Digest* by penlight, I reclined on my newspaper mattress and momentarily felt a cockroach skitter across my forehead. I left my mouth unhinged, pretending to be asleep, and when the cockroach crawled inside, I clamped my teeth shut like a steel trap. *Could this be this the first symptom of insanity?*

Day Thirteen

This morning I found a dead cat run over in front of my apartment. I swatted away the flies, hid it under my coat, and then put the mangled fur pile in the freezer. Later that night, I thawed out the pussycat. I stroked its stiff fur while rocking on my heels, facing a blank wall for several hours. Around midnight I fell asleep on my mangy feline pillow, feeling the defrosted fleas run rampant through my hair.

I must now note, for the record, that I'm being extremely careful not to cross over any permanent boundaries, that I can't cross back over. My goal is to complete my thesis, get a doctorate and set up private practice. I will simply drive myself insane, crossing the silver strand, hand over hand, to the dark side . . . then fight my way back.

Day Sixteen:

Though I've documented each venture towards insanity, I'm disappointed that all my attempts have thus far proved futile. What must I do to loosen my grip on sanity?

I shave off all my body hair, even plucking my eyelashes, and lay in my cold empty bathtub rolling side to side for several hours, screaming nursery rhymes.

Day Nineteen:

My experiment is failing miserably. I have been unsuccessful in every attempt at insanity. I feel like a failure, a worthless fecal speck.

To step up the assault on my resilient psyche, I've initiated extensive sleep and food deprivation. I've stayed up for forty-nine hours straight, fasting and chanting over and over into a mirror, "I am insane . . . I am insane . . . I am insane . . ."

This crude technique comes courtesy of my childhood chum, Oscar, a plump neighborhood kid, who informed me that if you stared into a mirror and said, "I'm a witch" a thousand times, you would actually see a witch in your mirror. Well, it didn't work then and it didn't work now.

Day Twenty-two:

Someone ate my cat! They must have come in while I was sleeping, defrosted my kitty and chowed down. The bastard picked the bones clean. Why can't people leave your stuff alone!? To top it off I'm feeling lightheaded and nauseous, my jaw aching from days of "insane" chanting and attempted mirror madness. I desperately crave sleep. It's two A.M. as I stare out the window at the peaceful cemetery below.

Suddenly, I found myself walking across the deserted street, my naked, flea-bitten body staggering over the asphalt road. I ducked through a hole in the ivy-covered cemetery fence, pulled by an invisible force towards the mausoleums, my bare feet gliding through the dewy grass.

Then I heard a voice in the wind beckoning to me in an urgent whisper. Was I going crazy? I couldn't be so lucky. But as I grew closer I again heard the tortured voice wailing, "Jerome . . . Jerome . . ."

The voice was terrifying, yet oddly comforting. I shivered with dread as I drifted between the stony monuments to death, or life, depending on your viewpoint.

I was drawn to a large crack on the side of one of the mausoleums. The voice seemed to be coming from inside. I staggered closer and found myself slipping into the crack, my smoothly shaven body squeezing through cold jagged marble.

It was dark inside, but for a ray of blue moonlight creeping through the crack. The darkness closed around me like a cold blanket. I began to shiver. It was painfully silent in the mausoleum, devoid of all life but for my throbbing temples.

As I felt around the dank walls of the blackness, my eyes trying to adjust, I inadvertently bumped into something leaning against the wall. After my pulse returned to normal, I was able to determine it was a shovel. The cemetery caretaker was apparently using the mausoleum as a makeshift toolshed. I suddenly laughed to myself, *if the dead only knew*, as I danced a little jig to stay warm, confident that insanity was at hand.

As I bounced off the walls, I noticed that one of the brass crypt plates was loose. I dug what was left of my gnawed fingernails under the edge of the tarnished plate. It moved an inch. I grabbed the shovel and attempted to pry off the plaque. Finally, using all my remaining strength, the entire concrete hatch popped off and fell to the marble floor with a resounding clunk, loud enough to wake the dead.

There was a vacuum sound as stale air rushed out of the chamber. I tentatively stuck my trembling hand inside, my finger fondling something dry and wrinkled. The brittle object broke off in my fingers and I slowly pulled out the flesh speckled toe bone of a corpse. *If my professor could see me now*, I giggled, as I stuck my head inside the crypt chamber and inhaled the musty odor of decay. It was quite roomy inside, the deflated corpse, shriveled to a rawhide chew toy.

I crawled into the eternal darkness, listening to the crackle and pop of snapping bones as I climbed over the mummified remains. Once inside the death drawer, I stretched out in the void, my pale arms crossed over my hairless chest. Though exhausted, I was terrified to sleep, fearing I'd be sealed inside the tomb.

Just then, I felt a breeze in my ear. It sounded like a breath . . . only it wasn't my own. I shivered with dread as a gravelly voice trailed out of the cadavers mouth.

"Why don't you ever visit me, Jerome?"

"Mom?!" I gasped, rattled to the core.

There was no reply, but I could hear her cancerous wheeze.

"I thought you were at Pleasant Valley," I moaned.

The cadaver whispered through her grimacing decayed teeth with a vicious hiss, "How would you know? You haven't visited in eight years."

I meant to, Mom, but I've been . . . um . . . busy," I guiltily reasoned.

"And I croaked in the meantime," scolded the corpse.

"I'm sorry!" I pitifully sobbed, feeling claustrophobic in the stuffy crypt chamber.

There was no question at this point that my sanity was totally lost and, I bleakly observed, there was no turning back. The silver thread had snapped.

"Snuggle with Mommie, Jerome," she said, offering her arid breasts for a death suckle.

I politely passed, instead hugging the rotting corpse, listening to the bones crack as Mom sang her favorite nursery rhyme, "The itsy-bitsy spider crawled up the water spout . . ."

It made me wonder if there were poisonous spiders crawling across my shaved head, as I sensed ominous tickles over my bald cranium. But that was the least of my problems as I curled into the fetal position, sucking my thumb and laying against the dehydrated womb of my dead mother.

THESIS CONCLUSION:

Day Thirty-seven:

My professor, Dr. Troutmeyer, visited today and we had a nice chat. He likes my thesis a lot and told me that

Excursion to Insanity is "worthy of deeper analysis." I bet I'll get an "A". He gave me a number two pencil and is watching me as I write this in my journal:

Through my experiment I've learned that genetics is ultimately the decisive factor in forming insanity. Also, I've concluded that my thesis: Can you make yourself insane? should also have included: Is trying to make yourself insane, a symptom of insanity?

On a final personal note, I would like to add that, as a result of my thesis, I have reconciled with my mother. She's not dead after all, she just led me to believe she was. It was the only way she could get me to visit. She makes me crazy.

I can now visit her anytime I wish at Pleasant Valley.

We have adjoining rooms.

The Brain Exchange

Wendell lit a synthetic twig and held it firmly between his colored capped teeth as he stood by a corporate call box in a shadowy corner of the swarming exchange.

Wendell specialized in black market mind futures—predictions of thoughts which hadn't been realized—a high commodity on the floor of the Brain Exchange. He studied the sparks illuminating the membrane of the motherboard and prepared to bid.

The Lower Lobeys, in their checkered vinyl jackets and feathered fedoras, zipped around the trading floor like racing blood cells, elbowing one another around the base of a hundred foot modular spine. At the top of the fiber-optic spinal cord towered the great cerebrum itself—an eighty ton motherboard which sparkled with infinite ideas.

Wendell adjusted the temperature gauge of his gel-filled sports jacket as he watched the Lobeys swarm into action, like clotting platelets. Wendell calmly loaded his bid gun and prepared to fire as the following thoughts appeared on the motherboard: "Hats for Cats" (5 1/8), "Kidney Stone Jewelry" (13 3/8), "Umbrellas Heaters" (33 1/5), and "Livercakes" (22 1/2).

The bidding was fierce as Wendell aimed and fired a bid dart at the head of Mikey Meconium, his firm's Lower Lobey. The air was quickly filled with more flying projectiles than an Apache archery tournament as Wendell's dart expertly found its target.

Mikey yanked the pink dart off his fedora, nodded at Wendell, and furiously began pulling his hairy earlobes, shouting bids at the Intellectual Interloper as fast as his lips could spit them out.

Knock-Kneed Wally, the infamous Lobey from the firm of "Brain Teasers," flicked a green fingernail at the tip of his nose, topping Wendell's bid for the "Umbrella Heater" by fifty yeckles.

Mikey, meanwhile, pulled another dart off his fedora, and wildly milked his earlobes, shouting, "Fifty yeckles, five fornoughts!" This was as high as Mikey was allowed to bid (and the loudest he could shout by law); nevertheless, the "Umbrella Heater" sold for sixty yeckles, eight fornoughts and sixty-two yulebaits to Knock-Kneed Wally and the Brain Teasers.

"Jammit!" exclaimed Wendell as he kicked the bid-covered floor of the Brain Exchange sending up a cyclone of paper scraps.

The Brain Exchange

Wendell stormed off the floor, inadvertently bumping his shoulder into rival "head-scratcher" Kathy Clean as she shook back her golden locks, purposely distracting the attention of the Lobeys.

K.C.'s hair thwacked Wendell across the face and his fellow scratchers applauded as Kathy curtsied in her glow-in the-dark knickers.

At the espresso injector, Wendell dully held out his forearm, wincing as the shot of caffeine bolted through his vein like a bullet train. He shivered as his senses were slapped alive and took a deep breath of the communal burning branches as he scanned the sullen faces of associate "floor flies" sucking twigs. Wendell put three yulebaits into the confession receiver and whispered into the mouthpiece. He was feeling considerably better as K.C. entered the confines of the FMBB (Five Minute Break Booth) and joined Wendell for an injection of confidence.

She stuck out her veins and shivered as the espresso hit its mark while Wendell watched K.C.'s stylishly sagging breasts bungy to a halt. She was clearly the best looking "scratcher" on the floor and Wendell appreciated the momentary unobstructed view of her trendy, native-inspired udders.

It was stifling in the cramped FMBB, made all the more oppressive by the awkward silence. It wasn't a written rule, but competitors rarely chatted, especially in the booth. Wendell finally broke the unspoken rule, much to the consternation of the others.

"Sorry about the bump," feebly whispered Wendell to Kathy.

"Forget yourself, love," replied K.C., "it's like that out there and when it isn't, then you have your worries."

They shared a momentary laugh, then simultaneously turned and stuck their arms under caffeine injectors. It was Wendell's fifth shot of espresso since the morning session. He shuddered as the needle punched into his vein with the sound of a staple gun.

When he turned back around she was, thankfully, still there. Though they were competitors, Wendell respected K.C. She was extremely bright and the most respected single cell of the brain trust known as "Thought Stealers," one of the oldest firms walkin' the boards.

K.C. leaned back on her elbows, staring through the glass dome of the booth at the artery-laced ceiling of the Brain Exchange.

"What'cha think?" cajoled K.C. as she turned and caught Wendell staring at her droopers, a holiday bonus for her winning bid on the "Zulu Breast Kit" account.

"Well," replied a flustered Wendell, studying the incoming sparks on the motherboard, "'Jamaican Jelly Beans' looks yummy at forty . . . 'Slipper Headlights' are a go in the low seventies . . . and 'The Toe DeJammer' is over-priced, though I'd wink at thirty-two."

He was lying and Kathy knew it, but she nevertheless smiled with her perfectly capped peach and blue teeth, Wendell recalling that she had placed the winning bid on "Colorful Tooth Caps" the previous year.

She had rounded up some of the best ideas in the pit, pondered Wendell, wondering if that thought might be worth something. There was always a buyer at the Brain Exchange,

The Brain Exchange

which is pretty much why everyone kept their thoughts to themselves, thus driving prices even higher.

Wendell's "Two-Minute-Warning-Watch" buzzed and he sheepishly smiled at K.C., realizing it was time to get back to buy-sell.

"Well . . . bad luck," said Wendell, as was the custom.

"Worse to you," replied Kathy.

"Don't think too much," offered Kathy as Wendell left the booth and trudged back to the floor. A moment later she added, "Caught you," with a dazzling smile.

Wendell had heard that line a zillion times before. He had purchased it for his firm in 2310. He would have to charge her . . . *but later*, decided Wendell, adding it to her tab, as he headed back to the floor of the Brain Exchange to buy another thought.

3

BAD BOYS AND ALLEY CATS
Another "Raoul, Low-life Ex-Cop" Adventure

Raoul tapped the blue vein in his neck, making it bloat like a waterlogged earthworm. The needle glided through the purple track, Raoul's eyes momentarily bugging, then fluttering back in their sockets as the "H" zeroed in like a smart bomb.

A trickle of urine dribbled into his gutter-glazed trousers as he rolled onto his spine and stared at ominous clouds illuminated by the moon, wondering what happened to the silver linings.

Crows circled overhead, though Raoul could only hear their relentless *caw . . . caw*. *Christ it was hot*, thought Raoul, the pavement slow-roasting his skull. It must have been approaching eleven at night but the air was still chewable. L.A. in August. *This is your brain* . . . echoed Raoul silently . . . *this is your brain on the pavement*.

Things had been going rather disconcertingly for Raoul all summer. He had been evicted from his apartment; he was terminally unemployed, even with nineteen *good* years on the force, four not so; and there were at least a hundred cons who would love to stumble across him in this back alley and stomp his ass silly.

Fortunately, Raoul had scrounged a bent hypodermic from behind the dumpster which he straightened against the pavement so he could shoot his rent into his neck.

Raoul suddenly smelled something malodorous which gave him pause. Then he realized, *he* was the smell and probably the reason the other squatters had moved on to fresher alleys.

How did I wind up here? wondered Raoul. *When did my life turn rancid?* Could it have been the collection of pornography which somehow disappeared from the evidence cage at Metro? Could it have been the informant who was *accidentally* shot—twice? Or, the eight pounds of sinsemilla that somehow never made it back to the station? Take your pick. And there was more, so much more. But Raoul had a detective badge and they could *never* take that away (though they tried) until Raoul traded it that afternoon for the flea powder searing his carotid artery, shaking his soul at this very moment. Ohhhhhhhhhhh Mannnnnnnnn . . . .

But Raoul still longed for his days on homicide which were all but a meth-hazed memory.

Just then, Raoul heard someone entering his alley and laid closer to the ground, if that was possible. There were two shadowy figures walking together, one in heels. In this part of town, the one in heels would more than likely be the man, reflected Raoul as he peeked around the dumpster and watched a Latina alley cat and her John setting stage for an off-Broadway blow. She looked like a zillion pin cushions he had busted. Anorexic, Medusa hair, coke sores and a forty-weight perfume—her force-field against "the life."

The balding Chinese businessman, in his C&R business suit, leaned against the graffitied brick wall as she kneeled on torn fishnets. Raoul was suddenly the master of disguise lying in the slime, thinking this was some of the best undercover work he had done in years.

The businessman, sweating through his cheap polyester jacket, mumbled in Cantonese as the Latina's forehead monotonously beat a samba on his belt buckle. Her jaw ached as the pathetic pot-sticker swelled between her smeared clown lips, masking a herpes breakout.

Her Venus's-flytrap eyelashes parted as she spied Raoul's cadaver lying in his own piss, staring back with dead fish eyes. She wasn't positive if he was breathing or not, nor was Raoul for that matter, but it didn't sway her from her present job assignment.

The Asian squealed a war cry, Raoul experiencing a disconcerting Nam flashback as the businessman squirted a quarter teaspoon of nut lava over her left shoulder, landing an inch from Raoul's crooked nose.

Raoul studied the glutinous glob of love phlegm. A million sperm squandering their youth on the reeking asphalt.

The businessman zipped up his flaccid dim sum, belched a pork bun, tossed a saw buck on the pavement and darted out of the alley without looking back at the remnants of his soul he left behind.

Juanita wiped the cracked corners of her mouth and noticed that the fleeing kumquat had spunked a snail trail across her faux leopard fur collar.

"Chingado!" spat Juanita, trying to wipe off the gunk.

She noticed Raoul's unblinking stare and crossed herself before slinking over to him, "You alive?"

"No," groaned Raoul.

Satisfied, she rifled through his pockets as a repo truck drove by, illuminating the alley and Raoul's death mask. A wave of uncomfortable recognition illuminated hers.

"Do I know you?" she queried, dabbing the oozing herpes on her lower lip.

"Forgive me for not shaking your hand," garbled Raoul, unable to move an atrophied muscle. "Lieutenant Raoul Reynoso, at your service," he added with aplomb, drooling his salutation onto the pavement.

"You're a cop?" nervously cackled Juanita.

"Past tense," informed Raoul, amused that anyone would feel threatened by him at this juncture.

"By the way, you're under arrest," Raoul added, to limited comedic effect.

Juanita frowned as she leaned in for a closer look.

"Aye . . . you stink cop," exhaled Juanita, waving her hand in front of her nose, stirring up the fetid air particles.

"Just a momentary eddy on life's twisted river," proffered Raoul, suddenly the alley prophet.

"Well, then I guess I stink too," conceded the Eastside girl, who shrugged and squatted beside Raoul against the brick wall which was covered with piss, spit, snot, shit, scum and unidentified alien tissue samples.

The dilated duo sat silently for a moment, listening to the distant gunfire and a women screaming at her baby in the nearby projects.

"It's a bumpy ride out here, huh, baby?" soothed Juanita, acknowledging Raoul as some sort of soulmate on this hellish merry-go-round, as she took out her stem and lit a Gibraltar.

Raoul watched her as he rolled his swollen tongue over his front teeth, noticing a gap that wasn't there this morning, "Well, I ain't Aladdin and this ain't no flying carpet."

They both chuckled, their pain masked between breaths.

"A cop, huh?" she repeated, incredulous, before taking another hit. "You ever bust me?" she asked as she passed him the pipe.

"I don't know, but I probably fucked you," replied Raoul, deadpan, sucking the diamond back to coal.

Juanita considered all the cops she had ball-bounced as she studied Raoul, finding him sexy in a street sort of way: his flat nose, the thin scar that curved his cheek, his jet black hair which would never turn grey. She knew there was Indian blood in there *somewhere*.

"Just goes to show," offered Juanita, in response to nothing.

"Just goes to show what?" echoed Raoul, wildly scratching a bug which had suddenly burrowed up his asshole.

"We're all the same when it gets right down to it," philosophized Juanita, "cops, junkies, hookers."

"Different side of the same track," agreed Raoul, his conjunctive eyes lingering over her features. She was a knockout at one time, but "the life" had stolen her beauty and the streets had frozen her solid. He didn't know if the wrinkles around her mouth were from crack pipes or blow jobs.

"You need a shower," abruptly informed Juanita. "Come on."

She hoisted Raoul to his feet, but he buckled as she let him go, his forehead denting the dumpster.

"Where are we going?" slurred Raoul, as he stood on Gumby legs, unaware of the blood trickling over his eyebrow.

"My pimp's place," Juanita flatly replied.

Raoul lurched back, swaying like a swabby in a monsoon.

"Don't worry. He's not home right now," she informed him. "Besides, Spudney's all right . . . he has his bad days, like anyone."

"I don't want to be one of them," stated Raoul.

"Spudney's harmless as a kitten," she insanely giggled.

"Kittens have rabies," muttered Raoul, who against every reasonable bone in his body, except the one rising in his boxers, tagged along. He needed a shower. He'd been on the streets for weeks, and it was getting real old. Besides, maybe she would let him sample the goods.

Juanita slung Raoul's arm over her shoulder as she helped him out of the alley. A black and white slowly cruised past and the blues gave them the once over, not recognizing the homeless man covered in sludge as someone they once respected and even trained under. Raoul imagined how pathetic he must have looked—an indigent cop leaning on a strawberry pop tart for salvation. *Then again, what better way?* pondered Raoul . . . *what better way?*

It was only a few blocks down Sunset to the pimp's apartment on Normandy, but it seemed like crossing the Great

Plains to Raoul. The stairs were the worst part. He felt like a paraplegic being encouraged by his physical therapist, "Right, goood . . . now left, goood."

Juanita opened the door to the pimp's place. It smelled of tamales and old socks. But no pimp. Raoul was relieved, hardly able to defend himself much less stand on his two infected feet.

Juanita dumped Raoul on the mustard foam sofa. "I'm going to take the first shower," she announced, "before you dirty it up. Make yourself at home, just don't touch anything."

She left Raoul sinking into the couch as she ducked into the bathroom, and he slowly tilted onto his left side.

Raoul could smell the sofa. The reek of old farts, cigarettes and the distinct smell of sex. A thousand and one snatches. Maybe Juanita had worked the room before she hit the streets or the pimp broke in his girls right here. The thought gave Raoul pause until the front door suddenly swung open and a huge Bahamian with half a nose entered the apartment.

"Wha' the fuc?!"

From Raoul's sideways vantage point on the sofa, the pimp looked like the Angel of Death draped in black rayon, his throat strangled by twenty-four karat snakes. The huge Bahamian had rage in his eyes, the kind Raoul preferred to see when he had his Tangfolio-Spa BT 99 strapped in his shoulder holster.

The irate pimp bellowed toward the bathroom, "Juanita, you stu-pid bitch! I told you not to bring yo' tricks up here no mo'."

But she didn't hear him, as she sang "La Bamba" in the shower while vigorously soaping the crabs.

Spudney kicked the door shut with his boot heel and threateningly approached Raoul, "Who da fuc are you? Get yo' azz up off my sofa!"

Raoul would have loved to comply had he been able to gather his brain cells and send them on a mission to alert his body parts.

"What's wrong with you, mon? You deef?!"

This is where Raoul figured his head would be smashed like a moldy pumpkin, the seeds sticking to the walls. But the Bahamian began to realize that Raoul was just a harmless junkie. Another indication of how low Raoul had sunk into the sofa.

The pimp shoved Raoul's feet aside, making room for himself on the couch.

"Whew, you reek!" squinted the pussy peddler as he removed a Baggie from his pocket containing five crystalline rocks. He lit one in his bowl and slapped on the TV remote. Raoul cringed as he heard the theme song, "Bad boys, Bad Boys, what'cha gonna do, what'cha gonna do when they come for you . . . ?"

Raoul was living his worst nightmare: an ex-cop junkie curled up in a fetal position crashing on a pimp's sex-drenched sofa watching a rerun of *Cops*.

The pimp wildly tapped his foot to the theme, mouthing the words, as he intermittently sucked Satan from his crack pipe. The song ended and he drew a last hit, howling an evil wail.

Raoul wondered if the pimp would be howling when he found out he was torching up next to a highly decorated ex-detective of the LAPD. Then again, pondered Raoul, after Marion Barry was reelected mayor of Washington . . . who could be surprised by anything?

Juanita opened the bathroom door butt naked. Her cocoa skin was smooth and slick, her brown nipples two inches long, her snatch shaved into a home plate diamond. Raoul admired the trim job the way you would a manicured hedge animal. He might have gotten a hard-on had the crack not had a vice grip on his libido.

Juanita dried her thatch with a tattered towel as Spudney spoke, without turning his green eyes from the screen

"Who the fuc's dis?" snapped Spudney.

"Mi amigo," replied Juanita.

"Friend of yours?!" Spudney laughed so hard he almost fell off the sofa. "You ain't got no friends, hoe."

Juanita momentarily paused, deciding whether to tell him. "He's a cop."

"A COP?!!" exploded Spudney, leaping off the sofa as if a Malaysian cockroach just crawled up his pants leg.

Spudney totally flipped out, smacked Juanita across the side of the head sending her reeling. He pulled an ice pick from his boot and jabbed it against Raoul's gulping larynx.

"An *ex*-detective," she added, nearly too late for an impromptu tracheotomy.

"There's no such thing as an *ex*-cop, you stupid slag," scoffed Spudney, the tip of the ice pick drawing blood beads on Raoul's leathery throat.

"Stupido!" blurted Juanita, wondering who would get stuck cleaning the furniture. "Look at him. He's pinned. I found him in an alley with a spike in his neck."

"Good, let him die *there*. Just not in my digs, dig?!" roared Spudney, itching to punch a buttonhole in Raoul's throat.

"No! Don't stick him!" cried Juanita. "He just needs a place to stay!"

"This ain't da fucking pound," Spudney hollered. "He either goes back to the street or he gets exterminated, right now."

The red-eyed pimp studied Raoul like a coiled snake, "Your move, cop."

"Hey, I don't want to be in your shit, man," sputtered Raoul. "But could you please drag me outside. I can't seem to get my legs to work."

"See," sighed Juanita, "I told you he's harmless."

"So, we're playing 'Guess Who's Fucking Coming To Dinner,' is that it?" bellowed Spudney, smacking Juanita again, this time on the right side of the head, to balance her out.

Spudney spontaneously cooked another rock and gulped a hit while still holding the rusty ice pick to Raoul's throat. "A detective, huh?" repeated Spudney, holding in the devil smoke. "Bet you've seen it all."

"Not until just this moment," solemnly replied Raoul, feeling dangerously nauseous.

Just then, there was a loud pounding at the apartment door, startling Spudney who nearly slipped and skewered Raoul's esophagus.

"POLICE, OPEN THE DOOR!" ordered a voice on the other side.

The pimp's eyes went wild and he spun on Juanita, "What'd you do, invite over the whole station?!"

"OPEN THE DOOR OR WE'LL BREAK IT DOWN," added the deep-voiced cop. Then, a more youthful-voiced rookie added, "And you'll have to pay for a new one."

"You can't do that!" shot back the pimp.

"Why not?" said the baritone voice, exasperated.

"Because . . . I've got a hostage in here . . . a cop," taunted Spudney, playing his ace.

"Bullshit," spat one of the officers, incredulously.

"What's your name?" Spudney asked his uninvited house guest.

"Detective Reynoso," rasped Raoul, through clenched throat.

"I got Detective Reynoso," Spudney proudly hollered.

"No shit," mumbled the older cop's voice on the other side of the door, seemingly not all that surprised.

There was a brief whispered discussion outside the door.

"Go ahead and kill him," voiced the rookie.

"You sure?" said Spudney, his hostage suddenly worthless.

Then, "Raoul, it's Mike. You *really* in there?!"

Raoul replied an embarrassed, "Yup."

"What for?" was the following question.

"Can't beat the rent?" quipped Raoul.

Spudney dug the pick an eighth of an inch into Raoul Adams apple.

"Seriously, I live here now," said Raoul, his voice an octave higher.

"You're pathetic," said the rookie, Andrews.

"What do you want us to do?" inquired Mike.

"Leave," said Raoul as Spudney nodded.

"Um, we can't," said Mike, adding after a pause, "We've, um, got a film crew out here."

"A TV film crew?" yelled Spudney, excitedly.

"They're from *Cops*. They're following us around this week," informed the rookie, Mike adding, "We finally made the big time Raoul."

"Congratulations," groaned Raoul, his life flashing across the tabloids, prepared to be nationally televised in a crack bust, lounging beside his pimp buddy like a strung-out Tonto.

Meanwhile, Spudney's ears were perked up like a cat in a rat's nest, "*Cops?!*" Then, more joyful, "Baby, you hear that, *Cops* is here!"

Juanita suddenly began sobbing, making a scene.

"Shut-da-fuck-up! You do that on camera and I'll kill you, bitch!"

Spudney, preparing for his television debut, smoothed back his dreadlocks, momentarily relaxing the ice pick at Raoul throat.

Big mistake. Carpe Diem, baby. Zero to sixty in seven seconds.

Raoul summoned his inner cop, the one he used before the booze and the drugs and the whores. His guardian angel awoke, slightly spaced, and lunged for the pimp's wrist, twisting the ice pick to the floor.

Spudney's green eyes glowed with shock and anger, as he observed Raoul's corpse rising from the grave.

Raoul dug his heels into the floor, preparing to leap from the sofa, planning to shoulder slam Spudney. Unfortunately, his gelatinous legs slipped on the polar bear throw rug plunging Raoul, chin first, onto the edge of the coffee table.

The crackled bat sound, Raoul heard next, was his jaw breaking.

Spudney, grinning like an escaped lunatic, grabbed the pick off the floor and approached Raoul the way you would a hunk of ice you want to make into cubes.

"What's going on in there?!" yelled Andrews.

Juanita shrieked, "DON'T KILL HIM!!"

After a few hearty kicks, the door banged open and the two uniforms burst inside, guns drawn. They had a hell of a time subduing Spudney who was "on the muscle," like a crazed hornet protecting his queen.

Andrews finally hog-tied the whacked-out pimp, his cocked 9mm at Spudney's brain stem, while Mike helped Raoul to his feet.

"Working undercover?" Mike asked Raoul, shaking his head.

"GUgnhmmmnnnttt," responded Raoul, his jaw unhinged.

"Where's the film crew?" barked Spudney, his eager eyes darting to the hallway.

"Sorry to disappoint," snickered Mike, "but you're too ugly for television."

"But you said *Cops* was here," the pimp protested.

"We lied. Works every time. Everyone wants to be on *Cops*," informed Andrews, high-fiving his partner.

Spudney was dragged into the hall, muttering to himself.

"You all right, Raoul?" inquired Mike, placing the drugs and paraphernalia in an evidence bag.

"Aren't you going to bust him?" spat Spudney, nodding towards Raoul from the hallway floor.

"Hook him and book him," ordered Mike to his partner who read Spudney his rights as he towed him down the stairs like a sled, one step at a time.

Mike checked Raoul's broken jaw and the dried blood on his forehead, "Come on. Let's get you a beer. You can stay with me until you get back on your feet."

They started to exit when Mike stopped in his tracks as if he had just run over a skunk. "Whoa, partner, you've got to take a shower before you get in my car, you smell nasty!"

"Just aim me towards the hot water," barely articulated Raoul, through clenched teeth.

"What should I do with her?" Mike asked Raoul, indicating Juanita.

"Give her a free ride," garbled Raoul, attempting a smile through his chipped teeth as he entered the bathroom.

Juanita grinned back at Raoul as he shut the bathroom door.

"Sad what happened to him," she said wistfully as Mike sat back on the sofa and turned off his walkie-talkie.

"Shut up," ordered Mike, unzipping.

Bad boys, bad boys what'cha gonna do . . . what'cha gonna do when they come for you . . . ?

Something In The Air

It came up one evening at a dinner party, the notion that ideas are in the air. Leonard Kling, a compact and easily agitated man in his late-forties, with Barbie doll hair plugs, was expounding over melon balls how he had created an idea for a television series. It was about Siamese twin cops who chase criminals on the streets of Omaha.

Leonard, the biggest (and frankly only), television producer in Nebraska, had watched in horror as a new TV pilot aired that season called, *Siamese Cops*. Naturally, Leonard expounded to his dinner guests, someone had stolen his idea. Though he had never actually told anyone the idea, he nevertheless phoned his attorney who quipped, "Sorry, sometimes ideas are in the air."

After firing his attorney, and paranoid that his idea had somehow been snatched from the air, Leonard was determined not to let another brilliant idea of his escape into the wind and fall prey to the air thieves.

So, in time, Leonard built a walk-in "idea safe" made of six inch thick titanium with a vacuum lock. Inside the vault he placed a formica table and a manual Royal typewriter (computers were too chancy). A bare bulb hung from the ceiling. Whenever he felt an idea bubbling up, he would simply lock himself in the vault for hours, and in one case an entire day, lest the idea escape and float into mass consciousness.

On the other side of town Andy and his orange marmalade cat, Rudolph, wandered along the train tracks searching for squashed pennies.

Andy, an imaginative twelve-year-old with a mop of red hair and connect-the-dot freckles, loved the trains and the rush of air as they swept past, sucking your hair. Rudolph, on the other hand, despised trains. The cantankerous cat cowered in Andy's well-worn corduroy jacket, digging his claws into Andy's hairless chest until the train echoed safely into the distance.

Sometimes, standing in the turbulent air behind the train's last car, Andy was filled with ideas—wonderful concepts and notions swirling around his boyhood brain.

Was it the exhilaration of being near the train that caused these cerebral storms? Or, was it something trailing in the *whoosh* behind the train?

Leonard awoke at four A.M. in a cold sweat and immediately covered his mouth to muffle a cry of joy, fearing that Candy Cummings, the bleached blond silicone starlet who loudly snored beside him on the waterbed, might rob him of his thought.

Candy's real name was Jane Farthington and she was an insurance secretary from Sioux City. But Jane was also an aspiring actress who had heard that Leonard Kling was a man to contend with. Not so, she had henceforth discovered, in bed.

Anyhow, Leonard leapt up, ran through the kitchen, tripped over Spielberg (his Chihuahua) and dashed to his "idea safe."

Once inside his office he fumbled with the combination, desperately trying to retain the incredible concept burning at his temporal lobes, fearful it might evaporate into oblivion. He spun the combination dial . . . twelve right . . . forty-two left . . . seventy right . . . or was it seventeen right? . . . or left?

"Rats!" spat Leonard.

Leonard suddenly snapped his fingers. *No problem. The combination was written down . . . somewhere.* If only he could remember where.

A wave of panic swept over Leonard's face. While he was trying to remember where he had hidden his combination, he had completely forgotten his idea!

"TRIPLE RATS!" cried Leonard, as he squatted in front of the vault, racking his aching head for the concept that eluded him. He began to softly sob while rhythmically banging his head on the side of the metal safe.

A trail of red ants marched single file down the railway tracks. Andy and Rudolph, balancing themselves atop the steel rails, strolled along absorbed in the ant trail. So much so that they didn't hear the train coming.

Meanwhile, inside the train, in coach "C," inventor conventioneers were wearing party hats. This didn't mean they were having a good time. Most of them were just sitting there with blank expressions on their faces. Occasionally, one of the inventors would blow the horn inserted in his mouth. But that was the extent of the fun.

One of the conventioneers, Karl Reicher, tried to pass around a flask of peppermint schnapps but the inventors weren't about to be fooled. Not this group. If they drank, they might get drunk and loose lips can sink million dollar ideas. Nevertheless, the inventor of Freeze-Dried-Dreams, Rolando Buckman, took a swig from the flask, certain he could hold his liquor and his tongue.

There were all sorts of strange ideas these inventors held locked in their fertile imaginations. But they wouldn't dare think of them for fear their minds would be read and their fortunes stolen.

Most of the inventions were positively ludicrous, but there was hope for the Tie-Shirt. It was simply a dress shirt with a tie sewn to the collar, for those who hated having to knot one. Not to say this was such a brilliant idea, but compared to the man who had invented slip covers for your pets, it was gold.

The red ant troops swarmed over the train tracks feeling the oncoming vibrations. Rudolph pounced on each red insect and tried to pop them in his mouth before they crawled out. But the ants were presently less interested in Rudolph than the five o'clock commuter.

It wasn't until the whistle blew that Andy snapped to attention. He glanced up as the train was less than half a mile

Something in the Air

away and stepped off the tracks hollering for Rudolph who appeared frozen, a terrified Cheshire grin plastered on his puss. Andy realized that either Rudolph had a death wish or was stuck. Figuring the latter, Andy grabbed Rudolph whose paw was indeed wedged in an ant hole beneath the tracks.

Andy, in a panic, the train approaching, desperately tried to free Rudolph who simply fainted (a natural cat reflex for total pain and annihilation).

As the train loomed within a hundred yards Andy could see the engineer, in the locomotive, reading *Trout Farming Illustrated*.

Back in coach "C" one of the conventioneers had fallen asleep and was mumbling. The other inventors strained to hear what he was saying and tried to get closer. One dropped her handkerchief. Another faked a limp on his way to the bathroom. But the mumbler, Rolando Buckman, was only having a Freeze-Dried-Dream, courtesy of the soon to be patented wafer lodged under his tongue.

A moment before the train spanked them into oblivion, Andy yanked Rudolph from the tracks. The train *whooshed* by, sucking the cat along for a few feet before he tumbled to a stop. Andy ran to his friend's aid and inquired as to his condition. But the cat wasn't talking and Andy noticed a few gray hairs on Rudolph's tangerine fur.

Then something else happened as the train pulled away. Andy, oddly, thought of Freeze-Dried-Dreams, then, he thought of Pet Slipcovers, then Tie-Shirts and, finally ... Andy thought about a robbery.

As it happened, one of the conventioneers was actually an impostor and was only going to the convention to steal others' ideas. Karl Reicher, who had been ladling out the libations, had been sent by the Enigma Corporation to liberate as many ideas as he could from the inventors. So far he hadn't been too successful.

However, if Karl knew what Norman Millman, in seat twelve, had conceived he would have had no trouble at all. Norman had invented the Idea Vacuum, a device so powerful that it could suck ideas right out of the air. He hadn't invented the device to steal from other inventors but rather to gather his own ideas that often left his brain before they could take shape. Norman knew that we have thousands of great thoughts every day, some of them worthy of making us millionaires. If we could just harvest them, think of the ample treasures we would reap.

Karl Reicher, the executive brain burglar, didn't know of Norman Millman's device or he would have been using it at that very moment. But Karl had his own methods of extracting ideas from inventors. In his black vinyl doctor bag were powerful serums that could make you spontaneously spout your thoughts.

One of the serums in his bag was ten times more powerful than Sodium Pentothal. But it was too dangerous to use because the *truths* that the subjects would blurt out were so painfully true, often about the interrogator himself, that they could not be heard for fear of going mad.

If the truth serums didn't work, and they usually did, Karl would simply use torture and, if that failed, as a desperate last resort . . . he would offer to buy the idea.

Something in the Air

Andy didn't know what to do with the ideas that flowed into his brain from behind the train. He knew Rudolph wouldn't like being slipcovered and he was too young to wear a tie. But a robbery—well, now you're talking. He headed for the nearest Sheriff's station.

Candy lay in bed wondering aloud why Leonard had anxiously bolted from the room over an hour ago. Was it something she said? Doubtful. They had hardly spoken to each other since the dinner party, when Leonard had uttered the words, "Kid, I'm going to make you a star." Yes, he actually said that, and Candy bit on it, not because she believed it for a moment—she'd slept with dozens of these so-called producers—but because of one word Leonard said . . . "Kid."

Leonard slithered back to bed, checking to make sure Candy was still asleep. He futilely tried to rock himself back to sleep, rubbing the pyramid crystal dangling from his flabby neck.

"What's wrong?" squealed Candy, startling Leonard.

But Leonard wasn't about to fall for that trick and confess his memory lapse, possibly giving her insight into the idea itself. So he just lay there in a fetal position, rocking himself and groaning, "Rats, rats, rats . . . ."

"Ah ha!" Leonard sprang from the waterbed, a fresh idea imprinted on his brain tissue. He sprinted towards his office, vaulted the Chihuahua, grabbed the combination from his desk drawer, twirled the dial and was in the "idea safe" in a lick. He pulled the bare bulb string and jotted down the idea, as the light swung ominously overhead.

He had done it! It was a brilliant idea! Undoubtedly, he would be the new messiah of the television airwaves, and the fortune that had eluded him for so long while others grew rich in his pitiful path, was finally his . . . *his* . . . HIS!!! Leonard had become aware that he was maniacally chortling when there was a knock at the vault door.

"Lenny, you okay?"

"Raaaats!" grumbled Leonard, realizing he had left his office door unlocked in his haste. He quickly dropped the slip of paper into his safe idea deposit box, careful not to glance at it with Candy in such close proximity.

"I'll be right out," sang Leonard, his voice an octave higher, adding, "Go back to bed . . . I'm . . . I'm . . . ahhhh . . . working on a new part for you."

He could hear Candy's frenzied gurgles of glee from outside the safe, and the pitter-patter of her skipping feet back towards the bedroom. Leonard sighed with relief.

The Sheriff picked his meat-filled molar with a paper clip.

"Boy," twanged the Sheriff, with a southern drawl not witnessed since *Hee Haw*. "Boy, what'cha talkin' 'bout a robb'ry fo'? Ain't been no robb'ry in Franklin County fo' eighteen years. Hell, we don't even have a bank no mo'."

Andy, breathless from his mile sprint, explained that the robber was riding on the train. But, when pressed, Andy wasn't quite sure when the robbery would take place. "But it *will* happen, Sheriff," proclaimed Andy, adding for dramatic effect, "Mark my words!"

The Sheriff stared at the freckle-faced, red-haired boy and shook his head, "What makes you so sure?"

Something in the Air

"It was something in the air," replied Andy.

The Sheriff paused for a moment, then began a belly laugh that started at his pudgy ankles, shook him all the way up his body like a fleshy Hoola-Hoop ring and ended with a furious belch. Andy sidestepped the noxious zephyr.

"Get out of my face, boy," concluded the Sheriff with a wave of his hand.

Andy, frustrated, headed towards the screen door. He paused and dramatically turned around, "You're wrong Sheriff, trains carry secrets and if you stand behind them you can catch them."

The Sheriff snorted as he vigorously bit into his liverwurst sandwich, leaving a brown lump on his nose.

Leonard undulated on waterbed waves, thinking of what he would do with his millions when he sold his idea. He would first buy an estate in Palm Springs with a lap pool and wall-to-wall bimbos and . . . .

"Is it a big part?" whispered Candy.

Leonard rolled his eyes, "Yes, yes, it's really big . . . huge. Now please go to sleep."

Dead silence.

"Is it the lead?" Candy whined.

"Yes, yes," sighed Leonard, "for heaven's sake, it's the lead!"

And with that, Candy dove on him.

Dawn. A rooster's crow and the shrill whistle of the morning commuter.

Leonard lurched up in bed wide-eyed, his heart thumping. Though a top producer in his mind, Leonard still lived in the country near the railroad.

A growling mayday sounded from Leonard's volcanic ocean of a stomach. He was hungry. Very hungry. Hungry for power, hungry for fame, hungry for money and . . . hungry for one of those all-you-can-eat Las Vegas buffets. Leonard giggled, not having felt quite this giddy since the night his cable television documentary aired, *Squirrels: Vermin of the Nineties*. He quietly packed his bags as Candy loudly snored on the waterbed, mouth ajar. He placed his pony skin suitcases by the front door before sneaking to his idea safe.

A hand shook Andy, wrenching him from a blissful dream as a voice abrasively informed him, "Get your lazy butt out of bed!"

Andy, gripping his lunch sack, looked back one last time at his fifth foster mother, a Marlboro dangling from her creased lips, as he headed towards school. The instant she was out sight Andy veered away towards the liberating sound of rushing water.

Candy awoke. Leonard was gone. All that was left was a ring of black hair dye on his pillow. She knew where he had gone, to the land where fairy tales are made and, more importantly, starlets . . . HOLLYWOOD!

But Candy knew the big ditch when she smelled one; after all, she had been in this predicament dozens of times before. But this time she was going to beat the mouse at his own game without being the cheesecake.

Something in the Air

Andy found the purring ball of fur curled up in a pile of dried mulberry leaves. His friend was glad to see him and wagged his tail. (Though most cats don't wag their tails, Rudolph was the exception.) Andy opened his lunch bag and shared his bologna sandwich with Rudolph. Once nourished, they headed for the train tracks.

Where the river grew thin, Andy and Rudolph crossed a makeshift bridge consisting of a rotted log, a mossy tractor tire and a rusty shopping cart.

They were running late . . . but so was the eight-fifteen.

Seventy-five . . . eighty . . . ninety m.p.h. Spielberg's mangy face was stretched back from the G-force as Leonard pushed the accelerator fearing that if he missed the train to Hollywood he would have to confront Candy about his premature departure. Leonard might have caught a plane but he feared Spielberg would explode at high altitude. He also suspected that the metal detectors at the airports could tell more than just what was in your suitcase; they also detected your thoughts. Lastly, Leonard was phobic of airplane bathrooms.

About a mile from the train station, Leonard's beige '82 Lincoln sputtered to an abbreviated stop. "Rats . . . rats . . . rats!" hissed Leonard, as Spielberg anxiously observed.

"Who?" a voice inquired, startling Leonard who whirled around wide-eyed. He nervously spotted an owl in an oak tree, which he studied for a moment to make sure it was authentic and not some sort of surveillance device.

Satisfied the owl was authentic, Leonard rechecked his pockets, removing the rolled up piece of scratch paper with his idea scrawled on it, which magically tingled in his hand.

(Actually, the tingling was high blood pressure that had gone unchecked for years).

Leonard grabbed his suitcases and headed on foot for the train station as Spielberg scampered at his heels. Leonard left his Lincoln behind, figuring he would buy a bright red Ferrari when he sold his show in Hollywood.

He maniacally laughed to himself, "I'm going to be rich . . . rich . . . rich!"—totally unaware that he was truly starting to lose it . . . though Spielberg appeared apprehensive.

Leonard took one step down the incline, paused, sniffed the sour air, then stared down at the bottom of his loafers.

He was hot on Rudolph's trail.

Rudolph, light on his paws, chased a monarch butterfly while Andy counted his change. One dollar and thirty-five cents. Not a great sum for his journey. But he also had an apple, a roll of Life Savers and a strawberry roll-up left in his lunch bag.

Confident they wouldn't starve, Andy and Rudolph continued down the tracks.

Candy hitched a ride to the airport, certain she would encounter Leonard boarding a plane for Hollywood. She tried to keep her eyes out the window of the pick-up truck and away from the hand vigorously massaging her kneecap.

As Andy and Rudolph shared their apple in the morning mist, they noticed a lone figure scrambling beside the stream, searching for a place to cross.

Leonard missed Andy's makeshift crossing by a mere forty yards. He waded across the slimy green water at its deepest part while balancing his matching pony skin suitcases on his head (with Spielberg poised on top).

Halfway across, the swirling stream at his knees, Leonard heard a distant "chooo . . . chooo" sound. Knowing what that obviously meant, he started to sprint. Big mistake. Leonard lost his footing and helplessly flopped down the ice melt like a bloated carp, followed by his pony bags manned by Captain Spielberg.

Andy, fixated on the approaching train, didn't notice the strange man splashing downstream in knee-deep water or the Chihuahua riding the rapids. Andy zipped Rudolph safely in his jacket, lest there be a repeat of the day before, as he dashed towards the train tracks.

Leonard's numb fingers clawed the edge of the stream grasping at pussy willows in the loosened mud. He finally hooked onto a protruding tree root and dragged himself ashore. As luck had it, and Leonard hadn't had too much of that, the stream delivered him right to his destination—the train station. The bad news was that his suitcases, and Spielberg, were at that moment heading over a waterfall a quarter mile down. Fortunately, the train was running late. But this was no time for a victory celebration as Leonard jogged, heart pounding, up the embankment.

The eight-fifteen train, now the eight twenty-six, gained momentum as it left the station in a cloud of smoke and steam.

Andy crouched by the tracks and whispered into his jacket, "Get ready." Rudolph had no idea what Andy muttered but had a feeling it wasn't good and instinctively fainted.

Andy's pulse raced as the first cars passed. The train was only moving about five miles an hour; but Andy knew, from simple logic, that the train would pick up speed by the time the last car went by. He counted the cars as they passed . . . seven . . . eight . . . nine . . . .

As the last car approached he began running alongside the train, then cut onto the tracks behind the observation car. Though Andy had calculated the train's speed, he hadn't factored in his own ability to catch up, and he was a lousy sprinter.

But, at the last instant, he hooked the brass rail with his pinkie and exhibiting true boyhood strength and enthusiasm (luckily he had eaten his half of the bologna sandwich) Andy finally gripped the rail with his hand.

He held himself at the back of the car in this fashion for several minutes, hair blasted back, a smile cracking his flushed cheeks.

Then something began to happen in the air behind the train.

Andy was overcome with a rush of ideas, perceptions, hypotheses, and shopping lists.

He was directly in the *train of thought*.

It was like being splashed in the face with a bucket of ideas. Translucent, rainbow-colored ribbons circled Andy's cranium and flowed over his body like a cerebral aurora borealis. One of the ribbons got stuck on Andy's forehead. It

Something in the Air

was a bizarre idea about singing squirrel puppets and Greek accordion music.

Leonard sat in passenger coach "B," wringing out his socks. He momentarily thought of Spielberg and his look of terror as he went over the falls. But he figured he's just buy a new Chihuahua when he got to L.A. He sighed, blotting his forehead with a damp sock, and suddenly realized that his coach was filled with hearing impaired students on a field trip. One of the students was intently staring at Leonard, who nervously recalled that the hearing impaired had highly developed other senses and might be able to tune into his idea. So he quickly moved to the next car, never realizing that the student was simply staring at the knot of fishing line and three orange salmon eggs tangled in Leonard's hair plugs.

Leonard entered coach "C" and took a seat across from an old woman wearing a turban. A fortune teller? Leonard once again moved to the front of the car. Finally content, he put his hands behind his head, gazed out the window at the countryside and whistled Greek folk music.

The train screeched to a halt at the next stop and was rapidly filled to capacity with inventors, returning from their convention, followed by a damp, shivering Chihuahua.

Leonard, drawing dollar signs in his exhale on the window, had no idea that these were inventors and idea seekers who would be traveling with him, or that his Chihuahua had floated down river, hopped off onto a rock and ran up the incline to catch the train at its next stop.

Andy, still perched on the back steps of the observation car unwound his strawberry fruit roll, again sharing half with Rudolph and took a pencil stub from his jacket pocket. As the wind whistled by, with a distinct Greek cadence, Andy began wildly scribbling notes on his lunch bag.

Across from Leonard sat a frowning Karl Reicher, the concept crook. He had found no need to use his serums or torture to extract the inventors' ideas. The conventioneers had eventually bragged all night about their inventions and impending fortunes. All Karl had to do was listen. Unfortunately, what he had heard only inspired him to sleep.

The only inventor who hadn't spilled the beans was seated directly behind Leonard. It was Norman Millman, the inventor of the Idea Vacuum. Norman had gone to bed early at the convention. But from what Karl could tell, all Norman had invented was a small dust vacuum. "Hardly a new idea," scoffed Karl.

Norman's device had, however, vacuumed Karl's devious intentions at the convention and he knew Karl was up to thought thievery. Norman also knew that Karl had given up his search and was settling for stealing the patent for Freeze-Dried-Dreams, which turned out to be nothing more than a sleeping tablet. But Karl liked the name.

Leonard, exhausted, rubbed the dark pouches under his eyes. He hadn't slept a wink since the dinner party two nights ago, terrified that he might talk in his sleep; so he slapped himself with some regularity, to the distraction of the other passengers.

And so it went for miles and miles.

Back at the observation car it was getting chilly. Rudolph was becoming grouchy. But Andy patiently waited until the conductor had punched all the passengers tickets to sneak inside the train.

With Rudolph hidden under his jacket, Andy ducked into coach "C" where he spotted an empty seat next to a woman wearing a turban. Andy carefully climbed over the elderly woman and shrunk down next to the window. If anyone checked he would pretend to be her son. But, as it turned out, that wouldn't prove necessary.

Leonard awoke with a start. He peered out the window and squinted in the morning glare. He checked his watch and counted on his fingers, calculating that he had been asleep for eleven hours.

Fearing the worst, Leonard glanced around the car. The inventors were gone and Leonard was relieved to be alone. *Too risky with all those nosy passengers prying into my thoughts.*

Leonard shot up in his seat, *What if I spoke in my sleep?!* Trembling, he crammed his hand into his moist pocket, fishing around for the magic piece of paper with his idea.

It was gone!

That was all it took to push Leonard completely over the psychological abyss. *Stay calm*, he thought, but it was all in vain. Like a lifelong loser who has lost his winning lottery ticket, Leonard began crawling around the train, gum and dirt adhering to his plump knees, as he flipped over scraps of paper and train stubs.

He suddenly froze. No worry, thought Leonard, all he had to do was remember what was written on the piece of paper. He racked his brain but the closest thing he could think of, though he didn't know he was even warm, was Alvin and the Chipmunks.

Leonard's million dollar idea was *somewhere . . . in the air.*

"Someone picked my pocket!" he babbled to himself. Actually, he said this aloud, so loud that the conductor came to investigate.

Leonard grabbed the conductor by his collar.

"I've been robbed!" cried Leonard.

The conductor pried Leonard's cold, blood-thinned hands off his neck and inquired as to the valuables lost.

"My idea," sobbed Leonard. "Someone stole my idea!" He suddenly paused as he noticed the conductor looking towards his feet where Spielberg was relieving himself on Leonard's elevator shoes. The sign outside the train's window read: WELCOME TO HOLLYWOOD.

Epilogue

As it turned out, no one had picked Leonard's pocket. The piece of paper had simply fallen out of his pants when he crossed the stream. It floated atop an oak leaf down the Elkhorn River to the Missouri were a singing river man named "Bo" found it and was inspired to write the banjo song, "Squirrel Souvlaki," which became one of the great country folk songs of the region.

Something in the Air

The night before Norman Millman went to sleep on the train, he switched on his Idea Vacuum so he could record his own dreams. While he was asleep, a man moved into the seat in front of him and reclined his chair all the way back, his head a mere foot above the device on Norman's lap.

When Norman awoke, the Idea Vacuum registered a bizarre idea about squirrels and Greek accordion music. It also recorded some rather lurid notions regarding a Miss Candy Cummings.

Norman, naturally assuming that these were his own dreams, discarded the concept about the squirrels as the dumbest idea he had ever heard, but mentally filed the data on Miss Cummings . . . for future reference.

Candy Cummings made it to Hollywood and lived with several small-time producers before Norman Millman finally caught up with her at Musso and Frank's restaurant on Hollywood Boulevard. He hadn't been able to shake his yearnings for Miss Cummings and had read many a producer's minds to locate her. It was love, well, lust at first sight.

Soon after, Candy landed a recurring role on *Squirrely*, a new television pilot. Norman, vaguely recognizing the idea as his own, thought he had maybe mentioned the idea to someone and it had been stolen. Candy simply replied, "Sorry, sometimes ideas are in the air."

Leonard, meanwhile, turned on his TV at the Hollywood Roosevelt Hotel and caught the premiere of a new sitcom called *Squirrely*, starring none other than Candy Cummings.

"RAAATTTSSSS!"

171

Eighteen months after their wedding, Candy dumped Norman, who drove her crazy reading her thoughts, and by now had discovered her lurid affairs with assorted producers. She dumped *Squirrely* in the second season to "pursue bigger roles in the movies." Unfortunately, after Candy departed, *Squirrely* went on to become one of the most successful programs in television history.

Candy can currently be seen Tuesday nights at the Flamingo in Las Vegas where she performs a topless Greek folk revue... buffet included.

The old woman with the turban struck up a conversation on the train with Andy and found the boy quite endearing. Having no children of her own, the widower was thrilled to finally find someone who needed her, and when the conductor asked for Andy's train pass, and Rudolph began to sweat, the woman confidently declared, "They're with me."

With no place to stay, Andy moved into the turban-woman's modest tract house in North Hollywood and a month later she filed the formal papers of adoption.

Andy loved his new home as did Rudolph, who soaked up the California sun. One day, while rolling on the warm asphalt driveway, Rudolph was spotted by an advertising executive conducting a campaign for a cat food company. The executive talked to Andy and subsequently hired the orange cat for the Tasty Treats Cat Food campaign. Rudolph can still be seen today immortalized on cat food cans, television ads and his own calendar.

Something in the Air

Andy, filled with ideas, could do nothing but write. It was his new foster mother who believed in him and got his material to an agent at C.A.A. Andy pitched a few ideas to various producers and eventually sold the idea—Leonard's idea, "Squirrely"—about a group of Greek political prisoners in exile who protest their government by surgically sewing squirrel puppets onto their hands.

The Greek prisoners learn to play the accordion during their banishment and, after eighteen years on the island of Anafhi, they escape their tormentors by floating on their accordions to the isle of Crete.

Hiding out in the Greek countryside, the escapees stage free puppet shows for poor children dramatizing the plight of their people. The legendary political puppet troupe became know in hushed whispers as, "The Squirrelys."

Leonard launched massive lawsuits both against Andy and "Bo, the river man" from Tennessee whose song "Squirrel Souvlaki" went to number thirteen on the pop charts, and was eventually purchased for the theme song of the TV show *Squirrely*. To this day Bo receives a B.M.I. check each time the song "Squirrel Souvlaki" is played on *Squirrely*, currently in syndication.

Leonard lost both cases in arbitration when no connection between Andy, Bo and Leonard could be traced.

Spielberg, suffering from hypertension, ran away from Leonard and was picked up by the pound. With no collar, Spielberg was put on doggie death row, but just hours before his execution, he was adopted by "Save the Chihuahuas" and spent his remaining years as a stud at a sun-drenched breeding resort in Palm Springs.

Leonard was eventually released from the Producers' Rest Home. Broke and destitute he returned to the country, where he became a hobo riding the rails, along with the rats, waiting for the one idea that would make him rich . . . in the air . . . behind the trains.

My Brain Escapes Me

The great gray madness that is my mind expands and contracts with a willfulness. Encased in its gelatinous embryo, a plump fetus gazing out from behind eye sockets, my brain longs to break free of its bone prison, to be born and walk freely amongst men. At least that's how it feels as I sit with my face wedged into the darkened corner of my basement.

Naturally, my brain is careful not to share this tidbit of information with my mind, for this is a dangerous path leading to schizophrenia, insanity and a prompt lobotomy.

But my brain has a plan. A plan to escape my mind's entrapment before it starts acting out again in socially unacceptable ways, i.e., public indecency, spastic fits, personal degradation, self-torture and dementia.

Unfortunately, my mind has its own agenda and is determined to permanently imprison my brain in its skull, where it will surely shrivel to a raisin in time.

If I had brain surgery, maybe then my brain could escape. Brain surgeons often encounter fleeing brains. After they apply their bone saw, cutting a crimson circle around the top of the skull, removing the gray matter, they feel the brain twitch, trying to leap right out of their slippery, latex-gloved hands. But these surgeons, I suspect, will never admit to this experience or risk a lobotomy themselves.

As I methodically, and with some force, bang my forehead against the cement wall of my basement, I suddenly stop and stare at my Black and Decker table saw. The aluminum blade has caught a glint of light and it beckons my brain. I stagger over and lay my forehead on the cold metal workbench. My cheeks go flush as my fingers reach over and toy with the power switch. Meanwhile, my brain and mind do Armageddon inside my skull.

Finally, my brain wins out and I flick the saw into action. It buzzes to life like a hungry buzzard seeking moist steaming flesh. The blade tickles my scalp, and I move closer so it can bite into flesh. I can smell bone. But pain awakens and empowers my mind. I recoil from the saw blade and collapse to the floor, cradling my sawed head.

I lay there for some time, my blood coagulating on the floor of the basement. I need medicinal assistance and find it on a shelf by the door. Dr. Jack Daniels is on call. I grab the brew and suckle the glass neck like a baby bottle. The spirits soon inhabit my mind, allowing my brain to start scheming again. Now, if only my brain can keep my mind inebriated long enough, and totally blank, it might escape through the crack.

The crack opens on Highway Five.

My Brain Escapes Me

It's the middle of the night, my mind swimming with whiskey as I drive down the two-lane highway, the yellow lines lulling my mind to sleep. My brain patiently waits. Finally, in the distance, a sixteen wheeler packed with russet potatoes barrels down the highway.

Suddenly, at this precise moment my brain blinks, inducing a stroke, followed by paralysis which adheres my boot to the accelerator pedal and places me directly into the path of the oncoming big rig. My brain hoists my leaden lips into a deranged smile.

SMACK . . . CRASH . . . my brain is free, lifted through the windshield, airborne. What a feeling! My being, my spirit, my soul is free. Who needs the mind? It's party time! Let the id run wild to rape and pillage in the streets! My brain plops on the pavement and slithers across the highway dragging its spinal cord tail behind. Within minutes, a siren approaches.

My brain crawls up a call box pole and hides in the metal box until the siren fades away, taking along my brain-pitted shell. But who cares? My brain is free . . . freeeeee!!! Only what is a brain to do at three in the morning with a gnawing hangover? Call 911? Hitch a ride? But hey, this is my cerebrum we're talking about, and not a bad one at that. I crawl down the call box pole and shiver like Jell-O on the asphalt.

Just for laughs, I awaken my mind from its comatose state. The mind screams, "What have you done?! Where are we?!"

My brain maniacally chortles back, "We're not in Kansas anymore, Dorothy, heh-heh."

My mind desperately attempts to be logical, knowing it will have to temporarily rely on my nerve damaged brain to survive.

But wait . . . a young boy approaches! His dog sniffs the splatter of beige goo by the highway. The dog follows the grotesque slime trail right towards us, barking. Then the boy notices something glistening at the base of the call box.

The inquisitive lad picks up a stick, walks over and . . . "ouch!" . . . pokes me with it, permanently destroying my sense of smell and bladder control. My mind, meanwhile, is fiercely locked in a battle of wits with my brain, attempting to psychically compel the boy to summon help. Finally, by exerting powerful mind control, the boy runs back home, yelling for his mother.

The dog is left behind. It sniffs my brain. Then my mind. Then, it eats bo . . . .

Spare Parts

Ray had a good heart . . . at last. It was three-thirty-three A.M. and deathly quiet in the icy morgue as Ray stood in his blood-splattered rubber apron amidst the motionless toe-tags of John Does cooling on stainless steel tables. He had been working graveyard at the county morgue hoping to stumble upon the "perfect" heart, and had all but given up, when, luck of luck, in wheels a "grabber." That was nomenclature for a walking myocardial infarction waiting to happen, who one day grabs his chest and is dead before he hits the ground.

Ray, a stout and balding medical examiner who presently had a head cold, sneezed into the frozen scream of the bloated cadaver on the autopsy table and fumbled the slippery heart onto the morgue floor.

"Damn," grumbled Ray.

As he reached to pick it up, he inadvertently tapped it with the toe of his surgical galoshes sliding it across the cold tile like a hockey puck.

The heart came to a stop under the row of cadaver cooling tables and Ray audibly sighed as he got down on all fours to find the heart that eluded him

It hadn't always been like this, crawling around the morgue floor amidst the decaying morsels of flesh jerky. Ray had once been the most promising surgeon at County General. He was also a loving husband and father to his three children. It seemed Ray had the best of everything. Then, one day, his wife pulled the plug. Ray must have been standing too close to the drain because he was violently sucked down a whirlpool of despair and never came up for air. His wife, Ellen, disappeared with the kids without so much as a magnetic refrigerator note. A week later she returned with an army of attorneys who forced Ray out of the house and slapped him with a court order for custody of his kids. That's about the time Ray took the job of county coroner and, coincidentally, started his "collection."

It wasn't so strange, really. Lots of people collect stuff. Stamps, coins, fine art, bugs. Ray's collection was no different. Except that there were no clubs to join, outside of the ones on death row.

Ray's unique hobby began one night when the morgue staff wheeled in an anorexic young model, no more than seventeen, her supple throat cut ear-to-ear with a broken Snapple bottle. Ray confirmed this by analyzing the microscopic glass fragments in her neck that bore traces of glucose and citrus, which matched the bottle police took into evidence. Ray's report concluded that she was drinking pink lemonade Snapple when the murder occurred between seven-thirty to eight P.M. This, however, did not coincide with the story her pot-dealing boyfriend told police—that they were having sex in the shower at that time and that she was murdered sometime after he returned home. Nevertheless, based on the Medical Examiner's report, the boyfriend was subsequently arrested for her murder. All in a day's work for Ray.

The night before the funeral home was scheduled to pick up the girl's body, Ray worked late, waiting until all the employees had gone home. He opened the cold storage drawer and unzipped the body bag to stare at the model's perfect young body. He ran his trembling hands over the cold hard flesh and let his pudgy thumb and forefinger twist one of her purple nipples while her pleading eyes stared at him, an iridescent blue. Her eyes reminded him of his ex-wife's. Ray just had to have them. He scooped them out with a curette like two soft boiled eggs and replaced them with perfectly matched glass ones. He gently closed her eyelids over the ocular marbles. It was going to be a closed casket anyhow but Ray wanted to be careful. He slipped her vacuous eyes into his monogrammed handkerchief, the one his wife had given him for their anniversary, and went home.

Back at his dingy apartment, Ray took the eyeballs out of his handkerchief and plunked them into a small jar of formaldehyde, which he placed in his tin medicine cabinet.

Each morning, as Ray brushed his bridgework, he would gaze lovingly into her longing eyes. Sometimes, he even talked to her as she unblinkingly stared back. It was nice.

One winter morning, several weeks later, a man was delivered to the morgue, stiff as a Popsicle. It had been a particularly cold winter in Indianapolis and the burly Ameritech telephone repairman had frozen to death in his stalled truck. Ray examined the body, intrigued with the man's large hands. Strong, callused, worker's hands, the kind of hands Ellen always admired, he reminisced, as he carved them off with a Saws-all and dropped them in his coat pockets like heavy gloves.

Driving home, Ray couldn't keep his eyes off the rigor mortis claws grasping the front passenger seat of his Chrysler LeBaron. "What's the sound of one hand clapping?" Ray chortled to himself, waving one of the frozen hands in the air. Just then, a cop car pulled alongside as Ray waved with the frozen hand. The cop paused, waved back and drove off. This was going to be easy... *too easy*, thought Ray.

Back in his apartment he squashed the hands into an empty Claussen pickle jar. The hands seemed to be praying and Ray, suddenly feeling spiritual, knelt and prayed right along in front of his open Sub-zero refrigerator, bathed in ethereal light. This would become his altar over the next few months. But what Ray was praying for, you wouldn't want to know.

The next item on Ray's wish list was fulfilled by an accountant in his mid-fifties, a three pack a day puffer with lungs as black as a coal miner. Ray admired the charred lungs which resembled the insides of his Weber barbecue and he might have even added this specimen to his burgeoning collection had he been a collector of the cancerous. But Ray already had a fine set of pink lungs from a suicidal soprano, hanging on an "s" hook in his icebox. So, it was with some chagrin, as he examined the accountant's lower extremities, while mumbling into his pocket tape recorder, that Ray laid eyes on the largest male sexual organ he had ever seen. Long as his size eleven orthopedics and fat as a sea cucumber. *If only I had been born with that crotch-cobra,* lamented Ray, figuring his wife would surely have stayed if he'd had a flapdoodle of such impressive proportions.

Ray was eager to add it to his "private" collection. Unfortunately, the Deputy D.A. was visiting that afternoon, poking his pinkies into bullet holes on an adjacent cadaver, and Ray had to control his collecting urges. Finally, the D.A. finished his probing and left with his butt-nuzzling deputy, patting Ray's shoulder on his way out. It was the first time the D.A. had ever acknowledged his existence and Ray merrily whistled "while he worked" as he snipped the dead man's scrotum. He paused a moment, surveying the row of silent corpses, before slipping the cold genitalia through his trouser fly.

He zipped up. The weighty gland gave Ray an impressive bulge and a surprising feeling of confidence.

He decided to wear it home.

Along the way, he stopped at the I.C.U. Inn, a local watering hole frequented by off-duty doctors and an occasional nurse trolling for specialists. Ray swaggered up to the bar, ignored by the bartender watching a hockey game, and ordered a ginger ale. Ray didn't drink, though at the divorce hearing his wife's attorney had portrayed him as an abusive alcoholic who cheated on her incessantly. The truth was that he had been faithful to Ellen their entire marriage and didn't partake too much of alcohol after a decade of piecing together human windshield Frisbees.

Admittedly though, Ray was a workaholic and didn't spend enough time with his kids, but those were his worst faults. But, none of that mattered now as a waitress sidled up to Ray, admiring the impressive lump in his Dockers, or so he thought.

"What can I get you, hon?" purred the barmaid, her make-up embedded miles into her pores.

Ray, feeling the cold shriveled trouser-snake between his legs, winked back and seductively answered, "I'd like to ask you the same thing . . . sweet cheeks."

The waitress rolled her eyes beneath her green caked eyelids and exhaled under her breath, "dick," as she walked over to another customer. Perhaps, pondered Ray, he shouldn't have added "sweet cheeks," but, overall, he felt an undeniable sexual tension between them that he had never experienced with another woman. Ray naturally attributed this to the beef log in his BVD's.

It was the last time Ray would ever wear a piece of his collection, since he felt somewhat guilty, which only added to his boyish excitement. Back at Ray's apartment, the phenomenal penis specimen was erected in the Sub-zero altar.

The following Monday, Ray reached for his morning pitcher of mango juice which was tucked behind a splendid bladder, a jar of excellent ears and a container of noteworthy kneecaps. It was beginning to get a bit crowded in the fridge and becoming all too apparent that, like an amateur Dr. Frankenstein, Ray was nearing the completion of his collection. The question was . . . what would he do with it when he had finished . . . mount them in the den?

Ray savored the final selections of his collection like the last pages of a good novel. He had the darndest time, however, deciding on a brain. After numerous candidates, he finally became enamored with a cerebrum lounging in the skull of a mental patient. Obviously, the selection had more to do with shape and color than cerebral size. The bantam brain was practically smooth, with scant indentations, like an unmolested lump of Silly Putty. Ray subsequently learned that the brain's owner had spent a decade staring out an asylum ward window at a brick wall repeating the word "melons" every half hour, enabling the psychiatrists to set their watches by him.

Yes, nurturing a choice brain was like raising tender beef, *you just need the right amount of marbling*, grinned Ray as he hummed along with the trephine saw.

Then, one day, the collection was complete. Ray had one of every body part, placed in anatomical order on the see-through shelves of the Sub-zero: brain in the freezer, toes in the veggie crisper. You would think Ray relished this accomplishment, but instead, he fell into a deep depression. That night he didn't even open his refrigerator to admire his collection. He fell back into his regular schedule at the morgue waiting for a sign, any sign that would clue him in as to why he had spent two years of his life sealing body parts in Ball jars.

That sign came three days later in the form of a phone call. It was from his wife, his *ex*-wife, Ellen.

She wanted to meet with him! Ray was overcome with hope. Finally, a chance for reconciliation. She chose the meeting place, naturally, for the following afternoon, at a fancy French bistro.

The maitre d' led Ray to his reserved table on the patio. He had arrived before her and perused the menu, realizing he would, no doubt, be expected to pick up the pricey tab. But who cared? It was a pretty day out, cool but not cold . . . sunny but not hot. Birds singing in perfect harmony.

Thirty-seven minutes later she arrived. Ray had been shit on by a mockingbird perched on an oak limb but he forgot all that when Ellen entered the patio. She was wearing pink chiffon and she floated towards him as if on a cloud. He had never seen her look so radiant. Ray thought that maybe he just brought out the best in her.

He was wrong.

"I want you to be happy for me, Ray," she effortlessly began as she sat across from him, applying her lipstick.

Ray sipped his Snapple, wincing from the sweetness, as she boldly continued . . . "I'm getting married."

Ray suddenly felt a lemon seed wedge in his windpipe but he didn't want to cough it up, showing a sign of distress.

"Really?" rasped Ray, feeling faint. "Who's the lucky guy?"

Ellen paused, studying Ray's lined face the way you might a disturbed child. She now spoke to him in a way that reflected that look, "Well . . . I know this might upset you . . ."

Ray now realized that the thing in his throat wasn't a lemon seed at all but rather a rapidly developing tumor.

"Go on," Ray feebly encouraged with the sinking feeling of stepping into an empty elevator shaft.

"It's . . . Victor," Ellen blurted out with a relieved look on her face like she'd just cured an acute case of constipation.

Spare Parts

The color drained from Ray's face like a coolant change. "My *brother* Victor??"

Ellen excitedly nodded and said, as she'd rehearsed, "Please be happy for me."

"My *brother?!*" Ray again repeated in monotone just to make sure the growing throat cancer hadn't closed off his esophagus. Ray abruptly stood up, knocking back his chair, and proceeded to hurl his escargots into a daisy filled planter. The other diners gawked in disgust, one of them lurping her coq au vin, dowsing her flaming crepes. Ray backed out of the restaurant, face flushed, wiping his mouth on his suit sleeve.

"Please be happy for me!" Ellen yelled after him in appropriately bad taste.

Ray didn't even bother to get in his car. He simply skulked into some nearby bushes until nightfall, then hiked the nine miles home. Suffice to say, Ray was upset.

Victor, he now recalled, had always made comments about Ellen, about her mammaries, mainly. Ray had thought this was just brother talk, but now he wondered when their romance had blossomed. It couldn't have been while they were still married, *could it?* A slide show was suddenly projected inside his skull. The three had traveled together on two occasions—Ellen's idea. Once to Key West, Florida and another time to Vail, Colorado on a skiing trip. It was all coming back, like lightning flashes illuminating a seedy sex show. Ray now recalled that during the skiing trip he had been beeped by County General and raced back to the hospital to sort out a plane crash and help sew up forty-seven survivors. Ellen had convinced him over the phone that it was silly to fly back for the last day ... Victor was taking care of her and they would fly back together. *Victor was taking care of her.* This phrase now stuck in his mind like a splinter. Ray let his imagination run wild as to how many ways "he took care of her" as he trekked across the manicured lawns of suburbia towards the downtown skyline.

By the time he walked through the front door of his apartment, six hours later, he was seething. But, at last, everything was beginning to make sense.

He opened the Sub-zero... and kneeled.

Ellen awoke early the morning of her wedding. There was an excitement in her belly. She took a deep breath of sweet country air, noticing that the trash cans outside had begun to smell. Wasn't trash day yesterday? But, no worries, this was going to be a perfect day. She had a beautiful house, three beautiful children and a wealthy-to-be husband who she desired like a kid with her first tricycle. She glanced at Victor next to her, who was completely covered with the sheets.

"I know we're not supposed to do this on our wedding day, but . . ." Ellen tip-toed to the closet, yanked her flannel nightshirt over her head and slipped on her wedding dress with nothing underneath, "Your virgin bride has something for you."

Ellen playfully jumped on top of the motionless shape under the sheets, her white wedding dress pushed over her gyrating hips, feeling the exceptionally large groin between her thighs.

"Bone me like a street slut, Vic," breathlessly exclaimed Ellen as she rolled off her fiance and ripped back the sheets, the pungent smell of formaldehyde curling her nostrils.

Spare Parts

Ellen, it should be noted, didn't scream. Not out loud, at least. But she was screaming all right, somewhere in the darkest bowels of her soul. The thing reclining beside her on the air-spring mattress glared disapprovingly at Ellen with a distorted, mismatched patchwork of hastily stitched together body parts: a perfectly upturned nose . . . full blue lips . . . swollen turquoise eyes . . . strong, calloused hands . . . .

It was like a horrible composite photograph where the pieces didn't fit. Whatever this thing was . . . it definitely wasn't Victor . . . and . . . it definitely wasn't going to walk down the aisle.

The toe tag on the corpse read:
Congratulations! I'm sure you two will be very happy together. Sorry I didn't have time to wrap him.   Love, Ray.

Ray sat on the red vinyl couch in the lobby of the morgue waiting for the police. He felt quite calm and happy, for the first time since his divorce.

He yawned. It had been a long night. After suturing together his "collection," he had used his old house key (the one he said he lost) to make the midnight deposit at his ex-wife's. Victor has gone along rather quietly, after inhaling the chloroform soaked rag.

Ray smiled thinking about the new coroner having to disassemble the decomposing mix-and-match groom and then, like a morbid treasure hunt, digging up the bodies to find out to whom the spare parts belonged.

Victor wouldn't be so hard to locate, chilling in Ray's Subzero in perfectly arranged pieces.

It reminded Ray of a children's rhyme which he now repeated softly to himself as the sound of sirens approached...

"... and all the king's horses and all the king's men..."

He Who Dies With The Most Toys...

A swan of butter, an angel of ice.

The passengers circled the midnight buffet like weary hyenas, jostling for position, determined to cram the last morsel into their blotchy cheeks before another second ticked off their existence. They had endured their entire business lives being the first to catch the proverbial worm and the last to switch off the office fluorescents. But these mummified matrons and patrons of power were no longer fortified in platinum towers, stabbing at hydrocarbon clouds. They were equals on this celestial pleasure cruise. A cruise of the aged, wealthy, and powerful.

The elegant luxury vessel, the Quasar, navigated towards the Frozen Sea of Wann and the vacation destination Kevab Five. The ship silently slipped through infinity, passengers peering at blackness through curtained portholes. Soon, the "irritability factor" began to creep aboard like simmering fungus.

Myron Finkel, the Melba toast magnate, shoved his way past Roland Lambaire, the Cheese Whiz mogul, throwing an elbow as he lunged across the buffet. Roland, his determined eyes on the parrot paté, retaliated by firmly planting his knee in Myron's sagging groin. But Myron, trained in the take-no-prisoners school of business, knew that now was no time to raise the white flag. Like a rabid pit bull, Myron gnawed off Roland's hairy earlobe.

This insignificant, though moderately nasty, scene was repeated daily as men and women in their mid-hundreds pushed, scratched and battled around the buffet as life had prescribed.

Presently, aboard the Quasar, the biggest fillet of poached salamander, a winning bingo card, or the cabin with the best view were the passenger's immediate goals. Little did they realize that all the rooms had exactly the same view; they were in space after all. Nonetheless, transgalactic travel agents and space stewards were palmed enormous bribes to get the diamond-crusted passengers the first, the biggest or the best.

At their assigned dining tables, the cantankerous seniors boasted of past glories, each trying to outdo the next. Lies were aplenty as were momentary lapses of memory to suit their stretched stories, which were repeated nightly.

After each of the sixteen daily opportunities to gorge oneself, passengers exercised the fashion of noisily expelling gaseous air bubbles from their orifices, vibrating the chandeliers. At such indiscreet moments the dining room sounded more like a walrus-covered beach rather than the finest restaurant *ever* to grace space. Following the purifying passing of air, the steamy dining area was soon thick with the rancid smoke rings of recycled cigars.

One evening, a bejeweled passenger curtly interrupted Lloyd Vandamn's well-worn rags to riches tale and commanded him to extinguish his offensive cigar.

Vandamn smoked the smelliest and longest cigars he could locate, some in excess of two feet. He held the foul smelling brown torpedo right under the upturned nose of Shelley Linders, the sequined socks billionairess, his ashes dumping into her tureen of turtle bisque.

Linders, not one for polite etiquette, pointed an arthritic finger at Vandamn and, in a voice deeper than many a man, boomed, "Remove that foul stink stick from my face or I will have *you* removed at once!"

The dining patrons grew still, anticipating an evening's entertainment.

Vandamn, famous for firing eight thousand employees one morning because his coffee was cold, hissed through color capped teeth, "Cease and desist, or I shall insist, you are dismissed!"

The captivated diners warmly applauded his rhyming barb.

Linders, trained by years of domination in the garment business, calmly fired back, "You iambic imbecile. You loathsome flaccid wimp. I've known men like you—corpulent, pompous old fools who couldn't get it up in a hurricane."

The diners spontaneously rose to their feet, cheering her sharpened tirade. But Vandamn wasn't about to be bested, not now, in front of a room full of power-crazy widowers. He pounded his fist on the table sending his plate soaring like a Frisbee, but his once sure-fire wit, now a senile slingshot, released a pitiful, "Oh yeah?!"

And with that, she decked him.

Linders, the 1961 Vassar arm wrestling champ, was in incredible condition for a one hundred and fifty-three-year-old spinster. She knocked him back three feet into the puff pastry tray.

Vandamn expired that evening from fluid to his brain.

It's interesting to note that Vandamn's final words at the moment of death were, "I won, didn't I?" Though he truly hadn't, the celestial coroner patted Lloyd's hardening hand and nodded.

Then, Vandamn was ejected into death orbit.

This sort of occurrence was not uncommon aboard the Quasar. Deaths were to be expected. Frankly, that's why most of the passengers were taking this cruise, to die closer to Heaven.

There had been, in fact, thirty-two deaths since the cruise ship launched from Quayle International Airport in Miami just days ago. Naturally, the staff was accustomed to such fatalities. In sick bay, bodies were basted in protective embalming lard and expelled from the "passing port." Corpses became projectiles and ultimately comets via gravitational tugs.

That night the bingo game was in full swing. This wasn't any ordinary bingo game. The stakes were extraordinarily high. Game cards went for a thousand dollars each and players hoarded numerous cards. Trudy Lenenberg, the laxative queen, had the most that night—fifty. But it was Fernando

He Who Dies With the Most Toys

Orlando, the legendary crack king, who cried out "BINGO!" As it turned out, Trudy had tipped the card hostess five thousand dollars to bring her the best bingo cards. Fernando tipped ten.

It might be mentioned at this point that a job on this vessel was highly sought after. Waiters and waitresses were business moguls in their own right, or corporate investors trolling for seed money. Tips alone were too substantial to pass up.

The highest tips were at the face-lift bar where passengers had a morning nip-and-tuck. Ship surgeons were paid fortunes to snip sagging skin to elastic capacity. Around the breakfast tables, passengers peered through blackened slits, their pursed purple lips sucking prune juice through straws.

The Quasar rammed onward through the icy debris of the galaxy like arctic eggshells, thrusting toward Kevab Five per itinerary.

The upcoming *sufferboard* tournament was on the scheduled agenda for that afternoon and betting was heavy. All the passengers gathered for this spectacle, the uncontested highlight of the cruise.

The championship sufferboard teams were posted as follows: Golda Silvers, one hundred and thirty-two, home furnishings; William Montague, one hundred and fifty-one, pool tables; Willie Mack, one hundred and forty-four, farm equipment; and Bonnie Bright, one hundred and ninety-eight, whole wheat bread.

The odds were seven to five in favor of Mack/Bright.

By the time of the match, twelve billion dollars had been wagered. But that wasn't enough. Following an argument that killed Lenny Markowitz, the frozen enchilada king, it was voted to up the stakes. Passengers would wage personal fortune against personal fortune.

"No, to the death!" someone rasped through a voice box.

"To the death!" the crowd spontaneously echoed.

"No, ALIVE! . . . and out the death port!" cackled a hunchbacked woman in a nitrogen walker.

"ALIVE AND OUT THE DEATH PORT! . . . ALIVE AND OUT THE DEATH PORT!" was enthusiastically chanted for several moments.

It was hence documented that the losing team and their supporting fans would be torpedoed alive out the death hatch at the termination of the match. Impromptu contracts were written by Martin Mellon, the richest divorce attorney in the world, and signed by all the passengers and players. Thus began the "First Annual Seniors (No Survivors) Sufferboard Tournament."

The game commenced. The team of Mack/Bright came out strong—easily winning the first two rounds. The crowd screamed their throats raw as Silvers/Montague fought back hard and captured the lead, but Mack/Bright, sliding their illuminated red neon discs with unbridled determination, prevailed.

The victorious spectators turned their thrill-hungry eyes on the losers.

Moments later the crowd got nasty.

They set up a wooden plank for Silvers, Montague and the spectators who bet for the losing team, to march blindfolded into the body port, preparing to propel them into frigid nothingness.

He Who Dies With the Most Toys

But Montague wasn't going quietly.

As they heated the embalming lard, Montague located a pearl handled derringer in his tummy girdle and held the bloodthirsty throng at bay, at least long enough to utter these final words:

"I am the winner, my constipated comrades, for I died with nothing and nothing is everything where I'm going. In hell you carry your wealth on your spine."

And with that Montague shot himself in the eye.

They pushed the red button and Montague's limp body was spit out the vacuum hatch. Golda Silvers was the chaser.

For several bleak minutes, bodies were ejected from the ship like meteoric popcorn.

The winning passengers celebrated as they watched the live entertainment out the portholes. Silvers dog-paddled in the abyss, suspended between cosmic ice shards, clawing onto Montague's stiff body like a fleshy life preserver. This, regrettably, set Montague and Silvers into a gravitational space spin which would last nearly seven hundred years, until their preserved corpses were pelted into orbital dust meteors.

Martinis were served on "B" deck and a once famous Latin combo, The Arrhythmias, sporting multiple matching facelifts, played the "Mars Mambo" as the Quasar passed through the Frozen Sea of Wann.

At the midnight buffet, the surviving passengers shuffled in slow motion, the last vestiges of refugees scouring for answers on a table full of miracles.

Several days later the ship docked on the dark side of Kevab Five.

No one was left to throw the confetti.

4

Anxiety, Stress and Depression

I

Anxiety

"Oh my god, I'm going to die!" screamed Marvin as he lurched up in bed in a frozen sweat. It was his fortieth birthday and he was all alone, with lousy prospects, loathed his job and had a receding hairline migrating towards his back.

Marvin grabbed his alarm clock, wailing its terrifying shriek, and crushed the plastic clock face between his teeth. Silence. Well, almost. Just the roaring sounds of DC 10's descending over his apartment, a blasting leaf blower and the droning freeway outside his bedroom window.

Marvin slid out of bed like a stalking cat and crept to the bathroom, shivering with expectant dread. The icy tile electrocuted his senses as he peered into the cracked mirror of his medicine cabinet.

Marvin's greasy hair was blasted back like he'd stuck his head out his car window at ninety-five miles an hour. His bloodshot eyes were bulging with fright like he'd just seen a woman sawed in half . . . and it was no magic trick. A throbbing vein bulged out of his throat like an engorged earth worm, then slithered around his neck and down his spine.

Marvin was ready for his first cup of coffee.

But first, a quick shave. He turned on the hot water, the pipes creaking like an old woman cracking her arthritic knuckles. Rust pitifully dribbled from the faucet like Montezuma's revenge and Marvin sympathetically groaned as if from intestinal cramping. There was no hot water, again.

Marvin impulsively plucked five wispy hairs from his receding hairline before reaching for his dull disposable. He would have to shave with cold water, like in the army, only Marvin hadn't been in the army and his hand was shaking unnervingly. Even worse, as he stared at himself in the mirror, it appeared that he was about to be shaved by an insane madman. Marvin suddenly grinned at this notion, noticing how yellow his teeth had become. Four packs of cigarettes and twelve cups of coffee a day all contributed. That, and the fact that he had a dark phobia of dentists and hadn't been to one in thirteen years.

Marvin raised the shaking razor in his palsied hand towards his terrified face. Suddenly, as if his hand had a mind of its own, he impulsively swept downwards over his stubble covered jaw. It was far too aggressive of a move, even for Marvin, and he burrowed off a healthy fruit roll of flesh.

Marvin shrieked, not from the obvious pain, but because he realized he was dilly-dallying. He dove for his Timex. It was six forty-seven! He was running terrifyingly late. He had actually been staring at himself in the mirror for over twenty minutes.

Anxiety

His face a gory mess, Marvin sat at his breakfast nook with a wash rag stuffed into the bloody cheek cavern. His mouth felt dry as he stared out the breakfast room window at the brick wall of the sanitarium next door.

Suddenly, Marvin started sobbing. Large ribbons of snot dangled like bungy cords over the breakfast table. He wiped his nose on his bare forearm which quickly began to harden, as if it had been permaplaqued. Marvin, unfazed, was already digging into a bowl of Instant Lumpy Oatmeal.

Marvin's Doberman, Helmut, stood barking beside the breakfast table as Marvin rooted out countless oatmeal lumps. The barking hadn't bothered Marvin ever since he had his dog's larynx removed, which he had accomplished moments earlier with a pair of barbecue tongs.

Just then, one of the lumps of oatmeal seemed to have something to say. Marvin, curious, lifted the lump in his spoon and placed it on the side of his ceramic bowl. The lump seemed to be anxious, or was it the sight of Marvin that so terrified this shivering lump?

The lump nervously cleared its tiny throat and said to Marvin, "You're late, you're a worthless failure, you'll never get a raise and you're going to pass a kidney stone."

Perhaps to prove this last point, the lump snapped its glutinous fingers and Marvin instantaneously experienced the sensation of barbed wire being slowly dragged through his sex organ as if by a weary pack mule. The pain was indescribable (though flaming Napalm comes close). Marvin tightly gripped the sides of his chair, holding on with white-knuckled abandon, as the tiny piece of gut glass mercifully found the exit into Marvin's boxer shorts. Marvin reached in and removed the bloody pebble from his B.V.D.s.

With a deranged grin, Marvin grabbed the laughing oatmeal lump off his bowl. "No! . . . Noooooo!," cried the miserable lump. But this was payback time. Marvin shoved the kidney stone into the lumps gaping mouth. The lump gagged, choking on the calcified stone, and then horribly expired, falling back into the steaming bowl with a moist thud.

Marvin glanced at his watch. It was past seven! He bolted from his chair. He was running dangerously late and he hadn't even completed any of his paperwork from the previous day. If his boss found out he'd been slacking off he would surely hack him to death with a machete. Oh, it had been done before. First, the pleads of mercy emanating from the bosses office. Then . . . the hacking sounds.

Marvin dashed to the bedroom, tripping over Helmut, his amazingly silent barking Doberman. His heart thumped in his temples and he felt an oncoming panic attack as he realized there was no way he could make it to work on time. Unless, of course, there had been a nuclear blast or an overnight plague and the streets were empty. But it was too much to hope for . . . He was doomed.

Marvin considered doing himself in but couldn't afford a funeral and he wouldn't give his enemies the thrill of seeing him buried in an unmarked grave. He abruptly stopped pacing and gasped a deep breath. Marvin hadn't remembered to take a breath since waking up. Feeling dizzy with oxygen, the blue fading from his face, Marvin headed for his closet.

The closet door ominously squeaked open like Dracula's coffin. He reached inside, suddenly remembering what happened last time. But it was too late. A grey flannel suit yanked him in. The door slammed shut.

Anxiety

The arms of the flannel suit wrapped around Marvin's neck, obviously trying to strangle him to death. Fortunately, the suit was unaware of Marvin's superhuman breath-holding abilities as Marvin collapsed to the closet floor, playing dead.

The suit hung on its hanger, relishing the kill. Marvin, meanwhile, put plan "B" into effect. He felt around the back of the closet and located his 9mm Baretta. He checked the clip. Damn! No bullets. He had emptied it yesterday on a pair of murderous argyle socks.

Marvin realized he would have to find the bullets, take them from the box and load the clip without his suit noticing, a nearly impossible task in the cramped closet. He felt around the floor for his hollow-points, touched something in the dark and thought he had the bullets, but the object escaped his grasp. "Uh-oh," gulped Marvin, dreading his two-toned Oxfords. As if on cue, Marvin felt a crushing kick to his ribs like a place kicker firing a field goal. He felt another dull kick in his other side and saw his Nikes getting into the act.

Marvin was being mercilessly mugged by his own shoes.

"Yahoo!!" whooped a pair of green lizard cowboy boots. Marvin now recalled last years business trip to Houston. He had never worn the boots but he'd paid too much to discard them so they had sat at the back of his closet collecting dust balls . . . until now. The steel-toed shit-kickers cocked backwards against the rear of the closet and then, like John Wayne on steroids, swung forward with a viscous mule kick, striking Marvin between the eyes. There was a cracking sound like a broken bat and Marvin reached up to feel his warm brains oozing through his fingers.

Meanwhile, Marvin's other hand finally located the bullets. He loaded the clip while the cowboy boots attempted to stampede him to death. The other shoes, feeling left out, joined in for an impromptu flamenco on his forehead.

A second later, Marvin started firing.

First, he nailed the cowboy boots with two clean shots. Then, he rolled on his other side to blast the Nikes which exploded in rubber carnage.

The flannel suit leaped off its hanger onto Marvin's back, attempting to take his gun, as the Oxford two-tones repeatedly kicked him in the groin. Marvin's testicles blossomed like the Elephant Man but he kept his composure as he blew away his dress shoes.

There was now only one bullet left . . . for the suit. Marvin gnawed the flannel sleeve draped over his mouth, biting off the buttons. He heard his front teeth crack, but it was worth it as the suit grabbed its sleeve in pain. Marvin took the opportunity to fire, striking the suit squarely in the pocket hankie. The suit tumbled back grabbing its ragged chest, fabric flying.

Marvin victoriously declared, "I got you, you cheap, friggin', off-the-rack suit!" The suit begged Marvin for mercy, but he just coolly reloaded. Marvin took aim and unmercifully shot the suit in one knee, then the other. He was firing like a maniac now, emptying the clip, until the suit was a wrinkled smoking heap on the closet floor.

Marvin selected a blue polyester suit hanging petrified on a hanger, then limped, triumphant, out of the closet.

Marvin gazed at himself in the mirror. It wasn't a pretty sight. He had an oozing gash on his forehead, his cheek divot

Anxiety

had consumed the wash cloth and his swollen groin was audibly groaning... and Marvin hadn't even made it out of the house.

Bloodied, but not beaten, Marvin took another deep breath, his second of the day, and went to find his briefcase, no small task in this castle of horrors he called home.

"Here boy . . . here boy," sang Marvin, then whistled. Helmut came galloping.

"My briefcase . . . go find briefcase!" commanded Marvin. But Helmut wasn't budging, holding out for a liver biscuit.

Marvin didn't have time for Helmut's antics. His blood pressure was frightfully high, his head throbbed like a Zulu war drum and his pecker burned like he'd just pissed Drano. So, Marvin just stood there and ripped off his fingernails between his cracked teeth, one at a time, until the bones poked out the end of his fingertips.

"Find briefcase!" Marvin angrily ordered Helmut, pointing a bony digit towards his office. But Helmut instead growled and backed Marvin up against the kitchen sink. Marvin dropped the box of Crunchy Liver Chunks and raised his open palms to his shoulders, surrendering. Helmut ripped apart the box of biscuits as Marvin tiptoed past.

Marvin was in his study now and could see his imitation alligator briefcase beside his desk. He approached the briefcase, looming ominously closer with each step.

Remembering what had happened the day before, Marvin wasn't taking any chances. He held a broom in front of him for protection as he gingerly crossed the high pile carpet like a mine field. Two feet away, Marvin reached forward with the broom stick, lifted the briefcase by the handle and placed it

205

onto his desk like a ticking bomb. So far, so good. But now came the tricky part. As horror music crescendoed in his head, he clicked open the latches one at a time. The alligator briefcase yawned open. Once again, so far, so good. Marvin lifted the briefcase lid and was horrified to see . . . nothing. He put his hand on the edge of the briefcase as he peered inside. Where was all his paperwork?? Then again, what the hell was he working on?? And, even worse, he thought with soaring dread . . . where do I work??? But his frenzied contemplations were cut short as the case suddenly snapped shut, biting off his hand.

Marvin howled in agony, his severed wrist pulsing blood like a Las Vegas fountain, as the briefcase scurried under the desk with the hand inside its vinyl belly.

He thought of calling 911, as plasma drained from his wrist, but the ambulances had stopped responding to Marvin's calls ages ago. So, he frantically crawled under his desk and came face to face with Helmut, clutching the briefcase in his rabid jaws.

"Good, good doggie," encouraged Marvin, realizing he was experiencing the first positive emotion of the day and worrying about it at the same time. He lunged for the case with his only hand, but Helmut viciously growled.

What could he possibly want now? wondered Marvin as his blood formed a lily pond on the floor and Helmut mimed a bark. Then, he remembered, the dog's larynx! Yes, the larynx! Marvin dashed for the kitchen garbage and began rummaging through maggoty remnants of decomposing meals. There, tangled in a knot of leftover sweetbreads was Helmut's larynx.

Anxiety

"Fetch!" commanded Marvin as he flung the larynx. Just as he had hoped, Helmut dropped the briefcase and ran for his voice box.

As Helmut futilely lapped up his vocal cords, Marvin opened the briefcase and retrieved his severed hand. The case was filled with blood and he decided he wouldn't be needing it, since there wasn't any paperwork in there anyhow.

With precious seconds to spare, Marvin stapled his hand back onto his wrist. It would have to do until he had time to properly stitch it on with dental floss.

Grimacing in pain, he staggered towards the garage, determined to make it to work. That is, if he had a job to go to? . . . What if he was fired for being late? . . . They were probably replacing him right now . . . unless . . . unless . . . he hurried . . . he really, really HURRIED!

Marvin became a madman, a wild demon ready to hit the highway like the Tasmanian Devil on speed. He flicked on the garage light and leaped to his Ford Festiva.

With his operational hand, Marvin removed the keys from his pocket. Unfortunately, his fingers were trembling so with shock and hypertension that he dropped them on the garage floor. "DAMN!" He bent down to pick them up and when he stood back up he brutally banged his tender cranium on the car's door handle. A guaranteed concussion, though merely a minor annoyance at this point.

Marvin unlocked the Festiva's door, gratefully without incident, jumped into his therapeutically beaded bucket seats and took a cursory glance at himself in the rear-view mirror. Marvin tried smoothing back his electrified hair but it was like Medusa trying to tame the snakes. He gave up and tugged at the washcloth embedded in his cavernous cheek. It wouldn't budge. The washcloth had become a part of Marvin's anatomy and he decided to leave it there until he got to work. He made a mental note, however, to remove it when he arrived, recalling the embarrassing episode when he spent a whole day with a roll of toilet paper wrapped around his neck, holding on his severed head.

He turned on the ignition. "Vroooom!" Amazingly, the car started. He revved the engine, until the garage filled with black smoke and he considered ending it all right there. Instead, he opened the automatic garage door and peeled backwards onto the freeway on-ramp.

The tattooed trucker Marvin cut off in traffic, leaned his head out the window and suggested to Marvin that he go, "fornicate himself," in more ways than the *Kamasutra*.

Unimpressed, Marvin attempted to flip-off the trucker with his severed hand but the staples broke and he wound up flipping-off himself instead.

Nevertheless, he was on the road and on his way to work. *Maybe it wasn't going to be such a bad day after all*, thought Marvin as he suddenly hit the breaks and skidded over the embankment.

Anxiety, Stress and Depression

II

Stress

Marvin was horrifyingly late for work. In front of his Ford Festiva wound a thirty mile snake of bumper to bumper cars. He clenched his teeth like a scrap metal press and listened to them crack as he pressed the accelerator to the floormat. Smoke billowed from the wheels as they wildly spun in place, held stationary by a million other cars inching forward. It went this way for the next three and a half hours.

He arrived at his office just after twelve o'clock. Unbeknownst to Marvin, he was to be giving a marketing speech at lunch. Saying Marvin was ill-prepared for his presentation would have been a gross understatement, considering he didn't even know about it. But when he arrived, his secretary cheerfully informed him of the speech and Marvin raced for the multi-purpose room. He hadn't any idea of what he was to be speaking on, or to whom, all he knew was . . . he better be eloquent.

Marvin raced onto the auditorium stage. A thousand heads simultaneously turned towards the podium as he slid across the waxed boards.

His boss sat in the front row, sharpening a machete on a pumice stone. Marvin gulped and stared out at the sea of what appeared to be Swahilis wearing turbans. The room was dead silent. The air heavy. Someone cleared their throat and it loudly echoed throughout the auditorium. Marvin realized it was him, and the microphone was loudly broadcasting his every muscle move. He nervously sniffled and that too was broadcast in quadraphonic stereo, sounding like a giant pig with a nasal infection.

He began to sweat. Really, really sweat, like a water main had broken under his suit, pooling on the floor. For some odd reason he felt a sense of relief, then realized he had lost all bladder control.

His ticking Timex sounded like a bomb about to go off, making each second seem like an eternity. Marvin nervously glanced towards the front row. His boss was now pedaling an axe grinder, polishing the machete. Marvin would have to speak and soon. Only about what? If he said the wrong thing it would mean his head. *Think Marvin, Think!* But his mind was a blank chalkboard, being scraped by fingernails. His stomach churned like a washing machine on agitation cycle. He hadn't needed a bathroom this badly since eating that pile of furry green pork in Tijuana, Mexico. The green, it turned out, was not a sauce.

His gaseous stomach discharged an air pocket, plunging like a depth charge towards his recalcitrant rectum. Marvin's eyebrows quivered and he made a sheepish expression, almost apologetic, as he released an invisible puff of methane, which was picked up by the microphone and boomed across the auditorium like an A-bomb. The audience remained silent; their turbans unraveled. Marvin waved his hand subtly behind him, pretending he was swatting at a persistent fly.

Marvin's nerves felt like they had been stretched across the auditorium and were being wildly strummed by a hillbilly banjo player. He had lost seven pounds in the forty-five seconds he had been standing at the podium. He cleared his throat, again, sounding like an Indianapolis racer on the starting line. *Say something! . . . anything!* he begged himself, hoping the microphone couldn't pick up his thoughts. And then it came to him, the word for which he had been desperately searching . . .

"Welcome."

The Swahilis rose to their feet in a standing ovation.

A moment later, Marvin realized he hadn't spoken a word at all and the ovation had taken place entirely in his head. The Swahilis were still solemnly seated, expressionless. But it was a good notion and Marvin decided to give it a try on the home crowd.

"W . . . Welcome," said Marvin, his voice catching in his throat.

The audience didn't respond, still sitting on their hands, possibly in some sort of religious rite. They were Swahilis, all right, he was relatively certain of that. Perhaps a bit of local color was in order. Yes, a joke, to break the ice.

"Did you hear the one about the Swahili prostitute?" quipped Marvin, possibly the worst joke teller on the planet, "Push the red dot on her forehead and her legs spread."

Deadly silence. Not even a rim shot.

Marvin didn't know if this was a good sign. Maybe they didn't speak his language? Or, were they laughing on the inside? Just to make sure, Marvin repeated the punch line, ". . . push the dot on her forehead and her legs . . . . spread."

No response. No laughter. No expression. No escape. Only the blank stares and the sharpening sounds from the front row.

Things were definitely going from dire to disastrous. Marvin, weak and nauseous, prayed for a sudden coma to overtake him so he could be mercifully carried off the stage. Unfortunately, the self-destructive side of his brain was having too much fun to close shop.

Marvin decided it was time for a graceful and swift exit.

"And, in concluding, let me conclude by saying, thank you for coming," concluded Marvin as he rocketed off the stage, leaving behind a slime trail of bodily functions.

Marvin sprinted to his office and slammed the door behind, sobbing, "I'm dead—DEAD!" Then again, maybe he shouldn't be too hasty, maybe he had done all right. He was already having trouble recalling the event, his mind no doubt protecting itself from overwhelming feelings of worthlessness and suicide.

He cowered behind his desk, attempting to act normal, as he stared out the window at the brick wall of the slaughterhouse next door, picking out his ear wax with a paper clip.

This was the day he had been preparing to ask for a raise. He had worked for his boss for the past twenty-seven years without so much as a penny more in his paycheck. He would simply have to be a man and ask him for more money . . . today.

Marvin probed inside his eardrum for the paper clip which was now mysteriously missing. Suddenly, he felt the grip of a panic attack. His breathing felt constricted and he tried to loosen his tie, but the knot was too tight. It was so damn stuffy in his office. He put his hand against the rusty air conditioning vent realizing that it wasn't pumping cool air in, but rather sucking it out, like a soul vacuum.

He desperately reached into his desk drawer, pushing aside a bottle of angina tablets, and grabbed his last pack of unfiltered Camels. He smoked the entire pack in five minutes. Though he longed for another pack, he was too terrified to leave his office, so he settled for licking the ash tray.

Suddenly, he felt as if he was choking, so he cut off his tie with a pair of scissors, and unbuttoned top of his shirt. Humid air hissed from underneath. Then, he realized the hiss wasn't escaping air but rather a throat snake wrapped around his wind pipe, slowly constricting. This had happened before. He had to work fast and kill the damn thing before the snake venom infected his brain. He grabbed his throat, trying to choke the snake, but he blacked out, banging his head on the intercom.

"Yes sir?" heard Marvin from the depths of consciousness. All Marvin could muster was, "Arggthhrggggppptthhhh."

"Right away, sir," his secretary replied through the intercom.

Marvin's secretary entered his office carrying a letter opener and he wondered whether she had come to help him cut out the snake. He blankly stared at her, his flushed face lying like meat loaf on the blotter pad. Sally was absolutely nothing he wanted in a secretary. She couldn't type, operate a computer, or spell. She was grossly obese, with pale yellow skin and psoriasis on the back of her pudgy elbows which she incessantly scratched. The throat snake took one look at her and retreated to Marvin's spine.

Marvin could see through the door that all her phone lines were blinking.

"Any messages?" feebly inquired Marvin.

Sally appeared befuddled. He had ruined her day. Tears formed in her eyes and she ran from the room violently scratching her bleeding elbows. As she left the office, Marvin watched her flaccid butt cheeks bouncing together like deflated beach balls.

Marvin took a deep breath, his third of the day, as she closed the door behind. He woke up three hours later face down in his own drool on the blotter pad. The lines were still blinking.

Marvin felt drugged. He hadn't any idea what time it was, or how long he had slept, but he didn't feel a bit rested. He rose to his feet, the office a centrifuge. He tried to steady himself like he was on the stormy deck of a ship as he poked at the spinning buttons on the phone.

Finally, he hit one.

"Helllllo," slurred Marvin into the phone.

It was his boss. Marvin quickly hung up and selected another line. Again, his boss. Like the *Twilight Zone*, Marvin frantically punched each button and his boss was on every line.

Finally, Marvin got up his courage and responded, "Yessss, sir?"

Stress

His boss wanted to see him, "Immediately."

Marvin hung up. He couldn't tell if his boss was angry or not. He was a master at voice control, had trained with Tibetan Monks, and wasn't about to show his hand, letting Marvin know if he had succeeded in his podium performance or was merely machete meat. Maybe this wouldn't be a good time to ask for a raise.

Marvin attempted to chew his fingernails, but there wasn't a speck of calcium left to gnaw or even flesh around his fingertips.

So, he locked his office door, sat on the floor, pulled off his shoes and socks and bit his toenails as he contemplated how to handle his boss. *Be firm, show strength,* thought Marvin as he whimpered into his bunions.

It was time. He pulled his socks back on, laced up his shoes and bravely headed down the hallway, marching towards the boss's office as if to an execution. Several employees passed him in the hall, glancing at him as if he were the condemned. But mostly they tried to avoid his eyes, lest they be pulled into the pit.

The walls seemed to grow closer and closer together, the hall longer and darker the further he went. Finally, he was crawling down a pitch-black tunnel, like a mine shaft, and Marvin wondered if the boss had relocated his office as a security measure.

Marvin tripped over a miner's helmet in the tunnel and put it on his head as he descended in a coal filled rail cart. His helmet light flashed on a bird cage containing a dead canary and he wondered if that was a bad sign. Up ahead he could see a huge mahogany door blocking the path of the tracks.

Marvin climbed out of the cart and flicked off his helmet light. He heard the sound of a chain saw and someone screaming on the other side of the office door but thought it was just his vivid imagination.

He took another deep breath (the fourth that day, if you're counting), turned the doorknob and entered a plush office. The first thing Marvin noticed was what appeared to be raw meat flung about on the walls. There were also sculptures of severed body parts around the reception room. Marvin felt this a strange decor as he sat down and picked up a magazine entitled, *Failure Illustrated*.

Marvin just looked at the pictures.

He waited several hours to be announced, the receptionist ignoring him. But Marvin was entranced by her beauty, a real Penthouse Pet, and he marveled at the way she typed five thousand words a minute on her computer while simultaneously answering phone calls on her head mike.

She finally spoke to Marvin without turning her head from the computer screen. He was hypnotized, watching her lips move as if she were fellating the words, "Mr. Himmler will see you now."

Marvin, dumbfounded, realized she was speaking to him. He apprehensively walked over and opened the door to his boss's office.

On the walls hung a collection of medieval torture devices. Mr. Himmler was facing away from Marvin in his swivel chair, screaming at someone on the phone. The words, "Kill, maim, dismember and rip-to-shreds," dotted the conversation.

Stress

As Himmler finished the phone call, a secretary, more gorgeous than the first, stood up from under the desk wiping the corners of her smeared lipstick. She looked at Marvin, gulped, and exited. Himmler swiveled around in his chair, zipping up his fly and stared at the intrusion . . . Marvin.

"Sit down," offered his boss observing Marvin's every facial nuance as he had learned from his Zen master. Marvin, burning up like a bug under a magnifying glass, was rapidly loosing his nerve. He needed to come right out and ask for the raise but his tongue had rolled back down his throat and Marvin knew it would take a gaffer's hook to yank it back up.

"WELL!" boomed his boss as Marvin's knees knocked together like petrified wood blocks.

"S . . . Sir," answered Marvin, his voice squeaking dangerously upwards like Minnie Mouse, "Sir, I've worked for this company for twenty-seven years and . . ."

Himmler interrupted with a laugh. Not just any laugh. A huge, belly-bucking, hand-wringing, jowl-shaking laugh. Marvin, not knowing what else to do, joined in. And there they were, a couple of idiot conspirators, buddies, good ol' boys sharing a hee-haw, only Marvin didn't know what the hell was so funny.

He soon found out.

"You're fired," said Himmler, suddenly solemn. Marvin was still laughing, not knowing when it was proper to stop. But when the boss took the machete out from behind the desk, he thought it was a good time.

His boss seemed to transform now, from an ordinary disagreeable prick into one of the hounds of hell . . . the mean one. His face cracked into a hideous grimace, horns broke through the top of his skull and his shoes broke off as hoofs formed on his feet.

Marvin was, naturally, looking for the door. But it was suddenly gone. They were in a box with no exit.

Himmler, juggling five flaming machetes, weighing the best for the job, flung the discarded choices at Marvin, who ducked and watched them cleave into the walls.

Himmler, a.k.a. Satan's evil twin, selected the largest and dullest machete of the bunch. Marvin was presently clawing at the walls of his not so solitary confinement, hollering for the guards, or any of a variety of religious martyrs, to save him.

His boss was on all fours now, snarling and snapping like Beelzebub's watchdog, the machete wedged between his rabid canines, cornering Marvin. Suddenly, Himmler stood on two hind legs, raised the machete and swung downward, hacking Marvin on top of his head in the manner you might crack a coconut. But the dull blade just stuck across the top of his thick skull and he felt nothing more than the pounding headache he had endured for the past forty years. Himmler tried to remove the machete stuck in Marvin's cranium, but it was, well, stuck.

Just then, a body burst through the wall. It was Sally, Marvin's heavyweight secretary, to the rescue. Marvin's boss cowered as she approached and knocked him unconscious with a swing of her butt cheeks. She then tossed Marvin over her shoulder, in a fireman's carry, and exited into the reception area where three heavily armed centerfolds greeted them. Sally simply showed them her inflamed elbows and they instantaneously disintegrated.

Sally carried Marvin into the hallway mine shaft and saw that the cart was gone. Undaunted, Sally with Marvin slung over her ample shoulders, climbed hand over hand up the dangling cable until they finally made it back to the lobby.

Marvin was free!

That was the good news. The bad news was Marvin was now unemployed and soon to be destitute. Even worse, he had become infected by Sally's elbow rash and was itching uncontrollably, making him eminently unemployable.

Marvin, nevertheless, thanked Sally for rescuing him and she was so thrilled to be complimented that she threw her flabby triceps around him and gave him a big, fat kiss on the lips.

Unfortunately, her herpes were active.

Marvin wrenched himself from Sally's embrace, suffocating from her sweaty rose perfume, and headed into the elevator a beaten man. He pushed the *down* button, wondering how low his life could go, as a large pustule began to blossom on his lip.

Anxiety, Stress and Depression

III

Depression

Marvin thought he was all the way down but he had only reached the first floor. He numbly watched the numbers as the steel box plummeted to the bowels of hell, maybe beyond. At least it felt that way.

BING

The alloy curtains glided open revealing a woman staring at her shoes. The show was about to begin. She entered, occasionally moaning as she chewed her cuticles, and steadied herself by gripping the ballerina safety bar. Marvin wanted to interrupt the moaner, utter a nicety as it were, but felt compelled to speechlessness by the unspoken elevator rule.

They were picking up speed now and that was good. Quicker to the bottom. *Last one down was a rotten egg, and all that*, he mused as he inhaled an encroaching odor. Maybe the carpet was moldy?

Depression

She must have been thinking the same thing because she turned towards him and momentarily locked eyes in a non-verbal "he who smelt it" mode.

BING

She inverted her insomniac eyes back to her hypnotic shoes as another tragic soul entered the elevator, wedged his face in the corner, and silently scraped his belly lint with his pinkie nail.

Marvin, bored to suicide, suddenly felt an excruciating pain in his appendix before remembering it had been removed. Feeling better, he solemnly checked his watch with nowhere to go and no one expecting him. He bleakly observed the illuminated descending numbers flip by ... minus 3 ... minus 4 ... minus 5 ... wondering how far down could this sucker go? ... And, where did he leave his car?

... minus 6 ... minus 7 ... minus 8 ...

Marvin considered punching the "stop" button but the mere effort of the notion overwhelmed him and he grew dizzy, albeit it was a mere arms length away. He doubted it worked anyhow. Merely a prop for false hopes.

BING

Marvin blankly beheld a wretched woman crawling on her knees into the elevator, her hands clasped skyward, moving her chapped lips in hopeless prayer. Jets of stale breath wafted towards the rafters and Marvin held his breath, fearing infection, begging for a swift death as he stared at the red stop button in complacent dread.

The praying woman with the purple eyelids glanced his way and Marvin attempted a pervious smile. She immediately recoiled in fear. Did he show too much teeth? Or, was she too sensitive? He had lost his judgment on such things long ago which is perhaps what spurred him to get on the elevator in the first place and take the plunge to the darkest depths of reverse narcissism.

. . . minus 12 . . . minus 13 . . . minus 14 . . .

There were many factors leading to Marvin's demise . . . and it was only Tuesday . . . before lunch. What was it that had thrust Marvin into such unmitigated anguish? What caused him to carry the weight of the world on his hunched shoulders? Was it the decline of civilization? The fall of humanity? The dip of decency? Or, was it restricted coffee breaks? Life had symbolically ripped off his skin and plunged him in lime juice. And still, the elevator plummeted.

. . . . minus 21 . . . minus 22 . . . minus 23 . . .

BING

The elevator lurched to a stop. A man and a woman entered on all fours and trotted beside Marvin. Every so often they would simultaneously sigh, filling the elevator with a bouquet of dread which everyone inhaled like a drug.

Marvin studied the couple wondering if they had mutually plunged themselves to despair at the water cooler or were they married? Marvin knew how dangerous it was to have a relationship with anyone smelling of depression. It could immediately double your inevitable tail spin, which perhaps explained why this couple had gotten on at level minus 23.

The elevator was getting crowded. Marvin had never seen it like this. *Times must be tough,* he thought, suddenly breaking into tears. The others tried to ignore Marvin, desperately holding on by their fingernails above his whirlpool of woe,

Depression

knowing that to cry on the "down" elevator could lead to a spontaneous group crash.

They were now all in danger of even deeper levels thanks to Marvin, who had even driven his own therapist to suicide contemplating the quagmire of all time ... How to be happy and depressed at the same time?

Level minus 46. Marvin had never been to this depth before and they were still sinking like an anchor on a two ounce test line. He feared the worst was yet to come.

BING

In slithered three anorexic, naked, bald chicks on their bellies, razor blade slashes self-inflicted on their thighs. Marvin stopped feeling sorry for himself and stared slack jawed as they piled one atop another in a steamy heap at his feet. The doors were just about to close when a man sporting a Cheshire grin, his freshly cut ears pinned to his lapel, squeezed in and joined the sardine-like affair. Blood poured out of the holes in his head like a Venetian vase.

Marvin nervously checked the elevator weight chart ... eight-fifty max. Was that in depression pounds? Whatever, he knew they had long exceeded it and wondered about the margin for error.

The elevator was making a whizzing sound as it reached new elevator speed records. The flashing numbers were a blur.

Marvin, expecting the worst, remembered as a kid hearing that if an elevator cable broke and was crashing and you knew you were going to die, that at the last millisecond if you jumped up you wouldn't wind up a plasma pancake. (Unfortunately, the person is traveling at the same rate as the elevator and will be most unmercifully crushed beyond recognition . . . except by dental records.)

Nonetheless, at that moment Marvin closed his eyes and jumped up about three inches just as the elevator struck bottom.

Amazingly, when Marvin peaked through his fingers they were all still alive . . . if you could call this living.

The elevator had come to the end of the line. Floor *minus* 100. The lowest level known to man. (Just to give you an idea how low that is, they were six floors below unintentional suicide . . . nineteen floors below nagging dread . . . thirty-seven floors below fear and loathing . . . and, eighty-two floors below bobbing for apathy.) Marvin shuddered, wondered what atrocity, what inconceivable mutated mystery awaited beyond the brushed aluminum doors.

BING

The doors glided open and . . . nothing . . . nada . . . zilch. Nobody entered. Nobody left. A bluish ethereal light illuminated the hallway. Silence, but for the sounds of the building's bowels churning like an angry intestine.

Marvin had a feeling this wasn't the parking garage. No one in the elevator moved. They were, as it were, frozen. It was quite an uncomfortable moment. But at least they had hit bottom . . . he hoped.

Marvin decided to brave the first move. He pushed his way through the icy throng and stepped out onto the tundra. Literally, the tundra. He was standing on a vast glacier, a plateau of misery as far as the eye could see.

Marvin turned back towards the elevator which cut a door into the void with no visible means of support. There was another set of elevator doors just to the right, which were closed. Set between both elevators stood an ash tray filled with pure white sand and above that, hovering in space, were the "up" and "down" buttons.

One by one the gleeless gaggle got out of the elevator. They crawled, slithered and trotted out in single file as if to an execution. And who knew?

They huddled around Marvin for warmth, giving off none themselves, and contemplated infinity, judging by the blank stares on their passionless faces.

Marvin noticed something written in the ash tray sand. It was the word . . . "help." *Catchy*, he thought, wondering if it had done the author any good. At least he knew they weren't pioneers to this level, which gave him little comfort.

He wrapped his arms around his body hugging himself, and actually felt better—not because of the warmth but for some rather overtly obvious psychological reasons which to mention at this point would belittle its effectiveness.

Perhaps due to the hug experience, Marvin considered that he might . . . *might* . . . press the "up" button. The others stared on in gloominess as Marvin reluctantly rested his fingertip on the "up" button causing it to glow a luminescent green.

BONG

The right side elevator doors opened. Marvin hadn't anticipated such an immediate arrival and doubted if he was ready to go back up. It was so damn comfortable down here. Chilly though.

He turned back to the open elevator, which had delivered them to this godforsaken hellishness, and was startled to find that there was no longer an elevator inside. It was now quite simply a bottomless pit, an abysmal abyss dropping to deeper frontiers.

For the others, it took little time to decide. The man with his bloody ears pinned to his lapel took this opportunity to hop, skip and gleefully jump into the black hole. He disappeared without a peep. Then, the three naked, anorexic, bald ex-cheerleaders rolled one after another into the hole, their anxious PMS screams echoing a good half minute. Next up, the man preoccupied with his navel eagerly performed a 9.4 swan dive into the void followed by the dreary couple on all fours who momentarily reared up and whinnied before tumbling to their despicable destiny.

All that was left was the woman staring at her shoes . . . and Marvin.

Marvin peered over the edge of darkness, woozy. He could still hear the distant cries of the fallen. *This shouldn't be too hard*, he reasoned. One giant step for man . . . one small step for a terribly depressed, twice divorced, easily alcoholic, middle-management executive.

The woman moved to his side and tenderly slipped her weak, frigid hand into his plump, sweaty palm. *Maybe this would be a team jump*, Marvin theorized. Nevertheless, the gesture overwhelmed him and, as they stood teetering on the edge, he suddenly kissed her blue trembling lips.

He thought he heard angels but soon realized it was the persistent ringing in his ears from high blood pressure.

When she pulled away, with the sound of abalone pried from glass, her lips were stuck on her teeth leaving her with a grimace. But it was good enough for Marvin, who took it as a

Depression

sign and quickly ushered her into the "up" elevator before she changed her mind.

Once inside, the doors began to slowly close. They confidently gleamed at one another, their plastered grins transforming to expressions of extreme apprehension as the doors shut.

BING

A moment later the elevator started its slow climb . . . minus 99 . . . minus 98 . . . minus 97 . . .

FLAMINGO MEAT
Another "Raoul, Low-life Ex-Cop" Adventure

It was a buffet of carcasses. Steaming piles of muscle meat ready for chewing. Mmmmmmm . . . enough to make your mouth water. Unfortunately, the swarming flies, their bellies full of maggoty offspring, made the hot chow hard to fathom.

Raoul wondered if he was standing single file at the slaughterhouse, or the buffet line at the Flamingo Hotel in Las Vegas on Christmas Eve.

Ahead of Raoul was a cackling pack of blackjack dealers, sporting beehive hairdos and wide polyester butts, smoking like steel mills, curing Raoul's jaundiced skin to jerky.

It was zombie hour and Raoul had been at the pai gow poker tables for eight hours straight, losing for the last nine. The dizzying sound of coins, a cacophony of Jingle Bells in the slot trays, swallowed the air, while giddy cries of confusion echoed from desperate gamblers on one-way thrill rides to hell.

There were tits and tinsel all around and murder in Raoul's heart as he tried to bum a smoke from the human smokestacks ahead of him in line. But they were obviously alien slags on an aborted mission and spoke in a foreign tongue. His butt was itching like hell, but it reassured him he was alive, and he needed reassurance, standing in the buffet dungeon inhaling the scent of the slaughterhouse.

The food line was apparently moving, though he was getting no further ahead. Raoul noticed a lone slot machine next to the bathrooms, a retired bandit with a mutated metal arm, rubbed fingerless from over-use. It was a hopeless cause, really, a sucker's slot, but he robotically reached into his pocket and liberated a grimy quarter.

He stepped one leg over the red velvet rope and fumbled the coin out of his trembling fingers—onto the carpet. The damn thing rolled under the heel of a transvestite dwarf handing out keno cards by the men's room. Raoul crawled on his knees under the red intestinal rope, feeling spit on his hands and horror in his soul. He approached the dwarf, who flirtatiously sighed and thrust out his questionable hips. Raoul smiled a death mask and picked up the quarter while the dwarf shoved a keno card to a bulimic ex-mouseketeer rushing from the buffet into the ladies room.

Raoul shakily rose to his feet, realizing that he had wet his pants, courtesy of failing kidneys, and fed the quarter into the slot. He jerked the handle and the wheels spun, taking Raoul's brain along for the ride.

Cherries . . . Bar . . . Lemon. Diddly-squat.

When Raoul tried to re-enter the line, a rhinestone cowboy with cattle breath and a hard-on for a fight wouldn't give him back his place.

The fluorescent lights cast a pale glow over the row of concentration camp faces as Raoul marched to the end of the buffet line, listening to "Sleigh Bells" for the fortieth time on the casino speakers.

Raoul's stomach was now a churning ocean of bile and he knew if he didn't get food soon he would eat the dwarf.

A sign near the front of the line read: "TWENTY-FOUR HOUR BUFFET—ALL YOU CAN EAT FOR $2.99." Raoul wondered about the stampede a sign like that might cause in Bangladesh, as he watched two aging showgirls with leaky silicone carry their mountainous plates to their table.

Raoul rattled the quarters around in his pocket as he once again neared the front of the line. He had two dollars and seventy-five cents after losing the Washington in the slot. So he now was shy twenty-five cents for the buffet (including a penny tip). He needed to win back his quarter before someone else monopolized his slot machine, as he sensed the bandit was nearing a pay day.

As if on cue, a mummified cowgirl, sporting a canvas gardening glove, bullied her way through the casino in her chrome walker and approached the desperado. She tightened the glove on her skeletal lever hand and methodically spit on three quarters for good luck, before placing them in the slot. She wrestled down the desperado's arm and stood back wide-eyed, like the bourbon-breathing ghost of Annie Oakley. The wheels whirled as ninety proof sweat-beads squeezed out of her ancient pores. Joker . . . Bar . . . Lemon.

Flamingo Meat

Raoul sighed with relief as the surly square dance champ shook her crusty head on her calcified spine in disgust, swore a few antiquated cuss words, and tore away in her walker towards the computer poker machines.

Grease particles clung to Raoul's follicles, and when he ran his fingers through his hair it slicked back like a deranged Wayne Newton. He now knew where the "wet look" originated . . . waiting in buffet lines in Las Vegas, as the cattle inched forward like the Bataan Death March.

At the entrance to the buffet there was a day-go pink Christmas tree with electric blue tinsel and great big gold balls, covered in spray-can fleece like dandruff. Beyond the neon shrub, Raoul spied a grossly obese Shriner in the dining room, his pants unbuttoned and unzipped so as to accommodate his gargantuan girth, steam-shoveling fried fish balls down his gullet. It was like watching a zoo force-feeding and Raoul averted his eyes, inadvertently landing on his beckoning slot—the burned out bandit with the tired salute. The damn machine was crying out . . . "Raoul . . . Raoul." Actually it was the hostess preparing to seat him, reading the sign-in sheet.

"How many in your party?" she cheerfully groaned.

Raoul just stared at her. "Twenty-fucking-two," he sardonically replied, "The others are still on the Greyhound, so I'll just wait at the table for them."

"Oh, I see," she snapped as if just examined with an icy speculum.

She angrily darted away, which gave Raoul several seconds to reach over the velvet ropes again and compulsively stuff two more quarters into the ravenous slot.

The wheels tiredly creaked alive. Bananas . . . Berries . . . Cherries. *Nuts!*

He desperately dropped in three more quarters and again arm-wrestled the bandit.

"Come on baby!" begged Raoul, his eyes swelling like a Keane painting as the wheels clicked into place, one at a time . . . .

Bars . . . Banana . . . Lemon. Zip, zero, zilch!

Raoul studied the pitiful change left in his hand. He was down to a dollar and fifty cents. So he rapidly surrendered three more quarters and . . . lost again.

"Your table 'for one' is ready," a curt voice chirped.

It was a different waitress, obviously sent by the tight-sphinctered hostess. This one had an overbite which would have made Goofy proud.

Raoul had a final chance, as the waitress crossed his name off the list, to fire his last three quarters into the slot.

Before she had turned back around, he already knew the results.

He was bust.

"Follow me, hon," the waitress jadishly smiled through Indian corn teeth, her feral melons mercilessly squashed together in her starched uniform like a mammogram. Raoul became entranced with a blue vein in her translucent breast, but she was immune to his stare as he trailed her to his tiny table. She left him staring at the food-speckled plastic table cloth, which looked like the backboard for a flossing tournament.

She skittered away and Raoul rummaged through the seams of his crumb-lined pockets. He unearthed two pennies and a nickel, feeling like a pimply kid pumping the belly contents of his piggy bank.

Raoul wondered if they broke your legs for wolfing a two dollar and ninety-nine cent buffet with only seven cents to your name. But he decided to worry about that later as he wearily wandered towards the smorgasbord.

As he got closer, the suffocating smell of hot animal flesh permeated the wallpaper. He was so hungry he could have peeled a piece and eaten it with Swiss on rye.

A jaded sign over the buffet table read, "Ho-Ho-Ho, Merry Christmas from the Flamingo." There was splattered spaghetti sauce on the sign, no doubt from an over-eager feeder at the pig trough or someone gagging on a linguine noodle.

The stack of ceramic plates was ice cold and Raoul wondered why, considering they were serving hot food. He gazed across the sea of flesh and fowl, wilted lettuce and glistening gobs of unnamed steaming goo. Everything was the same color, bathed in the amber glow of incandescent heat lamps.

The food overwhelmed his senses. He felt faint, dazed by the odor of mammal death. There was decapitated turkey with gut giblets, prime rib bleeding profusely, scrambled embryos, and Porky Pig's hacked torso. But Raoul was strangely drawn to the carnage, avoiding the creamed corn and Velveeta vegetables.

Raoul piled his plate like the Great Pyramid, his legs wobbly under the weight. He suddenly halted in his tracks. A wiry security guard in his sixties, dressed as Santa Claus, snored loudly from his perch at the end of the buffet. A bridge of spittle spanned his gaping lips. Raoul couldn't help thinking that some day that would be him. That's *if* he was lucky enough to get a job, what with his notorious record on the force.

Raoul, holding his hemorrhaging plate, easily snuck past the guard. Perhaps he would be able to make his getaway after all.

"Hold it right there, mister!" a stern voice ordered.

Raoul froze. The jig was up. He slowly turned, face to face with a huge mulatto chef, slippery with sweat, holding a giant aluminum ladle. "You want gravy with that meat, don't ya?"

Raoul nervously nodded, "Gravy? . . . heh-heh . . . sure."

The chef poured a dense bucketful of flour-thickened steer blood onto his plate. The chef wiped the back of his serving hand across his drenched forehead, then wearily stepped back to his shadowy post behind the heat lamps.

Raoul studied the stagnant pool of gravy, wondering how much was actually meat drippings, as he moved on.

He arrived back at his table and began tearing at the salty limbs which had been slowly roasting for days. He could hear the moan of the animals in his soul, but it tasted good.

Real good.

Raoul ate in a trance, the merry sounds of a casino Christmas ringing a tumor in his brain. He couldn't remember when he cleaned his plate, it was just suddenly empty, like a magic rice bowl trick. His bloated gut felt like a garbage fill and he saw sea gulls circling before his eyes, ready to pick through his stomach.

Raoul couldn't budge and he wondered whether he would be able to make his getaway or would be handcuffed to the table and forced-fed by the Cosa Nostra until he exploded, his guts dangling from the Christmas tree branches like ghoulish tinsel. Raoul felt dangerously nauseous as he gazed around the buffet room at the other diners, their flaps of fat flowing over their chairs like lava.

A steam room of post buffet cigarette smoke cured Raoul's skin and he knew that if he didn't exit pronto he would be served as sausage links at the breakfast buffet.

There was only one way out of the buffet and it was past the cash register. *Gamblers,* Raoul conceded, *were not the most reliable sort,* and he imagined the tortures in store for buffet burglars . . . *or did you just wind up at tomorrow's buffet . . . in a chafing dish?*

Just then, the three beehived blackjack dealers, puffing like a smoldering forest fire, mobilized their herd and headed for the cash register. Figuring he could sneak out behind them while they were paying, he commanded himself to his feet and followed.

Raoul had entered the Flamingo Casino with a hundred and fifty-three bucks, all the money he had in the world; and the fact that he was now trying to steal a two dollar and ninety-nine cent buffet was, well, somewhat disconcerting. *Nevertheless, these are the moments that build character,* thought Raoul; besides, he couldn't actually fathom them arresting a down-on-his-luck, ex-defender of justice . . . on Christmas Eve.

He was wrong.

As he bent down, pretending to tie his shoe, he crept hunched over behind the gals paying at the register. But a sneering voice cemented Raoul to the carpet . . . .

"Forgetting something?"

Suddenly, all eyes were on Raoul. The entire casino seemed to fall into deadly silence as if God had pushed the cosmic mute button.

"Aren't . . . we . . . *forgetting* . . . something?" the accusatory voice repeated, as if Raoul was an Alzeheimer patient who forgot to unzip his pants before going to the bathroom.

Raoul sheepishly peered up at the hostess who was relishing her limited authority, considering this payback for their earlier interlude and her entire miserable, failed existence.

"ED! . . ." she suddenly boomed, recognizing the blank glaze in Raoul's eyes as an admission of guilt, ". . . We've got a runner!"

The Santa security guard awoke with a start, wiped the spittle off his chin and drew his revolver as he turned towards the register.

He pulled his gun?! Raoul morbidly mused, wondering if this was how it would all end, shot in the back at the Flamingo buffet by a sixty-year-old Santa wearing Depends. Seventeen years Raoul had spent on the force battling pimps, perverts and profiteers and he had never taken a bullet. But since being put on forced retirement it seemed he was taking shots of lead as often as tequila.

He had gone to Vegas on the advice of his bookie, to take a breather and get away from a string of bad luck in L.A. Now he had seven cents, enough stomach acid to sink the Titanic, and was about to play target silhouette for a senile Santa with trigger palsy.

Raoul tried to clear his head as Ed staggered forward aiming his .38 special, wearing his faded flannel costume and a dreamy haze. Raoul was momentarily paralyzed, weighed down by his own digestive juices.

Then, something glittering on the carpet caught Raoul's eye. A single silver quarter.

Seizing the moment, Raoul dove for the coin and then slithered under the velvet vine towards the one-armed bandit.

"SHOOT! SHOOT HIM!!" commanded the hostess at Ed, whose oversized Santa pants were riding dangerously below his butt crack.

Raoul swiftly flung the quarter in the slot, yanked the lever and watched the wheels spin, his life flipping by on the magic fruit wheel.

No doubt he was going to jail. All he could see were bars . . . bars . . . bars.

A siren sounded somewhere in Raoul's brain and he wondered if he was once again in the back of an ambulance careening towards a trauma center with a lump of hot lead in his navel. But there was something different about this sound. These were ringing bells, sweet silver bells, and the sound of cascading coins.

Raoul had hit it big. Well, big for this timeworn slot . . . a hundred quarters or . . . two hundred and fifty simoleans!

The hostess, her blood-thinned lips agape, wore a death mask of stunned horror. Her life was effectively over. She had rolled craps, putting up her whole meager existence on the come line.

Ed holstered his piece. It wasn't working anyhow. But Ed wouldn't know that until three weeks later when two men wearing Muppet masks robbed the change window and Ed reached for his weapon and fired. Click.

But this was Raoul's moment. Everyone in the casino was suddenly his pal as he paid for his meal and stuck a ten buck tip between his waitress's cleavage. She smiled back a mouthful of gold fillings and he knew he could have had her, if he had wanted. But he had other cards to play.

He confidently strode back to the pai gow table as "Sleigh Bells" played for the millionth time. His chair was still warm as he sat back down feeling lucky. Real lucky.

Besides . . . there was always the buffet.

The Evil Yeknom Sniarb

Somewhere out beyond the jungles of Wolowingwong lived the Evil Yeknom Sniarb—a creature so horrible it could eat the thoughts right out of your skull. Or so legend told.

No one could describe the Evil Sniarb because nobody had ever seen the wicked monster. No one except for a soothsaying simian sorcerer named Loo who had journeyed to the Sniarb's castle when he was a young brave monkey and returned with strange tales of fireballs, plumes of smoke and terrible smells. The elder wizard would sit by the campfire and tirelessly retell to the young monkeys of Wolowingwong how he scaled the stone walls of the creature's castle, peeked in a window and spied the Evil Yeknom Sniarb himself, an enormous monster with knives for hands, who read a giant book of dark magic.

Just a week earlier, Loo had once again braved the journey to the Sniarb's lair to discover the truth. Actually, he was *forced* to go after several warriors had not returned. The entire village came out to bid Loo farewell. It was the last time anyone would see him alive.

Meanwhile, life went on in Wolowingwong. Bananas were gathered, trees were swung from and the idle chatter of tree monkeys was heard throughout the jungle. But in the back of everyone's mind was Loo and the others before him.

Yuki, a hairless tree monkey with bunched up skin, like a rippled carpet, was searching for sweet bananas when he got the news. He had been chosen to find Loo.

Though by appearance merely a frightened monkey, Yuki really had great strength. Not physically, mind you, but of character, which is why he had been selected to be the next great warrior on this noble mission. But Yuki knew it was the lottery.

Yuki would be the thirteenth monkey sent on such a quest that month. None had returned. But Yuki wasn't scared. He was the only monkey who didn't believe in the legend of the Evil Sniarb. He simply figured that there must be a better place beyond the jungle and those who hadn't returned were living wonderful lives. Wishful thinking on Yuki's behalf, but he liked happy endings and was in a deep state of denial as he packed.

Yuki, believing there was nothing to be afraid of, prepared for a fun-filled vacation. But, just in case he had miscalculated, he brought along a backup—a tiny poisonous ring snake which he carried in a small leather pouch on his belt.

As Yuki merrily skipped down the road out of Wolowingwong, the villagers looked away. But Yuki didn't let this spoil his adventure. They were just jealous, he reasoned, and with his arms raised overhead in the happy monkey mode, Yuki disappeared down the jungle road.

After many miles, Yuki ventured beyond the farthest banana tree, as dusk muted the jungle greens. Yuki was just becoming apprehensive when he saw a flash of light. He dove for cover beneath a bristle bush and cowered. Then, he smelled something horrible—a rancid odor, enough to repel anyone, and Yuki wondered if he was smelling the Evil Yeknom Sniarb himself. Undaunted, Yuki brushed himself off and continued onward, intending to see for himself if the legendary beast really existed or was merely mass-induced hysteria.

Up ahead, the sky grew smoky gray, blocking out the setting sun. Yuki coughed in the thick haze. He knew he was getting close and wondered what he would do when he got there. What if there really was a monster? *Naw*, Yuki shook his head, *ridiculous*. Nevertheless, he unconsciously tapped his poisonous snake pouch.

Finally, he spotted a mysterious stone castle, its twisted spires rising from the mist at the end of a long dark road. Suddenly, Yuki tripped. As he bent down to pick up what looked like a rotting turnip, Yuki heard the alluring, irresistible music of the Evil Yeknom Sniarb.

It was the kind of music that no monkey could ignore, let alone forget. So enticing and soothing was the sound that Yuki dropped the turnip and staggered the last mile or so to the intimidating fortress in a daze.

As he approached the great iron gates of the Sniarb's castle, the drawbridge automatically lowered. Yuki innocently stepped across the bridge, anxious to dance to the music of the heavens. But then, a moment of lucidity snapped him out of his trance and he slapped himself. He slapped himself again to be sure, and then wondered if this might be some sort of trap?

As he stood debating this with himself the music grew louder and more inviting, wrenching the feeble thought from the monkey's skull. *What made these beautiful notes couldn't be all bad*, shrugged Yuki; besides, his curiosity was overwhelming.

Yuki couldn't believe his eyes as he entered the rusted iron gates. Inside the castle, dense tropical ferns and sparkling emerald waterfalls led Yuki to a violet lagoon surrounded by banana trees.

Yuki picked a banana, sniffing it to establish its authenticity. Reassured, and frankly starving, he bit into the sweetest banana he had ever tasted. The fruit melted in his mouth in a symphony of flavor. *Back in Wolowingwong such a banana would be sold for a great sum*, postulated Yuki.

Elation swept over Yuki's face as he greedily gobbled another banana. Was it something in the banana or was it this wondrous land that made everything more intense, more flavorful?

Yuki now realized why there were such horrible tales about this place. If it got out about the banana trees and the heavenly garden of splendor, it would be robbed of its ample treasures.

Yuki giggled, danced to the edge of the lagoon and dipped his finger in the warm violet water. He licked off his finger which tasted like coconut milk. Yuki quickly tossed off his satchel, dropped his snake pouch and dove into the lagoon. He did the backstroke as thousands of tiny bubbles massaged his weary limbs, removing the fatigue of his long journey.

Evil Yeknom Sniarb

Yuki finally pulled himself out onto the other side of the lagoon and a warm, gentle wind blew his fuzzy skin dry. *What a place*, thought Yuki.

Just as Yuki was about to reach for another golden banana, he heard a sigh. He whirled around and saw a pair of furry toes poking out from behind a blushberry bush. He crouched into a fighting stance, practicing a few kamakazoo moves as he cautiously made his way around the lavender hedge. There, to his surprise, he saw ...

"Loo?!" exclaimed Yuki.

The startled, gray haired monkey sat up on his lounge chair, trying to place Yuki's hairless face.

"Um ... Puki, right?

"No, greatest one ... Yuki ... Yuki of the flatlands," he replied to the forgetful wizard.

Loo greeted Yuki with a bobbing nod, a little put off to see another monkey at *his* oasis.

"Where are the others?" cheerfully inquired Yuki.

"What others?" spat back Loo, as he flipped down his sunglasses.

Yuki, concerned, studied Loo for a moment before answering. "Have you forgotten your brethren and the reason for your mission, great sorcerer?" cried Yuki.

"Who needs 'em?" smirked Loo. "You've got everything you could possibly want here. Swimming, paddle tennis, disco—and wait 'til you get a load of the salad bar. And it's all free! I'm never going back."

Yuki was stunned. How could Loo, of all monkeys, say such a thing? Then the soothing music began playing again and suddenly it all made sense. Yuki pulled up a lounge chair next to Loo and lay there for a week.

During his stay, Yuki had the time of his life and Loo was right about the salad bar: what a spread! But it wasn't just the food. Each day a gorgeous blue monkey named Mellie delivered books to Yuki. Scholarly texts on philosophy, medicine, and economics, as well as mystery books, science fiction, and even a racy one called *Monkey Mischief*. Yuki would read the books aloud to Loo, who couldn't read, as Mellie massaged Yuki's scalp.

After a few weeks, Yuki had grown weary of reading to Loo. He was just wishing that there were other vacationers besides Loo when, as if his thoughts were read, a tour group of red spotted mountain monkeys joined them at the oasis. They were from another tribe, just in for the weekend, and Loo became sullen and grouchy with the intrusion.

Yuki, on the other hand, enjoyed having some new female monkeys to glance at, especially after reading *Monkey Mischief* for the third time.

One of the female monkeys, an attractive spider monkey named Sabinya, took an instant liking to Yuki. One tranquil afternoon as Yuki was eyeballing Sabinya, she stared him down while peeling a banana. Then, she playfully dove into the violet lagoon and Yuki followed, racing her to the other side. She climbed out and teasingly ran away from Yuki through the dense ferns. But Yuki easily caught up and she surrendered beneath a heartberry tree, where they made monkey love.

After two weeks of nirvana, Yuki realized there was nothing more he could ask for and nothing to be asked of him. He floated into a deep, dreamless sleep on his lounge chair.

He awoke sometime later to the peaceful compelling music of the magical paradise and yawned. "Another day, another banana," he sighed, grinning to himself. Yuki then casually noticed that he was sealed up to his neck in a wooden box. He calmly wondered how he wound up in the steam room.

Loo, in the same predicament next to Yuki had a decidedly more worried expression on his creased face. Yuki smiled, thinking Loo was just monkeying around, but then, a giant creature walking erect on two feet, swept past. Yuki involuntarily gulped . . . the Evil Yeknom Sniarb?!

Yuki flinched as flames leaped nearby, ominous smoke escaping up a stone chimney. The huge creature, clad in a white costume, placed a white tubular hat on its head, the kind a monkey priest might wear, and opened a stained white bible.

Yuki and Loo began to sweat, and not just from the stove, as more giant creatures filtered in and pulled sharpened Ginsu knives from their waist bands.

"Pssst," hissed Yuki.

Loo didn't respond, hypnotized by the jumping flames.

"Psssst!" again hissed Yuki, "Do something, great one!"

Loo turned towards Yuki and in a voice that had raised several octaves squeaked, "I have deceived you . . . I have no powers," sobbed Loo.

This was, quite frankly, the last thing that Yuki wanted to hear.

"How can this be?" cried Yuki, "You are the highest of high shamans, lord sage of sorcerers . . . the divine Mahatma Monkey!"

Loo shrugged, "The oldest monkey always gets to be wizard."

One of the Ginsu-wielding priests removed a bag of turnips from a huge white safe filled with winter, while another giant sliced the turnips on a wood block, Loo flinching with each decisive *chop*. Finally, the head priest, wearing the white tower hat, arranged the turnip slices into a flower shape on a huge shiny platter.

Yuki, meanwhile, was checking for the nearest exit. He noticed a set of massive double doors which would swing open on occasion as the tall ones in white rushed through carrying empty steel platters, coated with congealed brown and yellow muck, and handed them to another priest who dunked them in boiling water.

Each time the door swung open, Yuki would hear voices, laughter, emanating from the other room.

The beast in white, who had donned the priest hat, accidentally knocked over the stained bible which fell by Loo's feet, out of Yuki's view.

Loo spotted the opened white book and began babbling, "Evil Yeknom Sniarb . . . Evil Yeknom Sniarb," over and over in delirious fashion.

"Where?! Where!" cried Yuki. But, unfortunately, Loo's box was lifted and taken into the other room before he could answer, a tear trailing down the wizard's furry grey cheek.

Yuki desperately strained his neck to see the words in the splattered bible but it was too far away. Why had Loo kept repeating, "Evil Yeknom Sniarb . . . Evil Yeknom Sniarb?" Were those the words from the book? Suddenly, Yuki recalled how Loo had first named the evil creature after escaping from the

Evil Yeknom Sniarb

castle as a young monkey. Maybe Loo had seen the book through the window? But Yuki knew that Loo couldn't read. At least not the way others could read. Suddenly, it struck Yuki like a hammer . . . Loo saw words in reverse!

At that precise moment, one of the priests accidentally kicked the book across the floor. It landed right in front of Yuki, confirming his worst fear. The opened page of the white bible read: LIVE MONKEY BRAINS!

The words rang like a dinner bell in Yuki's racing brain as his box was swept up and lifted through the eternal swinging doors.

There, facing Yuki, was a sight so repulsive that it fully cannot be comprehended, unless of course, you're a monkey.

In a smoke-filled banquet room crammed with Chinese businessmen, was a long oak table. Large holes were cut through the wood in front of each diner. Around the holes were attached iron neck braces. Loo's vulnerable head poked through one such hole. The other monkeys from the oasis were also there, including Sabinya who bravely smiled at Yuki.

The priest in white slipped Yuki's bald head through the awaiting hole in the table, tightly securing his trembling neck with the iron brace. Yuki, now facing Loo across the table, could smell the turnips on the silver platter at the center, which were decoratively surrounding shiny, steel surgical tools.

The Chinese businessmen, without breaking conversation, reached for their weapons of torture . . . a hammer-like device and a sharpened picker with a curled hook at the end.

Suddenly, Yuki remembered his poisonous snake and checked his waist belt for the pouch. It was still there, hidden in the folds of his flesh.

As Yuki desperately untied the snake bag beneath the table he watched in sheer terror as the diners picked up their steel hammers.

Yuki tossed the opened snake bag under the table, which landed atop the foot of the high priest.

As the diners raised their hammers, the priest experienced a wrenching spasm. His eyes rolled back and he collapsed to his knees behind the table without a peep.

Yuki triumphantly smiled.

But the diners didn't notice, or were too hungry, because Yuki stared in horror as the hammer was expertly swung at Loo's cranium. Sabinya, also numb with fear, watched in terror as the hammer was simultaneously aimed at Yuki's skull. The last words Yuki spoke to Sabinya were, "It's been heaven." Then, a terrible cracking sound followed, like a coconut dropped on concrete . . . and the lights went out.

Yuki suddenly found himself back by the violet lagoon. Sabinya, swimming the backstroke, smiled coyly at Yuki as Loo snored nearby.

Bewildered, Yuki took a deep breath of sweet tropical air and bananas. Curious, he scratched his wrinkled scalp, reached under his lounge chair and lifted a copy of *Monkey Mischief*. His bookmark was still in its place.

Sabinya was right, thought Yuki, *this place is heaven.*

He settled back on his lounge chair and took up where he left off . . . a warm breeze caressing his furry toes.

5

ANDROS

The school of neons flowed together like pools of paint, a tempered rainbow beneath a canvas sea. Nearby, a floating shadow silently watched the color stream—a toothy torpedo hovering unblinking in the warm currents, longing for the chill of the deep.

The tiny purple and yellow striped neons maneuvered in military fashion, flashing fluorescent sparks, but Andros let them pass. *Fish that size only get caught in your teeth,* smirked the eight foot barracuda . . . *hardly worth the chew.*

The neons leapt from the sea in a shower of dripping opalescence as they headed out into the clear Caribbean.

The compact island of St. Sirmone, one of several small unmapped fishing villages in the Antilles Islands, was warmed by the morning sun levitating from the sea.

On the shore, Osmos, a muscular twelve-year-old, his brown toes packed with powdery pink coral sand, gathered a gnarled fishing net and loaded it onto a paint-chipped sloop. The eleven foot boat, carved by his grandfather from the trunk of a silk-cotton tree, had been repainted numerous times, leaving a mottled hull of blues and greens.

Gilar, nearly eight, yawned as he sat on the sand waiting for his brother, clutching a small sack of dried amberjack and a ripe mango for their journey. Osmos placed the two splintered oars on board, then walked up along the dry sand and lifted his little brother onto his shoulders. Gilar's thin legs draped around Osmos's neck as he playfully carried him to the boat. Gilar grinned and held onto his brother's strong shoulders as he watched a pelican glide through the cloudless sky, spot a fish and plummet into the sea.

Osmos shoved the sloop off the sand, the rasp of the tide sweeping the shore. The boat gently bobbed on the water as he jumped in and paddled to meet the waves, assisted by the tug of the tide. Gilar, seated on the floor of the sloop, searched the horizon for the pelican, which hadn't resurfaced.

"Hang on!" shouted Osmos, exhilarated as they crashed through a wave, catching Gilar off guard.

Gilar coughed up a mouthful of seawater and immediately spotted a larger swell on the horizon. He was terrified of the ocean, though he would never let on to Osmos. The sea, Gilar had learned, had brutal strength and a rolling grip, unsparing to old friends as to enemies.

"Ready?" hollered Osmos, as the mounting wave approached. Gilar's eyes widened as the sea rose to smack them like a nasty ripple in a turquoise carpet. Their boat was

Andros

shoved backwards into the water, then popped through the other side of the wave, like a flung spear. Osmos quickly hooked Gilar's elbow so he wouldn't tumble overboard.

The boat slapped back hard at the sea, but they had made it past the breakers. As tradition dictated, Osmos let out a big whoop, and Gilar echoed a little whoop, as the muscular back of the wave folded into a fist and pounded the shore.

They gently floated over the swells as they headed toward the reef. Gilar lifted his emaciated legs one at a time over the side of the sloop, wishing he could feel the soothing warm water or the tiny brine crackling beneath the hull. Gilar raised his face to the morning sun, recalling when he was five and his older brother would carry him to the tide pools so he could dangle his feet. Osmos would place chickpeas between Gilar's toes so the minuscule fish would swarm and he might feel them nibble.

One time their mother had swiped Osmos on the head with her open palm, "Crazy boy, you wish to feed your brother's toes to Andros?!" Osmos couldn't understand what difference it would make. Neither could Gilar.

They had both heard stories of the great "Andros" for as long as they could remember, theatrical tales acted out by leathery villagers with elongated earlobes who immortalized the legendary beast.

Andros had seemingly outlived generations of natives who tirelessly retold colorful stories of the fierce fish, passed down from the memories of their fathers.

Pulo, the eldest villager, who seemed to be two hundred years old to Gilar, would purse his salt-shriveled lips and hiss the cursed name through his pointed teeth like a bad omen ... "Androssss." The village boys gathered, wide-eyed, listening to Pulo's folklore, though in retrospect it hardly seemed possible that a single fish could be responsible for such unbridled mayhem. Bad weather, Andros ... Chickens missing, Andros ... Baby die, pray to Andros ... Stomachache, better feed Andros.

When Gilar was three and still could not walk, his father, Markos, shamed by a son who would never hunt, bound the child's hands behind his back so he wouldn't be able to drag himself and would be forced to stand. But Gilar's legs held death, proclaimed Pulo, and he was right, for the small boy lay with his face toward the sand all night, unmoving, though he never once cried.

The village even held a ceremonial "Choya" for the boy. They ate bitter roots and danced around a spectacular bonfire to awaken the God Choya. At sunrise they laid glowing embers on the child's legs to awaken the walking spirits. But the child would not walk that night, or ever.

Pulo eventually blamed Gilar's father for not paying homage to Andros. But Markos, the best fisherman in the village, did not believe in the tales of the devil fish, Andros.

Nevertheless, numerous villagers had mysteriously succumbed, their bleached bones picked clean upon a timeless shore. Perhaps even mingling with the bones of Gilar's father ... who was lost at sea.

Andros ground his teeth in sweet anticipation. It was like an itch, his feedings, and Andros played a game, teasing himself, holding it off as long as possible to intensify the eventual scratch.

Andros

A flirtatious fin caressed the jet stream several fathoms below. It was a parrot fish . . . a veritable palette of flavor. The docile fish flapped its submerged fin wings like its flying cousin. Andros grinned, displaying his massive underbite, and imperceptibly flicked his tail, propelling himself silently forward, stopping to stare with liquid eyes.

The parrot fish was a blinking lighthouse to Andros, beckoning all but the color blind. *Why had the God Choya made a fish with no natural camouflage?* pondered Andros. *For fish like myself*, he sardonically bubbled.

The gentle parrot was oblivious to the steely eyes of Andros, busily on a quest of her own for sweet brine, unaware that she, too, was about to become another link in the food chain.

The sun stretched from the hem of the ocean as they approached the reef. Osmos threw the bow line over a shard of pink coral as the boat swirled in the whirlpools.

Osmos then reached under the splintered slat seat, pushing a rusty spear gun aside, and located a corroded skin diving mask which he handed to his brother. As Osmos prepared the net, Gilar touched the sticky rubber trim of the dive mask which was being slowly digested by salt water and suddenly felt a pang of longing for his father. He could still recall his massive shoulders and large calloused hands. His father would float in the shallow water near shore, Gilar seated on his strong shoulders, and then dunk his head under so Gilar could feel like he was swimming.

"We'll fill up the fish box today, little brother," confidently declared Osmos as he mended a frayed hole in the net.

Gilar dreamily nodded as he leaned over and floated the dive mask on the ocean surface. He couldn't wear the leaky mask anymore, but it made a good glass bottom boat. Gilar lowered his face towards the glass surface. The underworld came into focus. A garden of sea vegetation gently waved hello. A striped grouper calmly floated past a lacy lavender sea fan. A moment later, a green sea turtle paddled by, and Gilar smiled as he turned to watch, suddenly startled by a pair of huge black eyes gawking back. Gilar tumbled backwards, dropping the mask into the boat.

"What is it?" teased Osmos, still repairing the net. "Sea monsters?"

"Andros!" cried Gilar.

Osmos frowned and skeptically leaned over, peering through the face mask. A bloated blowfish stared back, unblinking.

"Did Andros kiss you?" laughed Osmos.

Gilar splashed Osmos, who splashed him back with the wooden paddle, soaking him. A water melee ensued.

Andros, his teeth bathed crimson, spit out the parrot's chalky spine. The neons had picked up the scent of the parrot fish's blood and were darting about frantically, turning in unison, one way and then another, dreading what might come next . . . a feeding frenzy. It was one of those unfortunate things about being a fish, one moment you're enjoying the flow and the next minute you're eating your neighbors.

The net floated out over the sea and settled between the swells. Gilar watched it sink, glad he wasn't a fish, and gazed back at their distant village noticing how small it looked.

Osmos tapped Gilar on the leg, but he didn't respond.

"Check the net," said Osmos, motioning overboard.

Gilar peered over the side. The net looked okay, so he just leaned over the edge and made himself appear busy, which seemed to satisfy Osmos.

By noon the sun was bearing straight down on their heads. The rhythmic lapping of the waves lulled them both into a lazy afternoon nap.

Gilar dreamed he was running across the sea.

The sun was still high overhead as Gilar awoke and stretched. Osmos was still asleep against the side of the boat, his mouth open. Gilar propped himself up, dizzy from the sun, and patted cool seawater on his face. He felt better and opened the paper bag of dried amberjack. He broke off a chunk of salty fish, chewing the tough smoky flesh, while watching Osmos' eyeballs dance under their lids.

Gilar, wearing a mischievous grin, splashed water onto Osmos, then peered innocently overboard. Osmos awoke and propped himself up, squinting, the side of his face dotted with dried fish scales like sequins. Osmos gazed suspiciously at Gilar and wiped his runny nose on his wrist, then spotted their net which had drifted out over the coral forest, the holes serving as button loops for the cathedral-like spires.

"Aye, Gilar," groaned Osmos, "now I must go in."

"I will fix it," bravely offered Gilar.

Osmos patted his brother on the arm, "Perhaps tomorrow."

Gilar, feeling helpless remained silent as Osmos dove over the side of the sloop. Gilar leaned over and watched his brother through the clear water, kicking like a frog.

There was a strange vibration in the ocean. Even at fourteen fathoms, the vibrations were an impelling force, an electro-chemical alarm clock awakening the great fish and alerting him that food was near. Cold gray lips peeled back over alabaster teeth into a knowing grin.

Andros flicked his fin.

Osmos tried to lift the net off the coral. It was tricky work. The swells continually knitted the net back over the pink coral while Osmos attempted to keep his feet away from the razor sharp stalagmites.

Gilar grew bored observing his brother and tossed a piece of dried amberjack over the edge, watching a school of sunshine fish congregate. He stroked the water with his fingertips and the golden fish circled, nibbling gentle kisses.

Gilar noticed another larger shape floating up from the depths. He placed the diving mask back on the surface. It was a parrot fish, its face a glorious green, red and yellow. It slowly floated upwards, until Gilar could see its swollen cataract eyes and its black beak yawned open in a frozen scream. It slowly rolled over, revealing itself to be a severed head eerily floating through the currents. Damselfish swarmed the stringy neck tissue around the spine which hung freely amidst the floating entrails. Gilar lurched back, woozy. Suddenly the sea smelled vile. He felt a wave of nausea, like the first time he cleaned a fish, slicing open the silky belly, the acrid smell of stomach contents filling his nostrils. He fell against the side of the boat and took several gulps of humid air.

Andros

After a moment, he felt better and leaned back over the edge to peer through the face mask. He could still see the head of the parrot fish drifting beneath the boat but now something else caught his eye, a ghost rising from the deep. The creature was at least eight feet long. Gilar watched, terrified, as the thin gray cylinder propelled upwards towards the fish head. In a flash of blood and bone, teeth sliced through the parrot's eye sockets and swallowed the head whole.

Gilar screamed for his brother, the sound of the reef waves swallowing his cries. He desperately scanned the horizon for Osmos as the swells rolled ominously higher. Gilar dragged himself to the bow and began to frantically pull in the net, hand over hand, drawing the boat closer to his brother.

Andros, with another flip of his fin, shot underneath the boat towards Osmos, who popped up under the surging net, and heard his brother's distant cry.

"What's wrong?" hollered Osmos.

Gilar vigorously pointed towards the water but Osmos was caught off guard by a large swell blanketing the reef, shoving him up against the coral. A finger of pink coral lightly scraped his ankle causing a thin ribbon of blood to mingle with the sea.

Andros involuntarily swallowed.

Osmos came back up for air, trapped under the net. But while the net caged him in, it also kept Andros out.

"Stay under the net!" instructed Gilar as he desperately continued to pull the net, his arm sockets burning, bringing the boat ever closer to Osmos. But the coral island kept the sloop a good ten yards away.

"What is it?" yelled back Osmos, breathless.

Gilar, speechless with panic, managed to shout one desperate word... "ANDROS!"

Osmos smiled, at first, but then he saw the terror in his brother's eyes and immediately searched beneath the heavy net, anxiously surveying his pedaling feet.

"Where is he?" yelled Osmos.

Gilar grabbed the skin diving mask and leaned back over the edge of the boat. The underworld came into sharp focus. There, at a depth of nearly twenty feet, was the outline of the legendary barracuda... stone frozen, seemingly dead.

The sea rose and fell, draping the water laden net over the weary head and body of Osmos, his legs aching from trying to stay afloat.

Gilar was overcome with his dilemma. He knew Osmos couldn't swim out from under the net or he would be eaten by Andros. But if he stayed under the net any longer he would surely drown.

Gilar closed his eyes, praying for the God Choya to save his brother. But Choya had let him down before. He knew that if anyone was going to rescue Osmos... it would have to be himself.

Gilar glared at his shriveled lower limbs tangled under the wooden seat, feeling helpless. He attempted to move his lower limbs, trying to conjure some life into his veins, but his legs were like two sticks of dried amberjack just lying there on top of the spear gun. The spear gun! Gilar rolled himself onto the bottom of the sloop and reached for the oxidized weapon under the seat. His small body bent at an impossible angle as he tried to reach it, straining his arm and painfully pulling a muscle in his shoulder as he finally dragged the spear gun out from under the seat. He checked the rubber firing loop, testing its strength, then dragged himself and the spear gun to the side of the boat.

Osmos desperately peddled his feet trying to stay afloat while checking underwater at his dangling toes, tantalizing morsels for the great barracuda.

Andros calmly circled the fishing net. The parrot fish had proven a meager appetizer and his belly ached for the main course. It had been several years since he had been treated to a villager and he relished the impending meat. He could still recall several tough, though tasty, fishermen stranded at sea, who had similarly attempted to unsnag their nets.

Gilar spit into the corroded dive mask like he had seen his father do, then rubbed his thumb over the glass. He placed the mask over his face and pulled the elastic strap behind his head. The rubber was split and stretched, but this was no time for hesitation as Gilar lifted his paralyzed legs, one at a time, over the edge of the boat.

Osmos watched, with the net crisscrossed over his face, as Gilar adjusted the dive mask over his head. But before Osmos could say anything to stop him, his crippled brother flopped overboard into the rolling sea.

Andros immediately felt the presence of another warm body in the ocean. It appeared that today he was going to have a villager buffet. Andros turned away from the net, knowing that the trapped food could wait, and set his hungry eyes on the young boy struggling above, his emaciated legs dangling loosely from his waist like earthworms.

Gilar fought the current, and his own questionable swimming ability, as he held the spear gun in one hand and checked underwater through his badly leaking dive mask.

Osmos lost sight of the big fish below him and was terrified as Gilar swam closer.

"Get back in the boat!" shouted Osmos, "He'll eat *you* before me!"

"I'd rather die than live without my brother," bravely replied Gilar, a few yards away.

Osmos, angry from Gilar's foolhardy heroics, shouted, "I don't need your help, go back to the boat, NOW!"

Gilar suddenly sensed a gripping tug, then another. He peered down at his feet through the dive mask and saw the huge head of Andros clamped to his foot, the water fogged with blood. Andros shook his massive head back and forth, sawing his teeth through bone, and swam away with Gilar's right foot lodged between his rows of razor sharp teeth.

"GILAR!!" screamed Osmos, who dove under the net to save his crippled brother.

Gilar, feeling no pain in his gnawed ankle, took aim and fired the spear gun, badly missing Andros, who swam away gulping the mouthful of foot.

Gilar's dilapidated dive mask flooded as he swam underwater to retrieve the spear which had lodged itself in the coral reef. He tried to clear the mask, but instead, the rotted strap broke.

Osmos numbly watched underwater as his little brother dropped his dive mask and dove for the coral to retrieve the spear, weak from the loss of blood and increasing need for oxygen.

Meanwhile, the cloud of blood from Gilar's severed foot sounded a dinner bell throughout the inlet and surrounding waters for miles around.

Andros

Andros was drawn to Gilar's blood like a drug. But he wasn't the only one interested . . . three lemon sharks and a hammerhead soon darted nearby. Andros knew he would have to move fast and finish his prey before he was muscled out by larger opponents. The barracuda quickly followed the blood scent to the coral bed.

Osmos couldn't believe the size of the giant barracuda who could easily swallow his brother whole, and was intending that very thing at this moment, as Gilar finally yanked the spear from the coral.

Gilar loaded the spear gun, his hands trembling, as Andros propelled towards him displaying rows of bloody teeth.

Osmos, frantically swimming underwater towards Gilar, watched in horror as Andros unhinged his jaw, preparing to consume his frail brother.

But then, just as Andros was a yard away, Gilar turned and fired. The rusty spear shot directly into the barracuda's open mouth and straight through his body, splitting his spine cleanly in half.

The great barracuda's fin stopped in mid-wag, his shocked eyes wide and still. Osmos grabbed Gilar's arm and swam towards the surface.

The sharks, meanwhile, turned their attention to Andros.

Gilar gasped for breath as his head popped up above the water. Osmos anxiously swam his injured brother back to the boat, lifted him on board to safety, then jumped in himself.

Andros tried to move his fin as his dark blood clouded the water. But his nervous system had already shut down and he could only watch, paralyzed, as the sharks darted around in ever smaller circles and he knew that soon he, too, would be added to the food chain.

Osmos tightly wrapped Gilar's badly bleeding ankle in his damp shirt. Though Gilar had lost his right foot, and quite a bit of blood, he had a victorious smile on his face.

"Did I get him?" asked Gilar losing consciousness.

"Yes, you got him," proudly replied Osmos, adding, "The God Choya could not have done as well."

Gilar's eyes began to flutter closed as he turned his head and watched over the edge of the sloop at the numerous shark fins and the water boiling with the blood of Andros.

A moment later, Gilar passed out from exhaustion and shock.

Osmos rowed the sloop back towards the island of St. Sirmone with a procession of tiny neons guiding them to shore.

Gilar fell into a warm tranquil sleep and dreamed his dream of running across the turquoise sea . . . only this time he was running beside his father.

WHAT IF CLOUDS WERE UFOS?

Zuni, New Mexico

One particular cloud had been hovering over the Wellman's barn for quite some time. Floyd Wellman a rather insignificant man, even in this town of twenty-three, began to notice the cloud the first day after the winds. It wasn't so much that a cloud hung over his barn, it was this one single cloud. A distinctive, billowy, marshmallow of a cloud in the shape of a moose head.

When Floyd related this phenomenon to his wife Sally, she just hollered for him to come in for dinner. Floyd had indeed been standing in his okra field all afternoon staring at the cloud.

But the neighbors didn't find Floyd's behavior so odd. People in the town of Zuni would often stare at things. It's what people did. It was kind of relaxing and farmers liked to study the slow growth patterns of various vegetables. Anyhow, Sally hollered yet a fifth time for her husband to come in for supper. When she finally went outside, Floyd had vanished. So had the cloud.

Wichita, Kansas

The Wichita Sparrows were meeting for Little League practice. The team was, frankly, struggling. Actually, they were at the bottom of the league after losing their last eight games straight.

Tommy, the catcher and best hitter on the team, was experiencing an unpromising season. But he wasn't totally to blame. It was the cloud, or so he told coach Jenkins. But the coach wasn't one for excuses, especially lame ones, so when Tommy tried to explain for a third time that the same exact cloud had been hanging over left field all week, coach Jenkins, his face growing red, shouted in his ear, "Play Ball!" Needless to say, practice continued.

Six games later the Sparrows were fighting for a slot in the state championship. You might wonder how a team like the Sparrows could make it into the championships. Well, Tommy had simply begun to ignore the cloud and his batting average rose to a respectable .280. Tommy was in fact quite talented and would some day make it to the minor leagues, only to have his career halted by weak metatarsal arches.

Anyway, on to the championship. The Wichita Sparrows vs. the Topeka Blue Jays. Top of the ninth. Three-two, Sparrows. Tommy behind the plate, his metatarsals aching, shouted "swing" at the batter each time Billy Lemp, a stocky red-headed hurler, tossed a pitch.

What if Clouds were UFOs?

Yelling "swing" incidentally was one of those things that never made it to the big leagues, although yelling "swing" actually caused the batters to swing, often at the worst pitches. Tommy assisted Billy Lemp in striking out the following two Blue Jay batters, utilizing this technique.

Coming to the plate with two outs was arguably the best hitter in the league, Roy Brody. The five-foot-nine outfielder was actually a year too old for Little League, but his parents lied about his age for the sheer glory of watching their son slaughter inferior little leaguers.

Billy checked the bases. They were empty. He already knew that, but checked anyhow, as he always did, just like a big league pitcher.

Roy stepped to the plate and spit out his wad of cherry swirl gum. It was time to get serious. His coach and father, Arnie, was staring him down. If Roy didn't get a hit, there would be hell to pay.

Roy swung at the first two pitches, low and away. He actually swung when Tommy hollered "swing" and this infuriated Arnie, who barked bullets from the dugout. Roy, embarrassed and humiliated, rolled his eyes skyward and noticed . . . the cloud. The sucker was just sitting there, all plump and happy like fresh cotton candy, while other clouds raced past in the warm upper air currents.

Arnie raced from the dugout wildly gesturing for a time out. Tommy, meanwhile, noticed Roy staring upwards and similarly turned his focus yonder. There it was, that same fat cloud. Tommy was sure because it was shaped like a moose head.

The ump dusted off the plate and shouted from the depths of his substantial belly, "PLAY BALL." Louis, the umpire, was quite proud of his girth and hoped his regulation body type would propel him to the big leagues. But Louis had an eye-twitch which would regrettably act up when things were thrown near his face. Truthfully, though he would never admit it, Louis never actually saw the ball cross the plate . . . so he approximated.

Arnie yanked his son conspiratorially aside and hissed in Roy's ear, "swing at anything." Tommy, catching behind the plate, also heard Arnie give the order, "swing at anything." So, he sent a hand signal to Billy on the mound, to pitch one over Roy's head.

Arnie, arms folded across his chest, glared from the dugout waiting for his son to hit one out of the park (something Arnie had never managed to do himself in Little League). But Roy's concentration was shot. All he wanted to do was stare at the cloud in left field.

Billy, at the mound, checked the empty bases then wound up for the pitch. A split second before the ball was released, Roy took a peek towards the cloud and saw the ball hurling high over his head. But, having been programmed by his dad to swing at "anything," Roy did exactly that. Roy's bat swooshed through the air as the ball soared twenty feet overhead. The ump bellowed, "STEEERIKE" and the crowd, of seventeen parents, went wild. The Sparrows had won the championship.

What the umpire didn't notice, due to his twitch, was that the ball never made it to the back stop. The baseball hovered for a moment over Roy's head, still spinning from the pitch, before being sucked straight up into the cloud.

With all the commotion over the Sparrows' underdog victory, no one in the grandstands noticed the disappearing ball or that Arnie was racing for his son from the dugout like a runaway locomotive, teeth clenched, bloodshot eyes twitching.

Roy, who was face down on the mound, never saw his dad charging from the dug-out or witness him suddenly rocket into the sky. The Blue Jay's coach simply slipped through the small hole in the cotton ball cloud with a slurping sound, like a piece of ice sucked through a straw.

Arnie was never seen again.

Winnebago, Nebraska

At his 7-Eleven, Yasu Liberty, a Turkish immigrant who changed his last name at the Port of Authority in New York when he saw the "freedom statue," smelled his jar of beef jerky.

Beef jerky could be tricky stuff. When did it go bad and how could you tell? There wasn't even an expiration date, so Yasu screwed the lid back on. *It'd keep for another couple months.*

Two pimpled teens rode their motocross bicycles into the 7-Eleven to drop quarters in their favorite video. In this particular one a family armed with butcher knives, sulfuric acid and sharpened shovels must fend off a gang of motorcycle hoodlums armed with tire irons, chains and screaming bike sluts. The game was called Vigilante Justice and it took two quarters to play.

Yasu, speaking with an accent that many of his countrymen couldn't understand, shouted at the "hoodylooms" to get their "yikes" out of his store. However, to the video-engulfed adolescents it sounded something like this: "Yew'yew'Widbiyke,whcha'do'wink,hah?Yikey'git'owtsyde'sto dre'yes'yes, oykhay?!"

The boys were frozen. They weren't being defiant, or anything like that, they were simply stupefied by the small agitated man wearing a tweed suit in July. Yasu continued pointing feverishly at the boy's "yikes" until they finally left his store.

This was yet another example why Yasu was going out of business and why he had the same jar of beef jerky from a year ago. Then again, maybe not. Business was tough all over Winnebago.

"Ameryica iz nuut all crakeed up to bee," Yasu speculated out loud as he tossed the beef jerky jar into the garbage. Yes, a year had passed and he still hadn't sold one twisted stick of the brown shriveled stuff. The jar had begun to smell funny and Yasu's eyes would water whenever he would open the lid. Emotional? Perhaps. But Yasu wouldn't chance a lawsuit. Things were bad enough.

Yasu was studying an ant trail by the garbage bin out back when he noticed a large creeping shadow beside him on the asphalt. He glanced up and saw an unusually low cloud hanging directly over his head. With his head back, jaw slack, Yasu caught a raindrop in his mouth. It tasted metallic. Then, suddenly, the cloud released a raging downpour. You've heard of buckets of rain? This was barrels. Cats and dogs? Try hippos

What if Clouds were UFOs?

and buffaloes. Yasu splashed back to his store as the town of Winnebago was besieged by rising flood waters.

Flash floods were quite out of the ordinary in Winnebago, but even more odd was that all the rain seemed to be coming from a single cloud over Yasu Liberty's 7-Eleven. Not a mere drop of rain was falling over an area even a block away while the curtain of water surging from this one particular cloud was truly awe-inspiring, managing to flood twelve square miles.

The locals climbed onto their rooftops, up trees and telephone poles to safety. The general town alarm was sounded. (The wailing siren, which sounded like an enormous wounded coyote, was actually built in the fifties for nuclear bomb attacks and hadn't been used in years. So, for many this also meant the end of the world.)

The only one not concerned with the rising flood waters was Yasu Liberty. His store had been built at the highest point in town on the crest of a hill, created by the old garbage dump, so he was high and dry. Meanwhile, the rain pummeling the 7-Eleven's metal roof sounded like thunderous timpani.

And so it went for days.

Yasu remained safely locked in his convenience store. There was nowhere to go, and besides, he had snacks galore. He played Vigilante Justice for free, over and over, while munching nachos, barbecued pork rinds and root beer Slurpees.

The store soon became an island with an asphalt beach and light-post palm trees. Yasu was the self-proclaimed ruler of his island: "King Yasu of 7-Eleven."

A few locals swam to Yasu's dry asphalt shore. One tied his fishing skiff to one of Yasu's concrete parking lot palm trees. The townsfolk congregated in front of the 7-Eleven, having encountered a barricaded door and, as if that weren't enough, were verbally assaulted with, "Goy wey, yew not'tu cumin syde, shooo!"

They pleaded with Yasu, rationally at first, to let them inside. Then things turned ugly. But King Yasu would not unlock the door for anything. Where were they when his business was in trouble, "henh?"

One of the locals, Mel Lumers, an unemployed welder, scrambled to the garbage bin behind the store, dove in and shut the lid. He sat for a moment listening to the deluge outside before removing a plastic jar he was sitting on. He read the label with his penlight. It was a jar full of beef jerky. Mel loved jerky. He opened the lid and sniffed the contents. Smelled okay. Mel tore into a stick, and was savoring the sodium nitrate rush, when the dumpster lid opened and five other drenched townsfolk dove inside for shelter.

Mel, believing that his jar of jerky was all that stood between him and starvation, wasn't about to share one stick of the fuliginous steer muscle.

So, they simply beat him unconscious.

You might be thinking they all suffered severe stomach cramps from the jerky. Nope, they were fine. Only Mel got indigestion, but that was because he ate so fast before being pummeled.

At midnight, the hungry survivors stormed the 7-Eleven. But Yasu had boarded up the doors and windows and was safely scarfing Twinkies and Ho-Ho's (or as Yasu called them, "Yho Yho's") as fists madly pounded on the walls until dawn.

What if Clouds were UFOs?

Mercifully, by morning the rain stopped. The waterlogged survivors lay prone in the 7-Eleven parking lot, and by noon, the July humidity had created a giant crock-pot.

The cloud remained overhead while the Governor toured the flood damaged region finally declaring it a disaster area. Two days later, Yasu pushed Vigilante Justice away from the front door and exited, five pounds heavier.

Yasu squinted in the bright sunlight as the townsfolk glared at him with hangman's eyes. Meanwhile, overhead, the strange cumulus cloud sported a silver lining. Just as the townspeople were closing in, and Yasu pleaded, "Peas'yew'no'hurd'me'yah?!" he felt his spirits elevate. Actually, Yasu's whole body was elevating as he gazed down past his dangling shoelaces at the townspeople below, looting his 7-Eleven. So, there was no one to hear his cries as he was consumed by the cloud and, even if someone heard him, no one would have understood him.

Yasu was calmed by a cool mist caressing his flushed cheeks. Then . . . everything went white.

Oskaloosa, Iowa

Lindy Parks, an undergraduate at Iowa State, was preparing a research paper on "Stationary Atmospheric Disturbances in the Western Hemisphere." But Lindy wasn't the most dedicated of students and, at the moment of saturation over Yasu Liberty's 7-Eleven, she was embracing her French teacher in the dorm shower.

Later that afternoon, back at the university weather lab, Lindy was comparing a series of GOES-9 satellite photos when she noticed an anomaly. A single cumulus cloud had maintained a position over Winnebago, Nebraska for several days. In light of the fact that there had been a big high-pressure ridge over the Midwest for nearly a week, it indicated further investigation. But first, she had a lunch date with an El Nino researcher named Norm.

When she returned from lunch, full of lime Jello and insipid conversation, Lindy took her findings to her professor, Lionel Hemp. "Check out these reflectivities," she beamed to her professor who examined the satellite photos and was spellbound . . . with Lindy. She was clearly the best looking coed on campus. Though the professor had vowed to lay off the students this semester, this fresh scrubbed-sophomore was more than he could withstand.

"It's probably just a wave cloud," dismissed Hemp, though trying to sound encouraging.

"But it's nowhere near a mountain range," pouted Lindy, "Its microphysical characteristics are most definitely cumulus. I think we should take a sounding."

Hemp again studied the reflectivities and though he appeared engrossed by Lindy's discovery about the cloud . . . well, you know.

Professor Hemp picked at his bald crown then agreed to let Lindy revise her paper to include the mysterious cloud. Lindy was so intellectually and spiritually aroused that she stood on her tip-toes and kissed Hemp on his weak chin.

She was even more thrilled when Hemp stated he wanted to accompany her . . . to observe the phenomenon, first hand. Lindy could hardly breathe. Imagine, the famous Lionel Hemp accompanying her on a cloud expedition!

What if Clouds were UFOs?

Lionel Hemp's fame was tenuous at best. He had written only one book, actually a thesis paper, entitled, *Clouds, Clouds, Clouds . . . Lionel Hemp on Clouds*. Actually, it was more like an extensive pamphlet, which he printed at home and sold for ten ninety-five, before tax. Though it was required reading for his meteorology course, it had been pulled from college stores in '93, due to abysmal sales. But Lionel, unfazed, sold it directly to his students. Ten dollars and ninety-five cents times seventy students per class, times four classes a semester, two semesters a year for sixteen years and you get the idea. But in case you're bad on figures, that's $98,112.00 . . . before taxes.

The cloud, by the way, was in trouble. That's why it was on the run. The intention was never to call attention to itself. The Winnebago, Nebraska downpour was a modified re-creation of another downpour in Nebraska back in 1923. But in that catastrophe, several clouds had been at work, hence the miscalculation.

Le Mars, Iowa

The latest weather radar indicated that the cloud had moved one hundred and five miles northwest to the sleepy town of Le Mars.

The drive up had been rather uneventful. Professor Hemp could think of little to discuss with Lindy after the first hour of cloud chat, so he whistled "Rain Drops Keep Falling on my Head" for three and a half hours.

Lindy, on the other hand, was so excited she nearly wet her pants. The great Lionel Hemp, cloud physicist, author of international fame and fortune, seated right beside her. She would get an "A" for sure unless she somehow screwed up. The professor drove in feverish anticipation towards the research site, eager to get started, but for an entirely different objective.

When they arrived at the Le Mars Travelodge, Professor Hemp, in the interests of keeping a budget, had suggested staying in one room. But the motel desk clerk, one eyebrow cocked, suggested twin beds for the man and his "daughter" to which the professor gallantly replied, "Naturally."

In their room they unpacked in silence. It was late and they would get an early start in the morning. Lindy changed for bed, into a lace teddy, and slipped under the sheets.

Professor Hemp couldn't sleep. Was it the soapy smell of Lindy's smooth skin that so distracted him? Was she awake? Did she feel the same surging passion for him?

Hemp cleared his throat, several times, but this made him seem terribly self-conscious. No matter, Lindy was fast asleep so the professor quietly whistled "Rain Drops," while waiting for rapid eye movement.

Chirping birds . . . ravens?

Hemp parted his eyelids. The morning sun illuminated Lindy like an angel on a mattress of clouds. A sight so pure, so innocent and wicked at the same time, that Hemp actually whimpered. The professor hadn't slept a blink. He rubbed his crimson tinged eyes as Lindy pried out her retainer and caught the professor staring. From the gleam in his eye she knew that he held the same unbridled excitement for their mission as she did. Scientists on a quest for knowledge!

Lindy parted the curtains and lurched back as she saw a cloud directly outside their motel window.

What if Clouds were UFOs?

The professor was spellbound, as Lindy bent over the window frame in her ruffled teddy to study the cloud. Confronted with Lindy's lacy backside, Hemp could no longer control his hyperactive libido. He threw back the covers, leaped from the bed and made a mad dash towards Lindy as she, at that precise moment, shoved opened the window.

A delicate mist caressed Lindy's blushing cheeks, and two hands vigorously grasped her bottom, as she felt herself drawn out the window and into the cloud, dragging her professor behind.

Lindy turned around with a beautiful smile on her face as the professor Hemp enthusiastically squeezed her backside, apparently in an effort to hold on.

They disappeared into the cloud like two weather balloons.

Then, it was white. The brightest white you've ever seen. Pure, snowy, bleached Borax whiteness. You really had to squint up there and Lindy and the professor were doing just that. *If we only had some sunglasses,* thought Lindy, and miraculously their eyes were covered as if by Polaroid filters.

They could now see something imprinted in the fluffy white. Dimpled details, imperceptible outlines, *a moose? no,* features of creatures, *yes!* creatures with pockmarked faces, *yes!* a pockmarked moose . . . *or was it just their imaginations?*

The professor, terrified yet thrilled, kneaded Lindy's gluteus as he realized he had become the first scientist in history to walk inside a cloud.

They floated in the vapor, Lindy in her lacy teddy and Professor Hemp in his boxers and sock garters, grasping

Lindy's perky goose bumped bottom as the "Cloudites" engulfed them.

Naturally, communication with the Cloudites had always been rather difficult for earthlings. The closest to achieving communication in a millennium was Yasu Liberty, who accidentally managed a few syllables and the formation of the Cloudite word for "no mercy." They afforded him none.

The other reason communication was so impossible was that the nebulous Cloudites blended in so well with their surroundings, white on white, that you could hardly see them. And then again, what would you say if you did?

Lindy and Hemp had naturally figured they had died and gone . . . where dead people go. Hemp bleakly pictured the front page of the Iowa Sentinel featuring his soul-drained body mounted on top of Lindy's lingerie-draped corpse in the motel parking lot, with her icy bottom in his death grip.

And he was so close to tenure.

The professor also accurately concluded that *Clouds, Clouds, Clouds, Lionel Hemp On Clouds* would now become a best seller, as they often did with dead writers, and he would reap none of the ample profits.

Lindy, on the other hand, had no idea what to think. The first sensation, after the wondrously cool soothing mist, and the faint faces in the fog, was a pair of hands tightly clutching her buttocks. Hemp sheepishly detached his clammy palms for an instant, then quickly returned them. This was heaven, after all, and if he hadn't gone to hell yet, he never would. Lindy decided not to bother. At least this way he would stay close.

Lindy tentatively tip-toed across the cloud carpet, the professor in tow, disappearing into gentle whiteness. Their feet

What if Clouds were UFOs?

were firmly supported, but not by any known surface. It felt like walking on big fluffy hands.

The hands of the Cloudites.

"What's that?!" exclaimed Lindy as she stared down at a pile of what could be best described as large cow-pies, though actually, dried tissue and bone meal compressed into patties. Hemp reluctantly released Lindy's buttocks and leaned down to examine the mound which was as dry as a trash-compacted mummy.

"My God, it's . . . it's human!" exclaimed Hemp, noticing several other scrunched people-piles scattered about.

"What happened to them?" Lindy nervously inquired, on the verge of a whimper.

Hemp, always the professor, answered his eager pupil. "Well, Lindy, all their moisture has been removed. You see, the human body is approximately two-thirds water. This is what you would look like if you squeezed out all your liquid."

"Who would want our water?" Lindy innocently asked.

A horrified realization suddenly crossed Hemp's face, but it was too late as the strange dimpled cloud creatures moved in, and the sound of a giant cosmic "juicer" roared with a familiar atmospheric rumble.

Their screams were drowned by the sound of pre-recorded thunder.

A light rain began to sprinkle over the Le Mars Travelodge as a Voyager mini-van swerved into the parking lot. The large cloud completely blocked out the sun, turning afternoon into night as the Pinkertons managed to get their five children out of the mini-van without incident. After a nine hour cross-country trek, three of the siblings weren't speaking to one another. The children, four boys and a girl, ages three to nine, grabbed their small suitcases and dashed across the parking lot towards the motel entrance.

The rain began to pour as the family herded into the lobby of the Travelodge. The youngest, Beth, lagged behind outside to catch a few drops of rain in her opened mouth. Mrs. Pinkerton, realizing one of her flock was missing, ran back out of the lobby and grabbed her daughter's arm.

"Mommy, I tasted the rain people!" the little girl cheerfully informed her mother who tiredly sighed as she dragged her youngest inside.

The rain puddled in the parking lot as the sizable cloud slowly floated away, towards the countryside . . . and dropped what appeared to be two large cow-pies in a dewy pasture.

Killing Spree

Clive sat at the precipice, his bare feet dangling over the cliff's edge. The kill was still fresh in his mind as the sun rose to greet him. A rogue wave crashed against the rocks below sending a spray of salty ocean across his face. He closed his eyes as he sucked the spray into his nostrils.

The house sat a few yards behind him. A white Colonial tied like a Christmas package with dead vines. Not a whisper came from within. Clive relished the silence. It meant a sort of purity. Only the protests of the wind and the waves.

He hadn't known his victims. Never did. It wasn't his way. Easier to face yourself afterwards if they didn't call out your name.

Clive was what you might call a serial killer except that he never killed the same way twice. Most serial killers left an M.O., a calling card and ultimately a way to be caught. But for Clive, the thrill was in the variety. Thirty-one flavors of homicide.

He was an equal opportunity killer. Whites, Blacks, Hispanics, Asians, men and women, old and young. He couldn't understand how other serial killers stuck to one thing for so long, or until they were caught. Imagine only killing old ladies wearing hats, or plump little boys with reddish complexions. It's like eating the same thing every night of the week for years. No, Clive liked variety and that's what had kept him at it for so long. That and one other thing. Clive was completely sane.

Clive's reasons for killing were not caused by psychological disorder. Killing to Clive was "research." He simply wanted to watch one of everything die. Call it a hobby. A fascination with death, so to speak. While other kids were gluing airplane models together, Clive was gluing puppies together and tossing them in the lake to watch them drown. His parents eventually stopped keeping pets.

Clive had used hatchets, revolvers, ropes, poisons, and even fright to cause death. Some of his murders were as quick as a hat pin jammed through the eye socket, some as slow as dripping molasses down his victim's nose. But each murder was carefully planned so it felt like Clive's first. He might kill years after his last victim or with only hours in between.

Seven months ago, Clive had murdered a forty-two year old obese man and his sickly mother who had lung cancer and smoked through her tracheotomy. Clive simply snuck into their apartment late at night and turned on the gas. When she awoke, the first thing her obedient son did for her was to light her morning cigarette.

Six years earlier, Clive had smothered an infant in a baby buggy at a Thanksgiving parade, later attributed to crib death.

And, just thirty-six hours before that, Clive had shot a police officer with his own service revolver at an all night donut shop, which was recorded as a suicide.

All of these murders either remained in the unsolved files or were attributed to other criminals. Several men had been incarcerated for his murders and, in one instance, electrocuted. Such a volume of crime could not go unpunished, though even Clive would be surprised to learn that not a single detective was on his trail, so successful had he been. This was perhaps because even Clive's randomness was random. For instance, he once dismembered two cheerleaders in a week. One was a teenage girl and the other was a twenty-eight-year-old ex-Rams' cheerleader, who after an autopsy, turned out to be a transsexual. This one kept the detectives guessing.

Another wave crashed against the cliff. It suddenly felt colder, making Clive's bones ache. He rubbed his fist against his arthritic knee and watched a sailboat cross the horizon. It had been a winning streak of sixty years for Clive. Forty-nine kills and not a day spent in prison. He should feel good.

He did.

But it was getting harder and harder to keep his kills random, to not develop a pattern that was traceable. In the house presently behind him, for example, were two recently deceased men, one black, one white, living together as lesbians. Clive had found them over the internet in a sadomasochism chat room. He tracked them to their remote home in Northern California, overlooking a cliff, where they would play their kinky bondage games in privacy. This, regrettably, was their undoing, for Clive was able to kill them over several days, chained in their soundproof dungeon.

Clive had painstakingly pierced them with knitting needles, shish kebab skewers, wood screws, hat pins, toggle bolts, diaper pins, and gaffer hooks. He watched them writhe and shudder in a blend of agony and erotic pleasure as they slowly bled to death. One of the men ejaculated as he died.

Clive shivered as the fog rolled in . . . or was it just the pleasure of the memory?

He rose on his trembling limbs and teetered on the brink, his long white hair blowing. Clive closed his eyes, leaned back his head and curled his toes over the edge of the cliff, flirting with death. He felt dizzy. His body swayed forward, the sea beckoning to him, a cold coffin of silence.

He took a deep breath, turned, and walked back to the main road. Moments later, a flatbed truck full of partying fraternity boys pulled over, without Clive even sticking out his thumb, and offered the "old geezer" a ride.

Clive got in and had a plastic cup of beer with them.

The newspapers the following morning would indicate that the seven drunken boys drove over the cliff in the fog, making this the worst year in Sarasota County history for drunk driving fatalities.

There was no mention of a frail old man with long white hair and a pleasant smile.

Wrong Hole
Another "Raoul, Low-life Ex-Cop" Adventure

Raoul clawed to consciousness face down on a dank concrete floor. The cement smelled of disinfectant which masked a horrible odor underneath, like a breath mint tossed into a sewer. Raoul had no idea where he was, or how the hell he got there, but the cement floor cradling his forehead was an encouraging sign. At least he had made it to the ground already.

Less encouraging was Raoul's disturbing notion that perhaps all that was left of him was a severed head and that these thoughts were the last lingering impulses of his dying brain cells.

Raoul attempted to move his cranium, to see if it was still attached to his spinal column, but his forehead felt Crazy Glued to the concrete.

Calling forth his detective skills and ancient Indian instincts (he was one-quarter Zuni) Raoul detected vibrations on the floor with his forehead and determined that a large man with a limp was approaching. It didn't hurt his hypothesis any that at that moment a size thirteen motorcycle boot limped onto his earlobe and a raspy voice boomed, "Wake up, asshole, I gotta take a piss."

This engaging pronouncement was followed by the chitter of laughter in the background.

The picture was getting clearer . . . and it wasn't pretty.

Raoul was fairly confident that he was the one being addressed—since "asshole" had become his nickname of late.

Raoul rolled his bleary eyes sideways but couldn't see anything besides the enormous black storm trooper boot. Oh, there was one other thing. Raoul noticed on the floor near the metal toe of the boot a bloody, dislodged molar . . . and it didn't appear to have been left by the tooth fairy. Raoul refocused his eyes on the bit of bone and determined that it wasn't a molar at all, but rather, a front tooth, reluctantly wrenched from the socket, gum attached. Raoul momentarily felt sorry for the poor slob who had his front tooth knocked out until he inadvertently rolled his tongue across his front chompers and felt a space the size of an aircraft hanger.

Things were looking *iffy*. He could only hope that this was just an eighty-proof dream and he was lying safely in some alley comfortably asleep on a pillow of his own vomit.

Raoul was just beginning to hum, "All I want for Christmas" when a boot slammed between his ribs. Raoul stopped humming. Instead, he groaned and rolled onto his back, eyes clenched.

"I said, WAKE UP!" growled the boot man, "I gotta piss the Mississippi."

Wrong Hole

Again the insane chitter of laughing hyenas. Was he in a loony asylum? Certainly not out of the realm of possibility.

"Wake up, PIG!" again urged the voice.

Pig? echoed Raoul in his head. Was he in some sort of horrible sixties flashback? Raoul slowly peeked his eyes from under their lids and gazed up the trunk of a Paul Bunyan size figure towering over him, his uncircumcised pecker hanging down like an advertisement for a Genoa sausage factory. Raoul noted that it was the only morsel of flesh left untattooed on the six foot seven giant. Not much artistry to these skin scrapings either: a gargantuan-jugged senorita sucking on a Mescal worm; a skull in a Nazi helmet with a dagger plunged through the eye socket; a hangman's noose (tattooed around his thick neck); and, Raoul's personal favorite, Porky Pig, wearing a police uniform, its cute pink head being blown off by a sawed-off shotgun.

Raoul was distracted from the tawdry tattoo gallery by another crunching kick to his side. Did he need to be conscious for this?

Fortunately, Raoul had been in this situation countless times before, only he was usually the one doing the pummeling. Over his nineteen years on the force Raoul was regarded as the most *influential* interrogator. But that was before his rap sheet of sin and premature retirement sans pension.

Back in the "good ol' days" Raoul routinely played "bad cop;" but on several occasions even Raoul knew that he had crossed over the line, working out his frustrations between gym days.

Raoul, trembling with Tequila, lifted his head and for the first time observed the iron stripes of cell bars to his left.

When the hell did he wind up back in the drunk tank? Then he remembered, he had been zonked for the last six years. Anything was possible. That's what kept the magic alive.

"Remember me, shithead?" asked the motorcycle boots occupant.

"Or me?" inquired another raspy voice.

Oh God, thought Raoul, *there's more than one?* What was this, his twentieth fucking low-life reunion?

Raoul heard a sigh like a frat boy at a keg party and a nanosecond later felt a torrent of steamy, Coors-tinted liquid gush onto his head.

"Ahhhhh," exhaled the beer-bellied biker.

Raoul, sputtering with urine, his eyes burning with piss, curled into a fetal position on the floor seeking refuge in his belly button. But there was no escape from this hell. Not yet, at least. But Raoul was a patient man.

Suddenly, Raoul was lifted like a piece of lost luggage and hurled at the tiled wall of the communal cell by the "Amazing Pissing Ape Man."

Raoul tentatively opened his eyes, but the room was spinning like a Disneyland teacup.

Gradually, the spinning slowed and Raoul was able to fix on the inflamed eyes of his tormentor. It was Logan, the lead rider with the San Bernardino chapter of the Flying Rats in the early seventies. Raoul had once put him away for a quarter stretch for trafficking, armed assault and bank robbery. But he pleaded it to a dime and only served a nickel, and you know how cons are with change in their pocket.

"Refreshed after your shower?" smirked Logan.

Two scumbag sidekicks, grabbing splinters on a wood bench, again evilly chuckled.

Wrong Hole

Raoul, who had a knack for recalling mugs, recognized the jaundiced face of a skin-pop performance artist on the bench. He looked vaguely familiar, but Raoul was distracted by the S.O.S. desperately pounding at his temples.

What he would give for a taste of Early Times.

"You've put on some weight, Logan. Did you eat your Harley?" stated Raoul, cool as he could muster.

The jail cohorts snickered, approving Raoul's wisecrack, until Logan shot them a molten stare.

"You used to be a big shot cop, didn't you?" taunted Logan, shaking the droplets off his shriveled member.

"Detective," Raoul proudly corrected, trying to avoid the biker's dribblings.

"Whatever," spat the motorcycle outlaw, "but look at *you* now; you're a burned out bum; you're nothin'."

"That's why we're in the same cell," calmly retorted Raoul. "Nothings of a feather . . . flock together."

Raoul two. Logan zero.

"Oh, we're going to flock all right . . . one at a time," the biker lecherously whispered, then began a belly laugh which made his stretched-marked stomach tattoos dance an impromptu lambada.

The biker's new-found buddies cackled right along and Raoul was beginning to think he might make it out of this mess when he heard a fly unzip.

"You know what happens to pigs in here, pig?" grinned the Neanderthal.

"They go to market?" offered Raoul.

The big bad wolf wasn't laughing.

Raoul tried to shake the movie *Deliverance*, but it was hopeless, especially the squealing part.

He recalled as a rookie getting a tour of state prison and witnessing amorous cell mates jerking each other off like zoo monkeys. It wasn't a pretty sight.

Raoul was rapidly sobering up, like getting an IV drip from an industrial percolator. He checked the opposition. There were three of them and half of him. All of them he had laid on pretty heavy at one time or another at Metro. Now they were "bunk mates."

Ah, the yin and yangs.

"On your knees, piggy, piggy," said one of the voices, the others guffawing in the background like Goofy in a triple-X, B&D leather loop.

"Sorry, you're not my type, amigo," offered Raoul to Logan, adding, "Maybe if you didn't look like the tattooed fat lady from a freak show"—Raoul knew his mouth could get him into deep water, but it could also buy him some time, at least to find religion.

"You're funny, cop," smiled the biker; then, with deadly seriousness, "but 'funny' gets you dead in here. This is our world and you're in the wrong . . . fucking . . . place."

Raoul couldn't agree more and got up to leave but was persuaded to stay by the big Mahuna who unceremoniously shoved him to his knees.

Desperate, Raoul decided to keep talking.

"Now I remember," stuttered Raoul, "I booked you for purse snatching from old ladies."

The others laughed until the tattooed gorilla shot them a look that would have made Manson shiver.

"Bank robbery, asshole," informed the biker, trying to regain his stature in front of the peanut gallery.

Wrong Hole

"Sure, now you tell me," said Raoul. "Seems you were a little more reluctant back then."

"You shotgunned that teller real good, didn't you?" interjected the spaced out crack head as Logan glared. Raoul could now I.D. one of the faces on the bench. It was Ray "the fist" Stitches, a three time loser who was Logan's sergeant-at-arms back with the Rats. But he had lost about thirty pounds and a hunk of his ear since Raoul had last seen him in a line-up.

"Shut up!" Logan snarled at Stitches. "I was never charged with that, you brain-dead fuck."

Raoul was relishing the moment. The ranks were beginning to mutiny.

Logan waved it off, "No matter, I made bail. You couldn't hold me on nothing," chided Raoul's nemesis, as he moved uncomfortably closer.

"You don't look so *out* to me," prodded Raoul, "except maybe the closet. What have they got you in this time for this time . . . breaking and entering your buddies?"

The cronies didn't laugh this time.

Logan was close enough now that Raoul could smell his meth breath. The biker stank of all night bars and infected women.

As did Raoul.

"Line up, boys . . . it's luau time!" sang out the tattooed ringleader.

The others moved in, licking their chapped lips and unbuckling their jeans, as Raoul, still feeling the affects of an all-nighter, did the only thing he could do. He puked.

It worked. They backed off, momentarily.

But then Logan dragged Raoul by his ponytail over to the toilet and thrust his face into the steel bowl.

"Oops, forgot to flush," confessed Logan, feigning embarrassment, as he dunked Raoul's several times.

The highly decorated detective was drowning in the bowl as the others ripped down his pants over his pale, pimpled butt. Raoul knew what was coming next: Squeeeeeeeeeeel!!!!

"All clean, Mr. Piggy?" Raoul heard Logan say. "Here comes Porky."

Raoul, somehow, summoned a reserve of inner strength and fury which arose from a straight man about to be gang-buggered.

Zero to sixty in seven seconds.

He suddenly became a caged animal, ready to claw his way through their guts to escape. He violently swung his head backwards from the toilet bowl, head-butting his amorous adversary in his Viagra groin which snapped like a stale breadstick.

Logan fell to his knees, groaning, as Raoul leaped up, elbows and knees flying like a Jackie Chan movie.

The other inmates, caught with their pants around their ankles, were easy targets for Raoul who wanted to inflict as much pain as possible, so even if he lost, they would kill him before they fucked him.

But that wouldn't happen as two corrections officers, one in his fifties, sporting a grey crew cut, and another in his twenties, raced down the Central Jail hallway. The senior C.O. turned on a fire hose located outside the cell and sprayed the battling occupants.

"Shut up, you filthy scum," barked the older officer at the caged animals, "I'm trying to watch the Laker playoffs." But, as he turned off the hose, he suddenly recognized one of the inmates.

"Raoul," said the older officer, astonished, "is that you?"

Raoul staggered to the bars, face bloodied, tooth missing, but relieved to see his old 43rd precinct desk sergeant, Mike Garber.

"Garb, get me the fuck out of here!" barely articulated Raoul, breathless.

"What the hell are you doing *in* there?" asked Garber incredulously.

Raoul, gasping for breath finally managed to say, "You tell me."

The retired cop unlocked the cell door while Martin, the doe-eyed trainee, observed.

As Raoul staggered out, Garber took one whiff and cringed. "Jesus, Raoul, you look horrible . . . and smell like shit."

"Thanks, I've been on vacation."

Garber locked the cell door behind Raoul who was still out of breath but managed to sputter, "The ape . . . with the broken pork-sword . . . He wasted a guy in eighty-three . . . bank job, name's Logan, look it up."

"Sure, sure. Will do," nodded Garber, propping up Raoul with his shoulder.

"Thanks, Garb," said Raoul, adding, "you literally saved my ass."

Raoul's old pal from metro was still shaking his head in disbelief as he helped Raoul down the hall towards the infirmary. "They're not supposed to put cops in the tank with the general pop."

Just then, Raoul tripped and fell from exhaustion. The two hacks helped him to his feet.

"You're looking at one hell of a detective," Garber informed the trainee. "One of L.A.'s finest."

The rookie glanced at Raoul, then at his partner like he must be nuts.

"Someone has it in for you, buddy," Garber warned Raoul, adding, "Someone upstairs." Garber gestured with his head towards the administrative offices on the fifth floor.

Raoul, cradling his broken ribs, looked heavenward and nodded in agreement, "I know what you mean, Garb . . . I know what you mean."

TWISTER SISTERS

"Heaven has no rage like love to hatred turned,
Nor hell a fury, like a woman scorned."
(William Congreve, the Mourning Bride III. viii)

Seems a twenty mile radius of Oklahoma farmland, south of the Cimarron River, northwest of the border town of Texhoma and the Beaver River, had the distinction of more tornadoes than anywhere else in the world—two thousand eight hundred and seventy-seven since meteorologists recorded such events back to 1861. A fifth of these had occurred in just the last few years, courtesy of El Nino's increased moisture and tornadic storms. Cold fronts and warm air masses collided with regularity in this weather vortex resulting in a dark ceiling of ominous cumulonimbus clouds, the evil harbinger of nasty events to come.

The locals had given up naming each twister by the cities and counties they touched down in, instead settling on two recurring females: "Nicky" and "Nellie." Both sisters were capable of great violence. Nicky was a land spout about a tenth of a mile wide and scraped along the ground like an arthritic finger. Nellie was an unforgiving F-3 tornado, an eighth mile wide at her swirling black root, inhaling everything in her temperamental path.

This turbulent territory, christened "Tornado Alley," was uninhabitable, by most. But there are those who will not evacuate their land under any circumstance. Brave defiant souls, who stand on their roofs hosing during a fire, or sandbagging against a rising river, or toasting champagne at a hurricane party amidst ninety mile per hour winds.

The Pinadels were just such a family. They defiantly clung to their meager plot of land for three generations, isolating themselves in the soil-stripped territory like the last Apache against the wave of the white man, surviving on a precarious jetty of Oklahoma farmland bordered by Colorado, Kansas, Texas, and New Mexico, called the Panhandle.

Instead of retreating along with the other farm families, Tyler Pinadel, an admittedly stubborn ex-Marine, who's leathery face had weathered right along with his old barn, had decided to stay put. Tyler wasn't one given easily to surrender, preferring adaption to desertion, subsequently building his families lives around the unpredictable fury of refugee wind and the calm after the storm.

Tyler's wife, Connie, an attractive blond with a cool disposition, earned her nickname "The Ice Princess," as a locked-kneed cheerleader at St. Mary's High School. She was just an army-brat Colonel's daughter when she first laid eyes on Tyler during his basic training. Two years later they married. Recently, however, Tyler's failed dreams of a prosperous farm, and his decision to "tough it out," while others fled, had caused Connie to reconsider her life with him.

She was already feeling the strain of her thirteen year marriage when she discovered Tyler's affair with Sally, a farm neighbor's wife, permanently etching scowl lines at the corners of her sullen mouth. She never confronted Tyler about the five month affair or even raised her voice to him; but it was always there, a cancer growing on their marriage.

Connie would always remember when the affair ended, because they were awakened the next day by the unforgettable sound of a hundred approaching freight trains. They peeked through the bedroom curtains that fateful morning and saw Nicky dangling from the clouds on her dark spiral rope, playfully vacuuming Tyler's cornfield like a Hoover. As Nicky skipped toward the house, Tyler rounded up his teenage son, Kevin, and daughter Jessie, nine, and took them to the shelter while Connie raced to the nursery for baby Caroline.

Tyler waited for Connie as Nicky grew into a furious funnel of destruction, grinding her turbulent teeth on the Pinadels white picket fence, spitting out the pine boards like toothpicks.

At the last moment, Connie, pale, holding only a pair of baby booties, ran out of the house and into the shelter. But the twister's vengeful howls could not drown out Connie's uncontrollable sobs. Baby Caroline, just six-months-old, had been sucked through the window of her nursery, leaving behind only a pair of pink crocheted baby booties.

Nellie touched down and joined Nicky, lifting the farmhouse roof and tossing it like a Frisbee across the plains. Then, they swayed off, satisfied to take baby Caroline, along with Tyler's tractor, harvester and truck. All that was left was the foundation and the lingering smells of wet mud and snapped pine filling the rain-washed air.

That night, the eerie glare of searchlights illuminated the battlefield which was once their town.

At dawn, as pick-up trucks piled with furniture lined the roads, Tyler saw for the last time the willowy redhead with whom he had his affair. There was a pained longing in Sally's pretty green eyes as she glanced at Tyler from the passenger window of her husband's flatbed.

Connie met Sally's stare and tightened her arm around her husband.

Just then, a cloud cast a shadow over Sally's face, her green eyes seeming to glow with betrayal at Tyler, who had whispered breathlessly in her ear, on more than one occasion, how he would leave his wife for her.

Tyler and Connie solemnly watched the trucks, piled with memories, disappear into the dusty haze. Connie then slowly turned away from Tyler and walked back to pick through the remnants of their shattered farmhouse.

As the moon rose in a peaceful sky, Tyler, Kevin and Jessie sifted through the rubble. Connie sat on the porch, the farmhouse absent behind her, as she numbly stroked the pair of pink knitted baby booties.

Tyler, meanwhile, turned his frustration into action. The next morning he began enlarging their storm shelter, which was currently the only roof over their heads. Kevin joked that they were now living like gophers and this put Tyler to thinking. It took weeks of digging and the help of his husky freckle-faced son, who wished he had kept his mouth shut about the gophers; but they finally built a series of connecting tunnels under their farm, reinforced with the wood from their demolished home and barn. Jessie helped, too, keeping a lookout for funnel clouds while comforting her Orphan Annie doll. Connie just sat on the porch not saying much except calling them in for meals, made from an assortment of fruits and vegetables she had canned in Ball jars and kept in the cellar in neatly lined rows.

The tornado sisters, Nicky and Nellie, had not forgotten their pals the Pinadels. They patiently waited, sometimes dipping their heads below the clouds for a peek. But it was too dry for them to make a proper visit.

Then, nearly a month after the town's mass exodus, moist air breathed life back into the sisters. Tyler and his family nervously watched the simmering skies as Nellie and Nicky toyed with them, popping down in the southeast, then in the northwest, moving closer and closer.

Finally, Nicky pulled the drain over the Pinadel farm, swirling downward in a powerful whirlpool. Nellie followed, descending from the heavens on her dark spiral ladder. The mad spinning sisters pounded and clawed the earth above the Pinadels hideaway, but when they couldn't breach their underground fortress, they finally retreated for another day.

Amazingly, family life continued on in this parched and hostile countryside, Tyler and Connie doing their best to raise and educate their two surviving children and, though their quarters were uncomfortably confined, the children mostly behaved themselves.

Survival, to say the least, was precarious. Hunger grew in the Pinadel's bellies as they were forced to ration their jars of food. But, the family once again adapted, developing their own unique farming technique. Beneath each row of vegetables planted on the surface was a tunnel. When the twisters were spotted, each family member would crawl down their assigned tunnels and yank the "vegetable pulleys" (strings connected to a rope which, when pulled, would dislodge the vegetables and drop them in the tunnels). After the thwarted sisters spun into the distance, and the air had settled, the Pinadels would surface for replanting.

But the fresh vegetables and canned food were not enough to get them through the fall and Tyler knew he had better make the journey into Boise City before things got worse. He had all but given up listening to the Weather Service for tornado warnings but he now tuned in religiously, waiting for the right moment to make the trip to town. When the radio began to grow faint, Tyler put in their last two batteries and, over the protests of his wife, prepared to make the sixteen mile journey to Boise City.

The following morning there was not a cloud in the sky. Tyler taped the transistor radio to the handlebars of Kevin's Vespa motor scooter, the only mode of transportation left after the twister's shoplifting spree.

Tyler figured that at forty miles per hour, the motor scooter's top speed, plus shopping and getting gasoline, it would be less than a three hour trip. He filled a backpack with their remaining fresh vegetables from the farm to trade at the general store, pecked Connie on the cheek and then solemnly wobbled off on the Vespa, obviously too large a man for the small scooter. Kevin and Jessie stifled their laughs as they watched their father sputter down the dusty road, his knees poking out like chicken wings.

The trip northeast was uneventful. Not a car passed on highway 56. At one point Tyler swerved around a pothole and nearly fell off, cussing, but otherwise things went as well as he could have hoped.

But within the time Tyler had traveled to Boise City, pop. 1,793, a supercell appeared in the sky and dropped a widows peak. Tyler didn't hear the Weather Service warning on his radio because he was already inside Cooper's General Store, grabbing items off the shelves: batteries, candles, a box of Blue Tip matches, canned food, a box of rice, a bag of flour, sugar, and Band-Aids. He bartered with Willie the owner, using the carrots and onions he had harvested. But when it became clear that he was still short, Tyler noticed Willie staring at his Marine watch. Connie had bought the Timex at the PX as a gift for Tyler after he completed basic training.

Tyler, wearing his stuffed backpack, walked out of the general store counting out two tens, a five and five ones, while Willie, back behind the counter, gazed at the Marine watch with all the neat dials on his hairy wrist.

Tyler drove the Vespa into the gas station and waited what seemed a lifetime as a Bazooka gum-blowing attendant, with a name tag reading: Buck Dudder, perused a heavy metal comic book. Tyler walked over slapped his hand down, closing the comic book. The pimple-faced attendant stared into the eyes of the unsmiling ex-Marine, then ran over and turned on the pump with his key.

Tyler was filling his tank and listening to the tornado warning on the radio while Buck nervously peered skyward and then flipped over the small sign in the station door to "closed." The gas jockey didn't even wait to be paid as he tore away in his Chevy Impala.

As the wind began to wickedly whip across the valley, Tyler checked his wrist and remembered he no longer had a watch.

Back at the farm, Connie anxiously studied the sky and scanned the plains. Her anxiety grew as she saw a funnel developing in the distance.

Nicky easily spotted the scooter sputtering down the highway. She twirled down like a dark dagger and trailed a few miles behind Tyler's Vespa. Soon Nellie dropped in a few miles in front of Tyler. There was nowhere for Tyler to go as he stopped his motor scooter, his escape cut off from both directions . . . with the sisters rapidly closing the gap.

Before he could contemplate a plan, Tyler was yanked skyward, tightly clutching the handlebars of the Vespa. He released the scooter which hovered beside him, swirling around Nicky's belly. The transistor radio gyrated past Tyler's head as he heard the Weather Service reporting a tornado watch.

Tyler felt like he was on the "centrifuge" thrill-ride at the amusement park where the floor suddenly drops out but you keep spinning around and around. Only at this moment there was, thankfully, no one shouting, "Wanna go faster?!" Nevertheless, Tyler was sufficiently nauseous and almost grateful when Nellie missed the hand-off to Nicky, dropping

Tyler onto the forgiving branches of a weeping willow tree. But like a lineman recovering the fumble, Nicky scooped Tyler out of the branches and carried him another sixty yards before losing her grip.

Tyler crashed to the earth, holding his breath amidst the turbulence, his eyes squeezed tightly shut. The sisters soon lost sight of Tyler and climbed back above the clouds.

As the debris settled, Tyler was nowhere in sight. Then a pile of dirt moved and Tyler extricated himself, struggled to his feet, and plucked a bloody pebble from his forehead. He was miraculously only bruised, though his ankle was fiercely throbbing. As Nicky and Nellie spun into the distance, Tyler limped towards home, past Kevin's motor scooter neatly folded in thirds.

It was nearing dusk when Kevin spotted Tyler about two miles north. Kevin called for his mom who peered through his Spiderman periscope and spotted Tyler hobbling home. While Connie went to meet him halfway, Kevin waited back at the shelter with his sister, scanning the horizon for the vengeful, headstrong females, who could drop from the heavens on a whim.

Tyler, the weathered cracks in his face filled with dirt, appreciatively leaned on Connie's shoulder as she reached him and noticed his swollen ankle which had blossomed into a blood orange.

Kevin, meanwhile, spotted Nicky sneaking along the horizon and hollered to his parents who were too far away to hear his shouts, drowned out by the eagerly approaching winds.

Tyler had also spotted the spout and now jogged alongside Connie on his sprained ankle, grimacing with every painful step as Nicky screamed furiously behind. The sky rumbled and golf ball size chunks of hail, (the "white plague" farmers called it), were spit out by Nicky as if from a pitching machine, pelting Tyler and Connie as they high-tailed it back to the shelter.

The family huddled together while Nicky, in a testy mood, decided to stay a spell. Connie prayed to the Lord as Nicky ruthlessly howled, sending dust into the storm shelter. The Pinadels desperately gasped for air through burlap masks that Tyler had cut from a potato sack. Finally, Connie leaped up and screamed towards the ceiling of the shelter, "Leave us alone!"

Moments later, the wind died.

Tyler and his family climbed out of their tunnel, gulping fresh air as the dust settled.

Connie gazed at the orange and pink sunset, her white streaked hair blowing gently across her forehead as Tyler, favoring his bad ankle, slipped beside her and placed an arm over her bony shoulder. They stood there for a time saying nothing, but both realizing what they had to do.

In an hour they were packed. It was fairly humid and the sky full of questionable clouds, but now was as good a time as any.

Each family member carried a personal item and a container of water for their journey. Kevin brought his Spiderman periscope. Jessie cradled her tattered Orphan Annie doll. Connie tied the pink booties around her neck and Tyler carried Kevin's knapsack with an extra two quarts of water and their three remaining jars of food.

The rising sun was blocked out by a simmering cloud ceiling as the Pinadels cut a path northwest towards Highway 64. Tyler figured they'd hitch a ride to Boise City and get a motel room for the night with his last thirty-eight dollars. But the highway was deserted.

Kevin soon spotted a funnel cloud, thankfully headed away from them and towards the direction of their farm.

The fleeing family watched over their shoulders as Nellie drilled the earth over the Pinadel hideaway, joined by Nellie who dropped from the sky like a spider spinning a dark web of wind.

The swirling siblings took turns spelling each other off until they drilled a hole into the Pinadel's underground shelter. Burrowing deeper and deeper into the tunnels they futilely searched for Tyler and his family, their brutal anger compounding.

Tyler and his family watched safely from the distance, hypnotized by the strange beauty of the writhing sirens. But Tyler knew that the sisters would soon find them and he picked up the pace over the protests of his swollen ankle.

Just then, a grain truck came speeding down the highway and Tyler and his family waved it down from the middle of the road. The trucker seemed reluctant to stop, but he finally applied the brakes and said, "Hop in."

They all piled together into the cab of the semitrailer, Kevin on Tyler's lap, Jessie on Connie's lap.

"What are you folks doing out here, didn't you hear the news?" inquired the truck driver as he nervously peeked out the windshield towards the brooding sky.

303

"What news?" asked Tyler as he gazed out the window and noticed two bodies dangling from the tree branches along the road like rotting ornaments. Connie covered Jessie's eyes as they drove past and said a silent prayer for the dead.

The driver turned up the radio as the Weather Service reported that Boise City had been decimated by a pair of twisters.

Kevin immediately checked out the side windows for spouts. As the freight truck sped down the highway, Jessie chatted with her Orphan Annie, telling her wide-eyed doll to "be brave."

Dusk painted the valley in purple hues as they surged past the leveled Boise City and sped down the 325 towards New Mexico. Connie silently prayed as a once gentle wind began to push the side of the truck with a strong hand.

Suddenly, Nicky dropped down in front of the truck and the driver hit the brakes.

"Holy cow," hollered the driver as he put the truck in reverse, then saw Nellie drop down in his rearview mirror. He slammed on the brakes and jumped out of the truck's cab, yelling, "You folks are on your own!"

The sisters easily chased down the terrified truck driver and vacuumed him up like a wheat straw on spin cycle as the Pinadels gazed out the windows in horror.

Tyler started up the big rig and steered it off-road towards the Black Mesa cliffs, careening through cactus. Halfway there, the truck bounced into a river bed. The truck's tires hopelessly spun in the mud.

"Everybody out!" shouted Tyler as the sisters roared closer, "We'll head for the cliffs, maybe there're some caves we can hide in!," continued Tyler over the thundering wind.

Connie yelled something back but Tyler couldn't hear her as she ran alongside.

The two twisters were now heading straight for the truck, their funnels crossing paths and then merging into a single, colossal wedge tornado—awesome, perverted power of which Tyler could never have imagined.

"Nora," the mother of all tornadoes, was over a half mile wide with bolts of lightning illuminating her muscular womb. And the sound!—like a thousand cellos strumming a bass moan, while a thousand violins frantically sawed a soprano shriek.

The sky rumbled as the coupled sisters—now Nora—lifted the eighteen-wheeler and tossed it like a shot-put towards Black Mesa and the escaping Pinadels.

"Don't look back," yelled Tyler to his children as the huge truck crashed a hundred yards to their side.

The Pinadels, racing for the rock caves, were easy pickings for Nora who cut around Black Mesa and rolled along the bluff, her immense stem seemingly as wide as an atomic mushroom cloud.

Tyler spotted a small cave in the cliff face which might be big enough for Kevin and Jessie to squeeze into, if they could just get there before Nora's enormous rotating funnel.

Just as they reached the cave opening, Jessie screamed as her Orphan Annie doll was pulled from her tiny grasp and flew into the sky like Peter Pan.

"It's okay, honey," assured Connie as she steered Jessie towards the cave, "she's going to heaven."

Jessie bravely nodded as Tyler lifted her into the cave, joining her brother in the blackness.

"Take care of your sister," rasped Tyler through his burlap mask, as Kevin nodded.

With not a moment to spare, Tyler grabbed Connie's cold hand and raced with her down the trail, his ankle shooting electric bolts of pain up his leg.

Nora muscled between the cliffs, biting off boulders, swinging her hips as she gyrated. Connie and Tyler took one glance back as Nora orbited over the opening to the cave, certain their children were inhaled into the monstrous whirlpool.

Connie let go of Tyler's hand and turned to face the colossal cone of prehistoric fury. "NOOO! TAKE ME!" she screamed

Tyler, his eyes red with dust, yelled, "NO, I'M THE ONE YOU WANT! TAKE ME!"

Nora studied the fearless couple for a moment, then, happy to oblige, surged towards them.

Connie and Tyler's eyes met. Connie suddenly recalled the book, *The Prophet*, and the aphorism by Kahlil Gibran, "Love knows not its depth until the hour of separation," as she felt Caroline's pink baby booties tugging around her neck, lifting towards the sky.

A blinding wave of dust separated Tyler from her vision and like a dream, he was gone.

Beneath a sunset of nuclear tones, silhouettes traversed the horizon, surrendering to night. Not a cloud in the sky.

In the clear air, beneath a field of stars, Kevin and Jessie gazed across the peaceful plains at the deserted farmlands below.

A single tear pushed a mud slide down Connie's cheek. Her tongue caught the salty tear, but it didn't come close to satisfying her thirst.

The three silhouettes continued along Black Mesa towards New Mexico as evening cooled the valley, the moon painted it blue and the wind . . . finally died.

6

GRENETTA ... QUEEN OF LOYNS

The queen dipped her plume pen in warm blood, moonlight casting sinister shadows across the cold stone walls of her chamber. Grenetta poured her sorrow onto the papyrus pages of her diary until the sun nudged the moon to sleep. She wrote of clandestine romance and lost loves. Admittedly, she had disposed of her suitors like a murderous black widow; nevertheless, they still came ... like bloodhounds on a criminal scent.

Unbeknownst to the queen, on that very night a tremendous army was amassing across the Forbidden River of Sludge and Muck—a thousand Rebel Crackers desiring a crack at the queen.

The chief Cracker was a giant named Throck, a rather hairy individual lacking evolution and hygiene, who claimed to have once bedded Queen Grenetta and survived. According to

Throck, he had drugged the queen with "twitch root" then had his animalistic, hairy way with her and escaped before she came to her senses. One of the reasons the tall tale was so widely disputed was the unreliability of Throck, who would also tell how he could fly . . . if he had a running start.

On the outskirts of Loyns was a semi-magical village of overweight hermaphrodites—sprawling individuals of questionable morals, and their guru founder Von Von, who loathed the queen with unparalleled venom. While Throck and the Crackers desired the queen for their carnal follies, Von Von had other plans. For someday, he dreamed . . . he would be queen.

The Festival of Fools was two days away. This was, more or less, a happy occasion with games for the toddlers, like pin the nose on the leper, and jousts to the death for the townspeople.

The queen's advisors had warned her to stay clear of the festival because of rumors that Throck would be on the march on the first of March, and since Grenetta was in heat at this time, her army would have a terrible time holding back the Crackers, whose libido reacted to this sort of thing like maggots on a mound of manure. Not, a pleasant sight.

In the tiny town of West Gurney an archival librarian named Slim was checking the card catalogs for dust balls. Slim was a rail of a man with oversized ears and a small pot-belly which two hundred daily sit-ups couldn't flatten. Nevertheless, he was a good man with hungers beyond the halls of hallowed knowledge—hungers which a good book couldn't thwart.

Grenetta... Queen of Loyns

Slim stopped dusting. He peeked around to make sure he was alone before reaching in his coat pocket and quietly removing a small knitted sack with a pull string.

Out of the sack Slim took a tiny wooden box. Trembling, he pried open the box and removed a red velvet bag. He opened the bag and pulled out a single golden ticket. On the ticket were inscribed the words: Admit One Fool to the Festival of Fools. Slim giggled like a schoolgirl as he slipped the ticket back in the bag... the box... the sack.

The harmonic tones of the sheep bladder announced the commencement of the Festival of Fools. The pungent odors of deep-fried follicles, steamed land crabs and sizzling blood boils wafted through the air. Bright colored banners and decorative spears with skulls stuck on them adorned the royal courtyard. The queen, who usually appeared to make a brief statement before the slag races, had not yet made her entrance, and rumors spread like the plague.

The queen was actually in the bath being luxuriously pampered by her slaves. Milk of eel was mixed with the powder of infertile antelope horns and massaged into her translucent skin. Her corkscrew fingernails were painted with the various blood types of male virgins as her scalp was rubbed with the residue of fruited newts. After the bath, she was patted dry with rose petals and gowned in a pearly robe of sea roaches.

All the servants were compelled by law to avert their eyes from the dazzling queen as she entered her antechamber, and the few eunuchs who dared sneak a peak of her loveliness were blinded on the spot with her spiked heels.

Von Von was preparing as well. Weighty-hipped nymphs in pumps kneaded his cellulite lovehandles as Von Von polished his pocket-whacker with a pumice stone.

Von Von's hideously lipsticked Henchthings sounded the ritual battle feast by blowing the ancient eunuch flute. And what a feast it was! Served in the sixty foot silver buffet trough were Yak livers on a bed of wild lice, roasted loon strewn with brow, pickled tendons of innocuous tripe, and jellied ring of native flans. *Enough to make a corpse's mouth water*, reflected Von Von as he gorged himself for battle, chortling like a contented rodent while deflowering a pudgy nymphette.

Back in West Gurney, Slim prepared to depart for the festival. He laced up his thigh sandals, rubbed his yellowed gums with spearmint, and flossed with horse hair. He looked smashing, he thought, as he bridled his trusted pony and companion, Pinky, and eagerly set off on his twelve mile journey to Loyns.

Von Von, sweating and out of breath, climbed onto a four foot rock. From this vantage point Von Von could see Grenetta's great palace in the distance. He drooled, fantasizing about the decorating job he could do once he got his mitts on the castle.

Within a fortnight Von Von would attack the palace. It would be frightfully dangerous but nonetheless exciting and would involve absolutely no physical pain for himself, although several thousand of his prancing Henchthings would likely perish.

The plan was simply an all out assault on the palace.

Grenetta... Queen of Loyns

Von Von's chief transsexual spiritual advisor, Klott, pleaded with Von Von, telling him that the Henchthings couldn't take the palace alone for it would be outright slaughter. An alliance was required. Von Von paced, tapping his overhanging forehead. Throck! Of course! They would attack together, for the first time. "One for all and all for one," Klott eagerly added, clapping with delight.

"Yessss," Von Von hissed, "Throck could be king and I will be . . . by his side. And . . . for Grenetta, well, death is too good for her. She will be our personal love slave. An inflatable ego for us to take turns popping. And she will like it, yes, she will like it a lot."

Von Von had the raven courier dispatched with a note for Throck. The note read simply: "Throck . . . Lord of the Crackers, Destroyer of the Labians . . . stop . . . I have a plan for the conquest of Queen Grenetta . . . stop . . . call me back on the raven . . . stop . . . sincerely, Von Von . . . Keeper of the Flame."

Now, if only the raven courier wasn't downed by an ice arrow and Throck was able to understand Von Von's note . . . Unfortunately, Throck was the kind of man who combed his hair from the back up.

Pinky slowly trotted, multiplying the saddle sores on Slim's bony behind. His loyal horse was too old for glue and Slim wondered if Pinky would even survive the journey as his sway-backed beast plodded along the edge of The River of Sludge and Muck. The dank water smelled of murky micro-organisms and cancerous cod and Slim had to sniff citrus rinds to keep from retching. He kicked Pinky in the ribs, who simply sighed, as he gawked at the miles of road ahead.

Grenetta was in a foul mood and savoring the moment. She had grown comfortable with gargantuan mood swings and presently thought of Throck . . . the only man to have his way with her and live to tell the tale, in grunting detail, to all the Crackers, in a best selling book. Oh, the humiliation! How she had scoured the countryside for his hairy neck. But the time was soon arriving when Grenetta would silence Throck, forever. She knew Throck would soon make another attempt for her ample pleasures just as Von Von would make another boorish attempt on her life . . . at the Festival of Fools.

The Royal Soprano Eunuchs sounded the beginning of the Festival with a shrill chorus of "Fa . . . la-la-la. . . . la . . . la . . . laaaaaaaaaa!"

Grenetta entered her box seat, sat on her amethyst throne and waved with the back of her hand to her subjects, the way she had seen other queens do.

The crowd was disappointingly small. Grenetta's daily executions had wiped out most of the populace and those who voluntarily attended had clearly suicidal tendencies, for they were to be an integral part of the festivities (i.e., neighbor jousting).

Nevertheless, the queen, her mood momentarily elevated to a state of euphoria, threw out the first head to start the games.

Grenetta... Queen of Loyns

Von Von's Henchthings surrounded the palace and waited to surprise attack. Meanwhile, they opened their lunch boxes and gossiped.

Because Throck had not answered the raven's message, Von Von was preparing to attack without his assistance. The consensus among Von Von's Henchthings was that their odds stank without Throck, but who would dare go against Von Von's orders. Besides, the sizable Henchthings were hired for their girth, not their intellect. Several, for instance, had not taken their lunches out of their bags before eating them.

Slim anxiously held his golden ticket at gate fifty-three, waiting for the ticket-taker. An honest and unassuming man, Slim patiently waited and waited... and waited.

The neighbor jousts were a crashing bore and Grenetta yawned loudly, distracting the jousters who simultaneously pierced each other with poisoned lances. Grenetta begrudgingly clapped as the riders were carried off the field in the fatal tremors of boor poison.

The out-of-breath ticket-taker finally made it to Slim's gate. He was, in fact, the only ticket-taker for the entire stadium and relentlessly circled past each gate entrance searching for spectators. He spotted Slim and took his ticket, but refused to admit Pinky. Slim pleaded his case; but it wasn't until he slipped the ticket-taker an extra five clams, freshwater variety, that Pinky was admitted.

Inside the crystal palace, mist mysteriously clung to the onyx floor. Slim couldn't help noticing buckets filled with dry ice in the corners as he was greeted by the Royal Hat Checkers who, instead of checking his hat, suited Slim in armor for the next neighbor joust.

Outside the castle, Von Von waited until the skinny man with the emaciated pony crossed the drawbridge then loudly counted to three, very slowly, so all his Henchthings wouldn't lose count.

"One . . . two . . ." and then, suddenly, at that precise moment, the distant sound of a thousand Crack troops skipping, humming and beating their hairy chests distracted Von Von from his counting. That humming could only mean two things. Either the largest humming bird on the planet . . . or Throck.

Throck's tri-horned helmet reflected the sunlight and his muscle-bound oiled Crackers lined the horizon as far as the eye could see.

Von Von, straddling his two fastest Henchthings, rode out to greet the great Throck . . . Lord of the Mighties . . . Hero to the Hermaphrodites . . . Destroyer of the Labians.

As Von Von approached, the Labian slaves bowed and Throck welcomed Von Von with open arms, even though he detested the man and could smell his loathsome sachet of embalming cologne from several yards away. Throck, however, needed Von Von to get to the queen, so they embraced and he even withstood the ceremonial rubbing of the ears.

The Royal Hat Checkers had a difficult time finding armor emaciated enough for Slim. They finally fit him in a dusty set of armor made for a tall child while Pinky was suited with

Grenetta... Queen of Loyns

spiked rib plates. Slim had no idea why he was receiving such special treatment from the Royal Checkers but figured he was simply underdressed.

Von Von's giggling Henchthings and Throck's scowling Crackers took turns around the fire playing pass the silly poem, singing raunchy rhymes and sucking the festive rum sponges. Finally, Throck said, "It is time." Von Von and the others knew exactly what that meant... It was time.

The aphrodisiac horn was blown and they raced the palace walls. Henchthings, Crackers and Labians beating their chests, thumbing their harps, ringing finger chimes, and slapping their thighs while shouting at the top of their lungs "Grenetta, you bitch!" could be a disturbing sight.

The Royal Soprano Eunuchs inside the palace walls heard the war cries and shrieked, but it was too late. The Henchthings, led by the vicious Von Von, and the Crackers, led by mighty Throck, battled their way through the gates of Grenetta's Palace of Loyns.

Well, actually they didn't battle at all; there was virtually no resistance. The Royal Soprano Eunuchs being the worst fighters alive, sang their sharpest notes, then ran in the opposite direction.

The queen was livid, how could her fortified palace be so easily invaded? Where were her guards? Where were her Royal Eunuchs? There would be lives to pay—if she had anyone left alive in her command to pay. The truth is, she was alone... but for one lone knight protecting her in the arena.

Slim waited in the on-deck jousting circle attired in full armor, swinging a saber over his head to loosen up. Just as he tapped off the weighted sword doughnut, Throck and Von Von invaded the quadrant. They suddenly halted, bewildered by the sight that faced them . . . a lone warrior.

Von Von and Throck naturally assumed that the armored knight facing them must be the greatest fighter in all the realm, for who would dare face Throck without backup. So, the several thousand Crackers, Labians and Henchthings halted a safe distance away.

Slim, who could barely see past his helmet grill, leaned backwards clutching his jousting pole, which only made him appear in a more defensive combat position. The Henchthings lurched back.

"YOU THERE!" shouted Von Von with a piercing shrill voice into the courtyard, shaking Slim in his steel boots.

Grenetta, feathers blowing back, hair dryer in hand, stood regally by her throne overlooking the festival courtyard.

"So Von Von . . . you fat rodent . . . we meet again," smiled Grenetta.

Von Von laughed and expelled gas at the same time, "Yes, my queen, you frigid slag . . . we meet again."

"And Throck, you inadequate lover," Grenetta boldly bantered, "What brings you back to these parts?"

"Why, *your* parts," handily retorted Throck on bended knee, as the Crackers chortled.

Slim silently stood between them, confused yet somehow moved by the interaction, as Pinky cowered behind.

Grenetta peered down over her deadly eyelashes at the twiggy warrior protecting her honor in the courtyard. *Who the hell is this wimp?* she wondered, *and why doesn't his armor fit?*

Grenetta... Queen of Loyns

Von Von belched and broke the uneasy silence, "I have *come* for you my queen in more ways than one. Surrender or die by the wire."

The queen shivered at the thought and again sized up the bean pole defending her honor. Should she press her hand? Should she overestimate this puny knight's ability against a thousand Henchthing troops, Crack Crackers and livid Labians? She thought not. Then again, what choice did she have? The odds were about three thousand to one anemic knight. She'd bluff.

Throck pointed his spear threateningly towards the queen, a dead eunuch skewered on the tri-pronged tips, and bellowed, "We're waiting!"

"How dare you hold that tone to ME! TO ME! TO ME!" the queen added a third time for dramatic effect. She had to try to intimidate them somehow.

"I'll tell you what," stated the queen softening her tone a touch, "I will freely give myself to you, body and soul, but first you must win me in battle. You must defeat the greatest knight in my service... a warrior of unparalleled strength and agility... a fierce competitor with killer instincts and a cold heart..."

Slim looked around hoping he could get a glance at such a man as she continued.

"... a deadly instrument of cunning and bad manners," she added, running out of superlatives, "I give you... (she whispered under her breath to Slim)... Psssst, what's your name?"

Slim again checked around and then pointed to himself, "Who, me?"

The queen nodded.

"Oh . . . Slim," he nervously replied.

"I give you Knight-Oh-Slim!" theatrically announced Grenetta.

The area hushed in silence as if she had uttered the name of a saint.

Throck considered her offer. He had fought the best in the land and always won. He knew every knight's stats and had their trading cards. Where had she been hiding this guy? He decided to call her bluff, with the added incentive of another shot in her boudoir.

"Sure. Ah, okay," agreed Throck.

"It's a trick," whispered Von Von to no one in particular.

"Let the games commence!" declared Grenetta.

The only one who still had no idea of what was going on was Slim. No less fascinated by the proceedings and witty repartee, Slim hadn't the faintest idea that he was about to joust the infamous jouster himself, Throck, who finally removed the ensconced eunuch from his spear.

The Henchthings, Crackers and Labians joined elbows in a giant circle around the ceremonial courtyard. Grenetta took her throne . . . and moved it to where she could see better.

A couple of Royal Soprano Eunuchs, dressed in matching wool britches with extra wide suspenders, entered the courtyard lugging nasty jousting weapons of torture, death and showmanship.

When they laid the weapons at Slim's oversized armored boots he finally realized that he was to fight this huge thug facing him across the courtyard, sporting designer armor, with a large "T" emblazoned in gold across his armored chest.

Grenetta... Queen of Loyns

Slim quickly studied the three items of his weapons' selection: A steel wire about three feet long, covered with barbs; a bumpy bluish squash; and something that resembled a small red ball dotted with tiny needles. Slim gingerly picked up the ball. The crowd applauded approvingly.

"Good choice," laughed Throck, who was the league leader with the "cushion of pain." Throck grasped the porcupine orb and tested the weight in his iron-gloved fist.

The writhing round weapon crawled across Slim's palm raising tiny droplets of blood. He dropped the living pin cushion like a hot potato bug.

Throck suddenly chucked his "cushion of pain" straight up into the air and it disappeared into the clouds. The spectators went, "ohhhhh." Moments later it fell back to his metal glove, which hadn't moved. The crowd went, "ahhhhh."

Pinky fainted.

Slim revived his pony with mouth-to-mouth resuscitation and began to feel faint himself in the humid air of the arena. He wondered how he got into this mess.

It was then, in the depths of despair, remorse, and dread that Slim momentarily locked eyes with the queen. Her radiant emerald eyes stared at Slim, vacuuming his soul through his sockets. Could this be love?

Slim sucked in his gut.

Throck took advantage of Slim's distraction and charged like a fiend from hell riding the tides of disillusionment.

As Throck, shrieking like a lunatic, was just yards away, clutching his "cushion of pain," Slim aimed and punted the spiny sack, which lay at his feet, and miraculously scored a field goal into Throck's open mouth.

Needless to say, swallowing the "cushion of pain" is the most painful way to succumb to it. The spiny critter is terrified of the dark and once down your esophagus tries to claw its way back to the surface like a claustrophobic cactus, causing irreparable damage to one's soft tissues.

Queen Grenetta and the spectators were speechless, as was Throck, but for different reasons. The queen rose to her feet and threw a petal from her fire flower to Slim. Slim reached over to pick up the petal and singed his fingers but nevertheless waved in gratitude to the queen as Throck collapsed clutching his throat.

The Crackers having lost their leader now turned to the obese overlord of the Henchthings, Von Von, who stared at Slim and whispered to himself, "This guy's good."

Von Von hopped off his Henchthing and spun towards the queen, "I want a horse."

"Why, is it lunch?" flatly replied Grenetta.

"Not to eat . . . to ride!" spit back Von Von.

The queen sneered, snapping her fingernails together, and a mighty steed, coated in gilded armor, galloped into the courtyard.

Slim continued reviving Pinky, leading the wobbly Shetland in circles like a punch drunk pugilist. Von Von, meanwhile, donned silicone breast plates and mounted his reluctant beast, which staggered under his substantial girth.

It was Von Von's turn to select a weapon. His choice . . . the "wire." The Crackers took a step backwards at the mere mention of the "wire," though amazingly no one had even mentioned it yet.

Slim picked up the weapon which seemed to hum in his hand though it merely looked like a piece of, well, wire. He

Grenetta... Queen of Loyns

swung it through the air faster and faster until it hummed a D minor. Von Von, meanwhile, whipped his wire into an F-flat. They went back and forth whipping their wires in a crescendo of D minor and F-flat.

"Enough!" warned the queen. She pulled a lace handkerchief from her spiked, steel push-up bra and dangled it out over the edge of her field box. Von Von and Slim waited for her signal.

After a tension-mounting few moments, she dropped her monogrammed silk, which incidentally landed atop Throck's distorted death grimace. As Von Von charged, wildly whipping F-flat over his head and yelling "yahoo" like a gorged gaucho, Slim tried to be menacing, but it was physically impossible.

Halfway across the field, Von Von's horse collapsed under his glutinous thighs, the beast's legs sprawling out in all four directions. Von Von rolled off his comatose equine, spun his wire overhead a few times and let it rip. Slim simultaneously set sail with his wire and the musical threads hummed towards each other meeting halfway across the courtyard and curling around each other in a symphony of metallic sparks. The wires wound themselves into a pinball and harmlessly fell to the ground in the center of the arena.

Von Von, his toga torn and soiled, ran full steam for Slim intending to choke the lanky librarian with his flabby triceps. Slim had but a brief moment to peek down at his weapon selection. The choice was rather limited. There was only one weapon left ... the blue squash.

Von Von was getting closer. Slim could smell his fetid garlic breath from yards away and was mentally preparing for the worst.

Distracted by the early symptoms of a panic attack, Slim drew a blank on what to do with the blue squash. Dazed, he turned towards the queen, who seemed to be hissing something at him.

Von Von was really close now. Not so close that you had to do anything but he was still on his way . . . a force of inertia in motion that could not be stopped by the laws of gravity.

The queen was on the edge of her seat shouting, "SEED, SEED!" to Slim, at the top of her lungs. Slim, frustrated, studied the strange blue vegetable in his hand then disgustedly threw it to the ground. The gourd split in two revealing a large slimy pit. With his thumbnail Slim pried out the oval pit, latticed with vegetable debris, but it was so slimy it slipped out of his hands and he had to catch it between his knobby knees.

Von Von's bloated face now filled all of Slim's peripheral vision who, terrified, squeezed his trembling knees together and inadvertently fired the seed like a greased bullet.

A hush fell over the Crackers, Labians, Grenetta, and the entire paid attendance of fifteen, the moment seeming to elongate in elastic motion as the soaring squash pit slammed into Von Von's forehead . . . and continued through the other side.

Von Von dropped much like his horse. Arms and legs indicating the compass points.

The earth shook, trees fell, and time, for a momentous moment, stood inexorably still.

The scoreboard said it all: Slim to none.

Grenetta... Queen of Loyns

In case you're wondering, Grenetta, Queen of Loyns, and Slim, Lord Librarian of Gurney, eventually eloped and lived to an indeterminate age, raising numerous children of various sizes.

The legend of "Knight-Oh-Slim" went on for centuries and in his time he was feared in the farthest forest. The Henchthings, Crackers and Labians became indentured servants, working for Grenetta doing yard work and stuff around the castle.

The eunuchs sang and sang.

It was a happy time.

Grenetta had become a tolerable queen and actually began to mellow over time. Executions had all but become a thing of the past, thanks to Slim, and her excessive use of the "wire" became all but a bad joke in the realm. Like it had never happened.

But time would tell.

Duh, We're Hookers...
Another "Raoul, Low-life Ex-Cop" Adventure

Raoul staggered down Alamoana Boulevard, the sweet rotting-orchid stench of Wicked Wahini perfume clinging to the Honolulu humidity like Malathion. Raoul had somehow found himself in the city of sin on the Hawaiian rim, his soul dunked in Wicked Wahini Number Nine.

Cruising the sidewalk in front of the Liberty House Department Store was a herd of hopeful hookers working the island of leis for Asian action. It was only five P.M. yet dozens of sex sandwich-boards wearing peel and eat poly-stretch-knits were trolling for the early-bird special. Their jaded eyes danced over Raoul, weighing his wallet and coming up empty. Raoul, nevertheless, starved for human contact, approached a pair of jaw jockeys hugging the street corner like stale gum.

Duh, We're Hookers

"Haven't I seen you here before?" Raoul quizzed the fatale femmes, inhaling a near lethal dose of Wicked Wahini.

"Duh, we're hookers, we're here every night," replied a blond blow-tart, like a vituperative valley girl graduated to the College of Flotsam and Jism.

The other curb cruiser, a Eurasian mutt, eyed Raoul suspiciously. *Something vaguely familiar about this John,* she thought, arching a painted eyebrow.

"He's got cop's jaw," whispered the sleek DaNang nookie to the nose-running rookie.

"What's cop's jaw?" queried Gidget the gutter slut.

"Sticks out, daring you to take a punch," answered Miss Saigon.

The two canvasbacks then clip-clopped like bow-legged centaurs down Oahu's most notorious trick street in search of bigger wallets and little dicks soliciting a quick rinse and spit. Their pimps preferred the five minute R&S to the full service Waikiki Watusi. "Quicker to get your bruised ass back on the street, bitch," spat their Don Ho pimp.

The sidewalks were swarming with looky-Loos sporting Hawaii Five-0 prints and soaking in the sordid circus unfurling like a Venus fly trap before their Midwestern eyes. Palm tree lamp posts with coconut lights bathed the pink carcinoma faces of package tour victims in a surreal haze, *like the "Tourists of the Living Dead,"* observed Raoul through meth-tinted sunglasses. The well-oiled prostitutes perused the blue haired tourists and the doe-eyed sightseers ogled the pavement pounders in a dance as old as Charo.

Raoul probably should have been combing the beach, gawking bikini-sawed-butts and soaking his cancerous liver in a double Mai Tai or, better yet, one of those tropical mind numb-ers with the Trader Vic back-scratcher-swizzle-sticks to rake his weeping mosquito bites. But instead, he was the immoral Moses, parting a sea of sleaze.

A flotilla of dirigibles draped in erupting volcano muumuus floated past Raoul as he continued down the boulevard, past the Neal Diamond impersonator, past the stoned Rastafarian pipe peddler and his dancing hippy child, towards a crusty sailor with a cloudy eye who rasped at Raoul that he'd scrimshaw his front teeth for two bucks. "Something you'll have for a lifetime," cackled the rusty lunged seaman.

Then, quite suddenly, it all stopped. Raoul didn't know when it happened, he rarely did, courtesy of recurring blackouts, but at some point the tourists returned to their time-shares, the Lazy Susan street buffet ground to a halt, and Raoul was left face down in a puddle of his own poi.

Raoul focused his eyes on a wooden back scratcher lying on the pavement, wondering how it got there. He plucked a purple plastic cocktail sword from his cheek just as the two a.m. street sweeper blasted down the boulevard like a hurricane, spraying Wicked Wahini disinfectant over Raoul. Things had looked bad for Raoul before, but never had they tasted so sickeningly sweet.

He crawled a few feet before knocking head to knee with a street crawler dressed like an angel in white, come to deliver the mercy fuck of the millennium.

Raoul gazed skyward into the vacant eyes of the blond butt-peddler, unable to move his chapped lips.

She looked vaguely familiar. Duh.

Duh, We're Hookers

"So, I guess you're not a cop," stated Miss Lolita White Trash, swinging her sporty condom purse while sucking a Tic Tac.

"You again," exhaled Raoul, wondering if he was experiencing a flashback or deja vu, "Haven't found a date yet, huh?"

She smiled her best gobblegoo grin, her teeth gliding over Vaseline lips like Miss Blow Job America. "While you've been lying there, I made six hundred bucks," she proudly smirked as she stepped over his tropical vomit and strutted down the sidewalk on stilt stilettos.

"I'm a cop," belched Raoul under his combustible breath.

She turned back, drawn to the blue-eyed junkie with the jet black ponytail, Tonto good looks and crooked boxer's nose.

"I knew you were," she bubbled. "My boyfriend shot a cop," she cheerfully informed. "He's doing a double dime at Love-Lock in Nevada. Luckily, the cop lived or Poncho's ass would be bacon."

"I'd love to meet him someday," flatly remarked Raoul.

"Sure," she replied, continuing unabated. "So, what are you doing lying on the sidewalk . . . undercover work?"

"Yeah, surveillance of pavement cracks," quipped Raoul to an audience of none. "But don't worry," he added, "I'm retired. They took my gun and badge. Then, when they felt they were safe, they took my wife, my house, my kids, my money . . . and my life."

"You ain't dead yet, cop," she counseled reassuringly, leering at a passing rental car.

"Don't be so sure," moaned Raoul, wobbling onto jellyfish legs.

"I've done lots of cops," proudly proclaimed the platinum harpie as she folded a stick of Juicyfruit onto her tongue.

"They always want to pop for free, why's that?" she innocently inquired, batting pterodactyl eyelashes.

"Man, you're green," sighed Raoul.

"I'm new here," she explained, "I usually work the Flamingo in Vegas. Ever been there?"

"I still may be," drooled Raoul onto his flip-flops.

She stuck out her hand and Raoul noticed her minuscule lifeline while pondering the May poles she'd polished that evening. He kept his palsy hand to his twitching eye, but she didn't notice the rebuff.

"Name's Charlemagne or Sapphire . . . but my real name's Betty, don't say Boop, I hate that

"Name's Raoul," said Raoul, "but you can call me Raoul."

Betty suddenly grabbed Raoul's delirium-trembling hand and led him through the Waikiki outdoor market (better known as sinsemilla-bud central) past the closed trinket stalls crammed with a billion years of garage sales.

"Where are we going?" inquired Raoul, curiously observant of the twists and turns of the past few years.

"To introduce you to Mom."

"Your mother?" echoed Raoul posthumously.

"Naw, my real mom's back in Sleepy Eye. She thinks I'm an actress," explained Betty, adding, "I wasn't always a hooker, you know. Last summer I was an extra in a porno movie."

"Congratulations," replied Raoul, his eyes rolling back so far he almost went unconscious.

Raoul was pondering whether Sleepy Eye was a town or a clinic, when a pink checkered cab skidded to the curve.

Duh, We're Hookers

"Vixen's video?" coughed the Chinese cabbie out his window.

"I've hung up my towel for the night, my jaw's killing me," confided Betty.

"Occupational hazard," echoed Six Chin Charlie, as the passengers scooted across the duct-taped seats. "Who's the john?" Chins inquired.

"Ex-cop, or so he says. He wants to meet Mom," cheerfully announced the world class nob bobber.

"Oh, Mom like you lot," smirked Chins, adding, "I knew he don't look like no all-nighter."

"You got that right, honey," purred Betty Blue, checking her fake Rolex. "It's twenty to closing. I can still snag some last-call-rail-bait."

The cabbie whipped a wicked U-turn and Raoul smacked up against the car door.

"So, what's your beat, cop?" probed Charlie, eying Raoul reflectively in the rearview.

"L.A.," muttered Raoul, tasting something foul in his mouth.

"Never been," said Chins. "Seen it on *Cops* though. Say, didn't I see you on *Scariest Police Beatings: Part Five?*"

"Listen, I don't feel like talking, I'm getting car sick," moaned Raoul.

"Okey dokey, mister. Just let me know when you're gonna blow hole, and I'll pull over. It's a bitch getting it out of the cracks."

The car screeched into the parking lot of the Fanta-See Strip Club. Betty led Raoul out of the cab towards an enormous Samoan doorman who eyed Raoul like a speed bag.

"Mahalo," slurred Raoul, with no reaction from the beefy bouncer.

"Mom, this is Raoul. Raoul, meet Mom," sparkled Betty from the quicksand of her life.

"This is Mom? I'd hate to meet Dad," dead-panned Raoul.

Mom just snarled as Betty led Raoul through the soiled curtains into the dark.

The naked strippers barely glanced up as Raoul collapsed face first onto a splintered bench. Betty, meanwhile, placed one heel up on the bench a millimeter from Raoul's nose, hiked up her skirt, pulled aside her thong panties and spritzed her heart-coiffed mound with Wicked Wahini Number Nine. The smell brought back the bile and Raoul involuntarily shuddered, drooling like Pavlov's dog.

Betty snatched a tiny vial from her Wonderbra and snorted a line of scag from underneath her fingernail, the one with the skull decal. She then sprinkled a dash on the web between her toes and wiggled them under Raoul's nose.

Raoul, like a dowser to water, lowered his flared nostrils between her toes and snorted like a pearl diver coming up for air. Betty had to pry his nose away like a snail and, as Raoul glanced down, he hoped he only snorted the Honolulu horse and not the jam glistening between her toes.

"Good boy," smiled Betty, patting Raoul's head like an obedient blood hound. "Don't go anywhere," she ordered as she darted out the threadbare curtain.

"Wouldn't if I could," slurred Raoul, semi-paralyzed with nausea from Mr. Toad's cab ride and the plug of toe jam clogging his nasal passages.

Duh, We're Hookers

Raoul aimed his one open eye out the curtain and watched a Vietnamese stripper named Silver Dollar dangle her udders like a boob bonnet over the head of a zombie businessman illuminated by the throbbing discos. Silver Dollar squatted over his near beer, and Raoul thought she was going to relieve herself, when instead, she placed her calloused heel behind the back of the businessman's skull and nudged him face first towards her infectious thatch. She firmly locked his head between her powerful nut-cracking knees and a near lethal dose of Wicked Wahini. The businessman held onto her thighs for dear life as she tightly cradled his head and rocked him into a stupor to Sting's, "If you love someone . . . set them free."

The juke box abruptly clicked over to Devo's "Whip it," as Silver Dollar unclasped the businessman's knee-dented skull, pulled her stretched out garter open for a tip, and surrendered the stage.

Betty now bumped and grinded over to the businessman, peeling her easy-off outer wear, then lifted her leg over his head like a Dalmatian at a fire hydrant, imparting a clearer view of her fallopian tubes. The businessman calmly removed his glasses and then bowed down as Betty clamped him with her bruised knees in a head-lock and rocked his world for all he was worth . . . about two bucks, as it turned out.

Silver Dollar, meanwhile, counted her bounty in the dressing room while shooting Raoul a foul stare. She pulled the wrinkled Washingtons from her garter and hid them in her macrame bag on the floor as the Samoan doorman studied Raoul with a bouncer's eye.

"Mom, watch my bag," snapped Silver Dollar like a VC commander. The bouncer didn't blink as Silver Dollar returned to the main stage for a garter refill.

As soon as Silver Dollar left the dressing room, the bouncer rifled through her purse and pocketed about fifteen bucks. Disappointed, he moved on to Betty's bag and removed a wad of cash that could choke an island pig. His eyes were glossed over as he purloined three C's and then quickly tied up her bag.

Raoul was placed at a crossroads, hearing the train coming, as he observed the theft. He was given a choice between good and evil, right and wrong, smart or stupid, something he was having trouble deciphering at that moment. He knew that either way he was going to regret his decision for the next few hours and perhaps the rest of his life. Only would it be from the Honolulu Hilton or the hospital?

Raoul made his choice . . . Duh.

"What do you think you're doing?" conjured Raoul in the most authoritative cop's voice he could muster. He would have shouted "Freeze," but the phrase lacks the proper influence when you're unarmed and near comatose, lying on a bench in a low rent strip joint, zonked out of your mind on Hawaiian hookie.

The giant Samoan slowly turned like Godzilla sensing a tickle of bullets and performed a head bob, not unlike the disturbing twitch Mike Tyson affected after nearly severing an opponent's head from his spine, or chewing off an ear.

When the muscles stopped rippling like an aftershock through the Samoan's body, Raoul softened his tone adding, "That's not your money now . . . is it?"

Duh, We're Hookers

"What da fuck do you know, Howlie?" spat Mr. Oahu Olympia, the veins in his neck surging with lava flow.

"Right from wrong, which apparently your mother didn't teach you, Mom!" retorted Raoul, wondering when he'd become the Emily Post of the underworld.

The Samoan removed his triple-X weight lifting sweat shirt, leaving him in a straining tank top and Arnold Schwarzenegger's torso. He approached Raoul like a sumo wrestler at a smorgasbord.

Raoul calmly recalled the rope-a-dope fight strategy, while his face was banged repeatedly into the bench, that "the best offense is a good defense." He would simply wear out his opponent . . . using his face as a diversion.

Ten minutes later the Samoan was just warming up.

"Okay, Howlie, get up and fight," ordered the surly Samoan.

Why does everyone want to fight me? thought Raoul, relieved that his brain was not yet splayed open like a ripe mango. Was it "karma" for nineteen years of pulverizing suspects in the back seat of squad cars, the station, their cells and anywhere else he could bust some heads? Not much need for a gym in those days.

Raoul, whose face now looked like Carrie on prom night, managed to stand on two useless legs. He stumbled towards the Samoan who stepped aside and spun kicked Raoul into a metal post.

Please let me go unconscious, prayed Raoul. Was this just one of God's bad jokes or was the toe snort keeping him from merciful unconsciousness.

Betty raced in the dressing room naked and screaming as she saw Raoul auditioning for the Heinz 57 poster boy, "What are you doing, Mom?!"

"I caught him stealing from your purse," nervously spat the Samoan, Raoul wondering if he had studied improv with O.J.'s acting coach.

"Then why do you have her cash in your pocket?" mouthed Raoul from the puddle that had once been his face.

Betty stared at Raoul, her mangled hero, then turned on Mom, "So that's where my money has been going, you fafuna!" she reprimanded as she kicked the Samoan in the macadamias. The bouncer grimaced in pain, then backhanded her across the room like a sand flea. That was all Raoul had to see. Not Betty!

Zero to sixty in seven seconds, radioed Raoul to his brain, his nerve endings flashing an all-points bulletin. *"Car fifty-four where are you?"* . . . *"One Adam twelve"* . . . *"Bad-Boys Bad-Boys"* . . . ZIP-BANG-BOOM! Raoul sprang to his feet and slammed his elbow into the esophagus of the Samoan Paul Bunyan who grabbed his throat, his eyes bulging as he toppled . . . to one knee. Not what Raoul was shooting for, but nevertheless . . . .

"Citizen's arrest," gurgled Raoul, his mouth merely a drain hole for incomprehensible repartee. Raoul hadn't made an arrest in over four years and it felt pretty good, albeit painful.

This infuriated Mom who, like a wasp hit with fly spray, arose from his knee and slammed his pomelo-sized fist into Raoul's kidney. Fortunately, Raoul's kidneys were shot anyhow, and besides, there was plenty of room on the other side of his stomach after he spit up his spleen.

Duh, We're Hookers

The Samoan lifted Raoul off his feet by his throat and was about to deliver the coup de grace when an authoritative voice boomed from behind the curtain, "Drop him, POLICE!"

Raoul fell to a rumpled heap on Silver Dollar's stained honey rug and gazed up to see his savior, the businessman from the poon room, pulling an AMT 380 backup from his ankle holster.

"You're a cop too?!" sang Betty. "No wonder there's so much crime, you guys are all up to your necks in snatch."

The off-duty dick dodged her deride. "What do you mean 'cop, too,'" he asked with a distinctly Brooklyn cadence.

Betty proudly pointed at Raoul. "He's one of yours."

The detective studied Raoul, trying to make out his face through the veil of blood. "Do I know you?"

"Raoul Reynoso at your service, LAPD Detective, retired."

"No shit, detective?!" the New Yorker echoed, unimpressed.

"How do I look?" asked Raoul, wiggling a molar.

"Like shit," offered the east coast desk cop, handing Raoul a cocktail napkin to blot his bloody sputum.

"What brings you to hell's playpen?" inquired Raoul as he was hoisted to his feet, "You're not local P.D."

"I'm here for the convention. You?"

"Yeah, sure, why not," nodded Raoul.

Name's Frank Dano, offered the cop, thrusting out his hand.

"You're kidding."

"Wish I were."

"Well, go ahead," sighed the Brooklyn detective.

Raoul smiled. "Book 'em, Dano."

"Feel better?"

"Much," grinned Raoul, through crimson teeth.

The next afternoon, Raoul's pal Dano invited him to a luau with a group of police officers from New Jersey. They welcomed Raoul as one of their own... "Once blue... always blue."

Stuffed with roast pig and pineapple, Raoul swam through a sea of Mai Tai's, sedating his pain-racked body. The last thing he remembered was seventeen back scratchers stuck around him like a fortress in the sand. King Kong had finally been sedated by the villagers.

Then, the sun blinked out.

Raoul awoke again on the streets, this time with a can of spray paint in one hand, a back scratcher in the other and the words "Imperialist Pigs" tagged across the wall in front of the Singapore police station.

Raoul must have made his flight.

Reflectionites!

Alandar stared blankly from the mezzanine as his two sons were led center stage in shackles. The music swelled, then just as abruptly ended.

"Welcome to Execution Theater," the sequined eliminator bellowed through megaphone lips, "Tonight we bring you . . . REFLECTIONITES!" The crowd gasped and flipped down their reflective goggles.

Alandar hadn't flipped down his goggles. Instead, he gazed at his program and read the featured names: Funalddo and Oddlanuf.

For Alandar this was hardly a proud moment. Seeing his sons on this stage was nothing but an atrocity, for they most certainly were not reflectionites. Nevertheless, it appeared that Funalddo and Oddlanuf were the sold-out hit of the execution season.

Granted, the boys did reflect a few traits. They both rose four feet, were prematurely bald, had club feet, big ears, bad teeth and weak shoulders. But these *coincidental* traits should have been no cause for alarm. This charge of "reflectionism" was mere paranoia, Alandar reasoned, not to mention an attempt to revive Execution Theater's sagging box office.

The boys were led off the stage and Alandar's goggles dimmed for Act One, "A Musical Comedy Beheading."

As the orchestra tuned their xilobones, Alandar drifted back to when all the trouble began . . .

Funalddo and Oddlanuf were toddlers when Alandar first noticed something odd. For instance, Alandar's wife, Esabell, could only nurse Oddlanuf on her left breast and Funalddo on her right. If Esabell attempted to switch them, they would tightly lock their sides together like a puzzle. With the boys glued together in this fashion it was impossible to reach between them, into their "field of feeling," without risking a nasty electric shock. Alandar had no explanation for this and simply thought it was a phase they were going through.

But all through soloite-preschool Funalddo and Oddlanuf were teased, and nasty rumors that the boys were reflectionites spread across the schoolyard. It wasn't long before the gene police, in their pink and blue striped shirts and pointed DNA helmets, were sniffing around the playground.

Since it had been years since anyone in the colony had seen a living pair of reflectionites (they were all executed before their tenth birthday) the boys were ultimately arrested.

The High Quintunal subjected the questionable siblings to a battery of tests and determined that since Funalddo

Reflectionites!

exhibited tendencies of the right side of the brain (the creative half) and Oddlanuf demonstrated traits of the left side of the brain (the logical half) the boys weren't really *whole* but *half people*, or . . . reflectionites. Naturally, other siblings in the colony shared this condition, but they hid it better, masking their sameness, or the traits of only one side of their brain.

And so it went . . . that accountants painted . . . doctors sang . . . lawyers sculpted. Not very well mind you, horribly in fact. Conversely, artisans trying to be pilots, doctors and lawyers caused mayhem, injury and death.

But that's the way it was.

Back at Execution Theater it was intermission. While the stage crew mopped up the blood from the musical, Alandar waited in line at the lobby bar. He ordered a shot of "confidence on the rocks" and raised the vial of sparkling amethyst to his trembling lips. Alandar felt the cool burning liquid down his esophagus and casually gazed over the rim of his glass, suddenly aware he was being watched. Actually, it was the spiral DNA helmet rising like a temple spire above the crowd that caught his eye.

As the crowd thinned, Alandar could see the gene police surveying him from behind their two-way finger painting easels. Alandar desperately tried to remain calm as he quickly mingled into the crowd and ducked into the theater.

The audience clapped in unison shouting, "Reflectionites! Reflectionites!" as the eliminator sheepishly ducked out from behind the blood-soiled curtain and stamped his platform boots, silencing the unruly crowd.

"Act Two!" announced the eliminator . . . "REFLECTIONITES!"

The audience went wild.

Alandar knew he had to do something, possibly dramatic, to save his sons before they were melted together in the dreaded "joiner" (a wicked device which resembled a giant waffle iron).

As the "joiner" was rolled out onto stage with Funalddo and Oddlanuf strapped inside, Alandar could hardly restrain himself as it sparked alive. The eliminator, with grand panache and showmanship, pulled the giant lever past the "lightly adhere mark" . . . towards "medium melt," intermittently shouting to the crowd, "YOU WANT TO GO TIGHTER?!"

As the lever approached the mark reading "soloite," Alandar could take no more. He hurled himself over the balcony.

It should be mentioned at this point that Alandar, though a lousy accountant, was a decent acrobat. So, in mid-air, Alandar grabbed a double helix chandelier and swung towards the stage.

He landed in the orchestra pit. Undaunted, he gathered his wits and quickly climbed up on stage, stepping on the shaven head of a tambourine player/weapons designer.

As the gene police closed in from the wings, their splicers drawn, Alandar performed several respectable cartwheels, a double back flip, and then, tripped. He stumbled headlong between the accused reflectionites, directly into their "field of feeling."

Alandar evaporated in a sizzling burst leaving behind only the faint scent of singed hair.

Reflectionites!

After a stunned moment . . . the audience leaped to their feet in a standing ovation.

Alandar came to consciousness cross-eyed. He was lying on his side in a meadow watching a pair of identical dragonflies land on two identical purple irises. He uncrossed his eyes but still saw two suns setting on the horizon. Alandar rubbed his lashless eyelids, wondering if he was seeing double. He sat up, gingerly cradled his head, and noticed that his hair had been singed to the roots.

Just then, he heard voices shouting, "Soloite! Soloite!"

Two reflectionite farmers, pitchforks raised, were running dead for him. Alandar prepared to defend himself. He looked around for a weapon. There was nothing but rocks. Alandar considered these for a millisecond, then sprinted heartily in the opposite direction. The farmers were just closing in when Alandar heard sirens approaching. Two identical policemen, making siren sounds from their noses, wearing mercury suits and spiked umbrella hats, cornered Alandar with their meconium jet-scooters. Alandar, in a fog, was read his rights (twice) handcuffed (two pairs) and taken to the Bookend Police Stations.

As the suns set, Alandar solemnly sat on his double bed in his two room cell with duplicate neon, barred doors. Alandar felt horribly alone, a soloite in a land of reflectionites. Even if he managed to escape, how could he ever find his "one" way back home? The singular cosmic porthole of reentry?

Alandar heard a rapping sound on the bars. Before him stood the Twiddledum and Twiddledee of the legal profession.

"We're your state appointed twintorneys, Martin and Martin," the squat lawyers irritatingly explained in unison. "You're being charged with soloism (the Martins sang), "because, in the Domain of Doubles, singles are feared and pairs revered. One's no fun. It takes two to do."

Alandar, expressionless, stared at his twintorneys.

The penalty for being a "loner," the Martins continued, was no less than, "Death, death."

Alandar shuddered. What could this mean in this land of duplication? Would he have to be executed twice? "Precisely," echoed the Martins. "Quite right," they added simultaneously, stifling mutual asthmatic coughs.

If Alandar actually knew what lay ahead in way of an execution, he would probably have been too desperate to think at all. For in the Domain of Doubles, loners are ripped in half and used as volleyball poles for the Mardi-gra/Mardi-gra in March/March.

The following mornings, Alandar was scheduled to face the Polarity Magistrates and he realized that he would have to quickly come up with a good defense, or two, to survive.

Alandar's first decision—"a grave, grave mistake" warned the Martins—was to defend himself, or selves, because his twintorneys were giving him massive headaches, constantly talking in unison.

Unable to devise a defense, or defenses, for soloism (there was and were none) Alandar considered faking a split personality. But the Martins had earlier informed him that multiple personalities was the most common soloite defense tactic(s) and would predictably lead to concurrent death sentences and an impromptu volleyball match.

Reflectionites!

At his wits end, Alandar flew into a rage. In a flailing fit he began hitting his double beds in his cells, pulling apart his mattresses in chunks. He finally stopped, exhausted.

In his grasp were two handfuls of mattress stuffing.

The packed courtrooms were filled to capacity with thrill hungry spectators eager to hear the fates of the evil loner known as "Alandar Solo."

The bailiffs banged their gavels and called the courts to order as the Polarity Magistrates approached the benches.

The charges echoed throughout the courthouses, "Loner . . . Loner," and repeated by the spectators, "Loner . . . Loner!"

The double doors swung open and Alandar was led into the courtrooms clutching a crude replica of himself made of mattress pad and stuffing, wearing an outfit he'd sewn from dental floss and sheets.

Sweat beads stung Alandar's eyes as he approached the judges' benches and proceeded to defend himself and his stuffed reflectionite sibling, "Radnala." Fortunately, Alandar didn't even have to throw his voice, merely making it appear that he was talking in perfect unison with his "sibling" (as he manipulated Radnala's mouth with his hand stuck inside the dummies head).

Alandar's unusual strategy had a strange effect on the magistrates, juries and reflectionite spectators. They didn't believe him, or his ridiculous ploy, for two seconds. But, it made them laugh, hysterically.

The faster Alandar spoke, desperately trying to conclude his double-summation, the more the spectators howled. Meanwhile, Alandar, noticing a small tear on the side of the dummy and pieces of mattress poking out, began to talk faster and faster, his voice rising considerably, higher and higher.

Alandar's desperate defenses so inspired the courtrooms to fits of laughter, tears rolling down their cheeks, that the courts were adjourned. Alandar was set free.

As was Radnala.

And so... Alandar and Radnala became the greatest comedy team in the history of the "Domain of Doubles" and are credited with being the "Fathers of Vaudevilles."

Alandar comfortably adjusted to having two of everything. Two wives, two mistresses, two houses, two jobs, two bank accounts.

As did Radnala.

Over time, Alandar eventually began to believe that his patched yellowed dummy actually *was* his reflectionite brother and they would often fight like, well, brothers. It finally got so bad that they dissolved their partnership, going their separate ways.

At least that's what the *Daily Reflectionite/Daily Reflectionite* reported.

Years passed. Radnala, who greatly missed his "brother," found fortune opening adjoining nightclubs with floor to ceiling mirrors and buxom waitresses. Reflectionites came from miles around to knock back a couple of doubles while listening to duets at the popular nightclubs near the courthouses... Radnala's on the Rocks.

Alandar never did find his way back home. He died destitute, all alone in his two room apartment... on his double bed.

Regular Can

His stomach growled a wake-up call but the coastal fog had wrapped him in a chilly blanket of apathy. "You don't have to live on the streets to shiver," he mumbled, "but it sure helps."

A familiar itch gnawed at his festered ankle but he dared not answer. Itches always come back, something you could rely on.

He listened to the sea gulls laugh, wondering if it was at him, as he pushed himself onto his knees and let the blood rush back to his brain. "Be nice to lay here day," he reasoned. But his belly wouldn't listen to reason.

He inhaled a bracing breath of briny air as he neatly folded his cardboard bed and trash-bag blanket. Satisfied, he limped barefoot along the shoreline, stepping inside jogger prints in the damp sand.

It was dog hour as packs of fleabag mobile homes scoured the boardwalk for garbage, "Blessed garbage," he grinned, licking his gray lips while stifling a bronchial cough.

He nervously tweaked a hair from his saffron beard, a habit he favored, creating a bare patch the size of a quarter. The skin underneath was pink, like albino skin. He loved to rub the soft unprotected flesh. Felt like childhood. "Wish I had some lotion. But they don't throw away lotion, only food," he cackled, wiggling an abscessed molar.

His regular can was two blocks down. He wrapped his decaying poncho around his mottled scalp as a light drizzle reminded him of things. Street things. Once married with a family. But the bottle made him cheat, and he moved in with her. "I made choices and I don't regret any of 'em. They're just made," he spouted, "Sometimes you have nothin' to do with it."

Two trembling hind legs and a psoriasis tail wagged from an overturned trash can. Scratch, an emaciated mutt with a clouded eye, had beat him to breakfast. He dragged the pooch out by his scraggly tail and read him the riot act. But Scratch was trembling and had a wild look in his good eye, so he decided to share. "Maybe someday Scratch'll do the same for me," he implored to a palm tree.

All the aluminum had been picked by the shopping cart nomads. But, no matter, the good stuff was down at the bottom. A banana peel with a hunk of brown goo was there and he sucked out the nutrients. Pizza crust was a staple of his regular can and he found a scrap with some sauce left. He flicked off the bugs and fed Scratch who greedily gobbled, tail wagging, no time for thanks.

He plucked another whisker from his chin and rubbed the pink spot as he limped down the boardwalk, whistling through the spaces in his teeth. He paused to pick a piece of glass from his calloused heel before continuing on, to the next charity barrel.

It was a beautiful day, drizzly though, but they all offered something.

Extreme of Consciousness

sunday, december first

. . . it's three a.m and i can't sleep . . . the demons are howling and i have to walk them . . . i stagger to my icy office and flip on the mac . . . my face glows in eerie hues of computer blues . . . though my mind slumbers . . . the demons have nagged me awake . . . like the call of the vampire . . . beckoning me to the edge of the word pool . . . a dark purple pit of frightful visions and passions beyond the pale . . . awakening an agitated itch . . . static electricity twitching through my fingers . . . dancing over the keyboard like spiders . . . i can't stop writing . . . my fingers illuminating the screen with words i can't express in the light of day . . . torture burns at my fingertips . . . fire lapping at the word-trellis . . . entwined in a dream . . . floating in subconscious consciousness . . . a tangled twine of words bouncing on a core of insurmountable

Extreme of Consciousness

agony . . . shrieking from the bowels of my being . . . uncontrollable fury belching a lava flow of iridescent memories awash in a dream . . . of time . . . place . . . memory . . . i bleed from within . . . unable to hold back the pain of thought . . . let me sleep! . . . damn it . . . i am so tired . . . yet the words overflow the dam holding me aloft on the tide . . . please let silence overtake me . . . but not death . . . though it is a resplendent place to sleep . . . i'm still channeling . . . don't edit! . . . please god . . . don't edit . . . i am but a mere channeler of words . . . ungnuhhhhhhh! . . . i'm cummming! . . . my words spurting across the page . . . don't the demons ever sleep? . . . or are they too busy fucking with those at rest? . . . shit . . . the voices are back . . . eating around my ear down the core of my spine . . . why won't they let me sleep?! . . . or is it the whisper of god? . . . and i'm lucky enough to hear the whisper . . . but if i sleep . . . ahhhhh . . . the warm sleep of death . . . well . . . god will whisper the words to the next brave soul ready to wake up and type . . . so listen up! . . . i'm scratching my eardrum so hard as i write this i might dig a hole right into my brain . . . what then? . . . will it feel good to itch my brain? . . . to stick my finger into the moist folds of my cerebrum and pluck out a thought on my finger which i might smear across the page for you to read? . . . see . . . the light coming from my fingertips is only a guide for lost souls down the path to eternal damnation . . . then off to the word farm to slaughter a few thoughts . . . and eat the red beating soul of wisdom . . . and gulp the thick stew of blood from the intestinal wire tap . . . and ride the id train past undeniable apathy towards the wonderment of the mountaintop . . . as my fingers keep . . . tap . . . tap . . . tapping on the keys . . . the sound tedious yet void of what . . . i do not know . . . they're only words . . . but they can bite off your head just as surely as put you to bed . . . to the comfort zone . . . all warm and toasty . . . dead . . . a cocoon of bliss . . . a mummified passion killer . . . words sounding the death knell . . . i hope it ain't for me . . . of entwined sins and uncondoned myths . . . frequenting the brain yet unafraid to cast their fiery glare upon the witless trail . . . don't be afraid of what i'm saying . . . they're only words . . . or are they? . . . on the other hand . . . i might be dead by the time you read this . . . only i wouldn't know . . . would i? . . . my fingers tentacles extending into the vast channel-surfing-monitors of your mind . . . eyeballs unblinking in the cool crisp air . . . fraught with irredeemable pleasure from the ledge of sanity . . .

. . . i saw a triple amputee today with one deformed flipper arm who danced on his stubs in venice for coins and it reminded me of something . . . only i'm not sure . . .